THE CULPRITS

THE CULPRITS

ROBERT HOUGH

THE CUT PRITS

RANDOM HOUSE CANADA

Copyright © 2007 Robert Hough

All rights reserved under International and Pan-American Copyright Conventions. No part of this book may be reproduced in any form or by any electronic or mechanical means, including information storage and retrieval systems, without permission in writing from the publisher, except by a reviewer, who may quote brief passages in a review. Published in 2007 by Random House Canada, a division of Random House of Canada Limited. Distributed in Canada by Random House of Canada Limited.

Random House Canada and colophon are trademarks.

www.randomhouse.ca

Every effort has been made to contact the holders of copyright material; if any inadvertent omission has occurred, please contact the publisher.

Library and Archives Canada Cataloguing in Publication

Hough, Robert, 1963–
The culprits / Robert Hough.

ISBN 978-0-307-35564-5

I. Title.
PS8565.O7683C85 2007   C813'.6   C2007-902401-7

Jacket and text design: Terri Nimmo

Printed and bound in the United States of America

10 9 8 7 6 5 4 3 2 1

Life is more difficult than a walk in the forest.
—Russian proverb

ONE

Ahhhh, little one; ahhhhhh, my soon-to-be last-name sharer; ahhhhhhhhhh, the future pride and joy of Hank and *mamochka*. There's one thing I must tell you. Life is a deception. Oh yes—it's a ruse, it's a scam, it's a carnival shell game. When you peel back one layer of trickery, you'll find another and another, each one mossy and dark and underfoot-hidden. The good news is that these layers are there for our protection. If we could scrub away the lichen and peer at life with clear vision . . . well. Its entirety would overwhelm us. It would assault all our senses, like a subway-car bombing. It would come at us roaring, rendering us madmen. And so, we deceive ourselves and all others, if only to keep a grip on this thing we call sanity.

(And with time, little one, we don't even know when we're lying.)

But I digress. I am overly dramatic. It's my half-Slavic soul, drunk with attention. I'm a cranially enlarged Russian, with a soapbox to stand on. I apologize, I do; I'll sober up, and quit harping, and get on with this blather.

This, by the way, is the tale of Tushino and the bombs that went off there. To understand that day—to appreciate, in even the smallest of ways, the deaths that occurred there—you have to know one other small thing. None of this would have happened had a delusional stranger not shoved Hank Wallins, my six-foot-and-five-inch-tall stepfather, in front of a charging subway train.

This happened on May the fifth in the year 2002. Hank, then as now, worked the night shift for Quality Assurance, the country's second-largest provider of home and car policies. On a typical evening, he'd be given no more than an hour or two's worth of computer processing (issuing batch reports, distributing funds, testing systems), which he'd then have to drizzle over eight fluorescent-lit hours. "Boredom," his predecessor had warned, "will be a real bitch to deal with . . ." This, it had turned out, was an understatement: someone had to be there at night in case the computers stopped working, an event preceded, apparently, by a sound midway between a belch and an air leak. As this never happened (or at least never while Hank was on duty) time flowed like sludge through a gummed-up egg timer. Some nights he thought it would go on forever: the reading of newspapers, the drinking of coffee, the phantomlike strolling of dim and hushed hallways. Often, Hank felt more like a security guard than a computer operator, an impression in no way tempered when the actual guard, a type 1 diabetic, one night turned pale and started uncontrollably spasming. It took eleven yawning weeks before a replacement was hired.

But humans, they cope. It *is* what they're known for. So picture him, little one, each night of each workday, my red-haired semi-papa, chewing his sandwich as slowly as possible. Or tapping his pencil on his workstation desktop. Or rubbing his ears to soothe the tinnitus that plagued him. Or sighing heavily, and slowly, as though sadness was a thing he carried in his lungs. Oh yes, picture him—thirty-six years of age, a one-time sailor and now from-life hider, the airy whir of computers soothing the sounds in his eardrums.

Plus, there was smoking. It was something he could do with Manuel, who manned the freight train–sized printer in the room just one over. Every hour on the hour, they'd both go outside, where Manuel would chatter about thoroughbreds, and chinchillas, and other hare-brained schemes for getting rich quickly. They'd hear crickets, and transformers, and the whine of car tires against black, distant asphalt. At dawn, they'd watch the parkway bathe in the light of the low sun. And always, *always,* there were twin coils of blue smoke, one spiralling upward from sausage-like fingers, the other from a hand that was thin and bronze-coloured.

But I digress, once again. As I may have said earlier, it was the end of Hank's evening. He rose, wearily, reached into his desk drawer, and pulled out a pair of portable sound maskers; they looked like oversized lima beans, and they clipped to his ears with two curls of clear plastic. He turned on the volume, his ears now awash in the sound of air rushing—of all frequencies holding hands and making a warm, restful *shhhhhh*ing. This would help. Outside, in the real world, his maskers dampened the *ping*s and the whistles that sang inside his ears.

Thusly accoutred, he rode three storeys up to the Quality front lobby. He revolved through glass doors and stepped into hot, glinting white sun—it reflected off windshields, and hubcaps, and the building's brass facade. Hank winced, and checked his pockets for sunglasses; he found only keys, and coins, and a wallet so flimsy with use it felt almost weightless. He swore softly, and then trudged to the stop where his bus waited for him.

On board he squeezed. The smell was weighty and pungent, like the odour given off by a poorly kept barnyard. He sighed and gripped a pole. Whenever he adjusted his stance—a bend in the road, an unexpected braking—he left behind a residue that mapped his palm's lines and creases. Thirty minutes later, the bus pulled into the station. Hank de-boarded, and was immediately ingested by a march of commuters. This happened each morning: the stamping of feet against floors damp with water, the muffling of sound as they entered the station, the depositing of Hank at the edge of the platform. Here, he liked to lean forward and let tunnelling air flow over his hot face; as he did, he imagined what it would be like to dive forward, hands up and palms touching, the whole of his life before his eyes flashing. This possibility filled him with a warm, morbid comfort—it made him feel as though life was not a thing without options, and that if his ears and his mood ever got the better *of* him . . . well. He could always end it all with a quick alley-ooping. In fact, he was so busy imagining the moment of impact (apparently the smaller bones pulverize, and turn to a finely ground rock salt) he failed to notice the person skulking behind him.

Little one: he was wearing a fully zipped parka, a pair of worn tartan slippers, and a sort of Robin Hood cap made from aluminum foil. His pinprick-sized pupils blazed with divine inspiration, and he smelled, appropriately enough, as though he did the lion's share of his urinating in grimy back alleys. Oblivious, Hank embarked on an unwise course of action: he grew a pair of crimson horns, a tail that curled whip-like into a threatening trident, and a look of fulminating evil in his large, plaintive green eyes. This inflamed the man lurking behind him; he made the sign of the cross, gazed upward to heaven, and then pitched himself forward like a steroidal rhino.

Hank toppled, eyes wide and arms circling, his sound maskers propelled from each of his pink ears. Then, for the briefest of seconds, he hovered. His body turned veil-like, and his oversized sneakers turned lighter than chiffon. And though this wasn't noticed by those still on the platform, it nonetheless happened: his spirit turned weightless, and wafted like a leaf caught in an updraft. It was during these moments of floating that Hank was struck dumb by truths profound and eternal. It really was something: his soul flooded with joy, and his expression—normally so sober and burdened—gleamed like a child's on Christmas Day morning. Nothing, he now understood, was as precious a feeling as your heart beating calmly, or filling your lungs with air from a forest, or listening to the songs that come during daydreams. Nothing, he now saw, was worth more than life and the gesture of living.

At which point he dropped.

Oh yes—plank-like he fell, his ear *ping*ings replaced with screams and shouts and the loud screeching wail of metal on metal. He took the blow on his belly, which thank God had grown prodigious since his days as a seaman. His forehead landed inches from the electrified third rail. Little brown mice scattered everywhere squeaking. Then, for a moment, he lay nose-pressed and sooty. Above him, people were screaming and pointing and feverishly shouting; amidst this confusion, his assailant slipped away, triumphantly muttering. Hank lay still for a moment. Even though every bone in his body was aching, and a rivulet of blood flowed from a gash near his hairline, and his nostrils twitched at the stench of roasting brake fluid, he wasn't worried. He would survive, he just *knew* it, and it was this prescience that fired his underused muscles.

With the train ten Hank-lengths away and still grinding forward, he leapt to his feet and faced the platform determined. To his right, the train driver horn-beeped and arm-waved and generally looked frantic. In front, a dozen pairs of hands reached out toward him. They were pale, dark, olive-toned, hairless, ring-wearing, male, female, large, small . . . one was even missing a portion of baby finger, such that it looked more than a little like a wiener. With the train at five Hank-lengths, he took a long stride toward the wall of the platform. The very prospect of living—*of having more life!*—caused him to do something he did only rarely: Hank smiled, and smiled widely. This was unfortunate. The blood chugging from his hairline gelled in the space between his front teeth, granting him the look of an unbridled savage. The crowd gasped and stepped reflexively backward. Only two pairs of hands still reached toward him—one was pale and sinewy, the other light brown and wearing a gold ring.

    Hank took hold. His hands and wrists were squeezed duly. With the train sliding forward on rails hot and sparking, the two remaining stalwarts gave a galley-slave heave-ho. Hank gained a foot on the platform, and then straightened his legs so mightily that he almost pulled his rescuers onto the tracks with him. Fortunately, they were being held around the waist by the people behind them, who were in turn being grabbed by those in the third row.

    This extra bit of thrust saved Hank's life. Yet, as his right leg straightened, his left compensated by making a quick backward high kick at the moment in which the train was upon him. The crunch of small bones was lost to shouting, and screams, and the cacophonous grind of a train slowly stopping. Hank stood still, cupping hands over both ears. The air thickened and turned roux-like, and the whole of the world drooped like a painting by Dali. No one spoke. The only sounds Hank heard were the ones that his head made. In this *ping*-laden silence, he felt saddened all over— now that he'd survived, a new burden was upon him.

A second later he groaned, having shifted his weight to a foot in three places broken.

And so, Hank collapsed, his arms out beside him, his left foot pointed in a direction no foot should ever have to point to—it felt as though someone had heated oil in a saucepan and then upended it over the ball of his ankle. Still. Did Hank moan? Did he bellow, or howl, or claw at his face while screaming for mercy? Oh no. Now that his sipping at the grail of ecstasy was over, he reverted to the Hank who hated being the centre of attention. He swore through gritted teeth, and shut his eyes tightly, and cursed whichever bitch's son had just tried to kill him.

He now wanted one thing and one thing only: to go home to his chair, and his paper, and his Marsona DS-600 white noise generator. He opened his eyes. Turning his head to one side, he gazed at shoes and boots and open-toed sandals. When he attempted to rise, pain whistled through him. Hank shrieked, and fell back, and held himself shivering. The crowd surged forward. He was buried beneath jackets and sweaters, beneath blazers and sweatshirts, beneath a thick toddler's blanket and a Judaic prayer shawl and a Navajo serape that smelled faintly of wormwood; in addition to being spasmodic with pain, he now felt as hot as an incubated baby. An Evian bottle, descending from above, was placed to his mouth and gingerly tilted.

This felt good. He licked moisture from his lips and quietly whimpered. An old woman with a shopping buggy struggled to the front of those gathered. She lowered herself to her knees, her chin trembling with a slight, yet noticeable, palsy. Her breath was a steaming of garlic, cooked meat, and dill-infused mushrooms. "Is okay," she told Hank. "Is little fall, you have. Is nothing to worry about. The doctors they coming. This, I know already . . ." She stroked his forehead with a hand cool and yeasty. "Is okay," she kept saying, "don't *you* to worry."

Hank closed his eyes. His rib cage felt tightened, as though it were trying to choke him. He heard a garbled announcement, and the sound of footfalls coming toward him. The crowd made way for two paramedics. The old woman was suddenly rendered a figment; only her fragrance remained, gradually dwindling. Hank looked all around him, and then lay as still as was humanly possible. The younger of the paramedics, his hair tips as frosted as a child's breakfast cereal, dropped and placed three fingers against Hank's carotid artery.

Through chattering teeth, Hank croaked his name, identified the prime minister, and counted the trio of fingers rotating before him. When the paramedics eased him onto a white, cushioned stretcher, Hank's foot—which was largely unrestrained by ligament or muscle—from side to side flopped like a koi out of water. He gasped, and everything went blurry; it was as though he were viewing the world through a smearing of ointment. His heart quaked and trembled, his body warmth tumbled, and he felt as though death was finally coming. Meanwhile, the older of the paramedics (moustache, eyeglasses, the out-of-date haircut of a grown man with children) was cradling Hank's ankle while asking, "Sir . . . sir . . . can you stand this?"

There was a syringe in his hand, its tip pointing upward and bubbling with morphine.

Hank nodded. A bead of perspiration loosened and trickled down his neckline. His left arm was rotated and his shirt sleeve rolled up; this revealed a tattoo of a girl wearing a beret and tight sweater. A dot of blood welled like a jewel in her navel. The world turned soft, as though bathed in a twilight. The sirens in Hank's ears turned to coddling whispers. His eyes swivelled upward, and his thoughts turned to floating—no, no, to *hovering*—through skies that were blue, and warm, and with cotton balls dotted.

He awoke feeling woozy. His foot hung from a mobile of stirrups and pulleys, and his shoulder blades were sprouting blue, palm-shaped bruises. He lifted a hand and touched the gauze taped to his forehead. This caused him to wince—his pain was everywhere, in every fibre and corpuscle, flowing over his body like a breeze on a cool day. And yet, it was a strange sort of pain, Hank feeling its blaze and, at the same time, barely noticing its presence. It both stung like a hornet and caressed him like the hands of a compassionate lover. *You sir,* his ear-voices murmured, *that thing that you feel? That mild and yet all-over pressure? That's your pain, sir. That's what that is.*

Demerol, of course, was the culprit. Hank blinked, and was dazed by the colours that were through his room swirling: magentas and teals, mostly, with accenting swoops of a bright, bursting yellow. In those minutes (and hours) after wakening, smells registered as sounds, and sounds came as visions, and flat surfaces roiled with time and dimension. A half a mile off, his plump, purplish toes swirled like the tines of a beater. Above him, on the acoustic-tile ceiling, an amoeba-shaped water stain bubbled like mercury. Hank shuddered. In his ears he heard mad, hysterical laughter. With each breath, the curtains around his bed inflated, and turned from off-white to a shimmering orange. On top of all *that*—on top of his pain, and his loneliness, and his synesthetic visions—he needed a cigarette and he needed one badly.

Over the next twenty-four hours, Hank slipped in and out of a narcotic coma. He saw glimpses of heaven and floating bronze

Buddhas. He pictured his own death, as detached as a wise man. He comprehended infinity while, at the same time, couldn't have added two single-digit numbers. At some point, the doctors reduced the amount of Demerol coursing through his tight-sweatered French girl. Hank opened his eyes slowly, feeling nothing but pain and disorientation. A moment later it all came back to him: the sudden push on his back, those moments spent floating, that whiplashing smack against an oily, dark railbed. He closed his eyes and saw brown mice scattering, headlights getting bigger, and a dozen pairs of hands outstretched and waggling.

Hank's ears, in response, began acting up badly. As he lay trapped in bed, his head became a slave to a pair of high frequencies—the upper at twelve thousand hertz, the lower at eleven, both having been measured several times at the Canadian Hearing Society. Yet what depressed him most was the sound contained within those two frequencies, a sound that on most days was a *ping*ing but that on other days took on tonalities and textures that matched his own feelings, producing variants that were either distant and muffled or out-and-out blaring. Little one—he'd hear moans, or bleating, or low infant wailings. He'd hear large motors rumbling, or refrigerators running, or the shoulder-hunching crash of chinaware falling, or (yes *or!*) the luscious throat whispers of a French-speaking trollop. Today, however, it was his tried-and-true fallback—the *ping*ing of tapped stemware, of correct game show answers. Hank fumbled for his maskers, and realized they were still lying between the rails of the subway; he could picture them shattered and grimy with oil. His eyes reddened, and his ear *ping*ings turned into harsh cymbal crashes.

To his right was a chair covered in worn, dull brown fabric. On the ceiling, the water stain writhed like Salome. He turned to his left: above his bedside table, and next to his intravenous trestle, was a panel the size of a paperback novel. Two buttons protruded. The first was marked *bed*. The second bore the word that he wanted. Hank pushed, and waited. He cursed his damn ears and the torment they caused him. He was fighting the urge to once again press the button when the curtains suddenly parted. Hank, blinking, looked up at a woman whom everyone—from the hospital president to the lowliest scrubber of bedpans—knew only as Melba, the nurse who had worked at North York General forever.

Her arms were thick and dark-coloured, and they were folded beneath a bosom the size of twin bread loaves. "Now why," she asked, "you be callin'?"

"Sorry."

"Enough sorry. What de problem?"

Hank hesitated. Ringing in the ears wasn't easily described, especially to those who hadn't suffered its horrors. It even sounded fun—bicycle bells *ring*, ice cream trucks *ring*, laughing children join hands and run circles *in* them. But the reality was different. Oh yes—the reality was head pain, and ear pain, and a feeling like your eyes might pop from their sockets. The reality was dizziness, and hyperacusis, and nights spent awake, tossing and turning. It was a diet of Ativan and Zoloft and vitamin-enriched fruit drinks, along with hundreds of hours spent in a tinnitus support group, listening to tales of job loss and failed marriages and clinical depression, your head entombed the whole time by a cottony dry heat. It was tromping through the offices of audiologists and psychiatrists and those who pitched themselves as in any way holistic (the nutritionists, the aromatherapists, the shiatsu masseuses) before finally giving up and concluding that this malady—this from-hell-sent condition—had to be a punishment for being the person that *you* were.

The reality, little one, was wondering if there was a train, somewhere out there, with your name written on it.

"It's my ears."
Melba lifted an eyebrow. "Your ears?"
Hank nodded.
"What 'bout them?"
"They're ringing."
"They *ringin'*?"
"Yeah."
"What? You got tinnitus?"
Hank nodded.
"And it botherin' you?"

Hank blinked, and regretted he'd called her. He'd heard it all before, from a hundred and one doctors: that insincere concern, followed by advice just to make the best of it. (Or that it was all in his head, and that if he could somehow accept this, it would go away slowly.) He closed his eyes. In so doing, he missed the change in Melba's demeanour: she unfolded her arms and bent closer to him. Her face was so round it looked like an apple. "I *know*," she half whispered. "I know, I know. It a real goddamn bugger."

Hank opened an eye. She backed out through the curtains. A long minute later, she returned with an old humidifier. It was plastic and blue, and looked like a toddler's first potty. She placed it beside him. "*It*," she said, "make a nice bloody sound when it run out of water."

And it did—it gurgled and growled and made a soft, white-noise rumbling. The *ping* in Hank's ears got half lost in its sighing.

"Better?"
"Yes. Christ. Thank you."
"Anyting else den?"
He thought. "I could use a nicotine patch."
She neither smiled nor frowned. "You smoke much?"
"Yeah. Sorry."

There was a pause.

"Enough sorry. Just one gonna do it?"

Doctors came and went daily. He saw interns and specialists and arthroscopic surgeons. He saw an occupational therapist with a Gorbachevian birthmark. He saw a wall-eyed dietician with cold hands and a stutter. He saw a youngish psychologist who hinted that Hank's attacker hadn't really existed, and that his fall on the tracks was of his own devising. (*Thank God,* Hank thought, *I didn't tell them I'd floated.*) And though Hank was never quite sure who was in charge of his healing, he'd have wagered on a stoop-shouldered doctor named Jeffries, if only because he showed up more often than others. In he'd hustle, clipboard in hand, sparse hair tendrils waving, asking, "How are we doing?" in a voice thin and reedy. Without waiting for an answer, he'd start manipulating Hank's toes, which had downgraded from violet to the splotchy, anemic mauve found in Floridian condos. Satisfied, he'd tighten the bolts protruding from Hank's cast and then issue instructions that caused Melba to grumble.

Two visitors came. The first was a detective from 14 Division. He was hefty and red-cheeked and wore a bushy black moustache. He also had a talent for insinuation: "So, Mr. Wallins, you didn't see the man who pushed you? You didn't even catch a *glimpse?*" A pause for effect, lasting two or three heartbeats. "Tell me, Mr. Wallins. Do you use drugs?"

And Hank, who viewed this detective in the same way he viewed all people—as belonging to a sunnier world than the one in which he lived—rubbed his ears and looked through him.

"None that're illegal," he muttered.

The second was Manuel, who arrived on a day when raindrops splattered Hank's bedside window, and lightning filled the skies with sheets of white-purple. He came in soggy and grinning. "Hank," he said with a breathlessness that was typical. "Today I go to Woodbine. Tell me. Who do you like for the fifth? I like Fancy Girl, very good horse, muck-loving and quick and very good at four to one. You think, Hank? By the way, by the way, when are you getting out of here?"

Hank gazed at his workmate, feeling heavy and achy. "Tell me something, Manuel."

"Yes, brother?"

"Why are you always throwing money away on the horses?"

"Because one day I'll win. One day I'll hit the trifecta."

"You won't."

"Oh yes. I will. I *know* I will."

"Christ, Manuel, you won't. The odds are . . . what? Thousands and thousands to one?"

Manuel grinned, showing teeth orange and peggy. "And the odds of getting hit by a train and *living*? What are they, my brother?"

Hank sighed, and sighed loudly. Manuel's visit only underscored the loneliness that, over the last eight years, had gnawed at his life like a Grozny-dump mongrel. (Little one—the isolation that's *caused* by chronic ear ringing!) During the day, from his bed, while pretending to watch the television above him, he observed the families of his hospital roommates. His hearing was similarly in-two divided: as soap operas and game shows droned on above him, he listened to the languages that filled the room at all hours. He heard Greek and Italian, Vietnamese and Urdu, Mandarin and Farsi and even Amharic, each making him pine for the days in which he'd travelled the globe on a Canadian tanker.

At night he slept poorly, his dreams thin and drug-addled. In the morning he'd awake, feeling displaced and groggy. When his meal trays were late, he grew anxious. During his sponge baths, he felt helpless and babied. As a final indignity, he began to grow strange blue-green bedsores; they formed under his skin, and looked like singed flowers. With reading too difficult (there was still a little Demerol dripping into his French girl) he spent an excess of time looking up at the ceiling—soon he came to know the water stain's every curve and indentation, and every single one of its hue variations, from soft mocha brown to prosaic shit brown to the nearly black brown of a fetid banana. He spent long, boring hours watching clouds outside drifting. He yearned for the ear-calming whir of a mainframe computer. He had short talks with Melba, who complained about gout, and sore ankles, and a husband who loved her. And then, on the fifth droning day of Hank's hospitalization, *he* came—biliously snorting, face red and leathery, waving a cherrywood cane at anyone who came near him.

Behind him was the orderly who was pushing his wheelchair. Behind *him* was a young, skinny woman who (at least to Hank) wore the pale expression of a worried, grown daughter. They stopped by the bed nearest to Hank's. When the orderly took the patient's arm, the old man pushed it away and spat, "For Christ's sake, I'm no cripple!"

"Josef!" the young woman blurted. She turned to the orderly. "Sorry, please, he is very much in discomfort, he is usually much happier and nicer to people . . ."

She pronounced *happy* like "haypee," the *h* so loudly enunciated it sounded like a wind in the desert. The patient, meanwhile, had risen to his feet and was wavering like a sapling in a gathering tornado. His pelvis made an impression in his hospital-gown fabric. His legs were newspaper grey, and his posture was as bent as a six-foot coat hanger. He groaned, clamped his hands to his stomach, and fell on top of brown, scratchy blankets. The young woman yelped and rushed forward. The patient lay moaning, and still holding his stomach with hands old and twiggy.

"Josef!" she exclaimed. "You are all right?"

"Yes yes," he growled. "I'm okay, goddamnit." A few seconds passed as she helped him under the covers. When he spoke again, he sounded embarrassed. "Irina. I am sorry about this. About you having to see me this way. I wish always you saw me as a man who was younger."

"Shhhhhhhh."

"You are my angel."

"Shhhhhhhhh, rabbit."

"I tell you, I am feeling like a truck it has hit me."

"Shhhhhhhhh, rabbit. Save your strength."

"I tell you, when I get out of here—"

"Josef!" She giggled. "Best to think not so hard. Maybe you ripping some of your stitches."

"So what? They are in the sewing and ripping of stitches business here."

"Still, rabbit. Best not to get excited."

"I can't help it. I am an old man, but not yet a dead one. By the way, I am in love with your ass. It is an ass for the ages. I have told you this recently? Your ass it is like a sunset, whenever it comes near me."

"Josef!"

"Is true."

"Please . . ."

"Remember—if nothing else, I have the wisdom of age."

"You told to me this when they taking you to surgery."

"About the wondrousness of your backside, you mean?"

"*Da.*"

"You see? I forget . . . I was higher than a kite. If those butchers had killed me, it would have been the last thing to come from my lips. It would have been my final thoughts on life, which would have been fine with me. Oh, by the way, you have talked to the nurses?"

"*Da, da,* I talk."

"And what? Did they say when I get a private room?"

"I told you—they say soon, but who knows, is busy this place, look around, they are like chickens with their heads getting chopped. Is very much *crazy,* this place . . ."

Hank hung on each word—it was both a torment and a pleasure to see the way that she loved him. He swallowed, and took a quick glance to the left. In this way he watched the young woman bend over her rabbit, and kiss him in a way that was nothing but tender.

He came awake nauseated. Orderlies with big arms were delivering dinner—all through the hospital, hallways were filling with the scent produced by cod sticks, and bean mash, and carrots so over-boiled they liquefied when touched by a fork tip. These vapours then drifted toward ceilings, where they were greedily inhaled by the hospital air vents. Within minutes, even those browsing through *Cosmopolitan* in the ground-floor gift shop, or buying bouquets of roses at the mezzanine florist, or galloping toward visions of light during botched operations, involuntarily grimaced.

Hank sighed.

"Hey."

He turned.

"You can't eat either?" Josef asked.

Hank shook his head.

"Hah! I know what you mean! I'd rather starve than eat this slop. You know, these people, these *Stalinites,* they put me on zero-fat diet. Can you believe that? Zero, none, you think *yours* is bad? You should have a taste of mine. Not one ounce or gram or drop of flavour even. Everything, it tastes like egg whites—noodles, juice, this grey fucking meat, all of it, everything, like the whites of eggs. Oh, but I am in misery. By the way, my name is Josef, it could be some time before I get out of here, so I suppose we should meet."

"Hank."

"Okay then, Hank. I am pleased to make your acquaintance. Tell me, you are in here why?"

"Broke my foot."

"Really? And how would you be doing this? How, when there is no snow for skiing or ice for ice hockey?"

"It's a long story."

"I am not able to move, so go right ahead please."

"I had an accident."

"What kind of accident?"

Hank hesitated and looked sour. "A fall. A bad one."

Josef narrowed an eye. "Okay, so you not tell me. I get the picture. No need to. Is not my business anyway. Me, I have something wrong with my pancreas, is the large and the small of it. 'Can't you just take the fucking thing out?' I ask them, but apparently it's a part you can't live without. Or at least not for very long. I swear to you, Hank, this boredom will put me in the ground before my guts do. If it weren't for Irina . . . Tell me—you have met her? You have shaken hands with my lovely and inappropriately-young-for-me wife?"

"Your wife? No. I haven't."

"Well then. When she comes back, you will. Twenty-five years old, and all the way from Minsk. Yes, yes, my darling Belarusian. I tell you—without her I am . . ." He made a throat-slicing gesture.

"Without her I am one dead and bad-smelling old man. Tell me, Hank. You are married?"

Hank said nothing.

"Then . . . you do not have a wife?"

"Not that I know of."

"But why not? Every man needs a wife. I tell you, you should do what I did. From Russia With Love dot com. You can get a wife in no time—and young and pretty, like mine she is. I tell you, without Irina I am nothing. Of course, you are not old and goat-ugly like me—maybe you have lots of girlfriends, maybe you are playing the field hard, I don't know, is not my business, but you go ahead and you ask yourself: how is that ugly old yak supposed to get a woman who isn't an old and ugly old yak herself? But hey, maybe you don't listen to me. Who am I to say, anyway? Just an old man with bad teeth and some mangled-up insides, yes?"

Josef chortled. Hank looked over.

"You mean you didn't meet her in Russia?"

"In Russia! Ha! I have never *been* to Russia. I am Polish, and have been here fifteen years, thank you very much. No, no, she came just one year ago, not one word of English under her belt except for maybe *hello* and *my name it's Irina* and *my country it's a complete pile of shit*. Now I think she speaks better than I do. These young Russians, I tell you, they are as smart as they come. And trying hard, too." He laughed again, loudly. "Russia? *Ha!* No, no, thank you very much, remember, they ran over my country. I guess maybe I'm getting my revenge, by conquering one of their women, I don't know, this could maybe even be true except that these days she's not even Russian—not speaking strictly, anyway. No, no, I'll never go there. I'm from the city of Gdansk, in the North. A very nice place, you have been? No, no, of course not, Krakow or Warsaw maybe, but not Gdansk, nobody they go to Gdansk, you should see some of the things they do to it, making all the buildings nice, making all of the streets clean again. You should go there, is like the rest of Europe now and a hundred times better than Russia with that Nazi Putin who's ruining everything. In fact, I am thinking of going back to Poland sometime and maybe this time is going to be soon . . . Ah-hah! Here she is! Irina!"

She was hovering in the hospital room doorway. She was grinning, and she'd changed into a blouse and a black skirt worn tightly. Her heels clacked against the floor; she smelled of perfume, and shampoo, and the lavender cream she used to moisten her pale skin. She bent over and kissed her husband; when she straightened, his cheek wore a smear that was lip-shaped and vermilion. Suddenly she looked concerned. She rested a lily-white hand on his old, wrinkled forehead.

"Josef!" she exclaimed. "You are sick!"

"Of course I'm sick! This is a hospital."

"No, you fool. You look more sick than normal. Your food—you don't eat?"

"I swear, it's going to kill me. Listen, why don't you go out and get me something good? Maybe something Russian, like that shashlik you make?"

"Shashlik!" she exclaimed. "You crazy? Much fat, and heavy on stomach besides. Plus, shashlik isn't Russian. Is food from Georgia. Is food from *Caucasus*."

"Georgian, Russian, who the hell cares, on *this* food I'll starve—that is one thing I *do* know. Besides, shashlik isn't too fatty."

"Yes, is fat, is very."

"How about blinis?"

"Fat."

"Latkes?"

"You would swell and perhaps explode into thousand small pieces."

"Pelmeni?"

"A *million* small pieces, rabbit."

"How about borscht? A little cabbage can't hurt me."

She paused. "Borscht, maybe, okay, we see."

"Irina, you must promise!"

"We *see*, Josef."

"Irina, you promise, goddamnit!"

She stayed for the rest of the afternoon. She massaged him, spoon-fed him broth that she begged from the nurses, and gave him a sponge bath with the curtains drawn fully. She also read him the love poems of Anna Akhmatova; this caused Josef to quiet and gaze up at the ceiling, his expression both pleased and faraway-looking. Throughout, Hank couldn't stop glancing at the bounce of her curls, and the length of her legs, and the teardrop curve of her slim hips.

She left. Three hours later, with the lights a low ember, she crept back like a shadow. She wore running shoes, an overcoat, and a sneaky expression.

Josef lifted his head. "Irina . . ." he whispered.

She crossed his lips with a finger. "Shhhhhhhhh, rabbit. For once in your life don't say nothing. I sneak past nurses."

She pulled his curtains around them. A minute later the room filled with the scent of garlic and dillweed and meat cooked over charcoal. Hank heard Josef smack his lips and then say in a whisper, "Ah, rabbit, you are a miracle, a godsend, a gift from the heavens." She giggled once softly. This giggle would stay with Hank, as would the smell of the food, and the Pole's breathy chomping, and Irina's hushed and contradictory warnings: "Not too much, Josef, just little bit sour cream—is good, is not? Here, here, have little bit more . . ."

When Hank heard the coil of bedsprings, he knew that Irina had lain down beside her old husband. There came a thin murmur; though he couldn't quite make out what they were saying, he imagined they were discussing the sorts of things that pass between couples—whispered things, heart-touching things, things that only mattered in the world of two people ... things that Hank had once talked about in Marseilles, in the red and dark walls of Madame LaChance's, his one true love warm in the straw bed beside him.

Soon he forgot about Josef, his ears alive with the cawing of gulls and the tapping of heels on cobblestone laneways. His room filled with the scent of blustery sea air. Finally—this was past two in the morning, the moon framed shiny and silver by his hospital room window—Hank drifted asleep, only to be awoken by two hurrying orderlies. They cradled Josef, who was writhing and kicking and holding himself moaning. Onto a gurney they plopped him, causing him to curse in Polish and English. A half-minute later he was gone. The only remnant of his presence was a cloud of foul air, smelling of garlic and onion and burped-up green peppers.

Hank was fitted that day with a cast made of fibreglass. He was given crutches, a prescription for Tylenol 4s, and instructions to keep his foot dry while bathing. These came from the doctors. From Melba he received words of smart counsel ("Take a cab, silly bugger, and eat more vegetables"), and the touch of a hand that was padded and dimpled. He stayed one more night. In the morning, an orderly wheeled him to the hospital entrance, though not before helping him buy smokes in the canteen. "You take care," he told Hank, before leaving him outside, in the shade, on a bench filled with gowned patients.

It was a hot spring day. Everything looked sun-baked and hazy. Hank lit a cigarette. Smoke rushed to his lungs and his brain spun in circles. *One day,* he thought, *I'll give these damn things up.* There was a tree a few metres behind him and, in its branches, a cloud of brown finches. It was noisy here—he could hear birdsong and car motors and a nurse yelling at someone via her cellphone. Each and every one of these sounds mixed with the music made by words when they're happy and hopeful.

Ah, rabbit . . .

You are a miracle, a godsend, a gift from the heavens.

And so, Hank went home to his building on Wellesley, the elevator asthmatically wheezing while rising to his floor. He opened the door to his apartment and breathed in a scent that was his and his only. It was just as he'd left it: neat as a pin, though his plants needed watering. There was a small grey box on a stand near the window; this was his Marsona model DS-600, with its settings for Surf, Rain, Brook, Lakeshore, Waterfall, and—a perennial favourite among tinnitus sufferers—Warm Eve in the Country. Hank, however, preferred the pure white-noise setting; he set this to high volume, so that it sounded like a television tuned to a snowy off-station. He then hobbled to his chair and smoked with his bad foot propped up on an angle. Ten minutes later, when he still felt no better, he hopped to the bathroom and opened a medicine cabinet filled with tinnitus relievers—Ativan, Zoloft, Zanaflex, Nortriptyline, St. John's wort, ginkgo biloba, willow's bark, a few mild anticonvulsants, an Internet snake oil called T-Gone, an MAO inhibitor long since expired, and a mild neuroleptic that left him mouth-dry and shaky. His hand hesitated over this pharmacological buffet, Hank finally choosing a tranquilizer and swallowing it with water. This helped. Minutes and minutes passed. Sunlit thoughts of tomorrow came out of nowhere. He smirked. He couldn't help it; he was thinking of Josef and Irina and the way surprising things happen.

Over the next few days, he learned to dress while sitting, to push a grocery cart while walking with crutches, to cook rudimentary meals while hopping on one foot. He managed to take a cab to the Hearing Society, where he was fitted with a new pair of portable sound maskers. *Still.* Every trip to the kitchen meant foot pain and gasping and a surfeit of curse words. Every sandwich was eaten with a codeine side order (for he'd inevitably clip his foot against the door of his dishwasher, which tended to hang open like a tired man yawning). One night he went out onto his balcony; here he liked to sit and smoke and watch the lights of the city blink at him warmly. This took him forever, as his crutches kept striking the spring-loaded screen door. Finally he made it, only to realize he'd left his cigarettes inside. An ache arose in his throat, and he rubbed both of his eyes with the tips of his fingers.

One afternoon, after filling his bathtub, Hank waterproofed his cast in clear plastic wrapping and leaned both of his crutches against the wall by the counter. He then lowered himself to the rim of the bathtub. The room was misty and hot, and the skin on his face felt warmly moistened. He lifted his good leg and left the other supported. Before lowering himself into water, he stood for a moment, and that's when it happened, the culprit an Irish Spring sliver that had slipped from his soap dish. He fell backward, somehow flipping while airborne and landing face down in splashed-out bathwater. Air burst from his lungs. The breathing that followed was rasping and shallow. For the next few minutes he lay numb and dripping, a lump preparing to rise beside his beige head-wound bandage. And his ears! His damn ears! His normal *ping ping*ings turned to sad children's pleadings! He called out, but just once, as no one could hear him. He gritted his teeth and then felt himself shiver. Finally he struggled to his knees, his resolve to find himself a companion now having nothing to do with loneliness, or glimpses of wisdom, or hovering above subway tracks in air thickened with oil.

The next day, he awoke at about two in the afternoon. The sun curled bleary around thick bedroom curtains. He ate cornflakes, and drank coffee, and shaved his face in hot, soapy water. He dressed, an act accompanied by groans and deep breathing. Then he sat waiting. To kill time, he thought of places he'd been to, and bars he had haunted, back when he'd worked as a sailor on the *Antigonish Dreamer,* plying long ocean laneways between Hibernia and Europe. He pictured Andalusia, and the crazed, bustling ports of Cyprus and Corfu, where the smoke from street braziers formed greasy black spirals. He imagined North African shores and mossy-tipped mountains turned hazy by distance. He envisioned palm trees, and scrubland, and waters that reached for so far his thoughts often turned to what is meant by "forever."

He breathed salty sea air, hanging cloud-like and wispy over the deck of a big ship.

Later that day, he shouldered his way through the revolving front doors of Quality Assurance. After punching in his code, he descended three levels and hopped to his desk, wincing. (*This* despite the fact that he'd taped squares of foam to his crutches where they chafed against the sides of his body.) He surveyed the room, both relieved and resentful that nothing was different—the air still smelled of Freon, and his ears were still calmed by the whir of the mainframe. The room was so fiercely illuminated that certain things—bond paper, Hank's shirt, the disc-driver facings—shone with a tinge of fluorescent purple. His ankle ached. He took off his maskers and put them in his pocket. The toes of his left foot, though covered by a contraption that looked like a bonnet, tingled and felt chilly.

Manuel came toward him, his smile the result of a dentist-free boyhood. "Hank!" he exclaimed. "Look! Look what they brought *for* you!"

Sure enough, it was on his desk waiting, parked between his paper-clip well and his personal printer—a towering assembly of hyacinths, tulips, freesia, baby's breath, softball-sized hydrangeas, and, acting as a sort of billowing centre, a pair of white calla lilies bent by red plastic. He started opening the bouquet while standing on one foot. This was difficult; the plastic was sticky, and nicotine (at the best of times) affected Hank's balance. Still, he persevered. He hopped and fiddled and jabbed it with scissors. When he finally had it opened, he found a card in the foliage that had been signed by everyone in the IT department, most of whom he'd not yet had the pleasure of meeting.

He looked up at Manuel, and with a heartfelt nod thanked him.

How his evening dragged—he could no longer kill time by roaming the hallways, his profile reflected in dark office windows. Going outside for a smoke was likewise impossible; just coming to work had caused his ankle to swell and turn the colour of spinach. To kill time, he slowed his work to a pace that was emphatically snail-like: twenty minutes per batch report, fifteen minutes devoted to a single transmission, an eternity to issue an insurance claim cheque run. He and Manuel took their cigarette breaks in the nearest men's washroom, Manuel plugging the smoke detector with chewed Chiclet tablets. With no real work to return to, they smoked another, and another, lighting each Players with the tip of the previous, until their hands shook and their lungs felt as though they'd been with a coarse paper sanded. All the while, Manuel chattered about worm farming, and mink raising, and selling *TV Guide* subscriptions via an automated dialer, until Hank could stand it no longer and hobbled jittery back to his personal workstation. He lifted his pinned-together foot up onto his desktop and rested it, throbbing, next to a half-empty mug and a mounding of paper.

After a few days, his welcome-back flowers began to brown and turn wilty, such that a foul, swampy odour scented his pens and his papers. His stomach too was beginning to spoil, a victim of Tylenol 4s swallowed every couple of hours. He slept fitfully. Day after day, in his Wellesley apartment, he dreamt he was flying, over fields erupting with (of all things) ripe watermelons. This went on and on. A dozen times per night, Hank swooped and floated over fields of black, churned-up soil. And the sound that accompanied his weird daytime dreaming? It was the call made by wolves, thrilled by the moon's silver cascade. He began to feel like there was something inside him, something desperate to escape and glimpse clear shards of daylight. At night, at his workplace, he was often short of breath, his heart skipping a beat and then arrhythmically thumping. He began having headaches, and bouts of sadness, and a lusting for flight over subway-car railbeds. A week, and then another, passed slowly. He lost a little weight, for the first time in years, and dark, purplish bags formed under his green eyes.

And *then:*

On a night in which the muscles in his jaw hurt from teeth grinding, and the contents of his stomach churned and splashed upward, and the *ping*ing in his ears became a dead-of-night howling, and Manuel was asleep on his faux wooden desktop . . . well. Hank lifted his foot, and wheeled his chair to a PC hooked up to a modem. He pressed the On button. A desktop appeared against a blue, cloud-streaked skyline. He moved his Eiffel Tower cursor to the Internet icon. He clicked. He typed.

A new world bloomed like a tulip before him.

As he sat watching, the words *From Russia With Love* pulsed against a deep purple background. The font was ornate, and the letter *i* in *Russia* was dotted with a heart red and flaming. Meanwhile, a squadron of letters shuffled toward the computer screen's centre, where they danced and high-kicked and on their axis spun dervishly, before reordering themselves to read: *!!!Ten Thousand Women Are Waiting!!!* Below this, a bubble arose from the screen's inky colour. In it was the face of a beautiful woman. Her cheekbones were egg-sized, her eyes heavy-lidded, and her thin, glossy lips were the red of a plum stone. Hank swallowed thickly, for her estrous expression left no doubt as to what she was thinking—oh yes, under her picture was a double entendre if ever there was one.

Enter, it read, in letters as subtly pink as an in-season mandrill.

Hank clicked, and saw a full page of young faces smiling. He clicked again and again. His lips parted, and his eyes opened widely. He'd never dreamt so many women existed—and yet here they were, from age eighteen to forty-eight, an infinite array of come-hither expressions. Furthermore, they seemed to come from every nook and once-Russian cranny, from the North's frozen rivers to the South's arid valleys, from the corrupt Western cities to the East's wood-churched hamlets, from the lichen-coated taiga to the snowy-tipped Urals to the brown sandy wash of the *stan*-suffixed countries, and still, *still,* with each click they kept coming, organized by age or by birthplace, this procession of young women who all needed saving. His fingers sped. In his ears he heard French words. The quicker he Next-clicked, the quicker they kept coming, with their red-painted smiles and Meryl Streep noses, each one winking and lithesome and wearing a tight blouse. As Hank met each set of eyes, he felt a kinship with these women—no, no, with these *people*—there being nothing like the recognition of need to soften the soul, and quicken the pulse, and melt a resistance that for eight long years had been stone-like.

He logged off. Closing his eyes, he saw an afterimage, burning dark blue and hazy. It was 3:20 in the morning. He had fourteen cigarettes left, and enough change for five cups of coffee from the Quality Assurance vending machines. Other than that, there was nothing, not a thing, in the joke that was his life.

He surfed FromRussiaWithLove.com the following night, and the night after that, and then the night that came after. Embarrassed, he'd wait until Manuel was face down and dozing on the tops of his forearms. By his fourth online session, he'd noticed that the women tended to be photographed in one of three poses. There was the against-a-tree leaning, her dress short and thigh-hugging, her front leg bent and revealing stretches of young skin. There was the innocently smiling, her head tilted sideways so that her hair brushed one shoulder, her hands clasping some item evocative of childhood (like a flower, or a kitten, or, in the case of a young girl from some place called Chuvashia, the ribboned metal stalk of a cheerleader's baton). Finally—and this was a favourite of Hank's—there was the bending at the waist while looking up at you, as though you'd called her name just as she'd bent over to retrieve a dropped lighter. With a low-cut sweater, the gulf between her breasts looked like a deep snow-filled valley.

Hank would stay online for twenty-two minutes, or thirty-four minutes, or forty-seven minutes, until it got to the point in which he could kill a whole hour. Soon, *this* became his job, this patrolling of an eroticized Internet landscape. He proceeded systematically. One night he viewed Ukrainians only, with their freckles and snug dresses and lean, furrowed faces. Another night— his ears filled with *ping*ings and Manuel's pug-like snoring—he typed in *Belarus;* its women were leggy and pretty and lacking in pigment, as though raised under a sun blocked by particulate matter. He spent another night touring Baltic-state women, with their apple-shaped faces and lacy, fringed blouses. That morning, with Manuel outside and watching the sunrise, he toured ex-Soviet states that were arid and Muslim; these women looked Asian, with their black hair and round shoulders and complexions grown supple from prune and date eating.

He saw brittle-faced Muscovites and Paris Hilton–like "students." He saw ermine-wearing Siberians and the small, saddened faces of Far Eastern widows. He saw mostly blondes, but also brunettes and redheads and those whose hair was a multicoloured concoction. He saw the tall and the short and the smack dab in the middle; he saw the pretty and the plain and the spiritually radiant. He saw women whom most men would want, whom some men would want, and who would spend their long lives feeling lonely and hopeless. He saw the scarred and the gangly, the peach-faced and mournful, and playful young things who (so they claimed) still slept with their teddies. Without realizing, he saw women who'd inherited their mothers' martyr syndromes, and women who had married but were still gamely looking. He saw women who'd grown tired of men who were drunkards, and women who'd once baked Young Pioneer muffins. He saw women who were as lusty as badgers, and women who feared love as though it were something typhoidal. He saw women who looked at car crashes with their mouths hanging open, and women whose deflowering had come at the hands of sloshed uncles. He saw women who'd been children during the Thaw Generation, and who had swallowed fish oil during kindergarten recess. He saw women who remembered empty stores and articles in *Pravda* about the virtues of rationing, and he saw girls who had lied about their age and who knew only the wild west of post-Soviet Russia.

He *saw:* women who'd lost family in terrorist bombings, women whose brothers had been poisoned by FSB agents, and women who would do anything, *anything,* to leave Putin's Russia for five blissful minutes. Hank read their testimonials, he adopted their sorrows as if they were his own children, and he imagined the touch of soft skin against orange-stained fingers.

And then, oh yes *then,* Hank saw *mamochka.*

She was hiding in Girls from St. Petersburg, maintaining a low profile in Ages 18 to 30, keeping her head down amongst the Good-English Speaking. That evening, he had already gazed into a hundred or so pairs of sad eyes. He had already admired a hundred or so hourglass figures (Hank's tastes running toward the Sophia Loren–like) and he had already read a hundred or so testimonials (each and every one starting with "I am a caring and child-loving young woman . . ."). He was just about to turn it off for the evening: his eyes burned, his fingers felt achy, and he was beginning to tell himself that this idea might work for a cantankerous Pole but would not work for him, Henry Wallins.

Then she appeared, the resemblance uncanny, her left eye even wandering just the slightest bit inward . . . Oh yes oh yes, it was *her,* and in an instant he was back in Marseilles, reliving nights at Madame LaChance's, floating on wine and sea air and the sound of gulls cawing. His ears filled with a tune played on an accordion. He clicked on her name and watched the screen fill up with her—she was leaning against a tree, her sweater tight and mocha-coloured and just slightly unbuttoned. He gulped. He couldn't believe it. She had the same upturned nose, the same tousle of brown hair, the same lips and black eyes, all adding to a face that was *so* close to pretty. (And wasn't it this closeness, this tantalizing al*most*-ness, that had been the culprit, all those years earlier, in the port that every sailor most eagerly awaited?) She was twenty-one years of age, this girl from St. Petersburg. She studied marketing and English, and she lived with her mother. She liked pets and small children and walks in cool, leaf-strewn forests. In his mind he removed her glasses, and imagined kissing a face so young and so pale-toned.

Her name was Anna Verkoskova.

He spent three sleepless days, and three nights pacing on crutches. Finally (his longing having turned to a hurt that felt pleasing) he moved to the PC with the Internet connection. His breath came in tight spurts. His ear *ping*ing diminished to an apprehensive whisper. Hank logged on. He surrendered his credit card numbers. He rewrote his message five times before tapping Enter.

He logged off. The computer whirred and blinked at him. He actually felt relieved: nothing would come of this. This certainty both calmed him and left him feeling tired all over—he had seen enough of the world to know how it behaved, or at least how it behaved with respect to Hank Wallins.

In the middle of his next shift, around the time in which Manuel's eyelids softened and started struggling to stay open, Hank once again logged on, only to find a message in his From Russia With Love mailbox.

Dear Hank, it said, *please.*
My friends call me Anya.

TWO

And that, little one, was how it all started. His first messages were short and infused with a manufactured casualness—*I work as a computer operator,* he told her, *though I hope to start programming soon.* The next day he wrote: *I've always been fascinated by your country,* by which he meant he had keen memories of the 1972 Canada–Russia hockey series. Sometimes his emails took the form of questions—*Tell me, Anya, do you have brothers or sisters?*—and each time she would answer in a way that was youthful and breezy. *No, Hank, my parents they took one look at me and thought, okay, okay, is enough. Is very common reaction, here in Russia.*

With time, Hank forgot the goal of his emails, and concentrated on the pleasure each and every one gave him; each word was a balm, each sentence a bridge to the only time he'd been happy. He told her that, after not quite finishing high school—*Anya, what can I say? I was young and rebellious and that's something I regret now*—he'd signed on to a tanker called the *Antigonish Dreamer*. Though it was a job he'd enjoyed—*There is nothing, Anya, like the voice of the sea, whispering songs into your ears*—he told her he'd grown weary of travel, and the dictates of captains, and the rootless life had by all seamen. He also told her that if he'd had to reassemble one more sump pump, or weld together one more pre-start motor, or repair one more flange that had somehow come unflanged . . . *Anya, you know how it is, when your whole life needs changing.* What he didn't mention was the problem with his hearing—that *it,* and not any boredom or dissatisfaction, was the real reason for his career change. He didn't tell her that the whine of the turbines would spark a pain in his cochlea, and that this pain would knife down his cheek and into his jawbone, such that his last week as a sailor was spent in the third-level sickroom, holding his ears and quietly moaning. Oh no—in the myth he created for the new Henry Wallins, he wrote that he'd wanted something more stable, something that would enable him to settle down and, with luck, meet the right person. Shortly after, he told her, he'd applied to a computer school whose chief mode of advertising (*chuckle chuckle*) was paper matchbook covers. This led to his night shift with Quality Assurance, Canada's second-largest provider of home and car policies. *It's an okay job, Anya, it pays the bills and there's room for advancement though I have to say it can be slow, and because I work at night it's difficult to meet people.*

He wrote that he'd injured his ankle, and that it still gave him problems, though to make himself sound sporty he hinted at a mishap playing hockey. He told her that he one day wanted children, that he neither drank nor caroused, that he enjoyed winters and walks and the crackle of fires. He told her he needed a partner to feel happy, and that life was too short to get bogged down by problems. He told her all of this, his greatest deception coming in a single and mastodon-sized detail left out of his emails: *she,* Anna Verkoskova née Mikhailovna, looked exactly like a brothel-dweller named Martine who, for a time in Marseilles, had held him tight to her.

Hank, he one evening read, *please. If you would like to, come visit...*

Over the next month, he fought demons and nerves and vicious ear clangings. And yet, he did it—he booked a week of vacation and bought a discounted ticket on a cheap Russian airline. Three weeks after *that*, smack dab in the middle of a cool July evening, he packed a suitcase with clothing, the Eyewitness guide to St. Petersburg, gifts of ice wine and maple syrup, vials of lorazepam and Zoloft and ankle-painkillers, his Marsona DS-600 with a voltage converter, and the long-distance number for his tinnitus support group. He then tried to sleep, and spent six hours tossing.

Morning came. He bathed, shaved closely, and boarded an Aeroflot flight that transferred in Moscow. This, for Hank, was a new experience. Though he'd been all over Europe, on ships captained mostly by roughneck Acadians, he had never actually flown aboard a commercial airliner. As he boarded the plane, his ankle was throbbing. To fit into his seat, he had to splay his long legs or turn them dramatically sideways. Hank then noticed his big hands were shaking. *Damn,* he muttered, while closing his eyes and doing deep yogic breathing. The plane sat, and then taxied, and then jetted through skies with its nose pointed upward. Suddenly he felt better; the airy roar of the engines masked the *ping* in his eardrums. Outside the plane's window, the air was sparkling with colour. Sun glinted off the wings, leaving Hank dazzled. Beneath him, clouds stretched to the distance like ridged Arctic tundra.

There was something about being this far above the earth's surface that felt like floating (and that made his life seem puny and not deserving of worry). Hank leaned back and felt weightless; he drank tomato juice and ate pretzels and introduced himself to the young businessman beside him. "I *am*," Hank was told, "importer of shower curtains from Germany into Canada. Russian ones—oh boy, let me say, they rip, they tearing, they one hundred percent pieces of shit. Much better they are the German ones, manufactured in Singapore and not rippable or tearable and with them I make out-and-out killing." As the young man talked (and drank can after can of lukewarm Baltika) Hank listened and nodded. Oh yes—he listened throughout his pelmeni dinner, a pair of subtitled movies about hard Moscow gangsters, a breakfast of sweet rolls served with apricot jelly, and a descent so enthused the infants on board all started squalling. Then, and only then, did the young man stop talking.

Hank transferred to a domestic flight bound for St. Petersburg, the plane rising in pale sun and coming down in bad weather. He felt tired and nervous all over. He rubbed his big face till it was marked by pink splotches. His legs felt tingly and weak, as though conducting low voltage. Unbuttoning his coat, he walked onto the tarmac while favouring his ankle. Over his usual ear noises, he could hear trucks beeping and engines revving and male voices yelling. The lights of the terminal shone through warm rain; it looked grey and forlorn, as if newly abandoned. Hank kept walking, his eyes so narrowed against the weather that they looked barely open. He entered the terminal; it was smoke-filled and crowded. He retrieved his baggage and proceeded to customs. A green light flashed, and he entered one of the inspection cabins. Here he foggily presented his passport, his visa, his registry card, the letter of invitation that Anna had sent him, and finally his proof of medical insurance.

"Welcome," said the officer, without once looking at him.

And Hank, who had expected an FSB grilling, felt a wash of gratitude. He left the small cabin and, twenty feet away, saw large sliding glass doors. When he was two feet from them, the doors whooshed open and he saw her holding a sign with his name written on it. Hank approached smiling, his hand held out toward her; he felt her thin fingers slide against his palm. Meanwhile, he stared. She looked even more like Martine now that she was standing before him.

"Hello," she said.

"Hi."

"I am Anya."

"Pleased to meet you."

"Welcome."

(And Hank, oh yes Hank, could hear his ears singing.)

"So," she said after a moment. "We going now, yes?"

They stepped into a wet, rushing north wind. Anna seemed not to notice; she walked to the edge of the lot and held out a hand. Seconds later, a badly dented Volga pulled over, the car clinking and popping before giving a final hard side-to-side shudder. The driver leaned over to roll down the window. Anna's voice was lost to the patter of rain against metal. Every few seconds a gale would kick up and blow sheets of warm drizzle across the dark, gloomy car park.

She straightened and turned. "Is twenty euros. Is all right, yes? At first he want thirty, but I tell him is, mmmmmm, how you saying? Is robbery on highway, no?"

"Sure," Hank muttered, not really listening; instead, he was thinking that this feeling—this rapid heart *thudding*—was a thing that both frightened him and filled him with a yearning that felt almost ancient. The driver put Hank's bag in the trunk and then restarted the engine. The car smelled of smoke and wet nylon jackets.

Behind rain-dotted lenses, Anna's dark eyes looked like gems in a river. "Is old car," she said. "There are many like this, here in St. Petersburg. Also, are many fine and new cars, but many like this one also. But you will see . . ."

The driver revved three times before pulling onto the road that bordered the airport. The car rattled and jiggled and every few minutes backfired. He turned on the radio and the cabin filled with balalaika playing. "*There,*" Anna said, "is located museum commemorating seige of St. Petersburg . . ." and, a minute or so later, "This arch commemorates Russian defeat of Turkish army. Is very interesting, I think. Did you know, Hank, when Peter built this city, it look so different and royal and European that many people, who still mostly were peasants, they start to call it 'the unreal city.' Do you know this, Hank? The unreal city?"

Hank pried his eyes off Anna and took his first good look at her wet Russian city; it came through glass that was rain-streaked and warped and starting to turn foggy.

Anna kept pointing at the city's main features. "Is Nevsky, our most important street." Or, when the car again turned: "Okay, we are going in direction of Sennaya Ploschad, the old Tsar hay market . . ." Or, upon crossing a bridge that was marked by gold lions: "Is Griboedov, where lover of Gogol threw herself into water."

Each time she spoke, Hank's attention wandered and then went away fully. His heart, of course, was the culprit: it had become an antenna tuned to Anna's every gesture, and not the sense of the words coming from her mouth. She leaned forward and in Russian said something. The driver nodded, turned the wheel, and said *da da da* before stopping the car and peering at Anna. Hank glanced out. They were parked beside a slow-moving canal that was dark and (he thought) emitting the smell of frozen cucumbers. On the other side of the car was what looked like a hotel.

"*Here,*" Anna said, "is home away from home for next week. I do very much research for finding you nice place that is good and not so expensive. A friend of my uncle, he own it."

Hank stepped out. The driver was pulling his bags from the trunk. Hank gave him money and followed Anna inside, where she spoke to the woman who was at the reception. Hank put his bags by his feet. He looked around, at old wood and curled tiling and rusting wrought iron. Above him, a chandelier glimmered. Beside the concierge was a small cage-style elevator; it made a can-opener grinding when the doors slowly opened. As they rode upward, Hank noticed the scent of Anna's perfume—it smelled of lilacs and dew, and it made him all the more smitten. They stepped into a narrow and dimly lit hallway. Anna's heels clacked; her movements, Hank thought, were wondrous and graceful. They stopped before one of the rooms, where he inserted the latchkey and gave it a jiggle. Hank then stood in the doorway as she around the room darted; she checked the lights, the thermostat, and the spring to the mattress. From the bathroom, he heard the running of water and a cry that, to his ears, sounded muted and lovely.

She came out holding something. "Hank," she blurted. "What it is called such thing?"

"That?"

"Yes."

"It's a bath plug."

"Yes! Bath *plug*! Well Hank, I am proud to report you having one. Many Russian hotels are famous for not having, mmmmmm, bath plugs. I checked and it very well fits, so you may be having nice and long warm bath."

Hank grinned; she pronounced *checked* as *check-edd*, and somehow this made him giddy. Anna placed the plug on the dresser behind her and plunged her hands into the pockets of her vinyl jacket. Hank crossed the room. He put his suitcase on the bed, causing it to sag and make a soprano wheezing.

"Hank?"

He looked over.

"Only now I noticing you have . . . mmmmmmm, how you saying? When the foot it not functioning completely well?"

"A limp?"

"Yes! You have limp! I suppose is from hockey-playing accident—the one you mention in your email. It bothers you?"

"Not really. Only if I walk on it too much."

"Don't worry. Here, every car is taxi. We call them *chastniki* and they are everywhere. Is very easy to get around. Maybe in museum your foot it becomes sore. I don't know, maybe we go little bit slowly."

"I'll be fine. Don't worry about it."

"Many men in Russia have some sort of, mmmmmm, scar or physical problem. I do not mind this. I think it give, how you say, *character*? The Russian woman, she likes this. It shows that life has not, mmmmmm, let you go untouched. Is very important, here. Nothing should be perfect."

Hank bathed in the glow of her accent. He could almost see her words, rising into air and leaving a warm light behind them.

"I think maybe you liking to have little rest, yes? I have my studies, now, but maybe I later return and we having some small dinner and become better knowing of one another."

"Sure, all right. Sounds good."

"I am glad you have come, Hank. I am glad you came to meet me, here in St. Petersburg. I will show you many many things, this week."

"Thank you."

"So we meet in lobby?"

"Yeah. All right."

"At seven o'clock? I do not know when people in Canada they eat, but here I think is okay."

"Sure, seven."

"All right then, Hank. Have a good sleep."

She nodded and went to the door. The last thing she did was turn and give him a smile that was faint and self-conscious.

Hank lay on his bed, hands folded on his chest. Sleep wouldn't come; he worried that in one short week she would not learn to like him. Suddenly his good mood was gone, and his ears started *ping*ing. To relax, he tried the deep one-two-three breathing he'd learned in his tinnitus support group. When this didn't help, he rose and through his medicine kit rummaged. He swallowed an Ativan with a glass of cool water. He stood, peering at himself in the small bathroom mirror. He felt bothered—it was his pink, mottled skin, his spooling of red hair, the slight jowly padding that clung to his jawline. He sighed and, considering his size, swallowed a second white tablet. He then plugged in his Marsona and listened to fuzzy white noise as he lay gazing upward. As the sedatives took effect, he studied his tattoo, which had grown kelp green with age; sadly, he thought of the days in which his arms had been as big around as young tree trunks. He touched his lips to his French girl. Slowly his vision turned hazy, and his thoughts grew discordant. He felt Martine's skin touching him as though she were right there beside him. Deeper he sank into the balm that is sleeping, until a sea wave arose and washed through the window.

It spilled over the floor, shorting electrical sockets and dripping through cracks in the tiling. Slowly it built, till it dampened Hank's sheets and swallowed his mattress. Minutes later Hank was taken, his body now buoyant and his lips tasting sea salt. Oh yes—he was carried away on a swirl of blue current, from the cold Gulf of Finland to the rough, raging seas of the North Atlantic Ocean, and then, oh yes *then*, how a gentle smile graced those mottled Hank features, for the waters were warming, and the current was carrying him past the alehouses of England and the bullrings of Spain and the palm tree–lined coast of northern Morocco. And then he was in sun-drenched Marseilles, in another time and another place, wandering through the maze-like Arab quarter, his companion an Acadian sailor named Marcel who had been there before him and *who,* upon insisting that they explore the souk, had said, "'Ank, 'Ank, I know a place where the women are brown-skinned and curvy and 'otter than the white sands of the Sahara!"

"I don't know . . ."

"'Ank. They are going to wipe the frown even from *your* face!"

And so, despite Hank's reluctance, they'd set out, two Canadian sailors from the *Antigonish Dreamer* (a tanker now half filled with Hibernia's finest). They took turn after turn along cool stucco lane walls, and if you looked at them closely you would have noticed that the tips of their fingers were stained grey with oil, and that the whites of their eyes were run through with red lines, and that the skin on their faces had been worn rough by sea gales. When Hank stopped and asked, "Are we lost?" Marcel shrugged and said, "I don't know, maybe, a little . . ."

But who cared? *Who?* Little one—these were Hank's sailor days, his drinking days, *his days before ear* ping*ing,* and as they walked they drank wine from a dark, heavy bottle. Black-haired children trailed along behind them; their feet were crusty and their noses were running and their little hands were held out for centimes or dollars. Finally, Marcel said, *D'accord, d'accord! Où est la maison de Madame LaChance?* and they all threw up their hands and yelled, *Nous savons! Nous savons! Nous pouvons vous aider!* Off they went, Marcel grinning and Hank half-drunkenly stumbling and their gaggle of children in Arabic singing. After a bit they all stopped. They gave coins to the children. They also handed over the bottle, the children drinking and then handing it back grinning, the backs of their hands wiping lips stained and moistened.

Hank and Marcel entered a hot, clammy silence. They passed through a clay, sun-splashed courtyard, and into a room filled with pillows and divans and dark, dusty carpets. Sweat rolled down Hank's forehead and into his green eyes. Marcel and Madame yammered in French while laughing and gesturing and touching each other's forearms. *Oui oui oui!* she finally called, and clapped her fat hands together. Marcel grinned, and joined Hank on a divan. They both relaxed and leaned back and laced their fingers behind thick necks. The girls were coming out, one olive-skinned beauty after another, dressed in slippers and sheer pants and gold satin halters. Each was beautiful and Algerian and Naugahyde-coloured, with hugely orbed eyes offering quick-flitting glances—everyone, that is, but the last one, who was small and slightly cross-eyed and, unlike the others, only verging on pretty. Hank's gaze swept over this parade of enticement. His mouth went dry as pity rose in him. He couldn't help it—he felt he could love every one of them.

"Pick one," said Marcel, "or better yet, pick two . . ."

Hank found that he couldn't, he didn't know how to, he found beauty glaring and monolithic and at times almost frightening, and so finally he'd turned to Marcel and said, *Do any of them speak English?*, a question that caused Marcel to toss back his head and laugh loudly—*What? You are looking for conversation, 'Ank?*—and then turn to the Madame and ask her the question. Madame grinned too, *bien sûr bien sûr,* and with a scarab-ringed finger she pointed to the end of the row, at the small cross-eyed girl who was smiling, more or less, in Hank Wallins's direction.

"Martine," she'd said. "*Elle parle anglais. Oui, oui. Elle est* très spéciale."

Hank walked up to her. "Would you?" he stammered. "I mean, are you . . . ?"

Martine batted her eyelids. "Am I occupied? *Non*, monsieur, not at all, *pas du tout* . . ." And with that she reached out and touched Hank in a way that was replete with a warm, Christlike knowing. Marcel guffawed (for he saw only her wandering left eye) and said with a snort, *Only the best for my Henri*.

Ah, ignorance. Is there anything more blissful? Despite being men of the world (or at least the part of the world serviced by the *Antigonish Dreamer*) neither Hank nor Marcel knew that tales of this girl had circulated through all of France, and the better part of Mediterranean Europe. Furthermore, this had occurred even though she was not the most beautiful, or the swarthiest, or the most voluminously breasted among Madame LaChance's infamous stable. *She*, it was known far and wide, had her own artful flim-flam, her own carnival shell game. It was (they all said) a con that had never in a souk whore been so perfected. She led Hank up steps curving, and down a tight hallway lit solely with candles. She took him through a heavy latched door and into a room glowing softly. After washing his most intimate parts in water scented with tarragon, she laid him on a bed made of straw and hen feathers. Quickly, Hank hardened, for already he loved her.

"*Mon Dieu*," she opined.

Hank, blushing, covered himself up, feeling as though he had misbehaved somehow.

"*Non, non, non*," she said, smiling. "Ees not necessary. It ees a sing of beauty, *oui*?"

She took his hands in hers, drawing them away from his inflamed epicentre. She coated his face with soft angel kisses. There was stroking and caressing and swirling tongue movements. She hovered above him, lighter than the breeze that blew through the quarter. Then, slowly, she lowered herself on him, a motion followed by bucking and bobbing and pivotal rocking. When that critical moment came, the heavens ringing and church bells pealing, she called, *"Je t'adore! Je t'aime!"* in a manner so real and convincing that Hank, like a hundred lonely sailors before him, believed her. Oh yes, he believed everything she told him, the culprit a void that needed filling inside him.

They collapsed in a heap, more off the pallet than on it. Tightly he hugged her. Ten minutes later, to confirm her love for her big pink-skinned sailor, she threw in second helpings for free, and she did so while smiling.

Upon returning to ship, Hank discovered that the dockworkers had gone on strike in Algeciras, the next port of call, the captain deciding to stay docked in Marseilles until the problem blew over. Hank's heart burst into flames, and he went back to Madame LaChance's like an orphan who had found a source of free dinner. It got to the point whereby Madame, seeing him love-dazed and wandering the dimly lit hallways, pulled him aside and whispered, *Fais attention, mon petit, take care of yourself* before letting him go on paying and paying. He was there for over a week. Martine hired neighbourhood children to bring them chicken and couscous and wine in round, painted clay jugs. He left the brothel one time and one time only; when he returned, his new tattoo was still dotted with beads of warm crimson. Martine took a look, turning his arm this way and that way, and then loved him as though he were the last man living.

After that, they moved to a bulk-fee system. Every five or six hours, having enriched his blood with pomegranates and oysters, Martine would treat him to pleasures both old and inventive. His lips swelled. His skin became speckled with bruises, and his loins ached so badly he thought at times they'd been damaged. Her imagination had no bounds, which was startling for one who came across as so childlike. (Little one—is there anything more enticing than contradiction? Than asymmetry? Than two humanly facets that don't fit on the same page?) She showed him the Spread Eagle, and then afterward made mint tea and talked of her fondness for kittens. She performed a manoeuvre called the Flying Wallenda, and then showed him some lace she'd bought for her mother. On a night when the moon was a sulphurous lantern, and they were both full of absinthe and garlicky seafood, she unleashed an old strumpet favourite called the French Inquisition—a ministration that was profoundly erotic, just a little bit painful, and punishable by stoning in most Middle Eastern countries.

The strike in Spain was settled, and the captain ordered that the moorings be pulled and the engine restarted. Hank spent one final night with his courtesan lover. The moon settled behind clouds that were dark blue and misty. Madame herself cooked them kebabs, which they ate giddily and hungrily, like doted-upon children. He left for his ship in the morning, having been cuddled, and cooked for, and torn into shreds with fingernails hardened by polish. The salt on his wounds felt painful and wondrous.

Hank (being Hank) started wiring her money. In return, she wrote him letters, on paper as thin as the peels of a shallot. She expressed both her love and the things she planned to do to him slowly. One night, after working twelve hours, his coveralls messed with gas and sump water, he took one of her letters to the mess and read it alone while drinking black coffee. Then, because exhaustion makes one careless, he left it next to a ring of dark, cooling liquid. By the time he came back, the crew was passing it around laughing.

'Ank, they called out, *we never knew you 'ad it in you!* 'Ank, they kept blurting, *we never knew you were so much like a Frenchman!*

For the next three months, as the boat went from one port to another, he was called nothing but Romeo, or lover boy, or the six-and-a-half-foot-tall Casanova. And then, just like that, the letters stopped coming. Hank's face grew long, and his eyes sat half-closed on puffy grey pouches. He started making mistakes at work, and looking as though he'd given up shaving. His shipmates noticed and knew to stop teasing.

He had to wait two months before the boat again docked in Marseilles—two months of deck wandering, of up-at-stars looking, of long dreamless nights after which he'd feel tired. In Haifa, he tried to call the Madame; he was not at all surprised to find the number unlisted. Two days after *that*, following a shift in which there were fuck-ups and mishaps and too many problems to mention, Marcel sat him down and tried to help out by saying, "Ank—maybe it's better you forget about 'er, maybe she was, you know, takin' advantage?"

"I know that," Hank replied, looking into the distance.

The day came. The boat was pushed by a tug into dead-still port waters. The ladder was lowered for Hank and Hank only. He raced from the port and ran through souk laneways, the dirty-faced children yelling, *Bonjour, monsieur Hank*. Upon reaching the heavy wooden door of Madame LaChance's, he knocked with an anxious and hard-knuckled firmness. It was eleven o'clock on a cool, sunny morning. He saw a dark and miniaturized eye through the hole looking at him. The door flung open. It was the Madame herself, without her usual kohl makeup. Instead of a long flowing robe in a bright sunburst colour, she was wearing a drab baggy dress that made her look homely.

Her eyes were glassy.

"*Mon Dieu,*" she gasped, and put her fat arms around him. This felt so outside the rules that he almost recoiled. He returned her hug tentatively, his nose above hair smelling of tobacco and cassis. "Oh, 'Ank," she said. "I would 'ave write you myself, but I do not know the *name* of your boat."

She sniffled, and stepped into the lane and locked the wood door behind her. Outside, she looked older and worn down by sadness.

"Come. Please. *Come.* I show you the place where it 'appen."

As they walked past souk doors, and blue-trimmed souk windows, and falling-down old mortared souk corners, Madame LaChance began sobbing. "'Ere," she said at last. "It was *'ere* . . ." and they were right where the souk met the port, opposite the municipal post office. Hank knew the spot well—it was a place that teemed in the summer, its sidewalks alive with cafés and jugglers and white-faced caricaturists, not to mention gold-skinned mime artists who could stand still for hours. Hank heard gulls and close traffic. Meanwhile, Madame LaChance snuffled and at her red eyes kept dabbing.

"It was 'ere," she said. "It was 'ere. Oh, she was a good girl, 'Ank. A girl with nothing but love in her 'eart. Love, love, love— it was all she 'ad to offer. She was the only person I ever met who never, ever, once tell a lie."

"I don't get it."

She looked at him wide-eyed. "The *explosion*! You didn't 'ear?!"

"I've been at sea."

"So you don't know? You don't get the papers?"

Hank nodded, afraid of the answer. The Madame looked frozen, her face tight and staring.

"The explosion. The GIA, they put the bomb in a car. Those Algerian terrorist, they 'ate the French, yes? Oh, 'Ank, it was one of those little Russian cars, a Lada, you know? *How could you not know this?* It explode everywhere and Martine . . . Martine, she was . . . she was... and to *think,* by the 'ands of her very own people!" Madame held herself snuffling. "Oh, 'Ank. She was going to the post office. She go every day. Every day she would tell me, *Madame, madame, maybe there's a letter for me from 'Ank!* Oh 'Ank, 'Ank, it was so terrible... *and at the hands of 'er own people!*" Madame could no longer speak, her throat tightly jammed with sobs and half gurgles.

Hank stared at her, blinking.

"Thank you," he said, looking shocked to numbness in the bright Marseilles sunlight. He walked away, the Madame calling, "'Ank! 'Ank! Where you are going?" He moved smartly, as though pursued by wharf phantoms. He cut through the port, following truck lanes and sidewalks, and marched up the ship's ladder, hands on the railings, looking face-punched and older and not at all like Hank Wallins. He then locked himself in his berth and began around the clock sleeping. He was twenty-eight years old. He rose only to use the WC, or fetch food left outside his cabin, or to bellow at night over seas dark and churning. The captain, a well-worn sea dog who hailed from Rimouski, chose to indulge him; he had grown to understand when a man needs time to recover.

They reached a shipping lane west, and chugged toward the Atlantic. A storm kicked up in the middle of the ocean; the deck was pelted with water, and hail, and birds who had died while searching for islands. This went on for two days. On the morning of the third, sun slipped through the clouds like beams of white cotton. Inside his stateroom, Hank lay with his hands over his eyes. In the black space this created, his imagination went crazy—cars flying, people screaming, limbs falling through the sky and landing on house roofs. By the time he'd spooled it through his head for the one hundredth time—no, no, for the one *thousandth* time—he could see it so clearly that the flames blazed before him and the eruption pummelled his ears like a firing cannon.

Little one—he couldn't have made it stop even had he wanted.

He emerged from his cabin and padded along a yellow-lit hallway. His legs felt weak and a little bit shaky, and he was holding his ears, as though he'd been deafened. He took the accommodation elevator up to the officers' second-level quarters. Here he knocked on the door of the second mate, who was acting as medic on the *Antigonish Dreamer*. The man answered the door, a maritime Lebanese whose face needed shaving.

"What?"

Hank blinked; his features went ashen.

"*What?*"

Again Hank was silent. Seconds passed by. The medic looked at Hank as though he were crazy. When Hank finally spoke, his voice was shaky and weakened.

"It's my ears," he said. "I can't stop them. They're *pinging*."

But that was long, long ago. *So* long ago that it felt like a play, performed in a slim back-street alley. In his room at the Hotel Griboedov, presences nudged Hank with cold, gnarling fingers. He came awake groggy and thirsting for liquids. He got up, stretched, and trudged to the shower. Here his ears calmed under the drum of warm water.

Anna came. In a restaurant nearby, just down from Gostinyy, they ate shashlik and peppers and rice scented with saffron. Throughout the meal, rain musically pelted the window beside them. She kept glancing outside, as though she was seeing things skulking through shadows. This resulted in pauses that made Hank uncomfortable. Conversation, no matter how hard he tried, had never been his forte, and his biggest worry now was that he was boring her.

"Anya?" he would say, and she would look as though she was trying to remember what she was doing here with him. Then it would come, that same tentative smile she'd given him earlier.

"I am sorry."

"Everything's okay?"

"Yes, of course, is just my studies are very distracting of me in this moment. In two weeks we have exams."

"Exams?"

"Yes. Related to my studies in marketing."

"Jesus, Anya—you should've told me. I could've come after you were done with them."

"No—no. Hank. Do not worry. Is not big or serious thing. Please, enjoy your dinner, afterward we walk along Nevsky, is what we do here, please, do not worry, I still have much time to spend with you . . ."

True to her word, they went the following day to the Peter and Paul Fortress. Here, Hank's ankle started to throb around the time they passed the cell where Fyodor Dostoevsky was unjustly imprisoned. The day after that, they saw the statues of Peterhof, and the day after that it was the Russian Museum. It mattered little where they were: each time she looked at him, he felt numb in every place that wasn't his left foot; each time she spoke, the ground fell away, counter-clockwise revolving; and each time those slightly crossed eyes blinked, or those little hands gestured, or her young body hunched against the damp city weather . . . well. Hank learned there was more than *one* type of hovering. Oh yes. There was also floating with glee past Pushkin's Bronze Horseman. There was gliding on air up and down Nevsky Prospect. There was wafting on currents up the stairs of St. Isaac's. There *was:* slowly rising from your seat during a ballet at Mariinsky, Hank filled with a grace that left him giddily drunken.

And yet there he was, at the end of each day spent sightseeing, in the must-scented lobby of the Hotel Griboedov, under a chandelier made from silver and finely honed crystal, looking down at dark eyes through her rain-streaked eyeglasses, and yearning—no, no, *dying*—to bend over and kiss a girl who lived on in his memory. He could imagine it all: the warmth of her lips, the softness of pale skin, the transference of need between two hurting people. But then something would stop him, something that was cold and nerve-racking and not in any way pleasing. Perhaps it was something in Anna's body language—some slight stiffness in the shoulders, some slight corner-of-the-mouth drooping. Oh yes, her demeanour kept him at bay, Hank studying her face till he was sure he could see it—an obvious not there-ness, dulling the shine of her dark eyes.

He'd take a respectful step backward.

"Thank you for today."

"You are welcome, Hank."

"It was wonderful."

"I am happy you like it."

(*Hhhay-pee*, he thought. *I love how she says that.*)

"Will I see you, you know, tomorrow?"

And he'd *swear* he could see it, a slight indecision, as though the poor girl was being tugged in different directions. But then it would vanish, and her soft smile would come, and she'd look up at Hank and say, "Yes, yes, tomorrow I see you."

The week passed quickly. She had three or four hours each day of classes, and the rest of her time she'd spend with him, often arriving flushed and harried and with her hair wildly tousled. On his last full day in Russia, Hank ate breakfast alone in the hotel's small café. He then asked the woman at reception (who spoke enough English to half understand him) to arrange for a taxi to go to the Alexander Column. He arrived at eleven, and then waited, a half-folded map used as an umbrella. He hunched his shoulders and took quick, shuffling steps in the warm, misting gulf air. When ten minutes had passed, he crossed the square and took refuge under the Hermitage entrance. From here, he had a full view of the place where Lenin's troops had stormed the Tsar's Winter Palace. More time elapsed, each minute passing slower. *So that's it,* he thought. *So this is the way she's breaking the news to me.* He waited five minutes more, his ears *ping*ing loudly, and was just about to go inside by himself when he saw her, across the square running, her straight black hair swept away from her forehead. She reached the column and looked around and then heard Hank calling to her.

She darted to the museum, arriving breathless and soggy.

"Hank . . . I am sorry . . . I am late, and for this I am sorry."

"That's all right."

"No, no, please—is not, mmmmmm, excusable."

"No, Anya, it's fine."

"You are sure? You are not mad?" A moment or two passed. She wore an expression that made her look older. "All right," she said quietly, her voice lost to the rain that was falling around them. "Let's go."

Hank bought two entrance tickets. The museum was empty, and they walked through grand hallways. Hank gazed at the paintings, though to be truthful he cared little for Degas and Picasso, for Rembrandt and Velázquez, for Matisse's red and blue in-the-air dancers. What he cared about was Anna—her skin looked puffy, and her eyes looked red, as though she'd been stricken with hay fever. *Plus*—in Peterhof and the Fortress, in

St. Isaac's and the Russian Museum, in Mariinsky and the Church of the Saviour on Spilled Blood, she had talked volubly about her country, and its history, and every Russian's thirst for the genuine. Today she was nearly mute, managing little more than a quick gesture and, in a voice slightly rasping, *Is Caravaggio* or *This one, is Rousseau* . . . Each time she stopped to look at a painting, Hank would study the side of her face, as though *it*, and not Rembrandt, was what made the Hermitage special. (Meanwhile, inside, he was dying to tell her: *I love you, I always have, for eight years I've been waiting*.)

The cafeteria too was nearly empty; were it not for a busload of Scandinavian seniors, all of whom wore rain bonnets and chattered in Swedish, they would have been by themselves. They bought sausage sandwiches and sat at a little round table meant to be suggestive of Paris. They more or less ate in silence. Outside the tall leaded windows, the skies looked like grey and tangled wool blankets.

They left. They stood on the steps of the Hermitage, hoping upon hope that the rain would stop falling. An afternoon and evening still lay before them. Anna shuffled and gazed into the damp, regal distance. There was a long, awkward pause. She seemed to be thinking.

"Hank," she finally said without turning, "maybe I can show to you something. Something that tourists do not see ever. You would like this? You would like to see the *real* city?"

Hank nodded, and followed her across the great plaza. They walked along Nevsky to Gostinyy station, where he followed her through crowds and around large marble statues. They boarded a train, and rode standing in a car smelling of wood and potatoes. After three or four stops—the lights dimming each time to announce a door opening—they reached Baltiskaya station, and switched to a train with dark, grime-smeared windows. At the front of the car, a man in a raincoat was selling lettuce and lemons and three-week-old kittens.

The train surfaced, in a land of square cement buildings that went on forever, the only relief the occasional stand of white pine trees. Anna kept pointing and saying, "I have friend from school in that block" or "My aunt, she live in that building" or, finally, at a stop a half-hour from Baltiskaya station, "We are here." They stepped onto a dirty outdoor platform. "Keep your ticket," she said as they passed through babushka-manned turnstiles and stepped into a small outdoor market made with tent poles and sheeting. The vendors all had broad spider-webbed faces. There were dogs running in circles, and children playing rough games with each other. There was the burnt wood smell of braziers, and the squabble of chickens pecking at cages. The earth was soggy and covered with vegetable peelings, and Hank was stared at by drunks perched on crates and old lawn chairs.

"Come," Anna said, and then they were clomping through a field toward a procession of tenements. The ground was a mixture of dirt and grass and broken glass bottles. Upon reaching the roadway that ran in front of Anna's building, Hank looked in either direction, the buildings growing smaller and smaller as they neared the horizon. Together they crossed through a courtyard and approached a single rusting door wedged halfway open; its bottom was pressed firmly against chipped, broken concrete. Anna squeezed through, motioning at Hank to follow. The only light in the vestibule came in through the doorway; it cast a beam like a knife over spray-painted graffiti. He could see rising cement dust and a scattering of litter. Three feet ahead was an old elevator, stopped at mid-floor with its door seized wide open.

"Come," Anna said as she climbed a cold staircase lit by small stairwell windows. "At night, is necessary to have, mmmmm, hand torch, yes?" Without waiting for Hank, she climbed past chipped cement walls and scrawled Russian curse words and ghost eyes that peered through cracks and small fissures. She finally stopped before a door that was lined with locks and keyholes bored into metal. From the pocket of her jacket she pulled out her key ring; each lock required a surfeit of jiggling. Finally they stepped into a room so hot that Hank felt as though he was in danger of choking. Above them a light made an intermittent clicking.

"Is common room," Anna explained. "Nobody they use it. Come."

He followed her through a darkened hallway, past a *communalka* kitchen and a *communalka* bathroom and a row of *communalka* bedrooms, from which he could hear television sets and at least one baby wailing and the sound of a man for some reason groaning. "Is Mr. Yanofsky," Anna said with an eye roll. "He was in Chechnya. He is younger than I."

She reached a closed door and again went to work with her key chain. She beckoned Hank inside. He saw a sink, a dresser, a desk, a small refrigerator, a poster of some Russian rock star who was dark-skinned and brooding, and a sofa that (Hank suspected) folded out into the bed in which Anna slept with her mother.

"So. Is very typical, here. Is very *usual* Russian housing. Perhaps thirty percent of Russians still live in *communalka*. The rest they live in apartments not too much larger or, mmmmm, commodious, yes?"

"Who's that?" Hank said, pointing at the poster.

"Him?"

"Yeah."

"Is Viktor Tsoi. He is most fantastic rock star. He is amazing person and loved by all people. You do not know him in Canada?"

"I don't think so."

"I suppose not. Only in Russian he sings. But trust me—he is very good singer. Or maybe I should say, he *was* very good singer. He is dead now."

Hank moved to the window. From here, he gazed out over building after cloud-darkened building, the sky between them as grey as the soot of a chimney. *Bloody hell,* he thought, though he could barely hear himself think over the television babble, and the cranky babe wailings, and the sound of the ex-soldier being assaulted by nightmares. Then it happened. The sounds in Hank's ears turned to actual phrases. He listened intently, for they were words of guidance and faith, and they felt like a gift to him.

He turned. His face was half in the grey light creeping in through the window and half in the white light thrown by the fixture above him.

"You could visit me," he said.

Anna gazed at him palely. Time turned to a tension that invaded Hank's shoulders. A wordlessness grew louder than the sounds all around them.

"It's okay," Hank said. "It was just an idea."

Anna blinked as though startled. Seconds passed slowly as she turned to stare out the window. She seemed to grow paler as she gazed at the weather. Finally she turned to look at him. As she did, she brushed the hair off her forehead and mustered a smile that was wholly Martine-like.

Then, oh yes *then,* she hiccuped the answer that Hank Wallins yearned for.

Little one. There are moments remembered, and moments discarded, and moments that, when viewed from history's pulpit, burn with the brilliant white light of a supernova explosion. A man's first hovering is one of them. A man's return to life is another. Hank felt the terror that comes with promise and changing. It was a sensation that persisted through his last night in a room filled with phantoms, and it lasted during Anna's polite send-off at Pulkovo, and it flavoured every single minute of his stale-air flights homeward. He taxied to his apartment and slept for twelve hours, his dreams filled with a land where wolves brayed at soldiers.

When he awoke, it was midnight; the world from his balcony glinted in darkness. He felt fidgety, and breathless, and like he needed to do something. He ate crackers and cheese and sliced pickled onions; he swallowed Ativan and codeine and a glass of warm Molson's. He listened to a CD of Acadian fiddlers, and then put on a jacket and went outside walking, restlessness and joy being that evening's culprits. He trudged south along Yonge Street, any flaring of ankle pain lost to hard concentration. He walked past the Evergreen Youth Centre, where kids in torn jeans called out to him mocking; past the Dundas Street square, where unconscious drunks awaited gasoline dousings; past the intersection with Queen Street, where a thin Salvadorean asked him for food for his children (and Hank, being Hank, gave him all of his spare change). He strode past King Street (where a flickering gaslight lured brown bats and swallows), and Front Street (where squeegee kids made homes under shadowed bypasses), and Queen's Quay (which at this hour was pitch-black and lonely). Here he gazed like a sentry at choppy dark waters. Soon he was watching the red-blood rays of morning, and knowing, yes *knowing*, what it was he could give her.

The first house he saw had a cracking foundation. After dismissing it, he and an agent from RE/MAX climbed into her car and drove to an Etobicoke bungalow with a low, sagging roofline. They left quickly, only to view a bad-smelling row house in which a reclusive old woman had been partially eaten by house cats. These were his options on his first morning of house hunting; had his agent, a sibilant-voiced woman with nails like hawk's talons, not insisted there were *a thousand homes, just out there waiting,* he might have called off the whole thing.

Instead, she suggested they stop for a bite to eat. As she nattered about real estate prices, and the glowing accomplishments of both her grown children, Hank found himself picturing the place where Anna lived with her mother. This helped. Anything, he understood, would be a gift *to* her. Later, when they stopped in front of the small house on Craven, smack dab in the heart of the city's Little India, Hank decided (before going inside) that this was the house he would buy for his Anya. Maintaining this verve took determination: though the roof looked sound, and the foundation was solid, the windows were covered by tattered grey bedsheets. He walked to the back of the property and found a yard littered with dog shit and bottles.

"Now remember," his agent said as she opened the lockbox, "it *is* a foreclosure. It might need a little TLC." She unlocked the door and looked back at him while saying, "I'm sure it's nothing that a quick coat of paint won't—" Her voice stopped in mid-sentence, and she took a quick half-step backward.

Hank said, "Excuse me," and squeezed carefully past her. He too at first blanched and recoiled—grow lamps still dangled on wires, and the walls were still sheeted with aluminum foil. But then Hank reconsidered. He could overlook these flaws, just as he was willing to overlook the spray-painted slurs that covered the foil.

"I can afford this?"

"Yes," his agent said, having regained her composure. "This you can afford."

"And I could move in right away?"

She drew alongside him, arms crossed over her stomach. "I'm quite sure you could move in tomorrow."

He did, more or less. He bought the place for a song, packed up his belongings, and moved within a month of taking his first look. Afterward, he stood smoking, boxes piled up around him. He then rolled up his shirt sleeves and went to work whistling. In this way he spent the weeks before Anna's arrival—with a hammer in hand, with his arms smeared by paint drips, and with hope from his heart uncharacteristically gushing.

THREE

Little one.

If you haven't already guessed, your omniscient narrator is just that—a seer of things unseen, a hearer of things whispered, a comprehender of things without rhyme, context, or reason. Genetic inheritance is the unwelcome culprit: my toaster-sized head is a perpetual maelstrom. Oh yes—it's a whirlwind, a cauldron, a vortex of horrors. All day I chase away images that would put lesser ones under. To rid my head of Tushino and the bombs that went off there, I force myself to think of things brighter. Puppies, for example—I like their short, furry tails and the way that they wiggle. Or junipers, and the flavour they impart to a thimble of vodka. Or primroses, yellow ones, a predilection that's clearly my Russian half talking. Or dusks and dawns and the blazing colour they give us. What else? Oh yes. The fecund, earthy scent of an uprooted mushroom. The coursing of sweat in a stifling hot *banya*. Moments of revelation, as witnessed by lovebirds. *Or* (boys being boys): the skin-tight skating outfits of Irina Slutskaya.

I *think*, little one, of my Anna, of my beloved and near-pretty and *vor*-blooded *mamochka*—who, at the age of twenty-one, had wriggled free of Russia's bear hug just once and once only. This was to attend a marketing symposium in Helsinki. For one whole long weekend, she'd spent her days discussing market share and the loyalty paid to "brands" in Western economies. Her evenings, meanwhile, had been spent nightclub hopping and crisp-lager drinking and marvelling at the abundance of clear-skinned boys in a town that looked like a miniature St. Petersburg, minus (it goes without saying) the kiosks and gun violence and muffling air of displeasure.

In other words, *this* was the entirety of her experience with the world that was out there—dancing with non-pointy-nosed boys who spoke perfect English. *Ergo*, she was nervous. The fact that she knew two other women—*four*, if you counted friends of friends—who'd acquired Internet husbands was not at all a comfort, despite it having been one until three or four days earlier. What, she asked herself often, if they all were unhappy? What if they were being mistreated? What if Hank Wallins was hiding some diabolical weirdness?

It was ten in the morning. The other side of the bed had long stopped emitting the warmth of her mother, who had gone to her job as a public school teacher. (*Good,* Anna thought, *I'm not up to an argument this morning.*) Anna hugged herself softly. Her head was jackhammering. Her stomach pleaded for dry toast and hot black tea; the previous evening, her friends had taken her to just the sort of club where a fleeing *dyevushka* might enjoy her last night in Russia. And what a place it was—laser lights flashing, white clothes glowing purple, tribal house music booming over the massive sound system, pills of all shapes and sizes from tongue to tongue passing, crowded with expats and euros and Paris Hilton–like working girls who called themselves "students," all barely contained by a one-time Cheka bunker where, it was joked, Stalin himself had filmed acts of sadomasochistic bondage. It was in this bacchanal of pierced tongues, and bare midriffs, and the dance-music anthems of the Chemical Brothers that Anna—feeling more lonely and scared with each passing minute—tossed five Baltikas back, each turning frothy and warm in her with-fear churning stomach. The first two made her giddy. The third made her maudlin. The fourth made her emotional, and by the time her oldest friend Natalia bought her the fifth one . . . well. *Mamochka* began to weep, discreetly, her face contorted with worry. Natalia took her outside. The cool, moist air helped; her crying downgraded to a sputtering hiccup.

"Oh, Natalia," she managed.

"What *is* it, Anya? This is your *party*."

"I don't know."

"Tell me."

"I don't know, I think maybe . . . I think maybe I've made a huge mistake!"

"It's not true."

"Yes, yes, it's true."

"But why?"

Anna shivered, and then made a sound like a goat sadly bleating. "Natalia . . . I . . . I don't think I like him."

"What?"

"I don't think he's my type."

"Who . . . the *guy?*"

"Yes, yes, the guy."

"What's he like?"

"Quiet. Kind to me. Sad. He wears some kind of hearing aid. On *both* ears, no less. Otherwise, I don't know. Canadians are not like Russians—they keep everything hidden. Sometimes, I don't know, he looks at me and it's almost like he's seeing someone else. Oh, Natalia—I think maybe I've made a *gigantic* mistake!"

"So don't go."
"But I have to!"
"Why?"
"Because I promised!"
"So *break* your promise, little beauty!"
"But I can't!"

Anna put her hands to her face and once again wept with her small shoulders bobbing. On and on she boo-hooed, her back pressed against a cold and bass-shaking club wall. She paused only when Natalia crossed her arms and said, "I know what *this* is." Anna blew her nose and dabbed at the corners of her eyes with a fresh Kleenex. This smudged her mascara, and made her look slightly clown-like. "*This*," her closest friend said, "is all about Ruslan."

"No!"
"It is."
"No, Natalia, don't say that!"

"Oh yes, Anyachka. I know you, and I *know* this is about that damn Chechen and the simple and ugly fact that you, Anya Mikhailovna, can't get over him!"

"He's not Chechen," she peeped. "He's Dagestani."

"Chechen, Dagestani, who cares?"

"Natalia!" Anna howled, before cursing her friend's cruelty in a mélange of Russian, English, and the profane *mat*-language used by St. Petersburg youngsters. Two minutes after that, the women were hugging and patting each other's backs, Natalia saying she was sorry for being so presumptuous, and Anna admitting that it really *was* about Ruslan; she promised she would not only put him out of her mind but put him out of there forever. By this she actually meant two things (both of which occurred to her when she awoke the next morning). Number one: she had had it with her friend's bullying sermons. Number two: she would never,

ever, forget her dark and rock star–like Caucasian. Oh no. She loved Ruslan, and he loved her, and the only reason he'd ended their relationship was that he couldn't accept the joy she so thoroughly brought him. (In this one respect, she thought, he was typically Russian.) By the time she'd had a long shower in the *communalka* bathroom, her ears keenly listening for on-the-door pounding, she'd developed a plan that was practical, and workable, and best of all in defiance of Natalia's wishes.

She would see Ruslan, and tell him she was leaving forever. If this sparked even the slightest heart-melting—even the weakest *please think about this, Anya*—she would stay. If not, she would board her plane and piteously whimper throughout the safety demonstration, two in-flight meals, and both subtitled movies. But make no mistake—either way, she would see him.

So.

Mamochka—her hair a dark bronzy sheen, her eyes the size of eggs (albeit not quite working in tandem), her figure a wondrousness worthy of *Playboy*—stood foggy and head-throbbing in front of her Viktor Tsoi poster. Her hand was aloft, and holding a mirror. She shuddered. Her face looked reddened and splotchy. Her forehead was as shiny as a length of wax paper. To top it all off, she felt stupid—it was so *sovok,* so damned Soviet-*minded,* to get so out-of-her-head drunken. What will it be next, she asked herself. Reading *Pravda*? Wearing a hat made of lynx fur? Marching in pro-Stalin parades, face beaming and chest forward? She shuddered again and felt nauseous. At least her eyes were just minorly puffy. And, thanks to the existence of miracles, her three a.m. shashlik—which she had splashily vomited into the Fontanka River—had left minor blemishes only.

She breathed deeply, and then donned an Albanian brassiere so flimsily constructed it would accomplish little more than give her Viktor Tsoi–like Dagestani something to tear off her. This was followed by a pair of black stockings, a leather skirt that adhered tightly to her hips and her bottom, and the same horizontally striped sweater that had so entranced boys in Helsinki dance caves. With hands slightly shaking, she applied foundation, blusher, lipstick, eyeshadow, eyeliner, a Romanian-made mascara, and a hair mousse so watery it left her hands damp and shiny. Satisfied, she pulled on a pair of black high-heeled boots that raised the top of her head to the lofty height of five feet and six inches. Finally, she put on her cream vinyl jacket and attempted a full-body inspection by clamping the mirror's handle between her *Principles of Marketing* and her mother's leather-clad volume of *Famous Russian Icons*.

She crossed the room and observed her five-inch-high reflection. This caused her to swallow hard and fight tears—she looked like a cross-eyed, ex–Eastern bloc Barbie. This would never work. She turned to one side, and managed to look impish. She turned to the other, and batted her eyes like a slatternly midget. It was mid-morning. The Chechen veteran was already plastered and singing. The building's water-pipe clanging aggravated her headache. The smell that permeated the *communalka*—one part potato, one part dirty laundry—made her want to be sick and be done with the plan she'd concocted only twenty minutes earlier. That's when it hit her. She was going to Canada. The Unreal City had just about killed her; she needed the stink of its lies washed right *off* her. Her mission now was to visit her Ruslan and inform him that her heart was no longer a thing for him to play ball with. Oh yes—she was not only going to tell him she was leaving, she was going to tell him while grinning.

She took a deep breath, threw back her shoulders, and deposited yet another lipstick pucker on the already lipstick-pucker-smeared face of her Viktor Tsoi poster. Outside, there were dark skies and cool wet air blowing. She lowered her head and trudged forward, thinking: *The weather, pluh, that's the least of my troubles.* She passed the blue-tarped street market that sided the commuter train station, and tossed a few rubles at a gypsy child begging. She then boarded a train that rumbled into the city.

At Baltiskaya she switched to the metro. Fifteen minutes later, she surfaced at Sennaya Ploschad, which looked sodden and filled with hurrying people. As she crossed the open square—the wind in her ears making by-the-sea howlings—she passed clumps of people excitedly talking. Some, she noticed, were huddled around radios— the words *Chechnya* and *Nord-Ost* and *invasion* kept piercing the hubbub made by the city. Under normal circumstances she might have casually eavesdropped, but there was nothing about this day that was the slightest bit normal. By the time she crossed Ghorokhovaya and began walking through streets cloaked with dark shadows, she was all alone again with her sad indecision.

She reached a small plaza. She stopped and gazed up at the sky; it looked noble and gloomy, and it went on forever, shrouding the dome of St. Isaac's like a grey woollen comforter. Above her, the sky sat on old income houses, deepening the dull yellow facades of Sennaya Ploschad. She was now walking with her face tilted upward, like a tourist entranced by all the old buildings. As she gathered her jacket to her throat, she understood why old Fyodor had always lived in this neighbourhood, in corner apartments, a cathedral in view of his small, grimy window. It was this place. It was this wrecked and yet sensuous city, with its flesh and its stone and its falling-to-bits tramcars. *It* was his muse (and not, Anna thought smugly, that simpleton typist who helped pen *The*

Gambler). Above all else, it was the feeling in the air—that skin-warming grief, both painful and erotic—that the famous writer needed for his inspiration. Anna's ambivalence started once again flaring. She realized, with a start, she felt guilty for leaving. Prettying her life with North America would be . . . would be . . . would be like plunking a shopping mall in the middle of Sennaya. It'd be like a Russian ballet with characters by Disney. No! No! It was *worse*! It was a denial of the imperfections that lurk at the heart of real beauty. *Oh, Anyachka*, she thought, *how can you do this? How can you so easily betray your true nature?* For a brief and real moment, she came close to tearing up the plane ticket in her pocket and scattering the pieces over the cold, flowing Mayka.

She turned a corner. She walked up a side street, and then stepped into lanes lined with stalls and old brick walls. Her emotions again somersaulted. It was here, in the Apraxin Dvor market, eighteen months earlier, on a cheap shopping trip with her cruel friend Natalia, that she'd violated the cardinal rule when it came to Russian girls in Apraxin: she had talked to one of the Caucasians who crowded the laneways like ants on spilled sugar. (Aaaaaaah, little one: she'd done more than talked. She'd batted her lashes, she'd girlishly giggled, she'd thrust out her chest in that way of young women.) Yet how could she have not? How, when he'd had the same road-flare eyes as her favourite singer? When he'd had the same dark hair falling over his forehead? When he'd looked exactly like the lead singer of the Russian rock band Kino?

How, when he'd stepped into her path and smiled nicely while asking, "Is there something you seek?"

It was Natalia who'd answered.

"Get lost, Shamil," she'd said, insulting him with the name of the country's worst terrorist. It didn't matter—Anna's knees were already wobbly. Her friend's hectoring voice faded. *Let's go*, she barely heard. *Let's get out of* . . . And then it had failed to even be a voice, just a faint and far-off and indecipherable mutter.

"Yes," Anna told him.

"And what is it?"

"What is . . . I'm sorry?"

"The thing for which you are looking?"

Anna panicked. It was Natalia who had needed a handbag (and who was, even now, walking away grumbling). "Boots," Anna said, without even thinking.

"Then come."

He touched her elbow, and the two of them moved past the clothing stalls of Apraxin, past fake-Levis sellers and cheap-sweater vendors and hawkers of faux leather jackets from the sweatshops of Burma. Meanwhile, the young man kept nodding hellos at babushkas, and exchanging hand clasps with young, dark-skinned hustlers. Every few feet he turned to say something in his night-school-learned Russian. Finally, he stopped before a stall crammed with boots, shoes, and sandals. "This place," he said with an accent, "is the best place of places, a place with no rival and ably run by my cousin."

She'd looked, and then saw them—they were knee-high, and high-heeled, and not at all unlike the boots worn by the actress Elena Korikova.

"You like those?" he'd asked.

Inside she tremored, and thought, *Oh my god, oh my god—I'm here with Viktor Tsoi shopping!* "Yes," she said, the young man now loudly haggling in his strange southern language. On and on this went, a stream of brief pauses followed by heated, loud patter, until finally the vendor shrugged, took the boots, and passed them to Anna.

"How much are they?" she asked.

"They are nothing."

Anna blinked. "I don't understand . . ."

"They're free, you can take them, this guy . . . he owes me a favour."

"No, I can't . . ."

The young man smiled, and in that smile there were glimpses of fire and heaven and the flesh of the devil.

"It's too late, it is done . . . By the way, my name's Ruslan."

"Anya," she said.

"Anya," he said. "That's a pretty name."

She blushed, and could say nothing.

"Listen," Ruslan said. "I'm a little busy right now, but later, would you like to take a walk along the Neva?"

She paused, so as to not look too eager. "All right," she said. "But just for a little while."

The culprit, of course, was the month of April—that month of budding trees, and occasional warm breezes, and the return of life pulses that slow during winter. The river was sun-flecked that day, and the sound that it made was like a violin playing. Ruslan, of course, did most of the talking: he told her about Dagestan, and the way that he'd left when the fighting spilled over from Chechnya. There were boats on the river, and a blue sky above them, and people lolling on the banks looking pleased about springtime.

Ruslan, oh yes *Ruslan,* reached down and took her hand.

Thus started the happiest episode of Anna's life up to that point. Often she felt like she was on an exotic journey: the places he took her were dirty and wild and full of strange mountain languages. His room was subterranean and dusty, and there was more than one time—Anna entwined with limbs lean and dark-toned—that she could feel trains rumbling beneath her, their vibrations only adding to her verboten rapture. And every time he touched her? Every time he whispered in her ear, or told her she was lovely, or ran his tongue along the furrow of her belly? Little one—she sizzled, she smouldered, all the fire metaphors came to life and in hot flames engulfed her. Three and a half months it lasted—three and a half months of living for evenings, of dreaming of the way his lower back dimpled, of forgetting where she was in the middle of lectures.

And then it was over, a bomb dropped in her lap. Ruslan—who, yes, had been acting edgy and distant for about two and a half weeks—picked a café run by Azeris who carried guns in their jackets and served strange alcoholic drinks in mugs without handles. Here, she listened to every excuse in the bachelor handbook, *it's just that I'm so busy* sliding into *Anya, this is not right* tumbling chaotically into the most absurd of them all, *it is killing my parents I'm not with a Muslim*. This was the last straw. Fuming, she stood up. There were scythes tacked to bare walls, and the air was thick with the smoke from braziers. She began whispering at him, her voice growing in pitch and in volume. For the next five minutes she called him a liar and a Shamil and a user of young girls. As her Slav-language tirade grew louder and shriller, the faces of the other café dwellers turned and looked and, while understanding not one word, nevertheless thought, *Those Russian girls are such tigers.* It ended with Anna walking out and Ruslan wearing a froth of a fermented goat's milk.

Three days later, heartbroken and tired of Putin's assault on all that the country had fought for (she remembered cheering, alongside her mother, on the day that Yeltsin had faced Old Guard tanks with both his fists waving), she travelled with Natalia to the Peterhof gardens. It was a bright day in mid summer; sun flooded the train in diagonal columns. Anya stared out, watching the niceness of the weather compete with Soviet bloc tenements. It was the beauty of this contradiction that almost (repeat, *almost*) caused her to change her mind and go back home. Instead, they de-boarded and found a tree by a fountain where the light was agreeable. Anna leaned her back up against it, and bent her leg forward, and smiled at a camera belonging to Natalia's brother. She was wearing heels, a tight skirt, and a blouse snug and light brown. Passersby stopped, thinking she was some sort of model for a cross-eyed society.

Natalia took the picture.

"How is it?" Anna called. "Am I sufficiently beautiful to entrance a rich and kind North American who nonetheless needs to sleazily troll for young women on From Russia With Love dot com?"

Natalia inspected the photo, holding it this way and that way.

"Undo a button on your blouse," she called. "And this time, little beauty, try smiling."

And to think that once upon a time Apraxin had been a place she had always got lost in. Now her feet led her, past twists and around jogs and under low-sagging arches, as though the soles of her gift boots were doing the thinking. She stopped above a wood door that lay flush with ground level—the type that, in the days of the Tsar, had opened to cabbage-filled cellars and old gambling houses, but that now led to shops operating in fluorescent-lit basements. It was from this particular store that Ruslan's uncle sold TVs and stereos, all soldered together in east European countries and then given a brand name sounding vaguely Norwegian.

The stairs squeaked as she descended. Ruslan's uncle was at his work table, surrounded by spare knobs and picture tubes and disassembled speakers. Yet today he didn't seem to be working. He was staring straight ahead, listening intently to a transistor radio. He heard her and turned, his face immediately brightening. He turned the volume down till it was barely a whisper.

"Anya!" he said. "*Allahu Akbar!* Is it really you?"
"Yes, Dadya..."
"It has been some time!"
"Yes it has, Dadya."
"Have you been listening? Have you been watching the TV?"
"No," she said. "I haven't had the chance, what is it?"
"What *is* it? Anya! Where have you been? The Moscow House of Culture was invaded last night! Right in the middle of a performance of *Nord-Ost*! They're in there still, holding eight hundred hostages!"

Anna gasped. "Oh my god! Eight hundred! In the middle of *Nord-Ost*! I can't believe it!"

"It's true, it's true . . . it's all happening!"

"Who are the terrorists?"

"Who they say they are and who they *really* are—*bah!* Two different things, *dyevushka*. Two very different things. They *say* they are Chechens, but I bet they are Russians dressed to look like black-widow bombers. Putin probably needs some excuse to execute more atrocities in Chechnya—like the time he bombed his own buildings in Moscow."

"What's going to happen?"

"The victims are phoning out on their cells and begging the Russians not to storm the building." Dadya shook his head. "They're all there—FSB, police, Alfa Squad, the army, those cutthroat OMON. *Contraktniki* too, I'd bet, ready to do the dirty work. They'll storm the building, of course. It'll be a massacre—it's the way of the Russians. Praise be to Allah, I hate them." He stopped and looked sheepishly at Anna. "Sorry, Anya, sometimes I get carried away. I didn't mean what I said. The Russian *people* I have no problem with—it's just that government of yours."

"I know, Dadya."

"Listen." He turned up the radio. The room filled with reports of shots fired, and helicopters circling, and hooded black widows rigged with explosives. *"Bah!"* he cried. "I've heard enough. Think of the trouble this will bring to Apraxin . . . they'll be all over us, looking for scapegoats. Shaking us down for money. Taking away our young men. You think the police care that we're Dagestanis? No! Not on your life! Dagestanis, Ossetians, Georgians, Azeris, Armenians, *Chechens*—they don't care. If we have olive-tinted skin, we're all the same—a source of free euros. These are bad times for Caucasians . . . bad, bad times. Inshallah, they'll get better."

"They will."

The older man snorted and scratched his short grey beard. "How are you?"

"I'm fine, Dadya."

"Good, that can be difficult in this country. I suppose you are here to see Ruslan and not a withered old repairman?"

"Dadya!"

"Go ahead, go ahead. He's in the back, still sleeping."

"Really? Maybe I should—"

"No, no, you go. Talk some sense to him. He always did listen to you."

"I'm the *last* person he ever listened to."

"No! It's not true! It's not true at all! Anyway, you go. Give his door a good rapping. It's time he woke up, the lazy swine."

"It's okay?"

"Go! Go! Me, I have to go out for some groceries, so he'll at least have some company. Go!"

Anna swallowed. She'd changed her reasons for coming so many times, she now forgot if she'd ever really had one. (And anyway, it all now seemed so trivial, with this news about *Nord-Ost* and Chechens rigged with bomb packs. That was one good thing

THE CULPRITS

about living in Russia—no matter how badly you were doing, the problems of the country had a way of making your concerns feel not worth the effort.) She bent and kissed Dadya. She stepped over litter and dropped television parts before walking down a hallway with her heart firmly pounding. She reached Ruslan's door. She heard yawns and bedsprings. After a moment's hesitation, she raised her hand and knocked lightly. A second or two passed.

"What is it?" came his voice, the words in Avari.

"Ruslan?"

A few seconds passed. "Anya?"

"Yes. It's me . . ."

"Give me a few seconds," he then said in Russian.

Anna stood listening to more yawns, and bedspring squeakings, and the scratch of wooden drawers opening and closing. Finally she heard the creak of unoiled hinges and he was there, in all his black-jean and T-shirted glory—her blinking and handsome Tsoi-like Dagestani.

"Anya! It's you! How are you? How have you been?"

"I'm fine," she said, and for a few seconds they both stood there. Finally, Ruslan moved aside and beckoned her forward.

She felt some relief that it was all the same—same windowless cement walls, same tiny bed and battered dresser, same prayer rug lying flat on a grey floor, same poster of a snarling and knee-bent James Hetfield, lead singer of the heavy metal band Metallica. Yet it wasn't the arrangement of Ruslan's things that made her feel like a child who had once again come home. Oh no. It was the scent of cement dust, and laundry, and his own warm, unwashed essence.

"Have you been watching?" he asked.

"A little," she said. "With Dadya."

"What's happening now?"

"A lot of standing around, it sounds like. A little smoke and the odd burst of gunfire. Your dadya says the hostage takers are Russian soldiers in disguise, hired by Putin to make the Chechens look bad. To help justify the war."

"Dadya!" he said with a disrespectful snorting. "He sees conspiracies everywhere. He thinks *Putin* invaded Dagestan! He thinks *Putin* blew up his own buildings in Moscow in 1999! You know what I think? I think it *is* the work of Chechens. Remember, Dadya's been here for twenty years, so he forgets what they're like, the savages. Me, I still remember. Oh no. They're Chechens, all right. Probably the same fuckers who invaded Dagestan."

"Really?"

"Of course!"

Anna's head was a whirl. The urges inside her felt lovely and hurtful.

"I'm going to Canada," she said, and then glanced up at him. (*There!* She saw it—a quick flinch of the shoulders, as though he'd been startled.)

"To Canada? Really?"

"Yes . . ."

"For good?"

"I think, I'm not sure, I don't know."

"What about your mother?"

"If things work out, she'll rent out our room in the *communalka* and move in with her sister. That would be better for everybody. There'd be some money, finally."

"You have a Canadian?"

"Yes."

"What's he like?"

Anna shrugged. "He's okay."

"So this will work out for you?"

"Yes, I am hoping."

"Yes," Ruslan said, smiling. "I am hoping too."

Seconds ticked by. The floor swayed, and turned slowly. Cement dust rose with this motion—it settled on her skin, turning it clammy. Then it happened, just as she'd hoped for, Ruslan extending a hand and speaking to her in a voice low and deepened.

"I'll miss you, Anya."

"Really?"

"Yes, of course."

Joy crashed over her body. She felt olive-toned fingers touching her forearm. She then did the one thing she'd promised herself she would *not* do: she, Anna Verkoskova née Mikhailovna, weakened and weakened wholly. Her heart thrummed, her blood started simmering, the James Hetfield poster turned into a mandala of James Hetfields floating. When she felt Ruslan's lips land against hers, she didn't know whether to laugh, or cry sweetly, or succumb to her body's soaring core temperature. The culprit, of course, was the human thirst for debasement—she kissed the mouth she'd been thinking about ever since their sad breakup. She kissed the mouth that was just like a Georgian-born despot—regal and charming and lewdly commanding. Oh yes—she was Anya no longer, and she *was* a young thing who was lost to a moment.

"Has Dadya gone out yet?"

"Dadya," Ruslan answered, "doesn't matter."

It was off with her pointy Apraxin Dvor footwear. It was off with her vinyl, cream-coloured jacket (with a pause for more kissing and salacious touching). It was off with her striped and bought-with-euros tight sweater (and *oh*, the feel of his fingers, sliding under her bra strap). It was off with her snug skirt, with her lone pair of good stockings, with her fragrant and reddish-pink undies. She then lay beneath him, her dark Tsoi-like lover unzippering his jeans and off-pulling his T-shirt. She gave in to his Caucasian ardour, at first oh so gently, oh so sweetly, and then with the thirst of a wolverine rutting. They moved, and they rolled, and they flailed limbs while groaning. Her legs were alternately held, shaken, and throttled. Her cries were absorbed by the pillow, and the prayer rug, and Ruslan's damp neckline. The flickering light flickered, the wobbly dresser wobbled, and the walls shed dust and small speckles of mortar.

They finally collapsed in an intertwined heaping. She rolled off him and lay shining all over. They giggled, and sighed, and hooked baby fingers.

And Anna was so happy—with him, and only *him*, she could survive all that Russia had to hurl at her. She pictured her plane ticket, fluttering into the Mayka in small torn-up pieces. She felt her eyes brim, and her skin tingle, and her heart soar with thoughts of a gladdened, near future. Moments passed, Anna feeling only the slightest bit guilty about promises made to Hank Wallins. (She would write him, and make up some tragedy that had befallen her family.)

"Anya," said Ruslan.

"Hmmmmm?"

"Write me, okay?"

"I'm sorry?"

"Write me, when you get to Canada."

It was amazing, it really was, the speed with which the best moment of her life became the most awful. At first she felt stunned, and then her shock turned to fury. She swore and leapt up and landed on his chest, pinning his arms with her knees as she again and again smacked him. "You black ass!" she yelled. "You filthy Chechen bastard!"

As she girlishly slapped him, Ruslan could do nothing but call, "What did I do? What did I say?," an obtuseness that only enraged her further and caused her to flail at him harder. Within a minute she had worn herself out, her open hands now glancing at his chin and the occasional snippet of forehead. Slowly she climbed off him, and pulled on the lingerie she'd so carefully selected. She sniffled as she stepped into the skirt she'd so thoroughly mulled over. She wept as she donned the snug Finnish sweater she'd paid for with euros. She blubbered as she felt for her little wire glasses.

Ruslan lay wincing, his nose slightly bleeding. "Anya!" he cried as he watched her race from him. "What is it? Come back, come back, what is it, why are you so angry? Come back, you crazy little Russian . . ."

It was the twenty-fourth of October, smack dab in the middle of the city's rainy season, a day sufficiently damp that, in the city's Khrushchevian suburbs, the drains were overflowing and flooding the streets with rats and foul sewage. Meanwhile, on the sidewalks surrounding Pulkovo II airport, Anna blubbered in front of her friends and family (for only those with actual tickets were allowed in the airport). She dampened the shoulders of her *mamochka,* of her much older *tatya,* of her *tatya*'s kind and gentle second husband. She sobbed and felt silly in front of her twin niece and nephew. Her tears dampened the cheeks of schoolmates and cousins. Finally, she held on to her oldest friend, Natalia, if only because she was the only one who understood that Anna's tears weren't for them, or at least weren't for them *only.* Oh no. Natalia knew that poor Anna also wept for a man who didn't love her, and for a beloved papa who had disappeared into thin air, and for this de-evolved mess that was modern-day Russia. Most of all, Natalia knew that Anna wept for herself, and all the things that a not quite pretty *dyevushka* had to do to make life just a little bit better.

(Natalia, of course, had experienced these last tears, and knew the particular way they stung when rolling down cheeks red with sorrow.) It was a lot to cry about. Anna's sorrowful hiccups lasted through one airport transfer and ten airborne hours. Every moment not spent sleeping was devoted to snuffling. She accepted Kleenex from the hostess and the kind woman beside her. She made up stories about a dead favourite uncle, and she dried her crossed eyes just minutes before landing.

She then collected her bags and was greeted in Arrivals by a blushing Hank Wallins.

FOUR

The scent of the house was the first thing she noticed. She could smell lacquer, and paint, and floors newly finished. Her lower lip quivered as the second thing hit her: the walls were white, the ceiling was white, and the trim was a cream with aspirations toward whiteness. During those first, dislocating moments, she felt like she'd been dropped into a perceptual experiment: all around her was the white of snow newly fallen. As she walked through the house, she couldn't help but think of the neighbourhood surrounding Sennaya Ploschad—its burnt-yellow buildings, its jet-black wrought iron, its low, dark-hued skies the colour of pewter. She thought of its beauty and how badly she missed it.

"Hank," she said. "This it is your home?"

"This is it."

"And you have how long lived here?"

"Two months. I just bought it. You like it?"

She hesitated. "Is very clean, yes?"

She followed him up a narrow wooden staircase. Upon reaching the landing, Hank turned and entered the room in the middle. She caught up to him just as he was putting down her suitcase. There was a bed, a dresser, and a night table supporting a lamp and some water.

"It's small," he said. "I hope it's okay. I mean, the rooms in these old houses are all small. But I put in a space heater, in case you get cold. See? It's in the corner, brand new, I think you'll be okay."

She yawned, and sat on a brand new firm mattress. She looked at her feet, all the while thinking: Why couldn't *you* be dark, Henry Wallins? Why couldn't you be young, and alive, and even the *tiniest* bit Tsoi-like? "Yes. Is perfect. Thank you. Now, Hank, I am very much tired from my long and too-boring-for-words flight. I need to be having bath."

He nodded and smiled. Ten minutes later, Anna was in a tub soaking. She immediately felt better, for the water was steaming, and there was no one waiting for her to finish, and there was no hole in the wall uncannily formed right at chest level. Oh no— here, in Hank's tub, there was only quiet, and time, and all the hot water that had ever come from a faucet, and because of this her thoughts turned halfway hopeful. (*Who knows*, she thought, *with time and with patience I might learn to like him.*) She kept letting out tepid water and adding more that was steaming. When she finally got out, her skin was as wrinkled as linen. She crept down the hallway with a towel wrapped around her. In her room, she unpacked. With her clothes in her dresser, she picked up a portrait of her mother and held it at arm's length: the woman in the photo was young, attractive, and not so embittered. Anna's eyes moistened. She felt tired and guilty. How she and her mother had fought, all day and about all things, the subject always, as if by law, returning to her Dagestani boyfriend.

Ah, mamochka, Anna thought, putting her down on the dresser. *It's better, isn't it, placing an ocean between us? Squeezing a little time between you and me?* Ruefully she smiled. Two continents and one ocean away, she could finally tolerate her mother, if only atop a white (yes, white!) IKEA dresser. Her nose reddened, and like a spigot began dripping. *I'm glad,* she thought. *I'm glad I've escaped all that drama and sorrow.* She crawled between sheets bearing crisp package creases and laid her head on the pillow. Her breathing turned deep, and her thoughts disassembled, and all the sorrows in her world were by darkness swallowed.

She awoke much later; she could hear light traffic and a clock somewhere ticking. She dressed and moved downstairs, finding Hank reading a paper and dressed in his work clothes.

"Anya!" he said, and she could tell he was happy to see her. "You have a good nap?"

"Yes, Hank, I did."

He sat looking at her. They both searched for something to say to each other. "I'm late for work," he said finally. "But I wanted to see you before I went. I'd have left you a note if you'd slept much longer . . ."

"I am happy you did not, Hank."

"There's TV, or you could take a walk. But listen, Jesus, I'm late, I'll be home in the morning . . . Here, here, take a few dollars in case you want to do something."

He reached for his wallet and passed her a few twenties. Then he lingered, for just a few moments, wishing that a moment of hopefulness might pass between them.

Hank left. Anna sat on the sofa. She flicked on the television and surfed through its channels. *Pluh,* she thought, *nothing but stupid TV programs in which they all laugh at nothing.* She grew bored, and decided to follow Hank's advice: she'd take a walk and get to know the surrounding neighbourhood. She went to the closet and put on her cream vinyl jacket, her white cotton gloves, and the long leather boots that made her think of Apraxin. It was about eight in the evening. First she went north, past other small houses, most of which needed an all-over paint job (though there was one, she noticed, where an artist must have lived, as the yard was filled with sheet-metal sculptures). On Gerrard Street she looked in sari-shop windows, and smelled herbs she'd heard mentioned in Mongolian legends; she also shivered, and brooded, and bought a roast cob of corn from a Tamilian vendor. She ate it while walking home, her teeth spaces filling with ember-charred kernels.

The following morning, the two of them shared an awkward breakfast together. Anna had coffee, and Hank, who was hungry after a whole night at work, fried himself eggs and rashers of bacon.

"Anna," he said, "do you want to do something this morning?"

She peered at him. "Hank? You are kidding? You working whole night—you must having rest."

"You sure? I could just have a little nap and then we could, I dunno, go downtown or something."

"Of course not! Don't you worry, I am grown woman, you don't need to, mmmmmmm, how you say? Oh yes, *babysit* me. You go, you go. Have a good sleeping time. I see you later."

He went upstairs, and Anna heard him dial his Marsona to the pure white-noise setting. With nothing to do, she again went exploring, though this time she went a little bit farther. As she walked, she noticed a gradual change in the people, their complexions turning from a deep oaken brown to a canola-hued yellow. The restaurant signs changed along with them, from swooping round letters to jagged stick figures. When Anna tired, she went in one of them (her purse filled with dollars that Hank had given to her). She sat near an aquarium as long as a Lada. The menu had two hundred and eighty-one choices, and not one of them was written in English. Mutely, she pointed. Her soup came spicy, and filled with the sort of glistening grey meat that her mother had once bought at Soviet GUM stores. By the time she left, she felt homesick and mopey.

Still.

She had survived her first restaurant meal, and this in itself was saying something; in addition to an achy, all-over glumness, she felt a small burst of pride in that place that can sometimes keep you from quitting. This made her ambitious. Upon leaving the restaurant, she walked even farther, her near-pretty face lowered against cool autumn breezes. She reached the centre of the city. Here, on the longest street in the world, she was shocked. For the whole of her life she'd heard about North American riches—about the bounty that was the birthright of all who were Western. And yet she was here, on the most famous street of the city, and she could see nothing but McDonald's, and porn shops, and places that sold cheap, no-good watches. Where were the Givenchys? The Cartiers? The Louis Vuittons? The Saks of Fifth Avenue? Where were the fine wine shops that lined the walls of Gostinyy? Where was the glamour she saw every day on her very own Nevsky?

Not here, she thought, and glumly kept walking.

Over the next week, a subway map tucked in the side of her white coat, she explored the city, discovering pockets of Greeks and Italians, of Portuguese and Filipinos, of Sudanese and Ethiopians, of Guatemalans and Chileans and Poles and Chinese and Australians and Lebanese and, yes, oh yes, of *Russians,* whose presence had turned Steeles Avenue into a dill-scented homeland. The afternoon that she went there, she lunched in a Tim Hortons that served borscht and chilled pickles.

Little one—envision yourself in her shoes. Imagine what it must have been like those first days, our Anna passing long hours in shopping mall food courts, the air greasily doused by bubbling fat fryers, sitting beside gum-chewing girls and acned teenage boys. She'd pretend to read, her favourite authors being Polina Dashkova, Victor Pelevin, and that dirty-minded rascal Vladimir Sorokin (whose books had been torched back home by a pro-Putin youth group). Yet she couldn't concentrate. She'd be too busy studying the faces of those all around her, faces that sported every shape and skin tone and imaginable eye colour. Minutes would go by without her thinking about loneliness. Other times she'd walk, for hour upon hour, through neighbourhoods that were laid in maddeningly strait grids, as if the city had been planned for a battery of robots. She couldn't believe it. There were no curves, no streets that doubled backward, no closes that ended suddenly and without any reason, no bifurcating alleys that lent a city its character.

Her sadness rose and fell like moon-crazy sea tides. One minute she'd feel morose, and the next she'd feel hopeful. Inevitably, though, her mind would turn to Ruslan, and Russia, and the way the most crippling elements of life seemed to give the most pleasure. Scent memories were the worst. Passing a group of teenaged boys, her nose would fill with the essence of Ruslan—smoky breath, and old denim, and shirts left too long between laundromat washings. Passing a food shop, her nose would suddenly, and without any good reason, detect the scent of *koryushka*, a minnow-like fish that so populated the Neva in spring that St. Petersburg would smell like a smashed-up cucumber. Her eyes would redden, and her stomach would hurt, and her face would turn as white as the walls of Hank's small house.

Stop it, she'd whisper. *Just stop it, stop it, you silly* dyevushka.

Most days, she went shopping, her cart filling with pork chops and potatoes and other foods Hank liked eating. Or she would take the subway all the way to the Arbat, a delicatessen located on the north side of High Park, where the owner was friendly and didn't mix solely with Russians. (It had the additional benefit of being much closer than Steeles Avenue.) Here, she bathed deeply in the thing she probably missed most: her language, her tongue, her crazy and loose and gymnastic Slav diction. How rich it felt, when held next to English! How she relished the opportunity to use gerunds as nouns, or nouns as adverbs, or to take a plain boring sentence and at the wall throw it, jumbling up words until they emitted a music. How she missed the sonic improvisations that are forbidden in English. In fact, as her English improved, she began to believe it was language that was to blame for the simplicity of Hank's fellow Canadians. For the truth, little one, was this: There was something about the city's orderliness that exacerbated her turmoil. There was something about its cool functionality that made her lose her composure. Even the air felt thin, the soul squeezed out *of* it.

She'd buy all she could carry. On the subway ride home, she'd clutch shopping bags brimming with sausage and carrot salad and jarred pickled mushrooms; with rye bread and herring and all types of blini; with tubs of cold borscht and cakes topped with cherry; with Caspian fish roe that came in the sort of tubes used for toothpaste; with egg noodles flavoured with white Russian pepper; with dandelions picked from sloped Ural mountains; and, of course of course of course, with bunches of dill the size of small bushes.

She would find him, in his favourite recliner, reading one of three papers that were left on his doorstep.

"Hank," she one day asked him, "which paper you like it most?"

He shrugged his large shoulders.

"No, really. Which one is better than others?"

Hank peered at her. "I dunno—it's all the same crap, really."

And Anna, poor Anya, ran to her room crying. When Hank knocked on her door and asked if she was all right, she moaned something loudly in a guttural Russian. She couldn't help it. It was his obliviousness, his vacant Hank quality. It was the way he'd touch his fingers to his ears and stare into the distance, as though listening to a broadcast that was in and out fading. This was his life: he either worked, or slept, or on the weekend watched hockey. And yet, at the same time, none of these things seemed to actually please him. He truly was a strange man, always fiddling with those things attached to both sides of his head. Often, she wished she could sort out what was the weirdness of his being Canadian, what was the weirdness of his hearing disorder, and what was the weirdness of *him*, Henry Wallins.

She, little one, had been brought up to believe that one of the reasons for living was to sing the praises of the things that you liked (black tea! white nights! red Georgian wine! the soul-stirring music of Dmitri Shostakovich!) and to rail, red-cheeked and fist-waving, at the things that you didn't. To read three newspapers each day *and not form an opinion*? She did not understand this. It was a sign, she feared, of an inbred low IQ.

Evenings were a worry.

"Hank," she would say, "I have brought home food. You would like I cook for us something?"

"Really?"

"Yes, Hank. I make for us something."

"You don't need to . . ."

"No, is okay, is fine, I like to."

And so she would cook, the menu once in a while Western, though she was more partial to blinis or shashlik or hot, fresh piroshki. It didn't matter—every time she placed a plate of hot food on the table before him, he'd thank her with a gratitude that seemed too excessive. This was another thing that grated on Anna: his wholesale, and absolute, lack of entitlement, as though he'd spent his whole life with not a thing given to him. She'd lived with him for two weeks, and he still seemed totally surprised whenever she offered to pack him a lunch, or wash some of his clothes, or sort through the mail that came through the slot daily. Often she felt sorry for him, and there is nothing like pity to crush a sparking of affection.

And yet she could say *this* about him: in Russia they simply didn't produce men like Hank Wallins. He washed his own dishes, he cleared the sink of razor stubble, he never left socks or old shirts around the house lying. And the seat of the toilet? It was always left down, right where it should be. This, little one, was where it got really confusing: she'd find yellow tulips in a vase on her dresser, once Hank found out they were her favourite. Toward these she had no ambivalence—she'd sniff them and then hold them up to the window, the rays of the sun heightening the depth of their colour. It was then she would ask herself frankly: Did Ruslan ever give her flowers? Well, little beauty? Did he do it even once, even though (and here was the real insult) Ruslan worked for a florist, and all day drove around in a car *filled* with tulips?

Though Hank was no raging fire, she knew in her heart that she could do much worse. (Most Russian women did.) He was kind, and considerate, and he was always, always, giving her money. (*Anya,* he'd say each morning, *c'mon, take some cash, in case you need it . . .*) When the right light caught him, he wasn't even that bad-looking—he was rugged and worn, like a butte flailed for years by desert siroccos. And, yes, there were his eyes and the way a pathos shone from them; this light reminded her of her city, in the middle of winter, when the glow of the sun turned a sad, diffused orange. Besides—who was she to be picky? Who, when she was short, and not shaped like Paris Hilton, and had a left eye that veered just a little bit inward? Oh no, her life would be so, so much easier if she could learn to like (if not love) this odd Henry Wallins.

But then, each night after dinner, her lips sufficiently flavoured with white wine and garlic, the hour would arrive in which one type of appetite makes room for another. Yet whenever Hank approached her, images of Ruslan would pop up in her mind's eye. She'd make an excuse—*the dishes, Hank, so very they are dirty*—and he would resignedly go to work, leaving Anya to spend a quiet night in her bed, reading Pelevin or Sorokin or the mystery writer Dashkova. Or she'd turn off the light and, thinking only of Ruslan, would float off and away on a cloud of self-touches.

Or.

It was a desperately dull night, the sort in which the skin starts to crawl, and the mind cannot function, and a twenty-one-year-old woman starts to shriek for her freedom. Anna got up. She put on her nightgown and went down to the kitchen. She searched inside the refrigerator. When she saw nothing she wanted, she turned on the TV. This bored her even further. She flicked it off and sat there, arms folded tensely. A minute later she stood. Oh yes—she climbed the creaking stairs, moving slowly as though someone might hear her. She walked down the hallway, her feet chilled by wood flooring. At the back of the house was a little half room, where Hank kept a desk, a chair, and some old, unused luggage. She sat and gazed out the window; she saw houses, and power lines, and snowy back laneways, all of them lit by a moon low and hanging. After a minute—for it really was sort of lovely, this framing of the alley under a cold night in winter—she turned to the matter before her.

The desk's lower drawer was bin-like and locked tightly; often she had wondered what Hank kept inside it, and this was the night she was determined to find out. Over the desktop she ran fingers, sifting through papers and flyers and other detritus before finding a paper clip in a cup filled with pennies. She began straightening it, at first with her fingers and then with a ruler (an action she had seen many times in dark movie houses). She put it in the lock and felt for the tumblers. A minute passed, and she felt a spring of frustration spouting inside her; she cursed, and began to forget what she was doing. This helped—she was cursing and lip-gnawing when she heard a brief, muted clicking.

She couldn't believe it. She put a hand on her chest, and breathed once or twice deeply. Then she set to work. There were bank statements, and old tax returns, and thickets of receipts with rubber bands bundled. There were utility bills, fast food menus, and flyers from the Bay and Canadian Tire. Anna felt crushed—there was nothing of interest and nothing revealing. In fact, she noted sadly, each item seemed duller than the item before it. She leaned back, feeling cheated and bored and, above all else, sick of the curry smell that wafted down from Gerrard Street, invading every crack and windowsill fissure.

She was just about to quit when she saw it, lying face up on the bottom, beneath the mound of old papers through which she'd been rifling. She took a corner between each thumb and forefinger. It was an eight-by-ten photo of Hank when he was younger, and leaner, and blessed by eyes that were piercing. He was standing against a backdrop of boats and blue water, his arm around a girl who wore dark kohl eye makeup. And if Anna wasn't mistaken, the girl in the photo looked just a little like herself: she was small, and dark-haired, and hourglass-figured, and (oh yes, *and*) her left eye turned just a little bit inward.

So, Hank, she thought, *maybe you can't get this girl out of your head? Maybe this is the reason you're so sad all the time? Maybe this is why you emailed me—to make you forget an old love turned sour?*

Oh, Hank, she thought, *maybe you and I aren't so different.*

That Saturday, Anna came home from a walk and found Hank in the kitchen. She couldn't believe it. The counter was strewn with pots and dripping pans and cups used for measuring, and a downloaded recipe sat face up beside him. He was dressed in a nice shirt and pressed trousers, and his face was tense with a deep concentration. She approached. There was a large pot on the stove, and inside was a fish stew she knew from her girlhood. It simmered and bubbled and brought back days that were pleasant. She put her face over it. Steam filled her pores and made them feel moistened. Her nose ingested the smells of her grandmother's dacha.

Her heart was touched by what Hank was doing.

Little one. The wine that night was dark, strong, and Georgian. The music was soft, and nerve-soothing, and with just the right notes of wanting. The flowers were deep scarlet roses and *not* yellow tulips. The stew tasted like rock salt mixed with three-week-old porridge. It didn't matter; they both knew what this was, or at least what it could be. They both blushed slightly, and smiled often while eating. For dessert, there were strawberries on ice cream with lemony biscuits. They toasted their lives with a fizzy dessert wine. They then moved to the sofa, Hank too nervous to touch her given all the times she'd rebuffed him. But she could see it, she could, love for her pouring from eyes green and glistening. She could stand it no longer; perhaps something would rise up within her and by surprise take her. She nudged closer. Hank smiled at her. She kissed him, her mouth lingering against his and tasting Canadian tobacco. It wasn't *so* bad. She could feel his heart pounding. When his hand slipped up and beneath her wool sweater, his fingers felt tender, and warm, and by strong feelings guided.

Yet Anna felt nothing, no matter how hard she tried to summon any sort of reaction. There was no tingle, no burn, no rise in core temperature. *Ruslan,* she thought, both her eyes closing. *You are Ruslan, you are Ruslan, you aren't anybody other.* Never in her life had she exerted such concentration. Never had she so needed her imagination. In her head, she turned every kind movement into a commanding gesture; she converted every respectful advance into a Don Juan–like foray; she changed every soft stroke into an Errol Flynn parry. She willed, yes she did, that his hands were the hands of her Viktor Tsoi double. It didn't work. Anna grew desperate, her movements half-frantic. She reached toward his belt buckle and opened his zipper. It was then she discovered that Hank's size was prodigious. Her fingers bounced off him, as though they had touched something heated. She grabbed a third flute of bubbly. Her cheeks flushed pink, and her stomach felt woozy.

"Sorry," Hank said.

"No, no, is okay," and with that she inched up her skirt and sat down upon him. Hank blanched and closed his eyes as she hip-shimmied forward. With a labouring breath, she accommodated the first third of Hank's structure. It pinched, for a moment, and then went no farther. Hank looked guilty, like he was afraid he might hurt her. There was a brief dogged shunting followed by side-to-side movements; it was over with a whispered and barely felt shudder, Hank's house throbbing with the silence of cries not emitted. Anna leaned her face against his shoulder, disguising the fact she was about to start crying.

That was it. She now knew it. It would not, and could not, work out between them. Stress surged within her and felt like a knife twisting. This gamble was a failure, her whole future a question. Anna blamed herself in a way almost spiteful.

There was no one, not one soul, in this world who could help her.

And have I mentioned that, during this time of stress and dislocation, Anna was visited with memories that hadn't come to her in ages? There was one in particular: Anna, just a girl, maybe nine or ten years old, in those murderous days after democracy's arrival, sleeping on the fold-out in their one-bedroom apartment. Something disturbs her. She awakens and, in the room's dimness, sees her father lacing on his Adidas. He spots her big eyes, blinking sleepily at him. He sits down beside her. The gold chains around his neck clink as he does so; his shoulder muscles strain against cheap track-suit fabric. *Little Anya,* he says, stroking her dark hair. He is smiling, something he does often despite the madness that has come to the city—outside, lorries cruise around, collecting the victims of gym-shoe-wearing assassins. In Moscow, the embalmers of Lenin are making a small fortune, preserving the bodies of dead Mafia bosses. It doesn't matter. Here, next to *papochka,* it is safe, and warm, and sweet with his cologne. *Anyachka,* he says again, before leaning over and giving her a soft kiss. He then goes out for the evening, the kiss lingering for the rest of that day and the rest of her childhood and still, still, it sometimes comes to her, a warm and slightly damp sensation in the middle of her forehead.

She stood on Hank's porch, a parka thrown over her nightgown. A mug of hot coffee warmed the inside of her right hand. She was shivering, and gazing far off toward a blue, cloud-streaked distance. She felt an ache in her groin; it was the one and only remnant of last night's encounter. It was just after nine a.m., and already she had found herself crying at three slight provocations: a dog's lonely yelping, a child being pushed in a stroller, the sight of leaves collecting against house walls and fences. She felt lonely, and depressed, and dependent upon a man with an organ befitting a hippo. She went back inside. She finished her coffee and picked up a paper. She then went upstairs; from the other room she could hear Hank's Marsona DS-600. She fidgeted, and moped, and showered beneath hot, drumming water. With nothing else to do, she bundled up and walked south and took a Red Rocket westbound.

The inside of the streetcar smelled of damp wool and oil. She sat beside a window that was half an inch open—she placed her face in the breeze, streams of cold air rushing over her forehead. Only three or four people were on board; each stared out the window at the streets of the city. After a block, Anna sat back and watched the landscape change as they came nearer to downtown. Little wood houses turned to red-brick Victorians, before giving way to stores, Gothic churches, and glass office towers. She de-boarded at Yonge Street. Without really thinking, she walked to the Eaton Centre entrance. It was the middle of November; wind blew through the city like a dissecting scalpel. The square outside the mall was filled with peddlers, and bums, and teenagers smoking in tightly formed huddles. Off to one side, an evangelist was saving souls as he stood on a milk crate. She went in. Her melancholy spiked, there being something about crowds that exaggerates aloneness. She walked sadly along and gazed through glass windows. She heard loud hip hop spilling from every shoe store and kiosk.

She began to feel light-headed, and she noticed that the lights in the mall were starting to look spectral; it was as though they could at any moment come alive and somehow hurt her. Thinking that low electrolytes were the culprit, she bought a frothing orange drink at a stand near the food court. She sat on a bench sipping, her heart speeding inside her.

This helped. Her fingers stopped trembling and her pulse slowed down slightly. She took a deep breath, and dismissed the whole episode as flukish in nature. But five minutes later, while passing a rack of socks in the men's clothing section, it came back. Only this time it was stronger—her hands started quivering, and her heart started pounding, and she felt as though she, Anna Verkoskova née Mikhailovna, was beginning to vanish. She looked down and saw it: her body turning faint, her arms and legs fading. Trembling, she reached out and let her fingertips touch imported argyle. This made her feel a little bit better, the sensation somehow proving she still was a person—that she still had hands and fingers and the sensations that came from them. She turned the socks over, as though searching for holes and/or imperfections. She felt better still. She took a deep breath. With a single, smooth movement, she placed them inside her vinyl coat pocket; she could feel them in there, pressing against her, bringing all of her body back into existence. A wave of relief rushed warmly through her—her legs they grew back, giving her something to walk on. A calm overtook her, now that her vanishing had finished. The store's noisy babble became a sound softly muted, and the glare of the lights turned a warm, gentle colour. As she walked toward the exit, she felt possessed by a sudden and almost religious conviction: all existence had meaning, and that meaning was out there, just inches beyond her understanding.

Yet by the time she reached the street, her elation had dimmed, as though the wind whipping down Yonge Street had come up and seized it. She stopped, and felt nauseous. When passersby brushed against her, her arms felt prickly, as though pink and rash-covered. For a moment she stared ahead, the guilt in her throat a painful constriction. Her hand went to her pocket. She retrieved the socks and stifled a whimper. A half-minute later she threw them into a trash bin, atop pizza trays, muffin stumps, and damp donair wrappers.

Little one—with all that had just happened, she found she couldn't face her Canadian (and his sickening love for her). She also couldn't face her neighbourhood, the entire east end, and the rumbling red trolleys that moved through the city. And so she wandered, past record shops and peep shows, past head shops and roti joints, past noodle stands and leather shops and the homeless ragamuffins who loitered on the Evergreen front stoop. Doorway-clinging dealers eventually noticed her roamings, incorrectly assuming she was out looking for something. She soon found herself being followed by a skinny young man with bad skin and tight jeans. *Hey, sister,* he kept muttering behind her, *how 'bout some hashish? It's Afghani and green and it's got a badass kick to it.*

Her feet were hurting and she felt cold all over. The west side of the street was bathed in deep shadow; the east side was lit by a wintery silver. She stopped and imagined Hank at home: he'd be awake by now, pacing and smoking and worrying about her. And she should call—she knew this, it was the least she could do for him. She stepped up to a pay phone that looked to be working. She was about to start dialing when she realized, finally, what it was that she needed.

Anna hailed a cab that took her west to just south of the university, to a leafy side street across from a row of townhouses. Here, she was deposited in front of Holy Trinity Orthodox, a sad red-brick structure that was three days of the week Russian, three days of the week Greek, and on Sundays filled with the tall, brocaded hats of the Estonian clergy. She mounted six steps and pushed a tall door to enter. It was quiet inside—just a few lonely babushkas in the pews softly praying. Instantly she felt the sort of warmth known only to those for whom God has once been illegal. *She,* little one, was looking for an icon that might help to soothe her. Along she walked, gazing mouth-opened at all the symbols and martyrs. She saw Saints Boris and Gleb, and their old cohort Vladimir. She saw the Holy Physicians and the Forty Martyrs of Sebaste. She saw Cosmas, and Damicu, and the Seven Martyrs of Antioch. She nodded to the Prophets Jonah and Hosea and, of course, Zachariah. She saw the Burning Bush, and the Red Sea parting, and Jesus Christ on his cross, upwardly gazing. And then, oh yes then, she saw Saint Onuphrius the Great, who, for the whole of his life, had lived as a long-bearded hermit in the Egyptian desert. *He,* she felt sure, would understand. *He,* like her, had run away from his homeland and more or less vanished. She lifted her hands to a prayer position. Her eyes relaxed, and crossed more than usual. She lowered to her knees before the Patron Saint of Far-Away Running.

"O Onuphrius," she whispered in Russian, "please grant me your love, forgiveness, and pity. Please give me your grace, understanding, and affection. Yes, I have sinned. Yes, I have stolen, and I have no idea why I did it. Yes, I ran away, for reasons ignoble. But my great sin, O saint, is thinking I could flee things that are deep down inside me . . ."

On and on she went, rocking and trembling and to herself mumbling. At times her words barely made sense, though the gist was that she promised to never again pilfer. She left the church feeling calmer, and exhausted all over. Night had fallen. Its cloak was deep purple. When she finally reached home, she found a house steeped in quiet, and a note on the kitchen's Formica table.

Anya, it read. *Are you OK?*

She awoke early, bothered by the sort of worries that invade the mind when all around there is stillness. It would be another half-hour before the sun started to ease the thick outside darkness. She made coffee. By the time it was ready, Hank was home, his eyes halfway lidded and his hair looking tousled. He sat, and yawned, and had coffee with her.

"Hank. How it was your working last night?"

"All right."

"Sometime you must permit me to visit."

"All right."

"Because I liking to see what you do with your computers."

"Believe me, it's not rocket science."

"What is not rocket science?"

"What I do."

She peered at him. "Hank. I know this. You are computer operator, no? You are guy who keeps computers running?"

"No, no—it's something we say. It's an expression, for when something is easy."

"You say, 'Is not rocket science'?"

"Yeah."

"But is obvious, Hank."

And yet, even as they spoke, her thoughts ran in other directions. *Ah, dyevushka, ah, little beauty, no wonder you went crazy yesterday. You are bored! You need something to do! You need a time-filling project!* She looked around the room and was seized by inspiration. "Hank, maybe is okay I put little bit paint on these walls? I thinking maybe your home, which is very nice, could benefit from colour, yes? I thinking I could put up some nice pale yellow, if you want, like buildings in Sennaya I show you. Or maybe could be green, like Hermitage Museum. And also I could paint parts that, mmmmmmm, what you calling them? The parts that go around doors and windows?"

"The trim?"

"Yes! The trim! They could be, mmmmmm, *glossy*. How you would say to your house looking like palace? We could live like tsars . . ."

Hank paused for a moment. Then he opened his wallet and stammered, "Of course, of course, what do you need?"

He went upstairs. Anna waited for as long as her enthusiasm would allow—*yes! oh yes! to be busy with something!*—which in this case was a nerve-jangling hour. She put on her jacket and bustled to Queen Street and found a store that sold paint but that wasn't yet open. Anna stamped her right heel, and spat several curse words that came out in *mat*-Russian. She decided to cross the street and sit at a Tim Hortons, where she ordered a full sixteen ounces of American-style coffee, her energy further enhanced by a honey-glazed cruller. She sat. She ate. Her fingertips tapped the tabletop. Finally, she saw a little gnome of a man, wearing suspenders and black plastic glasses, come to the paint shop's door and turn the CLOSED sign to OPEN. She swallowed the last of her coffee, and recrossed the street after left to right looking. Once inside the store, she began flipping through paint chips. She picked out three colours. One was a deep green, one was a Dijon yellow, and one was the grey of St. Petersburg granite.

She went to the counter and dropped the chips in front of him.

"Excuse me," she said.

He looked at her slowly, through lenses so old they'd begun to turn milky.

"These colours. Which one you think is nicest? I . . . well. I liking *all* of them."

He looked at the samples.

"For what you use?"

"My living room."

"A living room . . . hmmmmmm."

THE CULPRITS

He breathed through his mouth as he compared all the samples. Finally, and with a sureness of movement, he held out the yellow.

"That one?"

"Yes. It reminds me of summer."

Fifteen minutes later, she was loading paint cans and brushes into the back of a taxi. At home, she covered Hank's furniture with clear plastic drop sheets. She began opening paint cans, and preparing her rollers, and imagining what life with new walls might be like. Then it hit her: she did not own clothes she could ruin with splatters. This left her with two options. She could dart to Gerrard Street and buy a cheap top and some dollar-store sweatpants. *Or,* she could turn up the heat, peel off her clothing, and get down to work in the clothes that God gave her.

She mulled for just seconds. The culprits were excitement, impatience, and the caffeine that had been in her large double-double. Upstairs, Hank slept, his room slowly warming. Downstairs, Anna rollered, while up and down jiggling. When the coffee wore off, she made herself more, the house filling with paint fumes and earth-scented Nabob. She worked through lunch. Through an error of enthusiasm, she left the drapes open, and at twelve minutes past two the mailman was treated to the sight of a young Russian wearing nothing but a paper hat perched on her head sideways. By the time Hank came down, the ground floor was covered with a pale, muted yellow. Anna was wearing a robe, and looking flushed with her effort.

"Hank!" she said. "You like?"

"Oh yeah," he said, unable to take his eyes off her.

"Really?"

He turned his head. The skin under his jaw wobbled just slightly.

"Is like buildings in the streets around Sennaya, no? Like the old income houses I show you?"

"I suppose it is."

"So, Hank, please, say you liking it . . ."

"It's great, Anya. It is."

She spent the next day like the first, this time displaying her lower-back dimples to the mailman, a deliverer of flyers, and a trail of grey-panted schoolboys, who spotted her through a window and muttered *Oh wow!* in Hindi. It came to an end when she was bothered by a pair of Jehovah's Witnesses; instead of ringing the bell, they stood on the porch while lasciviously staring. Anna, after a minute, heard the short feral rasps that infected their breathing; she turned, screamed, and covered up with hands that were far, far too little.

The problem was, she'd grown to like the feeling of paint on skin dripping. It made her feel free, and not burdened by life's problems. On her third painting day, she worked without sunlight, the inside lights on and the curtains drawn tightly. She finished the walls and started in on the ceiling, which she found made her neck sore. Still, she persevered, most of the drips caught by her round milkmaid bosom. (There were advantages, yes there were, to this in-the-raw working: just one quick shower and she was cleaned up completely.) By the fourth day she'd finished the first coat of the trim, and by the end of the fifth the entire first floor had been completely painted.

Yes, she thought, standing in the middle of the living room, *it's lovely, it's beautiful, you did good,* dyevushka. *Now all we need is a Christmas tree and some tinsel.*

But then her heart, which a moment ago had felt lightened, began to wilt like a plant left for weeks without water. *Why?* she thought, her head madly spinning. *Why, Anna Verkoskova? Why, Anya Mikhailovna? Why, you crazy and mood-sinking* dyevushka? A second later she understood: with the walls the colour of old Sennaya housing, she couldn't help but think of the market's mad clamour. And when she thought of Apraxin, when she thought of its laneways and alleys, its face-scarred vendors and egg-flogging babushkas, its fish alleys and graffiti reading *Viktor Tsoi Lives!!!* on walls old and crumbling ... well.

It was only a matter of seconds before she thought of a certain cement-dusty back room.

Her heart turned blue and cannonball heavy. She cleared a place on the sofa, sat, and placed her paint-speckled glasses on Hank's coffee table. She put her face in her hands. She gave a wail that was soft and a little bit spooky. *I am,* she thought, *going as mad as a cobbler.* Her sobbing, that day, was torrential as ever; her tears dripped through cracks in the floorboards and slowly formed a puddle in the cellar, providing a water hole for the vermin who lived scurrying lives down there.

When she finally stopped, her face was pink and mildly swollen. She donned a jacket, boots, and muffler. Outside, she walked south, her gait altered by heart pain. She entered the paint shop, to bells softly tinkling. The owner was at the back, where he liked to sit and read the paper. Anna, meanwhile, could feel herself fading. She looked down, and watched her hands turn translucent. Behind her, her shadow looked speckled and run through with sunlight. Little one—right there, in the store, in an aisle devoted to painting accessories, her body turned to mist before vanishing fully, Anna now nothing but a pair of eyes on stilts blinking.

That's when she pocketed a wood-handled paint scraper. Instantly, she felt her body reforming. She felt her feet regain the floor and her hands fill her pockets. It was the relief of these two sensations that caused her to start smiling just as she passed a display of Benjamin Moore paint cans, erected in a pyramid right beside the doorway. She left the store and started walking. Half a block later, she stopped, her feet cold as ice trays and her legs feeling wobbly. The rest came on quickly—shame and rank guilt and gutting self-hatred. She bent at the waist and then started gagging. A young couple stopped and asked if she needed a doctor.

"*Nyet,*" she gasped, "no," before awkwardly straightening.

A minute later, Anna reversed her steps—back to the store's entrance, back to the pyramidal display of Benjamin Moore paint cans, back to the aisle where the paint scraper in question no longer hung with the others. She replaced it, sniffling. The owner heard, and peered over his paper. Anna blinked, and bought enough green paint to coat a gymnasium (along with the scraper she'd both stolen and de-stolen).

Later, at home, she knelt on the floor before an imaginary Onuphrius. Upward she looked, eyes dark and misty, palms in front of her heart and touching in prayer. Her head glowed with the shimmer of imaginary candles.

"Never again," Anna pledged. "Never and not again *ever*."

It was a promise that lasted for five days and six hours; she had nearly covered all of the yellow when her arms and her legs began to turn slightly gauzy. She put down her paintbrush and thought that a glass of wine might help to calm her. It didn't. The sensation worsened, and a voice in her head started goading. *Why not take a break? A walk? A breath of fresh air?* The voices grew more insistent. *Anya, little beauty, can't you sense it? Can't you feel it? Your body, I hate to tell you, is right now growing dimmer . . .*

She breathed in the air of a city's long winter. She walked like a robot, chin up and grimly. A few minutes later, she stood before the cash at Iqbar's Fine Groceries, where she paid for cardamom pods, ginger root, basmati rice, mild curry powder, and a one-litre tin of syrup-packed mango. Meanwhile, a packet of garam masala was unsubtly scenting her vinyl coat pocket.

The next day, she took a *TV Guide* from a Sikh newsstand vendor. Five days later, she took an envelope pack from a post office outlet. It got easier—her highs became lower and her lows became higher. The only thing that stayed the same was the itch that came to her; *it* called the shots, rendering Anna a puppet. With a start she realized she *had* carved a new life in this orderly city: she painted, she cooked, she wandered the city. And when her cravings got bad, and her body translucent, she engaged in the art of the five-fingered discount.

(And one day, to tempt fate, she even walked out of a store with a Coke held in plain view. The store owner came running. She was smiling and nice and predictably Asian.

"Excuse me!" she called. "You forget to pay! Miss, miss, you forget!"

Anna looked down at a drink that she had always hated. "Yes, I am sorry, my head, I can't trust it . . .")

Having repainted the living room, she moved on to the kitchen. Hank, since the night of their calamitous mating, left for work earlier and came home much later. And yet, when he saw her, he was relentlessly polite *with* her. She couldn't stand this, and left the house often. At an Internet café, she received an email from her mother: the *communalka* had been rented to some displaced Ossetians. Her crossed eyes wept softly, and she feared, yes she did, her days would forever be like this.

Little one.

It was a Tuesday morning, and Hank was in his room, sleeping. Anna was nude and drinking tea on the sofa, her skin dotted all over with kitchen-trim colour. She heard the mail dropping.

After waiting a few seconds, she darted over. In the back of her mind, she had never stopped hoping for a letter from Ruslan, in which he admitted that he really did love her, that he wanted to marry her, and that he didn't care if all sixteen of their children were baptized as Christians. Through Hank's bills she sifted. She stopped. She couldn't believe it. There was a letter right there with her name in Cyrillic. She tore at the envelope and pulled out what appeared to be a lone sheet of paper. Her hands tremored badly as she began reading. And then, because there are moments in which even self-deception won't come to the rescue, and even the greatest of lies won't mute what is happening, her mouth fell open and her dark eyes turned glassy.

It was all she could do to stop from screaming with horror.

FIVE

Ahhhhhh—there it is. That word again. *Horror.* At the mention of these two syllables, I omnisciently backflip to the very near future. At the sound of its consonants, I take a tumble through time and land in a hot, stinking summer. And then I see it, replayed like a newsreel a thousand times over: the way the day looked, the way the air smelled, the way one of the black widows was oddly broad-shouldered.

I see Tushino, little one, and the slaughter that occurred there.

And you might ask, quite rightly—where does forgiveness come from? Where does a child's love perpetually spring from? Trust me—it comes from a mystical place, where iron will mingles with this thing called compassion. So don't be too harsh. Remember—Hank and *mamochka* didn't know what they were doing. They never once stopped to consider their actions. It happens. Think about it. Who amongst us is blameless? Who doesn't have one or two skeletons tucked in a closet? Take me, for example. If you were ever to see me, and could pry away your eyes from my less comely features, you also would notice that my skin is not like yours. Despite being blood of your blood, and kin of your kin, my complexion is not creamy, or glowing, or with light freckles dotted. Oh no. It's dark and purplish; in some light almost plumlike. It's the leathery hue of a Caucasus dweller, of an Apraxin Dvor vendor, of a handsome and Viktor Tsoi–like heartbreaker.

It is: the blue-bronzy tint of a half-Dagestani.

It was the day in which Anna had visited Ruslan to tell him she was leaving. Naked and bruised, he lay in his bed, thinking. His skin was still warm, his lips were still humming, and his gaze was still softened by unexpected pleasure. The market's noisy bustle seeped down through roof rafters. The chalky odour of cement dust was lost to her perfume—it clung to pillows, to his bedsheets, and to Ruslan's hurled clothing.

He smiled. *How strange,* he thought, *this life can be sometimes.*

He'd stayed out to four a.m. the night before. Now, after this morning's unscheduled romping, he closed his dark eyes and, in a moment, was like a contented pug snoring. He slept another two hours. Then he woke suddenly. He jumped to his feet, his arms and long legs a flurry of movement. He put on jeans, his black T-shirt, and his Apraxin Dvor jacket. On the way out of his room, he stopped to check himself in the mirror; here he stood, momentarily grinning.

Though late for work, he still sauntered. As he passed through the shop, he called good morning to his uncle, who was watching *Nord-Ost* coverage on a flickering TV set.

"Ruslan!" called the older man as Ruslan moved to step by him.

"Dadya, please, I am already late."

"Wait!"

Ruslan stopped. They spoke in Avari, the language of their homeland.

"What happened with Anna? What did you do to her?!"

"What do you mean?"

"She ran past me, I think crying. Her eyes were red."

Ruslan frowned. "I don't know. Maybe it was allergies. She never could stand the dust here."

"Allergies? Please. Nephew. I am not an idiot."

"Or maybe she was upset. How should I know?"

The older man snorted. "*She* was the one I always liked, even if she was Russian. She was one of the nice ones."

"I liked her too."

"She was a good girl. I don't like you treating her the way you treat all the others."

"*Bah,* uncle. It was nothing. Believe me, we are just friends. She just stopped to say goodbye."

"Goodbye?"

"She has an Internet friend. In Canada."

Dadya's eyes widened. "In Canada? She is leaving?"

"Yes. Maybe she was sad to go. How should I know? You may have liked her, but she was mad as a cobbler. Those Russian *dye-vushka*—they're so emotional."

"Maybe *you* made her crazy."

There was a pause long and quiet.

"Dadya," Ruslan said, "I have to go."

"You'll be back late?"

"I suppose. I don't know."

"For the love of Allah, be careful. The damned *militsia* will be out for blood. Look, they used some sort of gas in Moscow . . ."

He nodded toward the TV. Ruslan looked, and saw images of soldiers dragging out Russians from the cultural centre and tossing them like sacks into heaps on the sidewalk.

"They'll be all over the market now, asking for papers and revenge and a thousand humiliations. The FSB too, maybe, I don't know, they're such vindictive bastards. It won't be a good time to have dark skin in Russia, not for the next few weeks or maybe even months, not with *Nord-Ost* buzzing in their bonnets. Of course, it won't matter that Putin was probably behind all of this."

"Dadya, please, Putin was *not* behind all of this."

"I wouldn't put it past him—if he could blow up his own buildings in Moscow, then he's capable of—"

"You speak as though that's *proven*."

"It was! He was caught red-handed! They saw the FSB loading those buildings with bags of explosives!"

"They they they! Always *they!* Who are these 'they,' anyway?"

"The local police! In Ryazan!"

"And I suppose *you've* seen the footage? Honestly, Dadya, you see conspiracies and Muslim-haters everywhere."

"There *are* conspiracies and Muslim-haters everywhere. I tell you, if I was younger and didn't have all this—"

"You'd what? Join in the jihad? Please, Dadya, you'd pine for pork shashlik on rice at lunchtime."

"Bah!" exclaimed Dadya. "Just be careful."

"I'll be careful."

"You always say this."

"I always am."

"I don't believe you. At the very least, sew up your pockets so they can't plant drugs on you. All over the market, mothers are sewing up their sons' pockets, and if I was interested in being your mother I'd be sewing up yours too."

"All right."

"And euros? Do you have some? The theatregoers are dying already from the gas. If it had been only dead Chechens, then maybe rubles or dollars would do, but dead *Russians*? You'll need euros if stopped. More than usual."

"Okay, yes, uncle, I hear you."

"Yes you hear me. The problem is, it goes in one ear and comes out of the other."

"No, really, don't worry. Besides, what would they want from me—a bunch of primroses? Some daffodils, maybe?"

"How about your swarthy Dagestani balls? How about the pleasure of watching a *chorny* squirm? Sometimes I wonder about you, nephew. So busy with Russian girls you haven't got a clue what is going on all around you. You haven't got a clue about this war that is brewing. You know what you are, Ruslan? *Oblivious.* Why don't you pull your head out of your backside and get a Muslim girlfriend? We are a people under siege here. We need to stick together, and produce Muslim babies."

"Dadya, please, I have to go, Vakha he's going to kill me as it is . . ."

Dadya's jaw was gnashing. He wouldn't stop staring at his young, stupid nephew.

"Ruslan?"

"What?"

"What did you do to poor Anya?"

Ruslan charged up the steps to street level. Here he stood for a moment. The air in the market was colder than yesterday. Soon, he thought, winter would be coming. Despite *Nord-Ost* and Chechnya and the troubles they would both bring, Ruslan smiled. He liked winter—he liked the beauty of snow, and the way the city looked when by a white blanket covered. Plus—Dadya's shop was located near a row of Azeris who, with knives shaped like crescents, dismembered whole sheep that had been blessed twice by imams (the first while the animal was living, the second following a quick and expert throat slitting). In the long days of summer, when the sun didn't set until just before breakfast, this hacking dispatched a strong reek of offal. *This,* in turn, clung to Ruslan's dark clothing; from May to September he smelled like a butcher.

But in winter! In *winter,* in that beautiful and pure sky-blue season, Apraxin smelled like wood and warm charcoal, like a dacha's pine walls after a rainy camp cookout. This was good for business. His customers knew this smell, and it pleased them all greatly. The smiles at each door were warmer and wider. His tips, when he got them, were bigger and better. *Bozhe moi!* they'd exclaim. *Primroses for Christmas!!!* Ruslan again smiled. Between deliveries he planned to visit his latest Natasha, and he was glad he didn't bear the faint scent of innards.

Sweet Allah, life was good! Sweet Allah, living was such a continuous wonder! And it didn't matter one whit that he was a *chorny* in a country that hated all *chorny,* be they poor *chastniki* drivers or feared Chechen mobsters. Oh no—it was exactly this scorn that made him off limits and therefore irresistible. *That,* and one other thing: he, Ruslan Bhaiev, had the flukish good fortune to look exactly like Viktor Tsoi, the lead singer of Kino, a fact he hadn't appreciated until his escape from home three years earlier, his way lit by the moon and sulphur bombs falling.

His odyssey had actually started in Khasavyurt, a town that, for its sins, was directly across from the Chechnya border. It was a city so forgotten—so existing in a Caucasian yesteryear—that even its residents had trouble remembering its real name. For this there was a reason. The city was a ragtag assortment of Avars and Dargins and Lezgins; of Laks and Tabasarans and Rutuls; of displaced Ossetians and Chechens and Azeris; and, last but not least, of a handful of mountain Jews, who were known for visiting towns with sheepskin-filled ox carts. Each had their own name for their poor, thin-aired city: it was Khasavyurt, it was Kavasyurt, it was Vakasurt and Savakurt and Yasakurt; it *was* (much more often than not) "this Soviet shithole just in from the Caspian." It was such a problem that town council, an unwashed collection of bickering elders, devoted the majority of its time to arguing over civic pronunciations, and not over a problem that was infinitely more pressing: al-Khattab and his Arabs were storming across the border from Chechnya and lopping fingers off anyone who refused to join their Wahhabi uprising. In response, the Dagestani authority had started shooting back at Khattab, reducing Khasa-whatever to a city of craters, and pockmarked facades, and balconies left hanging by proverbial hair strands. And so, when Ruslan's father, a yellow-toothed wreck who looked twenty years older than his real age, informed his son that a plan had been devised to get him out of there... well.

Ruslan wept with gratitude, and kissed the stubbled cheeks of his papa.

"Not so fast," said his father. "You haven't heard all of it."

There were two drawbacks. First, Ruslan's chauffeur would be his much older cousin Soytiev, a man who had a business selling traditional vests in the north of the country. Ruslan disliked him, as did most people. He was a man who wore a necklace strung with bat's teeth, meditated in a circle of crystals, and had a third-eye tattoo on the palm of his left hand. Still, Soytiev had one redeeming feature: he drove to St. Petersburg at the start of each season, where he peddled his wares to stores catering to tourists.

"What else?" sighed Ruslan.

"You are nineteen," replied his father. "You are healthy and strong, and you have no papers of any kind. At checkpoints and roadblocks you'll be viewed as Shamil Basayev himself." Ruslan understood what he meant—riding in trunks was a Caucasian pastime. "You'll have your Walkman. You'll have a Thermos. You'll have enough woollen vests to burden an elephant. Believe me. You'll be okay."

The day came. They left in the pre-dawn, the mountaintops lost to thick, burly fog. Soytiev's car was a rattling old Lada, the passenger door shut with a bent-up coat hanger. There was weeping, and sad laughter, and the excitement of younger brothers and sisters. Ruslan was hugged by old, heavy-skirted women, and he was cried on by a mother saying goodbye to her eldest. Throughout, he couldn't wait to get going—he could almost feel it, through his lungs whipping, cold Russian air and the promise of freedom. They left just as the floor of the valley turned from black to dark orange, and vulture-sized crows began to caw at the morning. The car coughed and backfired and shot plumes of mauve air from its backside. There was less traffic than normal. In the distance there was shelling and a sky lit with flashes.

At the edge of the city, Soytiev stopped and, bat's teeth clacking, looked over at Ruslan.

"All right, all right," Ruslan said, and climbed into the car's trunk.

It smelled of oil and metal and old, worn-out tires. Yet the vests kept him warm, and his headphones blared with Metallica, Judas Priest, and early Led Zeppelin. He had a small penlight to use if he needed. He sounded out lyrics to songs shrieked in English. He played air guitar to all of the solos. Entombed in this dark place, he missed the beautiful landscape—blue valley streams, craggy rock chasms, the rising of smoke from storybook cabins. Instead, he got cramps in his limbs and sore, battered kidneys. Still, he didn't care, oh no he didn't, he was nineteen and male and escaping Khasa-however-you-say-it (and not only that, he was doing it in a manner that was daring and clever and, with any luck, *dyevushka*-impressing). He rode this way for hours. At checkpoints, he'd cover himself with vests in case someone asked to have the trunk opened. When he had to pee, he knocked on the top of his rusting enclosure; Soytiev would pull over and pace as Ruslan stood away from the roadway. And then it was back in the trunk, his Thermos refilled with potato and beet soup. On and on this went, the car slowing only at checkpoints and when they came near a village. At such times he'd hear roosters and stray dogs and yoked, lowing oxen; after a few jostling minutes these noises would fade and they'd be back in the country, the road thrumming beneath him.

Toward the end of the day, the car stopped moving. Ruslan turned off his music. He heard strange, magic whooshing caused by wind in the treetops. He could also hear the driver's-side door opening and closing. Suddenly he was squinting into a green, dwindling twilight. Above him stood Soytiev; his neck was now heavy with pendants and amulets and dangling yin-yang signs. He'd also changed into the sort of flowing white blouse worn by John Lennon during his 1969 bed-in.

He smiled weirdly at Ruslan.

"Soytiev," Ruslan sighed. "What the *fuck*?"

"A small and insignificant pit stop, boy. Come. Your edification, not to mention your salvation, awaits."

He offered a hand ornamented with rings; his nails, Ruslan noticed, were as horny as tree bark. Ignoring it, Ruslan climbed out. He felt stiff all over. They were next to a path that led into a forest. Ruslan looked around.

"Where are we?"

"Good question, cousin. Astrakhan, or at least a forest a little ways away. At the end of this trail is a baba, a wise woman, a world-famous *vedomye zheny*. She has her own website and, it is rumoured, a book contract with Penguin. Her métier is potatoes."

"Potatoes?"

"Yes."

"You've brought me to a potato witch? They actually *exist*?"

"She is a seer, cousin. A visionary. A modern-day wise woman. She is *not* a witch."

"For the love of Mohammed—we're going to have our fortunes told? You drove out of our way for *this*?"

Soytiev breathed deeply. "You are welcome to stay near the car."

Ruslan did. He leaned against the warm Lada while Soytiev tromped over ferns and tamped black earth. This lasted for a half minute; the light was low and dappled with shadows. When he heard the first howling of wolves, and the first rustling of wind in the treetops, and the first mangling of twigs by whatever was out there . . . well. He swallowed his pride and caught up to his cousin. There was a tightness in his shoulders, and his breathing was shallow.

"Aha!" proclaimed Soytiev. "I see you've had second thoughts! Wise choice, my cousin."

Ahead was a cottage surrounded by garbage and crabgrass and goats tethered to wood pegs. As the two men approached, the goats piteously whinnied and made runs at each other. Soytiev knocked. He listened. He knocked again, and the door creaked slowly open.

Ruslan had never seen a woman so old. She stood no more than five feet tall, or at least she would have had she not been bent so far over. Her hair, or what was left of it, stuck up from her scalp in crinkly white coils. Her eyes were milky blue orbs, and her face was as jowly as that of a bulldog. She moved to within an inch of the two men and looked at them, squinting; her scalp was covered with scrapes and dents and eczema patches.

"*Why*," she croaked in Russian, "you are bothering Baba?"

"Baba Mal," answered Soytiev, "we have come to have—"

"You have euros?"

"Yes," Soytiev said.

The baba nodded and motioned they should enter. They did. The door wheezed shut behind them. Her room was piled high with newspapers, rags, and plates crusted with old food. The walls were made of roughly hewn timber, the cracks insulated with a paste of mashed pond weeds. There was a cat, predictably black, pushing its nose through old turnip peelings. The whole place smelled of woodsmoke and yogurt. At the rear of the cabin was a large stone fireplace; the baba wandered over and spat a wad of forest green phlegm into it. The logs sizzled. She turned.

"Sit," she commanded.

The two men looked around before moving toward a table that was in the room's cluttered centre. They pushed away papers and dirty plates and then sat down. Even Soytiev now looked nervous. Next to the fire was a bushel of potatoes; the men watched as Baba grabbed two of them. "Who is first?" she grunted.

"He is," said Ruslan.

She approached the table and put the potatoes down on it. The handle of a cleaver poked from a pile of old *Pravda* copies. The woman seized it. A second later she yelped, and brought it down hard. A potato lay in halves, the hatchet stuck in the marred table surface.

"Hold out your hands."

Soytiev did so; the crone put a potato half on each of his palms. They waited. Ruslan worked hard at not smirking. After two or three minutes the old woman lifted the halves and regarded the meshing of lines and red creases that Soytiev's hands had left on them. She turned her head and studied them with the corner of one eye. "Hmmmm," she said. She cleared her throat once again, and fired another rocket of phlegm in the fire's direction. It sizzled for a moment, and then released a puff of light green smoke.

"Hmmmm," she again said. "I see prosperity, and much travel, and a good long lifespan."

"And what of love?" Soytiev asked. "Of marriage?"

"Hah! Don't make an old woman laugh. *Next . . .*"

She wrestled the hatchet from the table and brought it down hard on the second potato. Ruslan put out his hands, his smile now apparent. *I,* he thought, *am beginning to like this old Astrakhan ved'ma.* She placed potato halves on his palms. Ruslan grinned at his cousin; Soytiev had crossed his arms dejectedly over his thin chest. Two minutes passed. The witch again spat in the fire, producing another sizzle and a flame cool and greenish. She took Ruslan's potatoes and looked at them sideways.

"Hmmmm," she said finally.

Ruslan said, "What is it, O wise one?"

"Hmmmmm," she said again. "Bad news. I am sorry, but here goes. It says that you're damned with perception and all-knowing, and that your spurned-by-God soul is hell-bound because of it. It says you're a fury of demonic presences, and that the fires of hell burn deep within you. It says that your mind is possessed by devils, and that the very fibre of your being is scarred with malevolence, violence, and the rotting of garbage. It says that you're a vile and all-seeing vampire, and that your life brings ruin upon all who go near it. It says that, in a former life, you lived in the mountains and ate children who got lost there. It says that, in those days, you were a violator of women and a beater of stray dogs and a pusher-down of old people. It says that your body hums to the hymn of putrescence, and that your heart beats excitedly when nearing all that is ugly. It says that you are darkness, fever, and disease, all rolled into one, and that your comeuppance will come to you quite shortly and quickly. Sorry about that. Now get the hell out, before you infect Baba's cottage with your corrupting essence. Get out, get out, Baba needs her rest, get out before I hit you in the head with my splitter of potatoes. But first, that's fifteen euros for the two of you. Normally is ten each, but since the news was a little on the bad side, I'll give you a discount."

What could Ruslan do but laugh? All the way back to the Lada, he guffawed at having been frightened by the howling of wolves and the rustling of branches and the other sounds a forest makes when you're all alone in it. He laughed even louder as a pissed-off-looking Soytiev held the trunk open for him. Oh yes— he chuckled loudly, some might even say cruelly, all the way to Volgograd, where, the roadblocks long having since ended, Soytiev felt obliged to let him sit in the front seat. And still Ruslan sniggered about the old, spitting faker; every few kilometres he'd chuckle, and say something like *Careful, cousin, you're in a car with the devil* or *Perhaps I should be looking for wedding gifts for you.* After one extended period of silence, he leaned toward Soytiev and shouted *Boo!* at him. Meanwhile, Soytiev brooded and scowled and, somewhere near the outskirts of Moscow, blurted, *All right, all right, so I made a mistake! So she was an imposter!*

Ruslan snickered and turned up the stereo. The car filled with the roar of "Enter Sandman," his favourite song by James Hetfield's Metallica. Soytiev grimaced and drove and, once in a while, yelled "Pass me a sandwich" over the blaring of music. He dropped Ruslan on Nevsky Prospect.

"Find Apraxin Dvor," he said, "and ask around for your uncle."

Ruslan stood on the most famous street of the city, perhaps in all of Russia, his vision blocked by billboards for Givenchy and Cartier and Louis Vuitton. He stretched, and in his mind left home forever. He admired the long-limbed women who walked all around him. He admired the smell of progress that in the air hung like a perfume. Then, out of nowhere, he heard a strange high-pitched yodel—it was halfway between a shriek and a giggling—and he turned just as three blonde teenage girls came running up to him. Each was holding out a pen and a sheet of blank paper.

"*Bozhe moi, bozhe moi,*" they were calling. "Could we *please* have your autograph?!?"

That was three years ago. Since then, he'd had . . . praise be, how many Russian women *had* he joined beneath the covers? Was it three dozen? Was it *four*? It didn't matter. What did matter was that every single one of them was prettier than the Quran-spouting virgins who passed for women back home, in the dirt-poor hamlets of the Dagestani Republic.

You had to hand it to the Russians. Though murderous racists (if he had a kopeck for every time he'd been stopped in the street and called a damn *chorny zhopie*!)—he adored them when it came to their sexual mores. The truth was that St. Petersburg ran on one thing and one thing only. Oh yes—it travelled down Nevsky on heels high and teetering. It glared from every ad and sex boutique window. It was served up to Germans in breakfast-included packages. It permeated large hotels, where "introduction" services operated from clean lobby storefronts. It shone like red neon in darknestled corners. It was sold on TV like a furniture store clearout. It was what lit up the sky during the city's famed White Nights. It was the reason (Ruslan liked to joke) that its canals smelled like salt, sweat, and perfume. Oh yes—sex *was* St. Petersburg. In his mind, it was what made it so Unreal. Every fishnetted and midriff-exposed inch of it was out there, just waiting.

But the best thing? The thing that really made him question whether there was a limit to the luck a person could be granted?

THE CULPRITS

Viktor Tsoi had *died*! He was now deceased, no more, gone to rock and roll heaven! Oh yes—he'd got himself killed on one of the ring roads of Moscow, the culprit a driver who'd been excessively drinking. In other words, there was no more of *him* to satisfy his fans' earthly hunger (the vast majority of whom were female, and young, and liked to scribble *Viktor Tsoi lives!* in Apraxin Dvor alleys). Instead, the job fell to a young deliverer of flowers who just *happened* to have the same jet-black hair, the same sculpted features, the same famous dimples and lean, lanky body. The only thing Ruslan didn't have—or at least hadn't had during those first few months after arriving—was Viktor Tsoi's brooding air. No matter. He learned quickly to pout, and narrow his eyes, and obsess about things that were gloomy and distant, so as to claim his fair share of New Russia's biggest export.

A typical encounter: Ruslan is buzzed into a building just off Nevsky, a part of town afforded only by expatriate businessmen or Ural Mash mobsters. In his hands he carries a primrose arrangement. He knocks; his most recent Natasha (or Vanessa or Katya) answers. She is the physical intersection of Anna Kournikova and a cocktail bar hooker, and living in luxury for that reason only. She is also bored, furnished with an allowance that would make an heiress feel unworthy, and stoned on green hashish tinctured with opium. Above all else, she is resentful of her New Russian boyfriend, who has five other such women in five other such apartments. Yet the final straw? The insult that drives them toward a Lothario like Ruslan? The card on the flowers is always (and only) made out to *My Rabbit,* just in case there's a mix-up in the paid-for delivery.

And so. The primroses (or calla lilies, or orchids, or tulips) are tossed aside blithely. She eyes Ruslan coolly, noting his dark hair and Viktor Tsoi likeness, her interest expressed by a tilt of an eyebrow. *You are busy?* she says in that way that Russians pose questions. Before Ruslan can answer, she invites him for coffee, or a drink, or a bowl of green hashish. Then, noting his purple-tinted skin and Caucasian accent (for he does nothing to lessen it around his young Katyas and Tanyas), she smiles and asks his name and then asks, "It is Chechen?"

Ruslan's reaction was once to blurt, *Do I look like a hoodlum? Do I look like a gangster? Do I look like a murderous, kidnapping phantom?* Yet he has learned to narrow his eyes, and throw back his shoulders, and say in an accented Russian, "*Da*, yes, is right. I come here from Grozny . . ."

Out comes a lighter, a pipe, a square of tinfoil. The hash is green and Afghanistan's finest. Yet it also has flecks that are white and inspiring of out-of-body experiences. There's a blue butane flame. Dark smoke comes up in a spiral. Then, after they've rolled on the carpet like a pair of cats fighting, Ruslan pulls on his jeans and says, "Maybe, who knows, another time I will see you . . ."

He pulled himself out of his reverie; today, of all days, he had to keep his wits about him. Though he hated to admit it, particularly where his paranoid and Russian-loathing uncle was concerned, the old man was probably right—it *was* only a matter of time before the *militsia* descended and started demanding bribes from every Chechen, Dagestani, Ossetian, Ingush, Georgian, Armenian, and Tatar they could get their cold hands on. He hunched up his shoulders and walked through Apraxin Dvor faster, his boots dampened by slush and gurgling black water. The heavy rain of the morning had turned to something lighter, and misty, and bordering on ominous. He pushed through the door of Vakha's shop. His boss was sitting at his table, trimming some roses. He looked at Ruslan over cutaway glasses.

"Ruslan!"

"Yes, yes, I am late, I know."

"I know, I know—always I know. A little less 'I know' and a little more 'I do,' please. We have orders! We have orders for all over the city!"

Ruslan rolled his eyes. "Vakha—speak Russian! You have been here . . . what? Twenty years? Learn to speak the language!"

"Russian? Why should I speak Russian? You have forgotten your own language all of a sudden? You have forgotten Avari? You know what your problem is? Too much Afghani hashish and tall Russian girlfriends. They both poison the mind and pollute the soul. Remember, we are Muslims."

"We are *Sufis*, Vakha! We are *supposed* to smoke hashish. And meditate, and dance the *zikr*, and idolize saints, and chant the Quran in cemeteries, remember? We're mystics, thank God. That means we get to have a little fun."

"It does *not*."

"It does," insisted Ruslan, who was by then smiling widely.

"It does not. You young people. Every time you do something bad, you cry, 'Oh, Sufi let me do this' or 'Sufi let me do that.' I tell you, it makes the sin double, blaming it all on religion."

Ruslan tut-tutted. "You better be careful, Vakha. You're starting to sound a little like your son. You know, I saw him the other day."

Vakha stopped what he was doing. "You did?"

"Yes! I was in Gostinyy Dvor shopping. All of a sudden he was there, in broad daylight no less, looking like Cat Stevens at a public burning of *Satanic Verses*. You should have seen him, with his djellaba and his long beard and his *Allahu Akbar*s every ten seconds. He wanted me to come to some meeting. I told him—"

He stopped. Vakha's eyes were moistly glinting. Ruslan immediately felt guilty, and with himself disappointed.

"So he's alive," Vakha said softly.

Ruslan nodded. "Don't worry, boss, I was just teasing. His beard wasn't that long. This war, it'll make crazy persons of us all."

There was a pause. Two years earlier, Vakha's son had started visiting a small Wahhabite mosque somewhere out in the suburbs. He'd started spending less and less time at home, until finally, five or six months ago, he disappeared altogether.

"Did you talk to him? Did he say where he was living?"

"No. I'm sorry."

The older man sighed. As he turned away, he upset a crate of daffodils. Yet instead of yelling at Ruslan to pick them up and get going, he sighed a second time and dolefully looked at them. Ruslan felt more chastened than if Vakha had hollered at him. He grabbed an armload of orders, each one cone-shaped and wrapped loosely in plastic. His guilt vanished the moment he breathed the damp air of the market. His thoughts were now on one thing and one thing only: visiting his most recent, and luscious, Paris Hilton–like Russian.

So.

Through the market he swaggered, the old beetroot vendors calling "Hello Ruslan!" to him. Each time he'd grin widely without at all slowing. He turned down a laneway too narrow for vendors. After twenty metres he turned once again, reaching a small niche bordered on three sides by brick walls. There was barely four inches of space on either side of the Volga. He unlocked a door marred with dents and deep scratches. He reached his arm inside, rolled down a window with his chin pointed upward, and threw his orders into the back seat (exhibiting a carelessness that would have left his boss fuming). He climbed in through the window, careful not to strike his head on the door frame.

The car had been backed in, which explained all the scrapes that streaked the door panels. Just ahead was a small lane, tinted by light that came squeezing through roof gaps; this in turn led through an arch and into Apraxin Dvor's clamour. In other words, he was more or less hidden. He reached beneath the passenger seat and felt for a hole in the car's rusted chassis. His fingers touched foil. He grinned, and fumbled for his lighter. Thirty seconds later he was contentedly puffing. And oh, it was wonderful, this bounty that defined post-Gorbachev Russia! How glorious it was, this immediate access to all Western pleasures! After a few lungfuls, his eyes bulged and widened, and his head filled with the music of a dreamily played zither. The flowers in the back began to glow a pale yellow. Off he went on his rounds, red-eyed and whistling.

He had to take lilacs to Vasilyevsky, roses to Petrogradskaya, tulips and daisies to Prospect Vyborgskaya, orchids all the way to the Primorsky parklands. And *primroses* . . . to every nook and city cranny, to every small urban corner, to every far-flung ethnic pocket. (No matter how long Ruslan worked in St. Petersburg, he would never, ever, understand the Russian adoration for this small and understated flower.) When he ran out of orders, there was barely time for a cup of strong kiosk tea, in which he steeped a little more of Afghanistan's finest. Then it was back toward Apraxin's mad bustle. This was the way he spent his last day to be envied, his little car chugging on light blue air currents, the slosh of canals in his ears softly humming, the wrought iron lamps looking like monks on a tightrope. With his mind filled with green smoke, all of the city was a dream . . . a fantasy . . . a beautiful and thuggish and sad Unreality.

And then, because it was the middle of the afternoon, and Ruslan had been toiling for five solid hours, and the traffic would soon thicken and stop altogether, and he was taking an order to Tavrichesky Garden . . . well. He checked his dark locks, and suitably mussed them. He grabbed a fistful of flowers bound for the widow of some old ex-apparatchik who had no power to hurt him. He left his car in a courtyard lined with Audis, and Hummers, and a few glowering Chechens who were paid to keep an eye on them. He entered the building with the code she had given. Smugly, he waited. *Ahhhhhh*, he thought, *this is the Russia I wish to have someday*—a Russia of crystal chandeliers instead of low-wattage light bulbs, of velvet wallpaper instead of *mat*-laced graffiti, of swooshing elevators instead of clanking monstrosities, of penthouses acquired through extortion and murder.

He was buzzed in. A doorman—a *Russian*—resentfully nodded. Upward he rode. Brass doors hummed open. He stepped onto burgundy carpet and then walked along a sound-dampened hallway. Here, oh yes *here*, there was no echo of television, no blaring of radios, no groans of old men who'd all day been drinking. Oh no—here was the blissful and oh *so* peaceful Russia.

He stopped and knocked lightly. In a moment she was there, in her long-legged Slav glory. Her skin was pure white. Her lips were the same colour as her pink fluffy slippers. Her blonde hair was up, and her dress was a sheeny and tight silken nothing. Her left hand held a cigarette, and in her right she had a dog who looked like shredded white Kleenex.

She arched an eyebrow. "So, my flower-delivering Chechen. We have come for a visit?"

"Nice dog."

"Ivan bought it for me. He thought I wanted one. His name is Boris. He is a Shih Tzu. It's all I can do to stop from strangling the little fucker. Please, come in. Maybe you can help me drown him in the tub."

She stepped to one side. Ruslan entered a foyer where a real Marc Chagall greeted all visitors. She passed him and he followed, his feet touching a rug fashioned from a Siberian tiger. Natasha put down Boris, the little mutt yelping.

And then, oh yes *then,* came a stalking by the room's other tigress; she circled him in a way almost predatorial. There was the smoky hot press of lips painted thickly. Meanwhile, Boris yelped and yapped and took small sharp-toothed nips at both of Ruslan's ankles, until finally Natasha said *Enough, filthy mutt* and hurled him into the bedroom. Her dress fell down a long hipless body. Two bodies fell to a floor made from Javanese hardwood. Then it was Ruslan avenging every Russian atrocity ever visited upon the Caucasus, from the strafing of Grozny to the slaughter at Samashki to Stalin's deportation of every Dagestani man, child, and woman to the barrens of Kazakhstan. Oh yes yes yes, how sweet it was, this mustering of DNA-encoded resentment, this turning of tables on a hundred-pound Russian, this pinning of wrists over a head from side to side tossing, it never *once* occurring to our hip-thrusting Ruslan that this moll, using a dialect heard in the wilds of Archangel, was grunting *Fuck me, you Chechen, you Shamil, you ruthless and goddamned* chorny *bastard . . .*

They caught their breaths on the back of the spread-eagled tiger. The dog was still in the back bedroom yelping. They smoked a small bowl of al Qaeda's finest, the chandelier twinkling like the sky in mid-winter.

"Hey, Chechen."

Ruslan turned and said nothing.

"I did it."

"You did what?"

"Enrolled. At school."

His eyebrows raised. "Really?"

"Yes."

"You are really going?"

"Yes."

"What does Ivan think?"

"He doesn't know. Maybe I won't even tell him. The college is in another city."

"What will you study?"

"What do you think? Russia has been liberated by democracy, and for this I have the luxury of foregoing mathematics, and science, and literature, and medicine, and music, and all those other useless, frivolous pursuits. Now that totalitarianism is gone, I have the glorious freedom to study marketing, along with every other ambitious young *malchik* and *dyevushka* in all of the country."

Ruslan laughed. Though he'd never before thought about it, she was really quite witty.

She gave a low, rueful chuckle and waved a bangled arm at him. "Maybe, someday, I'll leave all of this." Turning her head, she kissed him, her breath a charcoal-ish blend of Winston Lights and green hashish. "Maybe one day," she said, "I'll be with all of this finished." There was a pause. "You had better leave," she said. "Ivan will be returning soon. If he catches us, he'd make us do it again, only this time with him taking pictures."

Again Ruslan chortled. "You are funny."

"I am not. That's the sad thing, Chechen."

Ruslan's throat felt dry. He sensed it was the last time with this particular Natasha. "You know, I hate to tell you, but I'm not really Chechen."

"Yes you are."

"No. I'm Dagestani."

"No, you're a Chechen all right. We all are. I am, you are, Ivan is, even that yelping cur Boris is. We are all Chechens. Each and every one of us in Putin's New Russia . . ."

THE CULPRITS

And because Ruslan was now good and confused—*You're all crazy*, he thought, *all you spoon-fed Russians*—he chose this moment to stand, pull on his pants, and tell his Natasha that maybe, oh yes *maybe*, he'd see her later.

He crossed the courtyard of her building in late afternoon shadows. He climbed into the Volga feeling more stoned than usual. As always, he had to pump the gas pedal and play with the choke until the motor came to life with a long bout of coughing. He revved, and felt relieved—there were probably a dozen angry calls from Vakha on his cellphone, and the last thing he needed was his vehicle dying.

He put the car in gear and exited the courtyard. The city was darkening; what was left of the sun refracted off grey, stony buildings. He liked this time of day, for in the weakening light everything had a hazed, tinsel quality. He thought of Natasha's thin body and Anya's small, curvy figure—not bad, he thought, for a Dagestani living without residency papers. (Or at least without real ones.) He smiled, but did not feel that happy. This perplexed him. He filed back through the last hour, only to find that his memory was as hazy as the air of the city. At a red light it hit him—it was that thing that she'd said, that thing that had made him feel so oddly burdened. He could still hear it, a voice in his head that was smoky and jaded.

You, me, Ivan, the dog . . . we are all Chechens . . .

He forced a laugh. *Bah!* he thought. *Easy for you to say, with your white skin and your legitimate papers and your easy access to New Russian money.* And yet, no matter how hard he tried to dismiss it, her statement tunnelled deep into Ruslan's consciousness. Once there, it began to taunt and to tease him; yet every time he was on the cusp of grasping its meaning, it would once again speed away, until his head was criss-crossed with the vapour trails caused by his strained, buzzed-out thinking. And then, for just a second, it hovered just long enough for Ruslan to take it in—this ephemeral notion that Chechens (*and* Dagestanis, *and* Ossetians, *and* Ingushetians) weren't the only children to feel a slap from Mother Russia. Oh no, he was now understanding. The Great Bear had more than enough hostility for all of her cubs. *Ahhhhhh,* Ruslan thought, *the husbands she's had: all those Romanovs and Leninites and paranoid Stalinites, all those reformers and oligarchs and track suit–wearing gangsters, all these grubby little pinch-faced Putin-lovers. It's no wonder,* he thought, *that deep down she is bitter.*

With all of these thoughts through Ruslan's head whizzing, his driving skills (which were never of the highest order, Ruslan having purchased his licence from an Armenian with a card-laminating business) suffered. He sped along the Sadovaya, his accelerator flat to a floor marred with rust holes, his tires hitting slush and shooting up plumes of ice water. He played with the radio, finding only more news of the *Nord-Ost* gassings in Moscow.

He let his mind settle. He thought again of his good luck. Two Russian *dyevushka,* and both before sundown—he smiled at the prospect of more days just like this one. He found a rock station, and sang along loudly to the Stone Temple Pilots. Outside, the sky was rapidly darkening. Minutes passed by, in a full bloom of glory. The light at Moskovsky was a bright, waiting orange. He noticed it only as it turned red and suddenly became the *whole* of his vision—oh yes, it was like a nova erupting, like a flash pot exploding. He knew he was speeding. To make matters worse, the pavement was slick with rain and dripped oil, and his car brakes worked in a way that was grudging. With all this in mind, he made a sudden and naive and drug-addled decision: he held his breath, accelerated, and said a quick prayer to benevolent Allah.

A second later it appeared, a blue and white car with its rooftop light swirling. Ruslan cursed and pulled over. At least it was just the police. If it'd been the FSB (or, God forbid, the OMON), then yes, he would have a problem. But the police? The stupid and paid-off *mil-it-see-ah*? He breathed once or twice, and remembered all the times he'd been in the last year pulled over. Each time it was the same. The officer would look at Ruslan's residence permit, which was about as real as anything in this theatre piece called Russia, and then shake his head gravely, only to extract a small bribe that went straight to his wallet. It was a formality, a charade; it was the price of doing business when your name was Ruslan and your skin bore the tint of a ripened Bing cherry.

Two officers emerged, both backlit by low beams. One of them came forward and leaned in the car, scowling. And oh, how Ruslan had to stop himself from grinning—the sheep was so *so* Russian, from his dart-tip nose to his beady mole eyes to the hair gooped back off a long pimply forehead. Yet what really amused Ruslan? What *really* made stifling laughter a struggle? To show that he wasn't a sheep through and through—to show that he hadn't been *totally* co-opted by a life of bribe taking—the officer wore two rings in his right ear, like an E-swallowing kid on his way to the Tunnel. In the face of this ludicrousness, Ruslan clenched his jaw and felt his face pinken. He couldn't help it. Two golden earrings on an Unreal City copper? It was like dreadlocks on a Cossack, like a tube top on a babushka. Behind the first sheep, the other sheep hovered. Though he was younger, and less subtly pimpled, he too suffered from oily white skin and a gelatinized hairdo. The biggest difference was the language of his body: he was hunched in the cold and from foot to foot hopping, as if to say, *Yuri, please, let's go, I am hungry . . .*

"So," said the Yuri-sheep. "How is your night, Shamil?"

The smallest bubble of fear rose through layers of cockiness. It passed, and passed quickly—calling him a Shamil was just another insult, like *Chechen* or *chorny* or *you black chorny bastard*. As long as he kept his head, and was careful to dampen his accent . . .

"I apologize," he said. "I think I went through that light, and I am sorry."

"Papers."

"Yes, yes, of course . . ."

Ruslan, feeling only that he wanted this all to be over, produced his licence, and his residence permit, and twice the number of euros than he normally gave them.

The sheep took the money. "Wait," said the sheep.

The two walked to their car. Ruslan's thoughts churned with green hash and worry. All he could see was two orbs shining a hostile white light in his cracked rear-view mirror. The word *wait* echoed through his head, taking on substance and a fear-causing meaning. He fought the impulse to peel away and try to make it to the maze of Apraxin. Instead, he took a deep breath and fought off the paranoia caused by the times and this moment. *Calm yourself, malchik, they're just trying to make you feel rattled.* He drummed his fingers on the wheel and tried to stay focused. As long as he played along, wide-eyed and courteous and more than willing to hand over another handful of euros . . .

"Shamil."

Ruslan started. The older sheep's face filled the window.

"This licence. It is yours?"

"Yes. Of course." Ruslan swallowed. "Has it expired? If it has, I am sorry, I'm sure there is some way that—"

"Tell me, Shamil. Where did you get it?"

"I am sorry, officer, I do not understand."

THE CULPRITS

"Your licence, Shamil. Where'd you get it? From one of your hoodlum *chorny* friends?"

He couldn't help it—his face fell and his body started to tremble. "I don't—"

"And your residence permit—it is unreal too, yes?"

"No, officer, if there is confusion, I am sorry, but I was born in this city."

"Then why do you look like a *chorny*? Eh, Shamil? Why are you stuttering like one?" He chuckled, as did the other sheep, who stood hidden by shadows. "Why don't you *inform* me, Shamil, please, really, I am interested. You tell me please how this could, mmmmm, transpire?"

Ruslan knew that the secret of lying was to produce lies without pausing, a trick he'd employed on dozens of young Russian women. "My mother," he said, "was born half-Italian." (And the moment he said it—the *moment* it passed from his lips—he knew his good luck had turned sour.)

The sheep and his partner both started laughing. "So that explains it, your *mamochka* ate garlic and spaghetti? Why didn't you say so earlier, you lying and full-of-shit Shamil . . ."

Ruslan stared ahead numbly. "I'm from St. Petersburg," he said.

"I'll say this clearly. You look like a fucking Chechen terrorist."

"I am not. I am sorry. I deliver flowers. Look at my back seat. There are still orders there. The floor is covered with leaves and thorns and bits of plastic. Please, I don't want any trouble."

"You don't want any trouble?"

"No, sir," he said, his voice growing weaker.

"You don't want any trouble, is that it, wop?"

Ruslan nodded.

"Then *prove* you're Italian."

Ruslan was silent.

"I *know*. Why don't you sing for us. It's the one thing Italians and Russians have in common, yes? The love of opera, yes? So sing for us, Shamil. Give us a song."

"I don't know any."

"Oh, come on! You're telling us that your *mamochka* didn't sing to you while wiping your *chorny* shit-covered ass? Yes, sing for us. Sing Verdi! Yes! I always was fond of Verdi. Sing *Tosca*. Don't be bashful. Go ahead—open that *chorny* mouth and sing!"

Ruslan looked stricken. "Officer," he said. "Please, *pajalsta*, I am sure there is some way we can resolve this small matter."

"There is!" the sheep bellowed. "You can fucking well sing! You can sing some fucking Verdi! Sing for us, you Shamil, you *chorny*, you son of a cock-sucking Italian . . . open your god-cursed mouth and *sing*."

Ruslan stared ahead, mournful. It was as though he had gone deaf, his ears hearing nothing but sad recollections. Mostly he pictured days back home in his country—tromping over hills, and through valleys, and past streams slowly trickling. He watched the misting rain turn to wet snow, and landing like blobs of gel on his car's rusted bonnet. He noticed a man with an umbrella pass by walking quickly, his boots making no sounds even though he was striding. It was strange. Everything had gone silent. Ruslan shivered, and sent out *help* thoughts to all those who knew him. When the volume returned, it was so intense and ear-numbing that he wanted to curl up and sleep through whatever was going to happen.

The sheep opened the driver's door and grunted, "Get out of this fucking and about-to-be-towed-away shit heap."

SIX

Aaaaaaaaaah.
That moment of arrest, in a place where arrests have become famous. The act of apprehension, in a country where it's practised as an art form. You are hurled from one state to another. It is a shattering thrust, a violent expulsion. You burn, you boil, you're a man set on fire. A chasm forms and swallows time's passage, leaving you gasping and back-arching in a soul-crushing present.
Little one.
You wither, you turn inward, you stand a hundred miles off, gazing at yourself.

They led Ruslan toward headlights. The whole time, he pleaded that he'd committed no wrongdoing—Pajalsta, *officers, please, the back seat of my car, you can see, it's covered with dried petals*—though of course it didn't matter, for in his panic he was no longer able to tamp down his accent, his vowels now long and muted, his consonants now like a brush against leather. Even as he protested his innocence, he knew—yes, he *knew*—he only sounded like more of a *chorny*. They pushed him against the side of the police car. He felt the cold of the metal transmit through his black jeans.

"Hands behind the back, Shamil."

He tried once more, *Please, officers, please—you have mistaken me for someone else,* and so they grabbed him by his hair and slammed him onto the car's hood. He lay bent over and wincing as they roughly handcuffed him. His head throbbed so badly he wondered if something was broken. As they shoved him into the car, Ruslan started sobbing.

The back seat smelled of smoke and old vinyl. As they drove, the officers chatted about some light opera they'd both seen at Mariinsky. *Sergei, did you notice what nice tits the maid had? Yes, yes, Yuri, and also I liked the libretto.* They chuckled. Ruslan gazed out the window. A thinness in the air seemed to sharpen every detail, bringing every spire and cornice into high resolution. Never, Ruslan thought, had the city looked quite so pretty. Even its colours—leafy green, glossy black, dull amber—achieved a depth that made his heart feel less heavy. He could see the far-off dark outline of the dome at St. Isaac's, and the illuminated tower at Petrogradskaya. Ruslan's tears dried and left salt tracks along his pale, egg-shaped cheekbones.

Southwest they travelled, through thick, snarling traffic. He heard the younger sheep say *We've got another* into the radio. The city turned into suburbs and then thick white pine forests. The moon rose and shone so fully the sky looked jet-black in contrast. The car took a turn, two or three times in quick succession, enough that Ruslan, in his state, lost track of his bearings. They were now driving along country roads, through small, sleepy villages with old wooden churches. This went on for an hour, the *militsia* smoking and joking and after a time turning quiet. Finally, in the middle of a forest, they turned onto a track deeply rutted by tractors. They drove slowly, the car up and down jostling. This too went on for an hour. Ruslan's back grew sore from the relentless bouncing. Finally, they stopped in front of a low concrete building, its windows like beacons in the dark of the forest.

"Get out."

The *militsia* walked him toward the front entrance, a hand clamped tightly to each of his long arms. They went in. Though he kept his head lowered, Ruslan once or twice glanced up. The building was abandoned and, judging by the misting of his breath, without heating. The floors were messed with papers and wires and discarded food wrappers. Ruslan heard laughter from somewhere, and the clinking of glasses. The *militsia* walked him along a cold, filthy hallway. They stopped. He was put in a room that might have once been an office. There were an old metal desk, a pair of chairs, and more papers and wire strewn all around them. Ruslan sat. The younger of the sheep taped his ankles to the chair legs. He then took off the handcuffs and fastened Ruslan's hands behind his back with a stripping of duct tape. He finished the job by taping Ruslan's trunk to the seat back.

"Move one muscle," said the older one, "and personally I will shoot you."

Ruslan was left alone. He didn't bother struggling. Time passed. Once or twice he called out, and was answered with silence. The cold hurt his joints and caused his body to shiver. Hours passed. When he could hold his bladder no longer, he released it, his liquid at first bringing a warm, relieved comfort. Yet after a minute it turned cold, and stung the inside of his legs. Another hour or so passed. His limbs turned numb. He would fall asleep for brief, tortured seconds, only to waken every time his head collapsed forward. He heard owls hooting and trees swaying. In the middle of the night an FSB agent walked in, confirming that this nightmare was both real and unending.

He was carrying a folder, which he threw on the desk as he sat in the free chair. He lit a cigarette, and stared at his prisoner through eyes thickly lidded. He didn't say a thing. Ruslan looked down, his gaze coming to rest on the streaky grey desktop. After a bit he lowered his eyes further, till they fell upon the papers scattered around his taped ankles. He heard smoke come in whispers. When he tried to stop shivering, he found that he couldn't.

"Look at me."

Ruslan did. The agent had thick, greying hair and a nose red and bulbous. Again he said nothing. This went on forever. He finally opened his folder and took out dozens and dozens of eight-by-ten photos. He spread them on the desktop. "So," he said. "These are your bastard Wahhabi friends. The ones from *Nord-Ost*. Please. I invite you. Have a look."

There were forty in all, each with a bullet hole in his or her forehead. Each expression was messed with powder, and blood, and the calm acceptance that comes when your life has just ended. Yet the thing that most haunted Ruslan was the fact that, already, the photos were wrinkled and marred with white creases—he wondered how many Caucasians had already looked at them that night.

The agent smiled. His teeth were orange and crooked. "So," he said calmly. "You want to take your war to the big cities? That is it, yes? Okay, Chechen, you are welcome here. We are happy to be your hosts."

He yawned, and pulled another large photo from the desk's metal drawer. He placed it before Ruslan. In that instance Ruslan understood why a bribe had not worked, and why he'd been taken away, and why he was being interrogated in this cold forest building. It was Khassan, Vakha's son, wearing his beard and sunglasses and his long-flowing djellaba.

"Do you know this man?"

THE CULPRITS

"No."

"Do you know this man?"

"No."

"How long have you known this man?"

"Please," Ruslan muttered. "I don't know him."

"How long have you known this man?"

"I don't know—"

"Do you know this man?"

"No."

"Do you know this man?"

"No."

"Yes you do."

"No I don't."

"Yes you do."

"No, please."

"We have pictures. Of the two of you. Together. He is your boss's son."

"We've never met."

"How would you know that if you don't know who he is?"

"I . . . I beg your pardon."

"How would you know that you'd never met him, if you don't even know who he is?"

"Please . . . I am tired."

"We have your filthy Chechen boss too."

"No . . ."

"He told us differently."

"No . . ."

"He told us you were the best of friends . . ."

"No . . ."

"He said you were bum-buddies. Homosexuals. *Infidels*. He told us you sucked each other's cocks."

"Please..."

There was a pause.

"Do you know this man?"

"No."

"How do you know this man?"

"Please."

"How long have you and this man been fucking one another?"

And so it went, on and on, the agent refusing to believe the answers given by Ruslan. After an hour he said, "Very well, then. Have it your way."

Ruslan was alone for the next five or ten minutes. A different man came in; he wore a headband, and tattoos, and a bandolier that was straight out of a Sylvester Stallone movie. Ruslan saw this, and felt what it was like to die while still living—this man was *contraktniki*, a thug hired to do whatever the Russians did not have the stomach for. Ruslan had heard of them, from both family and friends, though he'd always wondered if they really existed. Now he knew. Not only did they exist, but—judging by this one—they carried lengths of hose filled with sand and capped tightly at both ends. The man came closer, from ear to ear grinning.

"So, Shamil."

Ruslan said nothing. He heard a *heh heh heh* come to him, along with a puff of warm breath that smelled like Bacardi.

"So," the man said again. Ruslan looked at his scuffed boots. For a moment, time stopped. One of the man's laces was untied, and this would forever exist in Ruslan's mind as a snapshot.

"SO!" the man yelled, and gained a firm grip on Ruslan's thick hair. He snapped Ruslan's head upward. "You fucking, fucking *chorny zhopie*."

The man's smile was filled with tin, light brown stains, and dark depthless spaces. He lifted the hand holding the filled tube.

Ruslan closed his eyes. The *contraktniki* hit him while laughing; it felt like every bone in Ruslan's face had been broken—the pain was a ball hit hard at him, ricocheting through his cheeks, jaw, and forehead. His brain felt like it was bursting. His eyes hung from his head on thin, sizzling wires. The man struck again, this time choosing Ruslan's sternum: his ribs expanded, and jetted across the room with a loud, imagined clatter. He couldn't breathe, he started coughing, he felt his organs and muscles recoil in terror. And the *contraktniki*? The man whose job was to administer this punishment? He snickered, and raised his arm, and brought the tube down on the top of Ruslan's legs; this time the shock travelled through his spine, issuing a bone-cracking pain to every bodily crevice.

By the time it was finished, Ruslan's body bloomed violet and orange, loose teeth trickled down his throat like a stream of rough water, and his kidneys leaked blood into the rest of his body. His eyes were so swollen the room appeared to him slit-shaped. Oh yes—by the time it was finished, Ruslan was handsome no longer, and would never again be mistaken for the Kino lead singer.

The *contraktniki* cut Ruslan away from the chair. He fell to the floor and lay on his side, gasping; his hands were still duct-taped behind him. Other boot steps approached. He heard a voice say, "Good work," in Russian. He was lifted to his feet and a burlap bag was placed over his head. He was dragged into cold air and thrown onto the back of a half-ton, where he lay on hard metal covered with ridges. His world darkened further, and he imagined that the flat bed had somehow been covered. An engine rumbled beneath him; he smelled diesel and rags and rank, leafy water. The truck started moving, the wheels bouncing heavily over deep-rutted laneways. After a time Ruslan slept, his head filling with images of tombstones and bomb squads and swooping vampires.

He awoke as the truck's speed diminished. It stopped. He could hear men talking to each other in Russian.

There was a pull on his feet and he was dragged from the flat bed. After falling, he was stood upright, his taped-together hands affecting his balance. Beside him some men were cigarette smoking. They pulled off his sack. Ruslan whimpered, for he knew immediately where he was—they called them "filtration camps," and they were used to weed out those deemed a threat to the nation. And while they existed mostly in the South, at times of crisis they'd pop up in the forests surrounding Russia's two biggest cities.

Ruslan looked upon a clearing in a moon-brightened pine grove. In it was a large canvas tent with a light burning inside. Beside it were holes, a couple of dozen or more, each one freshly dug and as deep as two coffins. And while this scared him (he was a Caucasian, after all, and he'd heard all the stories) it was the sound coming *from* the pits that caused him to drop to his knees and start pleading for mercy.

Little one.

The men in the pits, having heard the truck coming, started moaning, and wailing, and for help loudly calling.

He had a thin, threadbare blanket. The only food he was given was dark, hardened bread scraps (which they threw in his pit after whistling to him). The soil was alive with worms and beetles and ants that looked reddish when viewed in the daylight—these became his friends. He chatted with them to help pass long hours. When screams came from the tent, he'd say to Comrade Worm or his friend Boris Beetle: "Hey! Do you hear that? I think that they're having a Georgian!" Or, if the moans sounded at all Asiatic, he'd comment, "It's an Azeri, I'm sure of it, you can tell by his shrieking . . ."

THE CULPRITS

He tried to escape often, clawing and scraping at the walls of his enclosure; this brought earth tumbling down and made his pit even smaller. To pass unendurable hours, he learned to look up at clouds and at swaying pine branches; late at night, he often thought, they looked like the arms of dark, friendly giants. One day passed, and another. It was on the afternoon of the third day that they pulled him out by his armpits, Ruslan screaming and moaning and begging for mercy. He was then treated to techniques originally applied to Middle Ages witches, the torturers wearing the robes of medieval clergy. Their efficacy, of course, was now honed with practice, and electricity, and an improved understanding of bodily mechanics. But the worst part? The part most diabolical and blithely inhuman? The tent was *warm*. They had heaters made in Bulgaria, which they ran off the same generators that powered their flesh prods. When Ruslan was led back to his freezing, dark earth pit, an uncontrolled shivering overtook his thin body, and cold seeped through his wounds like a strong, airborne vinegar.

He never knew when they'd come for him. He'd go for a better part of a week without a session, and then have two in one day, for no reason he could think of. At first he would pray they'd leave him alone, his knees pressed against earth and his eyes peering upward. This didn't last long; God, and his love, died right before him. In the absence of hope, he turned bone thin and obedient. He drank his own urine, and choked down earth to quell stomach rumblings. He survived thanks to the presence of a ruthless camp doctor, who calculated how much Ruslan's body could suffer. He began to look upon his life as Unreal—as something chimerical and far off and glimpsed in a daydream. After a while he wondered if death had already come to him, the camp an afterlife punishment for hedonistic Muslims. This helped, just a little: he imagined that one day it would stop, and he would float into the air and face a forgiving Allah. He stopped counting the days, or the time between feedings.

On the nineteenth day of his internment, he was led from his hole, Ruslan muttering and trying to find strength in his scarred legs. He was tied to a chair. Five minutes passed slowly. As he waited, he adjusted to the warmth of the tent, his body convulsing and voiding itself and registering pain more effectively.

The camp doctor came with a syringe pointed upward. "Hold out your arm."

Ruslan offered a forearm that was thin and bug ravaged.

"You won't feel this," he stated, to which Ruslan said nothing.

Little one. It was a serum devised by CIA-employed pharmacologists, and used on Viet Cong prisoners to extract information (only to be abandoned because its effect was not what they'd planned for). Later, it had been traded to the Russians for certain KGB data, and labelled *N20* in the labs of Cold War–time Russia. It was a solution that released the whole of the universal subconscious, such that the victim's brain was flooded with every scrap of knowledge ever held by anyone in our planet's long history. In so doing, this drug—this evil N20—rendered its victims instantly omniscient, and by extension spit-drooling and mad as a cobbler. After an hour of howling (trust me: that first rush of clarity is a mind-tripping doozy) Ruslan was led shaking to the cold of his earth pit. Visions of all things blazed before his eyes. He held his poor head as it erupted with knowledge. He covered his ears, which screamed the secrets of living into the depths of his blown mind.

When the FSB came a few hours later, Ruslan was wet-nosed and snivelling. What was left of his mind thought, *Now they will shoot me.* They pulled him up, his body caked with black soil. Sure enough, he was led in a different direction. *This is it,* he thought again, *I am glad, now they'll kill me.* With all of his might, he tried to open his mouth and jitteringly thank them. He trudged through leaves and low green ferns. In the back of his mind he thought of his brothers and sisters, whom he wished he could hug to his frail, trembling body. He thought of his two doting parents, who'd spent all of their money on his flight from his homeland, there being nothing for a young man in the hell called the Caucasus. He thought of friends that he'd had in his big northern city—young and wild, every one, their capacity for joy heightened by the horrors behind them. He thought of the women he'd bedded, including little Anya, the one who'd left behind Russia to forget all about him. He thought of watermelons, and wildflowers, and the crags of ancient, squat mountains.

He felt a humility before all things that he wished he'd known more of.

They reached a rutted track. Again a sack was pulled over his head. He waited for the gun crack that would put life behind him. It didn't come. He stood there waiting, and begging forgiveness from Allah. He heard lighters flicking and two *contraktniki* chattering about last night's DVD movie. (It was the one in which Stallone was a skilled mountain climber.) Despite knowing everything, he couldn't sift through all of the information inside him and decide why death hadn't yet claimed him. He smelled forest, and cigarettes, and diesel fumes spitting. He heard a loud, clanking chug and then brakes whining shrilly. He was thrown in the back. He lay there, his mind a fiendish wild cloudburst of every known colour. Sleep came in fits and in spurts while the truck was in motion. He came awake fully when he heard sounds of the city.

The lorry stopped. Ruslan was dropped amidst cold Russian chatter. Every part of him hurt, though he didn't much notice. He heard a motor's loud gunning, and the cry of old women. People rushed to him, and someone pulled off his hood gently. He was on an Apraxin laneway, his body lying in slush that was dirtied with oil. There were cries, and loud weeping, and dark-skinned hands reaching toward him. To his feet he was lifted, his arms on the shoulders of two Apraxin stall owners. In this way he was walked to his uncle's TV store, his ears ringing with shouts of, "Ruslan's alive, *Allahu Akbar,* please, Dadya, come now and see him!"

And then it was Dadya, running toward him with both his arms outstretched. He kissed Ruslan's cheeks and wept, "Oh, my nephew." And Ruslan—he cried, before all those assembled, thinking how odd it was that Apraxin would be in the Hereafter. He also noticed one thing that struck him as funny: in heaven his dadya had grown his beard longer.

His uncle hugged him again and into his ears whispered, "I have missed you." He then led him inside. He closed the cellar door to the street's outside clamour. As Dadya dropped to his knees and offered his gratitude toward Mecca, Ruslan looked at the shop's once-cluttered stock shelves. They were now empty, Dadya having sold everything to pay Ruslan's ransom. Ruslan wiped away tears, his head erupting with thunder and lightning bolts flashing. When Dadya was finished praying, he once again hugged his nephew and in Avari asked him: "You told the *contraktniki* nothing?"

Ruslan shook his head no, and in a way this was truthful. He *had* told them nothing, even though he'd pleaded to make a confession. *I'll tell you everything!* he'd called out every time that they burned him. *I'll confess to anything!* he screamed every time they genitally seared him. In response, they'd just laughed and drunk more Bacardi. In fact, the more he offered to help, the more they seemed to relish the hurting. So no. He hadn't talked. He had wanted to, but hadn't. His torture had *had* nothing to do with his talking. (Little one, there was nothing he could have possibly told them.)

Dadya hugged him tighter.

THE CULPRITS

"Oh my son," he said, for in the houses and dachas and yurts of his homeland, every loved man is a son, no matter his father. "You have distinguished yourself." He then leaned so close that Ruslan could smell cumin, and garlic, and cherry-scented tobacco. "You are sick. But don't worry. Inshallah, we will make you better. Then we will make them pay. Trust me, my son, it is the way of our people. They all will pay dearly."

It was like being in two places. At the same time he hung from his uncle's thick forearms, he was pulled by cruel hands from his pit in the cold ground. At the same time he was carried through an empty TV shop, he was dragged by the heels through a snow-covered forest. At the same time he was put to bed by Apraxin babushkas, he was dumped into his pit, his cold body covered with wounds raw and gaping. At the same time he felt the warmth of his small bed, he felt the comfort that came late in a session of torture, when the soul leaves the body for places that are unreal.

Trauma and N20 were the tag-teaming culprits. He was never quite awake, and never quite sleeping. He was lost in two places, a ghost between planets. At times he was conscious of old kerchiefed women, brought in by his uncle to care for poor Ruslan. ("Oh good," he'd hear them say, "the boy he is sleeping.") Other times *they* would be there, in his Apraxin bedroom, laughing as they touched hot tongs to his body. This went on for weeks, Ruslan hovering and floating and never landing in one place. He cried like a baby, and wet his bed often. He soaked his pillow with the sweat that came from his fevers. He sat bolt upright in bed and began loudly shrieking, his eyes reflecting an image of tall pine trees swaying, his neck muscles distended as he screamed in the darkness. His screams would then set off a macabre chain reaction, for all through the market young men were going through the same process, be they Ingush, Ossetian, Dagestani, or Chechen. Upon hearing Ruslan (or whomever) they'd all open their mouths and produce screams in concert. And when *this* happened, all of Apraxin Dvor would awaken, and listen to a choir of men suffering.

But then, little by little, each day infinitesimally better, Ruslan began to exist in one place more than the other. He'd hear a dog barking, but in Apraxin Dvor only. He'd hear the sweet giggle of little brown children, and not transform these sounds into something despicable. He'd awake to babushkas changing his bedsheets while saying, "Don't worry, it happens," and feel only a modest degree of terror.

Or he'd open his eyes and find his uncle with strange men wearing beards and djellabas, and he wouldn't confuse the faces of these visitors with the faces of the *contraktniki*. Friends visited, too—tall, young, dark-haired men whose cocksureness would melt into something nervous the moment they took a look at what had become of their Ruslan. The only other visitor was a kind Georgian doctor, brought in by Dadya to check for signs of infection. Ruslan took one look and raced to his room's dusty corner, where he muttered and whimpered and held himself, rocking.

With time, he started asking for small things: water with lemon, warm bread with honey, a chance to speak on the phone with his worry-sick mother. But then he'd slip back, and have another hard night in the forest, followed by a morning in which he wanted only an end to his short life. It was a matter of three steps forward and two and a half backward. And then, on a day in which the city had a blanketing snowfall, such that the lions of Griboedov looked to be wearing twin white shawls, Ruslan opened his eyes and was *just* in his bedroom. He saw white walls, the lonely dresser, the poster of a handlebar-moustached James Hetfield (and he remembered his favourite Metallica song was called "Enter Sandman"). Oh yes—he finally knew where he was, and he wept just to be there.

He tried to make sound. It came as hoarse coughing. Again he tried, and heard footsteps approaching. The door of his room opened. Dadya entered and crept over to him and held on to him tightly. After a time he released him, his eyes turning glassy: the boy was so thin, so all-over trembling, so permanently scarred with N20 madness.

"You have survived."

"Yes," Ruslan whispered.

"You are the son of my sister and I love you."

Ruslan looked at him.

"Rest, son. Rest."

"Dadya?"

"Yes?"

"They have Vakha?"

There was a pause.

"Yes, we think so."

Ruslan's eyes welled, and prophetic visions streaked before them: bombs and rock concerts and his uncle drinking tea with men quoting the Quran.

"Dadya?" Ruslan peeped.

"Yes, son."

"What will happen to me?"

"You will honour yourself, of that I will make sure."

Ruslan slept around the clock, waking occasionally to eat and visit the bathroom. Though he was now in one place and one place only during his waking hours—the city, Apraxin Dvor, his little TV shop bedroom—the filtration camp still came during intense blood-soaked nightmares, Ruslan waking in a sweat while shaking all over. The babushkas would come running, and place cool, dripping cloths on his sweat-dampened forehead. Days passed. He began spending some of his time listening to music. He began to eat normal meals, though he was subject to bouts of fear and confusion. One afternoon, when eating a lunch of hot rice and chicken, the rice started to wriggle like the bugs in his cold pit. Another time, he decided he was ready for a walk in the market; though his uncle was with him, the crowds and the noise left his nerves badly jangled. Instead, they walked to the canal, where Ruslan stood and watched N20 thoughts dart past his sad eyes, their depth and intensity reflected in water.

Though Ruslan had never been a great reader, his uncle brought him books, mostly about history, and war, and the South's liberation struggle. In this way Ruslan read about the original Imam Shamil, who led the first war against the Russians two centuries earlier. He read about the great WWII expulsion, when Stalin accused every Chechen and Dagestani of sympathizing with the Nazis. He read of the Cossack general named Yermolov, who famously said, "The only good Chechen's a dead one" (and then later, in a gesture of diplomacy, the Russians would build a statue in his honour in the middle of Grozny). Ruslan couldn't understand a word. The words on the pages fell apart into fragments, and then floated away like moths in a strong breeze. Still, he pretended. When asked what he thought, he'd say, "Thank you, I liked them."

More rest. More short walks truncated. More beetroot soup and pieces of cold chicken. More nightmares invaded by bandoliered Russians.

More: time.

One afternoon, with Ruslan feeling groggy and shaky all over, Dadya came into his room and sat down beside him.

"Ruslan," he said, "I have people for you to meet."

"People?"

"Yes. They would like to speak with you."

There was a pause. "Dadya. I am tired."

"It is important."

"Will it take long?"

"I don't think so."

Another pause, this one awkward.

"All right."

Uncle thanked him, and called "Okay" to those outside. Three men entered, all wearing djellabas and prayer caps and beards long and bushy. Ruslan, meanwhile, had the feeling he'd seen them before, huddled at the fringes of his fever-caused daydreams. He gave a cautious "Hello." Two men answered with a nod and said, *"Asslam-o-Alaikum."* The third, however, came closer. Ruslan felt sure he knew him. He sat on the bed right beside him. Ruslan puzzled, and stared, and felt his eyes blearily crossing—he saw that the man, despite his beard, was little older than he was. And then, just like that, he knew how he knew him: he was his boss's son. He was the lost son of his lost boss. Yes, he was sure: he'd seen him in Gostinyy, a full lifetime earlier.

"Hello, Khassan," he said weakly.

"Asslam-o-Alaikum," Khassan answered in a voice warm and gentle. "It's good to see you again. Much time has passed since we last met."

"Yes . . ."

"Many things have happened since then."

"Yes."

"You were buying *wine*."

Ruslan craved sleep, and food made by babushkas.

Khassan bent closer, as if to exclude all the others who were in the room listening. "I underestimated you," he said.

"That's okay."

"I am sorry."

"That's all right," Ruslan said, yawning.

"Ruslan." Khassan's deep-set eyes were burning. "You have a decision to make."

Ruslan blinked. Khassan's face half came into focus.

"If you wish us to go," Khassan said, "we will do so." He glanced over his shoulder, indicating the two others. "But if you wish us to stay, you'll walk with us. You'll become one of us. You will be one of God's soldiers. You'll make the infidels pay for what they've done to you. The decision is yours and yours only."

Ruslan felt pain in every joint, bone, and tissue. He struggled to think through his N20 madness. Though ninety-nine percent of him wanted to fall asleep forever—to close his eyes and drift away, as though in a canoe on a river—there was also the one percent the *contraktniki* hadn't got to. Oh yes. There was the lone one percent born of Caucasian spirit—the one percent that was halfway responsible for three centuries of warfare. As Ruslan lay hurting, that one percent seethed and railed for attention. That one percent became a hot and flame-spitting culprit.

Little one—it was *that* one percent that caused Ruslan to open his mouth and whisper, "Don't go, my brother."

He walked in a shuffle, a blanket over his shoulders. The moon was lost behind a matting of black clouds. Already he'd forgotten why, or where, he was going. Still, when they opened the trunk of a Mercedes S-series, he lay down in the darkness and felt at peace with the movement. For an hour they drove through the city, circling and backtracking to make sure they weren't followed. Thinking himself dead, Ruslan fell asleep smiling. They finally stopped. The trunk was opened, and Ruslan was helped from it. He was standing before a falling-apart building. And though it may have looked like every other building in the city's bleak suburbs, it wasn't. Here, on the whole second floor, women wore burkas and men dressed in djellabas. All the meat was halal and washed down with juices. Arabic was spoken with every manner of accent, and walls bore the portraits of Palestinian martyrs. Music was forbidden, as was wearing a watch on your left wrist, or buying supplies from Semitic grocers. So fervent was the adherence here to the majesty of Allah that the power brokers of Peshawar had deemed this floor already liberated by the Islamist revolution—an honour likewise bestowed upon the Belleville district of Paris and the neighbourhood surrounding Finsbury Park mosque in east London.

Ruslan, of course, knew nothing of this. He knew only that his feet were cold, and that he whimpered as they led him up a crumbling, dark stairwell, the walls kaleidoscopically tagged with pro-9/11 graffiti. They walked along a dim, littered hallway. Children stopped playing and looked up at Ruslan, their bent, dirty fingers inserted in noses. The four men then stepped into a hot, dank apartment. A half-dozen Wahhabis were sitting cross-legged on a silk Persian carpet. Six funnel-shaped beards lifted toward him in concert. Ruslan, in turn, felt lost and embarrassed. Though he'd been told where they were going, the information had been swallowed by N20 confusion; it now whipped round in circles, like house shingles torn off by a force-four tornado. His ears reddened, and his breathing turned shallow, and suddenly he was straddling two places at the same time, the old men sitting before him in the filtration camp forest, their words accompanied by the *shoosh*ing of pine trees and the shuffling of animals who stayed awake in cold weather. He fought tears, and failed. They broke free one by one, till his thin face was dampened. The old men sipped tea and revealed no emotion.

"This soldier," announced Khassan, "has suffered indignities at the hands of the infidels." There was a consoling murmur. "Inshallah, he'll be an aid to our cause." This time there were head nods and murmurs and a few solemn *Allahu Akbar*s.

"Come," Khassan said. "Please, Ruslan, come. The women have made a bed and it is now waiting for you."

The council returned to their meeting. Khassan led Ruslan toward the rear of the apartment. They passed a bedroom clearly in use as an office; he saw a computer and fax machine, and he heard the soft bubbling sound of an aquarium screen saver. His room was at the back, at the end of a hall covered with curling linoleum. There was a dresser, a Quran, and a small bed adorned with a bright-coloured blanket. It was ten o'clock in the evening. Ruslan closed his eyes; his head filled with screams and pleadings and the horrific sizzle of purplish flesh burning. And the *smell*—that diabolical mixture of snow and skin charring—oh yes oh yes, with the stress of this move it was all coming back to him. Ruslan put his face into hands drained of colour. Khassan didn't touch him. He stood next to him, waiting. His voice bore a tone that was hushed and yet clinical.

"Ruslan," he said. "I have seen this happen before. Many times. You are not the first, and you are not the last."

"I'm sorry," Ruslan managed.

"You will stay here with us. Your care will be good, and you won't ever see doctors. This I promise you."

These were the right words. Ruslan's tremors eased and his flashbacks receded. Two or three moments passed.

THE CULPRITS

"Would you like anything?" Khassan asked.

"No."

"A cup of tea? A sandwich?"

"No."

"We have tabouleh with pita."

"Please . . ." Ruslan said.

Khassan left, though not before adding, "There are nightclothes in the dresser."

Ruslan took a few steps to the window. It overlooked a cracked concrete yard and, beyond that, a roadway. He opened it. He heard the whine of car tires and a radio playing. He crossed the room to the dresser; in it were three or four djellabas. He pulled out one made with a heavy material. Before slipping it on, he held it to his nose: it smelled like lemons and Egyptian cotton. In a moment he was dressed like an Arab Wahhabi. He crawled into bed and covered himself with the thick woollen blanket. Sleep then toyed with him, a wave warm and salty, carrying him away and then, after a few blissful moments, returning him to shore with a soft, sandy landing.

His sleep here was different. The bed was better, and the room didn't smell like old clothes or concrete. It was also quieter than Apraxin; when Ruslan slept, which was most of the time, the children were told to play away from the apartment. As a final benefit, he no longer feared a second *chorny* roundup—not here, in the suburbs, a universe away from the Apraxin Dvor market. His sleep grew deeper, and less nightmare riddled, in this place of tea drinking and five daily prayers in the direction of Mecca. Whenever he woke, women in burkas brought him toast and tea sweetened with quince jam. When he was hungry, he had kebabs, and baba ghanouj, and a lovely spiced rice with raisins and saffron. Khassan came and went, as did the clerics who'd assembled for Ruslan's arrival. The two men who'd accompanied Khassan to Apraxin seemed to live here; their names were Ahmed and Ayman, and they spoke Russian about as well as Ruslan spoke Arabic. Instead of chatting, they took turns playing dominoes with Ruslan, their water pipes filled with apple-scented tobacco.

The passage of time was all Ruslan now expected from his life. Dadya visited every few days, and spoke to him slowly. (No one else knew of his hidden location.) He was treated with ointments, and poultices, and fortifying juices; Ayman gave him long, manly back rubs that left him dizzy all over. Though still pale, he gained enough weight that he no longer looked starving. And while he still suffered the symptoms that are the hallmarks of trauma—confusion, and memory loss, and brutal attacks of heart-pounding panic—he nonetheless took the occasional walk outside. Ahmed and Ayman would give him a few rubles and then gesture with an empty milk carton, or show him the butter dish that needed replenishing. In this way he began doing simple chores. At times he'd forget what he'd been sent to the store *for*, and he'd return empty-handed; Ahmed and Ayman would smile as though nothing was the matter. Less often, and more frightening, he'd come awake at a roadside, light snow on his shoulders, with no idea how he got there; he learned to keep the address of his building on a card in his pocket. And yet, on other occasions he'd be fine: while walking, he'd release tears he had stockpiled and hadn't wanted the Wahhabis to witness.

One afternoon, he came home from a walk with a bag full of chickpeas. In the kitchen he found Khassan, smoking a cigarette and drinking strong coffee. He gestured hello and invited Ruslan to sit with him. He passed over a cigarette and lit it for Ruslan.

THE CULPRITS

A half minute went by, the room clouding with Turkish, blue-burning tobacco.

Ruslan put his cigarette down. He felt ashamed all over. "Khassan," he said softly, "I can't help you."

Khassan inhaled and said in fluent Avari, "Yes you can. You already are."

"No," Ruslan said, his tired head spinning. "No, I'm sorry . . . not with the way . . . not with the way that I—"

"Ruslan," Khassan interrupted. "You would not be here if I didn't think you could help. I will explain."

He butted his cigarette and lit another one slowly. There was a certainty in his eyes that Ruslan found calming.

"Ruslan. We are an al Qaeda logistical support cell, and you are now one of our members. Our primary function is to raise operational funds. These funds are then distributed in three ways: they support the day-to-day operation of our network, they are paid to the families of martyrs, and they finance what we call 'specific works.'"

Ruslan could barely follow. "Specific . . . uhhhh . . ."

"Yes. That is right. Specific works."

"*Works?*"

"Yes. Functions. Operations. Related to the worldwide jihad and most importantly the jihad in Chechnya."

There was a long, painful pause. Ruslan held his head, in a way almost pleading. "Chechnya?"

"*Ruslan,*" Khassan said. "You are our brother. You know this. We feed you, and share with you our ambitions. It is an honour to help you, and assist your recovery. In return, we have assumed that you would gladly help fund a work that is in the planning stages." Khassan's voice was rising and falling like a radio transmission on a road in the country.

"I don't have money."

"You know those who do."

"No. I don't. I'm sorry. Please, I am now tired."

"Yes, Ruslan. You *do*."

Khassan rose and stood on his toes to reach a high cupboard. He opened it and took a brown paper folder. He sat back down and said, "We've already been in communication."

He casually opened the folder and turned it around on the linoleum surface. Ruslan looked, and swallowed—Khassan's voice had been replaced by a soft, buzzing white noise. None of this made sense. He only knew that looking did not at all hurt him. Far from it. For the first time since being dumped in a lane in Apraxin, the corners of his mouth crept a tiny bit upward. He ran his fingers along the eight-by-ten photo. It was a girl, leaning against a tree, her sweater worn tightly. He lifted it up, and gazed at her fondly. He knew her from somewhere, and that memory sparked pleasure—memories of curves and crossed eyes and a touch by love guided. Little one—he was holding the very photograph that *mamochka* had supplied when, heartbroken, she'd uploaded her picture onto the From Russia With Love website.

Khassan spoke.

"You are a hostage of the Caucasian Revolutionary Guard, committed to fighting the repression of Islam. Welcome. We will treat you like a loved one. She"—he tapped Anna's photo—"will pay for your release. Our sources say that she still loves you, and will do anything to help you. She is living with a rich Canadian. As I say, we've already been in contact." He let this news settle. "By the way, the next time you go out, remember to lock the door. Nothing is safe, not with all the damn gypsies out there."

And Ruslan, he looked right through him, through several thousand kilometres of continent and ocean, and in the whirlwind of his mind's eye he saw Anya, his little and affectionate Anya, staring at a note that was straight from the movies, the words torn from the pages of *Izvestia* and *Kommersant* and that old Soviet rag they had the nerve to call *Pravda*. The words had been pasted on paper, where they so crudely formed the following message: Her first and true love, her dark, handsome Ruslan, was being held at the hands of mujahedeen killers. If she did not personally deliver twenty thousand euros, he'd be tortured and then chopped into masticable pieces, so as to satisfy the appetite of pigs good and hungry.

For a moment, Anna stood frozen. She could hear the refrigerator running and, from Hank's room, his infernal snoring. This letter, this *thing*, didn't make sense, not for one second. She moved to Hank's telephone. Her fingers trembled as she punched in twelve digits. For a few moments she listened to scratchy phone raspings. An operator came on and asked her questions in Russian—there were more scratches, and whirrings, and fax machine–like screeches, before a man finally picked up and said, only, *Privyet?*

She tried to speak and, hard as she might, could say only, "Oh, Dadya."

"Anya?"

"I got a letter! In the mail! It's a—"

"Yes, I know."

She struggled to catch her breath. "Dadya, what is happening?"

"Anya, I'm sorry."

"It is true?"

"Yes."

"But I don't under*stand* . . ."

"He's been gone—a few days now."

"But how? It doesn't make sense!"

There was a pause; the phone line sounded hollow. "Damn sweeps. Damn *Nord-Ost* gassing. Damn Muslim zealots. Damn Russian body traders. Damn *everything*. Anya, this is what I heard—the FSB picked him up and then traded him to the Wahhabis. Now the Wahhabis want money for his release."

"How can they be? The FSB are *fighting* the Wahhabis!"

"Fighting with, doing business with, *bah*—in a war this corrupted, it's all turned into the same thing."

Anna trembled while listening. It happened, it did, Chechnya's famed trade in bodies having spread to the cities of Russia. There was crackling and an echo. Anna heard her own cries volley back to her.

"What do we do?"

"We pay."

"But—"

"If we can." Dadya's voice started racing. "Anya," he lied, "the *militsia*, they came here. They took all of my televisions and they did it while laughing. I'd sell them to pay the ransom, but my store . . . Anya . . . it is empty, nothing left. So now the Wahhabis are turning to *you*. I have nothing but empty shelves and my anger."

"But how did they . . . Oh, Dadya, where am I supposed to get that kind of money?"

"I don't know," he said. "Somehow they found out about you. Maybe Ruslan told them, I don't know, who knows what they've done to him. Anya—what about your Canadian, maybe he would—"

There was a click, a silence, and then a long-distance dial tone. She hung up and frantically began hitting buttons; this time she got nothing but a series of pulses, and she knew that the lines were all in use or broken. She put down the phone and pulled on the clothes she'd left on the staircase. And oh, how she wept—tears streamed down her face like rain on a windshield. She wept for her handsome ex-lover (whom she'd never stopped loving, not for one second). She bawled for White Nights spent in his small room love-making, their skin turning blue from concrete dust falling. She wept for those three and a half months in which the two of them, Anya and Ruslan, Ruslan and Anya, had been a couple. (One time, for a lark, they'd smashed a champagne bottle on Vasilyevsky Island, and then kissed as though they had just been married.) Yet the thing that made her cry the most? That made her feel the worst all over? She couldn't be sure the whole thing was not a deception, not with all the dodges and scams and flimflams in Russia. But then she remembered: Dadya would have to be in *on* it, and she knew that such a thing couldn't happen.

Finally she stopped sobbing, her eyes as dead as an Unreal City statue. For the rest of that day she was unable to do anything (or at least anything productive); she slept, she paced, she prayed to the wisdom of Saint Onuphrius. When he awoke, Hank noticed her distraction. "Anna," he said. "What is it? What's the matter?"

"Nothing," she said without looking at him. "I not feeling very well. Is my woman's time, Hank."

The next morning, for no real reason she could think of, she phoned the number of her aunt's house. She waited as it rang; the tone sounded distant and fuzzy. Her mother answered.

"Privyet?"

She tried to speak but couldn't.

"Da? Privyet? Da?"

Anna, ashamed, said nothing and hung up. She stood looking at the phone, her body turning to air under the weight of her worries. This made her feel fearful all over. After fidgeting for a few minutes, and flipping through all of the television stations, she put on her coat and stepped onto Craven. It was early December;

Christmas lights hung from eavestroughs and windows. She trudged north. At Gerrard she turned east, and wandered past sari shops and curry houses and a theatre showing the latest Bollywood romance. She stared straight ahead as she walked, oblivious to everything but her own disappearance.

She stopped in front of an establishment called Dhaka Fine Jewellery, and slipped through the door like a gusting of warm wind.

It was the middle of the day, the store so filled with rich Asian women that many of the display cases had been left invitingly open. Anna strolled up and down, her boot heels making no noise, trying to give the impression of a woman just browsing (while inside her, her *need* was like a blast furnace raging). Her eyes darted everywhere. Her hand jetted sideways. There was a sensation of warmth and regeneration, her left pocket now host to a gold-plated Cartier. A split second later, she came face to face with a frowning saleswoman. For a few tortured seconds the woman said nothing—the dark pools of her eyes did all of the talking, as did the fold of her arms against the front of her sari.

In a rich, honeyed accent, she asked, "May I see what you have in the pocket of your jacket?"

Anna hung her head. The woman reached behind a display case and pushed a small plastic button. She then took Anna's elbow and led her politely to the manager's office. She sat her in a room littered with catalogues and papers. A look of exhaustion took hold of Anna's features. The saleswoman saw this and asked, "Would you like a cup of tea while you are waiting?"

Anna shook her head no.

The woman sighed, and sat across from Anna. For the next few minutes nothing was said between the two of them: one woman sat reading a magazine, the other fought a pain that was nearly exquisite.

But these, oh yes *these,* are not important details. You don't need to know what the police officers looked like, and you don't need to know about *mamochka's* expression when she was taken away, face down and eyes moist and wrists clasped with handcuffs. You don't need to know what the weather was doing, or a description of the bright winter light when she was helped into the back seat of the cruiser. You don't need to know her dark worries (for I'm sure you can imagine) and you don't need to listen to the officers' banter as they drove her away to the nearest police station. Likewise, you don't need to know that Anna was released after a stern and bullying caution—she hadn't left the store with the watch and therefore it hadn't been a real robbery.

What *is* important, however, is that, when asked if there was someone she wanted to call to come and get her, her first reaction was *No, no, I am alone, my father disappeared when I was a little little girl, and so there is not one soul in this world for me.* But then, after a few cautious seconds, she reconsidered.

"Yes," she said weakly.

He came within twenty minutes, his shirt half-untucked, his bootlaces loosened, his orange hair standing in wavering tendrils. Up she walked to him, and wrapped her thin arms around his large and once-hard chest. Her face rested against flannel; she could smell smoke and burnt coffee and the scent spawned by tension.

"Jesus," he said. "You all right?"

"Oh, Hank," she said, weeping.

And then, because the energy between people is an amoral minefield, and Anna came from a place where lies are a currency, and Hank would never, ever, fund the release of the only man she had ever loved *really.* She cursed herself mutely and said the only thing she could think of.

"They have him," she blubbered.

"Who?"

(And she said it, she did, a lie so putrid and raw it left a foul taste in her mouth.)

"My brother! My eighteen-year-old and much-loved-by-all *brother*. Oh Hank, oh Hank, he has been kidnapped in Russia!"

The rest was the truth, or at least it more or less was.

SEVEN

And have I mentioned that love, like life, is also a deception? That Hank knew this in the most fundamental way possible? That he was brought up to distrust it, in a house ruled by whispers? That he grew up in a place where joy was viewed with suspicion? That most people, at the age of seventeen, do not wander into an office of Employment Canada and ask for a job—*any* job—that takes you away to faraway places?

Have I mentioned, my littlest of little ones, that you don't go to sea *without damn good reason*?

As he sat in his Craven Street living room, listening to Anna blubber and babble about the trading of bodies in her de-evolved country, and how she needed twenty thousand euros to save her poor brother, you could see it, you *could*, without looking closely: his face muscles tensing, and the lobes of his ears growing pinker and pinker. When he could stand it no longer, he held up a hand and said, "Please, Anya, for chrissakes, I may be a fool, but at least I'm no idiot."

He stood and slowly went to the closet. He put on his parka and headed into the night air. Anna (if that was even her real name) yelled, "Hank! Please do not go!" over and over. She shouldn't have bothered. He could barely hear anything over the loud, mocking laughter that filled both his eardrums. His thoughts, likewise, were an accusing maelstrom. *At least this explains something. At least this explains why a girl like her, with soft skin and dark hair and a Martine-like figure, was here in the first place . . .* And still, *still*, she was out on the porch step, hands cupped around her mouth, hollering, "Hank! Hank! Please tell me! You are going where?"

Hank trudged away from her, feeling mournful and near-dead and as though he'd never once floated. He had to hand it to her. In his life as a mechanic on the *Antigonish Dreamer*, he thought he'd heard every con that existed—every three-card monte, every bait-and-switch come-on, every *Meester, hey meester, my sister is waiting around this dark alley corner.*

But this? A kidnapped brother? Who needed to be ransomed from Arabs? Had he been wearing a hat, he would have taken it off to her. Back in Russia, he thought, they must have swindles that are in a league all of their own.

Oh Anya, he thought, *if you'd needed money, you could have just asked me.*

(And meanwhile, from the house, a cross-eyed girl was still calling out to him, her voice growing fainter and fainter in the cold air of winter.) He kept moving; his shoulders were hunched to his ears and his breathing was rapid. He walked down to Dundas and held out a hand like a dumb-with-love sucker. Here he waited, his feet making snowshoe-sized impressions in slushy wet pavement. A cabbie pulled over; his tires slowed with a sound like a brush rubbing leather. Hank climbed in and asked to be taken to the august and time-honoured drinking establishment known as the Canada Tavern.

The driver nodded and drove west through damp, silver flurries.

And for Hank, this felt like a return to the days when beer halls were the places he felt most at home in. Oh yes—this was the old Hank, falling back on dead habits. In his ears he heard the clinking of glasses and the chatter of hard men and the sad, luring mutters of girls wanting money. The cab drove through streets that were dark and spotted with drunk Natives stumbling. They stopped at the southwest corner of Queen Street and Sherbourne, a neighbourhood not in any way known for grace or refinement, and that *was* known for the pawnshops that stood, like fluorescent-lit sentries, between the northeast corner and the Salvation Army. Hank crossed the street, inviting the honking of car horns. He pulled on the handle and stepped into dim, smoky, stale air. He lumbered to the bar in the hunch-shouldered way of men who knew, with a certainty that doesn't come often, that every last cent of their paycheque would be drunk up that evening. He moved around tables of Indians, and skinny-legged rubbies, and bulbous-nosed men who were staring at nothing. He smiled as it all came back to him: he saw thin, lank-haired women with tattoos on their fingers, and the sort of men for whom a night out is not a night out without an eruption of brawling. He moved past a stage that, on Fridays and Saturdays, hosted country bands, or cover bands playing the tunes of AC/DC, or the occasional stripper with legs nicked with track marks, but that, on this night, was empty and lonely and criss-crossed with mouse tracks. His *ping*ing subsided as beer-scented air seeped into his lungs. This was the world of his youth, and it felt deliriously real to be once again in it.

He sat at the bar with his wallet in hand. Across from him a wreath was haphazardly dropping. The bartender came over; he had a mole on his cheek and a thick head of grey hair.

"One shot of rye whisky," Hank said. "And the coldest bottle of beer that you got."

Hank began drinking. He practically guzzled. Oh yes—he embarked on a tear spawned by love and deception, two things that go hand in hand with a predictable closeness. He was a big man, and he still had a tolerance for alcohol that some might have described as impressive. As the night wore on, the bar became crowded, for it happened to be the day on which welfare cheques were issued. He drank a bit more, and hummed songs to himself that were twangy with sadness. He caught himself looking at his hands, trying to remember the story behind every rope burn and scar and bent-to-one-side knuckle. It was around this time that a guy sat beside him; he wore a thick red-tinged moustache along with a ball cap that kept his eyes in a permanent shadow. They started talking, the guy launching a tale that was long and convoluted but that had, at its core, a wife who was cheating, a six-year-old daughter he hadn't seen for ages, and prison time spent in the city of Kingston.

And because Hank was a kind man, and a man who genuinely felt sorry for people, he listened carefully—it was the least he could do for this hard luck guy beside him. When the guy was finally finished, Hank peered at him through eyes that looked as though they'd seen all things.

"Oh yeah? You wanna hear something?"

"I'm all ears, bud."

"*I* have a Russian who's playing me for a patsy."

Hard Luck's eyes widened. "What?"

"She came all the way from Russia to bilk me for money."

"No!"

"Oh yeah. Some story about a brother who's been kidnapped, and how she needs me to pay the ransom. And the hell of it is, I just might give it to her."

Hard Luck tapped the neck of his bottle against Hank's Molson Stock Ale. "Been there, bud."

"Yeah?"

"Everything but the Russian part. Bet you fuckin' love her."

"Fuckin' do."

"I know ya do."

"I know I do too."

And then, because Hank and this stranger had opened up to each other, and had felt a kinship in their respective emotional suffering, they ordered more bottles of beer, and more rounds of rye whisky, each time arguing over who would be paying. Eventually it occurred to Hank that the room was slowly revolving, yet in a way that was friendly and warm and rekindling of memories. (*Martine*, he thought with a pain that felt lovely. *I can still feel your touch, all these years later. I can still smell your perfume, as though you were next to me . . .*)

"Hey," Hard Luck said, pulling Hank from his reverie.

"Yeah?"

"Wanna go outside?"

"What for?"

"Smoke us a hash spliff. You should see this stuff—when you hold it up to the light, it's green and covered with white flecks."

"Oh yeah?"

"Yeah. I tell ya, it kicks like a mule. I think it's got something in it."

Hank hesitated, though just for a moment—street drugs had always had a way of pouncing upon him, turning his world to either a light-flashing circus or a dyed-in-the-wool torture. But then he figured, what the hell, it's my night out, ain't no way I'm gonna feel any worse than I do at this moment, and besides . . . wasn't it Martine who said I had to learn to relax more? Wasn't it Martine who said I was a man who feared good times?

They stepped out the back door and into an alley. There was garbage and broken glass and the smell of old french fries. Hank was transfixed by the way the snow looked when caught by the street lights; mounded in banks, it was speckled, and mysterious, and alive with a million star twinklings. There was something about this that made him feel maudlin, and as though there was a reason for all things that happened. Hard Luck lit up. He took the tiniest of inhales and passed the toothpick-sized spliff to his new drinking buddy.

"Careful," he warned, "this stuff'll tear your head off."

But Hank wasn't listening—he was thinking of Marseilles and Martine and all the dark wine he'd drunk with her. He took two or three lungfuls while summoning the soft sound of her voice. *Ah, Christ, you never once lied, did you, Martine? With you I knew the score, didn't I, Martine?*

He puffed once again, and held the smoke in his lungs till there was nothing left of it.

Oh Anya, oh Anya, I wish you were just like her . . .

He passed the spliff back to Hard Luck just as the sky erupted in streaks of purple and orange. Everywhere he saw starbursts and the faces of children. He heard Hard Luck inhale, the sound like air hissing from a leak in a tire. Hank giggled like a child and felt cold all over.

"Oh yeah," said Hard Luck. "That Russian of yours."

Hank's ears perked up. "Yeah?" he said, his own voice echoing forever inside his head.

"I've known women like her."

"Yeah?"

"Yeah. Complete bitches, every one of 'em."

"Whaddid you say?"

"I said she sounds—"

THE CULPRITS

... and Hank grabbed Hard Luck by the collar and raised one of his fists into the night air, where it shook with a rage about to be enacted. His face bloomed scarlet, and his breathing grew so fierce it sounded like mountain air howling. Hard Luck shrank beneath him, hands covering his face and his voice a high bleating, *Christ, bud, Christ, I didn't mean anything by it,* and Hank would have hit him, he really would have, for a frustration had been building inside him forever, when something strange happened. Oh yes—as Hard Luck hung like a limp-with-fear rag doll, Hank was visited with a memory from his long-ago boyhood. Hank, a boy of six or maybe seven, on a Saturday afternoon when the sun outside shone brightly, lay on the living room floor, next to the sofa on which his father sprawled sleeping, and he lay there for hours, hoping against hope that his father would waken and take him outside to play ball or have ice cream, and yet no matter how long he waited, his father never stirred, sleep being his defence against a world he found overwhelming. Eventually his mother came and whispered to him, "Hank, leave him alone, he's tired, he couldn't sleep all night, come and have your tea." But in the meantime, as Hank stayed flat on his back in that house filled with silence, he let his imagination provide all that was missing. Oh yes—he let his ears fill with song and happy talk and loud, raucous laughter. He let his ears ring with the sounds that all young boys yearn for.

Hank's eyes, which ten seconds ago had smouldered with anger, turned sad and depthless. He lowered his fist and released Hard Luck's collar. The cold air felt like a knife in his lungs. He bent over, and coughed, and wished upon the stars he hadn't smoked that green hashish; he could see it, in the snowbank, a small red-headed boy lying beneath whatever alien imposter had laid claim to his father.

Hard Luck looked at Hank and realized he was peering at problems that can take a whole life to crawl out of. (He knew these sorts of problems. In a place like Millhaven, they're the only things owned by each of the inmates.) He stepped gingerly forward. "I know, bud, I know. Life'll do this to you."

Yet when Hard Luck put a hand on the back of Hank's shoulder, Hank spat *Fuck off* and pushed it away as though it were a thing come to hurt him. He stood upright, his mouth halfway open, and groaned like a bear with its leg in a steel trap. *Fuck you,* he yelled, as though an enemy lurked somewhere in the dark clouds above them. *Fuck you fuck you fuck you,* he howled as Hard Luck backed away slowly, saying, *Okay bud, take it easy bud* before re-entering the Canada via the rear door of the barroom, leaving Hank to howl and swing fists at the demons that plagued him.

When Hank emerged on the street, he was unable to walk straight. And his ears! How they raged! How they scoffed, and hectored, and shrieked insults at him! He lifted a hand, one foot in the gutter. Three or four taxis passed by, afraid to stop for him. When one did, Hank climbed in, a sloppy, incoherent drunk with a thicket of red hair.

"Subway," he mumbled.

The cabbie looked over his shoulder, not liking what he saw. "Queen Street okay?"

"Yeah," Hank blubbered. "Yeah, bloody hell, go."

And *that,* little one, is where he was taken.

Hank stepped from the cab and felt snow fall on his face. He paid the fare, and stumbled downstairs beside giggling teenagers. He crossed his hands over his heart and lurched to the edge of the platform, his size-twelves resting on raised yellow pebbles. Here he drunkenly wavered, one grey train after another passing inches before him. Only this time there was no madman to do the job for him—no madman to raise bruises on the back of Hank's shoulders. In this absence, Hank thought of the last time he'd mustered the strength to do something monumental—*Christ, Christ, it was going to Russia*—and it was this memory that convinced him of the futility of living. So he waited, his head still crazed with green poison, thinking *The next train, goddamnit, the next train I'll do it.*

That's when it happened, yet another part of this story that *you*, little one, might have trouble swallowing. As Hank stood with his head turned toward the dark tunnel entrance, he heard shuffling footsteps. He turned, and saw an old kerchiefed woman moving toward him, pushing a bundle buggy filled with groceries and clothing. She was bent over so far she had to lift her head to look at him. He watched her approach; her face sported a smile and a hundred deep wrinkles. Closer and closer she came, the two of them suddenly alone on this section of platform. Hank looked around, wondering where all of the teenagers had run off to.

"Tell me," she croaked. "Is going this train north? My daughter she living near Sheppard station. This train . . ." She looked in either direction. "To Sheppard station is going?"

She looked up at him and smiled, her breath smelling of garlic and dill-infused mushrooms. Hank inhaled and stared at her; he knew her from some other place, a place that was similar but different, and he associated this place with hope for the future. His throat constricted and his face drained of colour. The old woman raised a hand and placed it on his elbow. Even through his coat he could feel the hand's kindness.

"Hey," she said. "Is okay. Is not to worry. Is little bit bad night, you having. Is something happen to everybody. Go home and sleep. Tomorrow maybe things they looking better, yes?"

A train pulled up and a crowd of kids in their twenties got off at the door nearest to him—there must have been a dozen of them, in from the suburbs and wanting a night in the city. For a moment Hank was surrounded, his nostrils filling with the scent of gum and cheap perfume and Smirnoff Ice coolers. He listened to their chatter as they mounted the stairs from the platform; it was only when they'd gone, and he looked up and down the chilled subway station, that he realized the old woman had disappeared from his view. He looked all around him—into thin air she'd vanished. Hank sighed, and looked down. A trio of mice scurried over the railbed.

Twenty minutes after *that,* a cab pulled up to the small house on Craven. Hank got out, paid the driver, and stumbled to the front door. He went inside, feeling empty and unreal. He took off his parka and crept upstairs slowly, his footfalls as light as he could possibly make them. With each step the stairs beneath him groaned slightly. He pushed open her door and crept over to where she was sleeping. She was lying on top of her blankets. He stared at her near-pretty face, and bathed in the need coursing from the whole of her being— he could hold out his palms and feel the warmth of it on them. Her mascara had smudged and down both her cheeks dribbled. For minutes he stood there, gazing at Anna, thinking about the way in which love and sorrow had always ganged up to hound him. Oh yes yes yes—he thought about his life, and all that he had once wanted to do with it, and how he now spent his days just trying to get through it. As he continued looking at Anna—at the way her chest was falling and rising, at the way her hair fell over her forehead—his feet grew light, and for a moment or two started off the floor hovering.

He awoke clothed and hurting all over. His eyes ached when they opened, and his mouth felt as though it had been filled with warm gravel. And his *ears*—sitting hunched on his bed, he remembered why it was he'd given up drinking. These were clangings, not *ping*ings. These were church bells, these were dinner bells, these were the crashing of pots by a chef French and angry. Hank moaned as he clipped on his sound maskers. He limped to the bathroom, where he swallowed Tylenol, Ativan, a daily ration of Zoloft, and a capsule or two of ginkgo biloba. He then gargled with a mouthwash that tasted like spearmint. This helped, but just a little. He dressed, went downstairs, and called out for Anna. As he did, he winced, for nothing could now hurt him like those two syllables together.

There was no answer. He choked down toast and a pot of black coffee. He smoked one cigarette after another. As he sat at the table, he saw the ransom note, with all its damn Russian characters. He picked it up and stared at it, his fingertips trembling, until the figures and squiggles began to rotate before him. He closed his eyes and felt nauseous. He put down the note. He called out Anna's name; it echoed through his head, growing fainter and fainter, until the only things he could hear were bells clanging and dishes breaking and the concussive clash of hammers on metal. He wondered where she was. It felt as though she had never existed—that every moment of her life here had been something imagined.

Hank washed away this feeling with another cup of strong coffee. Though there was much from last night he no longer remembered, he keenly recalled the moments he'd spent floating by her bed. *That,* and the way the street light had crept into her room through a break in her curtains—it had been a little like a beam from a maritime lighthouse. He also remembered the decision he'd come to while bathed in need and near beauty. The problem was *how.* Over the last few months he'd purchased a house, new furniture, a pair of return plane tickets to Russia, and more than enough paint to twice coat St. Isaac's. With all of these expenses, he was now barely surviving from paycheque to paycheque.

It was Sunday. That night he went to work in a beleaguered fuddle. He fell asleep on his desk, and dreamt of windfalls and lottery wins and unexpected promotions. Midway through the shift, while standing outside in an unbuttoned parka, he mentioned to Manuel that he not only needed money, but needed it quickly.

"What for, brother?"

"Anna."

"What about Anna?"

"She . . ." He paused; his head still echoed with loud ear-made noises. "There's a crisis back home. In Russia."

"Oh yes?"

"Some sick aunt or something. I dunno. She's all upset. She has to go back."

"How much do you need?"

"Lots."

"Lots, or *lots* lots?"

"Lots lots."

"Hmmmm." Manuel thought as cigarette smoke from his nose and mouth billowed. "Chinchillas," he finally said. "They can be raised in your basement. I have a cousin in Ilocos who—"

"Chinchillas?"

"Yes."

"Tell me something, Manuel. What exactly *is* a chinchilla?"

"It's like a small hamster, only it has very soft fur. You make coats out of them."

"And how many would I have to keep?"

"Maybe . . . I dunno. Maybe . . . a thousand? But my cousin says they can live many to a cage."

"Look around you, Manuel. When was the last time you saw a woman wearing a fur coat in this city?"

"They wear them in China. And India. They wear them in Singapore. Wherever there are rich women who before had nothing."

"But it's hot in those countries."

"Doesn't matter, brother. The women still love them. Shows they're rich. In Manila we see them all the time. Especially when the monsoons come. You see them walking around, looking like drowned yaks. Besides, in parts of China it gets cold."

"And how're you supposed to kill them?"

"You don't. You harvest them."

"Huh?"

"You don't say *kill*. You say *harvest*."

"Okay, Jesus, how do you harvest them?"

Manuel thought. "I dunno. Maybe you hit them on the head."

"With what?"

"I dunno, maybe they have a small mallet you can buy."

"A mallet?"

"A little one, yes, maybe, I dunno."

"A chinchilla mallet? Ah, for chrissakes . . ."

Manuel looked at Hank. "Why you so mad tonight, brother? Why you so touchy? Tell you what. You could always come to the track with me. We'd make a bundle in no time."

"You know I don't gamble."

"You don't gamble? You ask a woman from Russia you barely know to move to Canada and live with you, and you say you don't gamble? Hank, brother, we all gamble. Some of us are just a little more honest about it."

They went back inside. Hank sat at his desk with a far-off expression. A day went by, and then another. In that time Hank grew more determined, and as he did he grew more and more anxious. The reality was this: you don't work for eight years at a dull job without dreaming of taking money that is *not* on your own paycheque. (The culprits, you ask? How about fantasy? How about desire? How about the need to keep the mind nimble and the soul a little more lifelike, despite all of the drudgery that is thrown by life *at* us?) Hank had actually thought up the scheme a couple of years earlier—it had come to him one night during a period in which he was more bored than usual. He'd then waited for the day in which Quality Assurance would change the glitch that made Hank's scam possible.

And that day, little one, had never come.

So.

A brief wait, for Manuel to grow tired and his head to lower slowly to his printer room desktop. At exactly 2:43 a.m., a large batch transmission started—stock dividends mostly, along with end-of-year bonuses—to be deposited in bank accounts all over the country. Hank watched numbers and figures march across the screen of his computer. These squiggles showed one thing—the transmissions were moving from the mainframe (where they were guarded by security codes and firewalls and two different types of protective software) to the server (where, for the next three minutes and fifteen seconds, they were *not*). Hank looked around. In his ears he heard sirens and the clanging of cell doors. He opened the server file, and there before him, ripe for the proverbial plucking, were thousands of account numbers, all receiving money. He picked one that was sizable and moved his cursor to it. All that was left, in the minute or so still available, was for Hank to exchange that bank account number with his own, thereby filling his empty coffers with almost thirty-seven thousand dollars. His fingers were poised, but then started shaking. He pushed his chair away and sailed across tiling. He, little one, may have been a high school dropout, and a user of brothels, and a disappointment to everyone who had ever really known him, but the one thing he was *not* was a criminal. He rubbed both his eyes, and felt ashamed of his cowardice.

He went home that morning not at all richer. As he walked down his street, he saw lights turn on in kitchens and in small upstairs bedrooms. His house was quiet and cool and he could hear floorboards creaking. He made coffee and sat drinking. As he did, he decided he would devote every ounce of his attention to the way the hot cup felt in his big hands. For a moment he felt okay. He rose, and went upstairs. As he passed Anna's bedroom, he stopped and listened to her slow, heavy breathing. He stood for a while; he felt the floor under his feet, and the clothes on his body, and the heart in his chest beating slowly and firmly.

He reached his small office. Sitting, he heard the bark of a dog and the sound of cars starting. He looked through the same desk that Anna had once broken into, gathering bank account balances and RRSP statements and any other financial data he thought might help him. Just as he was about to pack these into a satchel, he came across the photo of Martine and himself, taken years and years earlier in Marseilles. He sat looking at it, for minutes and minutes. His ears went silent, and for a moment he felt a calm overtake him.

Hank walked for an hour that day, through light snow and high winds. When the cold started to make his hands and feet tingle, he didn't notice—there's a numbness that comes when you're all-over tired. He reached stone bank arches at just after ten in the morning. His face was windburnt, and his hands felt deadened. After trudging inside, he asked to see a loan officer, and was led to the cubicle of a recent MBA graduate.

"Please," said the boy, "have a seat."

Hank sat, head pounding.

"How can I help you?"

"I need a loan. And I need it right away."

"A loan?"

"Yeah."

"What kind of a loan?"

"What do you mean?"

"We have many types of loans."

"The kind where you give me money."

The banker looked at him. "Let's talk about your needs."

"Let's."

"How much are we looking at?"

"As much as you can give me."

"Could you tell me what it's for?"

And here—oh yes, *here*—Hank couldn't help grinning. What should he tell him? That he was borrowing money so that a Russian could cheat him? So that he could pay off a ransom that was completely fictitious? *That there were women from Russia who felt they had to do this?* "Lookit," he said, "I just need some money."

There was a long pause. The boy's face grew slightly furrowed. "Do you have any collateral?"

Hank dumped out the contents of his creased leather satchel. "There," he said. "That's it. The whole lot. The whole nine yards. As you can see, I have a few RRSPs and a house. Other than that, I'm finished. I need some cash to get me through. That's why I'm here. Go ahead. Have a look. You decide. Say yes or no, though I'd prefer a yes. I don't mind waiting."

THE CULPRITS

The banker looked through Hank's papers. He looked at Hank's bills, and bank records, and credit card statements, most of which had bottom lines that were encased in brackets. He perused his employment record, the deed on his house, and, last but not least, the real estate assessment performed after Hank moved in. The officer looked as though an ulcer was bothering him.

After a minute of thinking, he took a pen and a paper and wrote down a figure.

After signing some papers, Hank went home in a taxi. He stood on his sidewalk, gazing up at his small house, thinking how ironic it was that he was going to have to sell it just to pay the money he now owed the bank *on* it. He went inside. Anna was napping on the sofa, a comforter around her. Her face looked drawn, as though she'd that day grown older. Hank, meanwhile, felt unusually tranquil. There were good deeds, and there were bad deeds, and it felt good to be certain which one this was. In his ears he heard nothing, not even the mildest of *ping*ings.

She awoke, and rubbed her eyes. "Hank. You have been where?"

He didn't answer the question. He sat by her feet and waited a few minutes as she came awake fully. He then wrote a cheque and on the coffee table placed it.

"*There,*" he said, "is your money."

She didn't touch it. "No, Hank, it was not proper to ask for such thing."

"Take it."

"I cannot."

"You can," he said. "Take it. I don't care, I don't want it."

She touched the cheque with her fingers. She picked it up slowly. "Hank," she whimpered. "Is too much, here."

"You'll need some for a plane ticket."

"Is too much."

"You'll need some to get started back in Russia."

"No, no, is far too much."

"Consider it an early Christmas present."

She put the cheque down beside her. A few seconds passed. She shuddered, and looked toward him through eyes red and puffy. "Hank," she said, sniffling. "Sometime I think maybe you coming from different place, or from different time. Sometime I think you coming from place where people are to one another much kinder."

"Trust me," he said, his smile nothing but rueful. "I'm not."

"Hank. I will go home."

"I know."

"You *know* I must do this."

"You can always come back."

She stiffened. "It will not happen. I am like fish here, without air for breathing. Is terrible feeling, this."

"I realize that."

"I am sorry. Is not good place for me, this Canada. Is too pretty and nice for girl accustomed to Russia. For a girl with Russia in her blood."

"I know."

"I am so, so sorry."

Hank was quiet. "If you ever wanted, you could come back and stay with me for a while. Just for a visit, if you ever wanted."

"I am sorry," she said again. "This . . . mmmmmm . . . arrangement, it did not work out. We both trying, I think, but it did not. Do you understand? I hope so. There is one other thing. I will return to you this money, every dime and nickel and kopeck. It will require much effort and time, but I will do it, or never I will live with myself again. Hank, no one has *ever* done to me anything this nice."

Hank trudged to his room and fell asleep with his clothes on. He slept like the wounded, and awoke in a dwindling, bronze daylight. He listened, intently, to Anna moving around on the first floor. He pictured her, putting on her cream vinyl jacket, slipping on her little white cotton gloves, checking her hair before going out somewhere. That day he went to work early. When he returned the next morning, she was still in her bedroom. Days passed this way—Hank avoiding Anna, Anna avoiding Hank, both avoiding the failure that was theirs and theirs only. If they happened to pass in the hallway, they'd both awkwardly smile and say, "Excuse me." Soon, Hank realized that the silence in his house was an exact duplication of the silence he grew up with. *What goes around comes around*, he thought to himself grimly.

And then, on a pale afternoon, Hank awoke to a house that was totally different. His ears were a howl of arid winds blowing. He lay still, struggling to hear noises that weren't of his own making. He switched off his Marsona DS-600. He could hear the shout of some neighbours, an icicle dripping, the rush of forced air through dusty old air vents. Other than that, there was nothing beyond a slight, saddened *ping*ing. His throat felt prickly, and he tried to cough away the sensation. He could feel it, he could, a density in the air caused by her absence. It weighed on his chest, and made his lungs feel full of liquid. He could smell it, all around him, the mustiness of absence.

He rose. Downstairs, he saw it—a folded piece of paper with his name written on it. He held it in fingers stained a pale orange. Despite knowing what it would say, he opened it anyway.

It read:

Goodbye, Hank. I am sorry.

EIGHT

And oh, little one, the fantasies *mamochka* had had of her first, trumpet-blowing trip back to Russia! She had screened it in her mind so many times, it had become like a movie in which you cheered at the ending: her cute half-Slav children, adoringly holding each of her small hands; her beaming in-tow husband, whom she not only adored but who was tall, dark, and Tsoi-like; her left eye corralled by some Mount Sinai surgeon, such that her beauty was now whole and not partial; a career that was the envy of all of her girlfriends, most particularly her oldest (and bitchiest) friend, Natalia.

And the gifts! Dozens of them, boxes and bags and colourful packages, each one bought in the district of Yorkville, spilling off a trolley, and all for her family. And *then*, at Pulkovo, when the glass doors slid open, they would be waiting, tearful and cheering their prodigal daughter, their warm arms embracing a girl *who*, they couldn't help but notice, bore an air of maturity she hadn't had when she left them.

She told no one she was coming other than Dadya. She was ashamed, depressed, saddled with an obsessive-compulsive disorder, and, like an Unreal City mobster, carrying about thirty thousand euros in a Samsonite suitcase. Her plane rose into the sky. The clouds beyond her window looked wispy and golden. Far off, she could see the day's failing sunlight—it was thin and dark orange, and for a while its beauty was a distraction from the whole of her failure. It changed in a moment, the sky turning from a phosphorous glow to a velvety purple. Anna squeezed her eyes shut against all of her worries, first and foremost among them her one true love, Ruslan. She'd heard all of the stories—there were videotapes in circulation, of terrorist Chechens lopping off fingers—and it took all of her will to stop herself from imagining what they might be doing to him. (*No*, she thought, *they couldn't, they wouldn't need to, not when we're paying . . .*) When she finished trying not to think about Ruslan, she started struggling not to think about Hank and the lie that she'd told him. She would pay him back someday. It was all there was to it. As she sat hunched in her seat, it was hard to say whom she felt worse for—her thoughts leapt from Ruslan to Hank and then from Hank back to Ruslan, the process accelerating faster and faster, until her head began to form a composite image, a handsome and yet orange-haired *Huslan,* who was kneeling before her, hands out and pleading.

Anna leaned over and took hold of her handbag beneath the seat in front of her; it was pink, and zippered, and about the size of a toaster. She opened it and rooted through bags of salt peanuts she'd stolen at one of the kiosks. She finally found a Kleenex that only verged upon soggy; she blew her nose and stared once again out the plane's window. The sky's velvety purple had turned to pitch darkness. Her fears turned to strange thoughts, which then turned to dreamscapes. She slept through the meals and both gangster movies, awaking only when the plane began descending in Moscow. She changed planes, her second flight landing in the middle of a gloomy mid-morning. She packed up her things feeling deadened and weary. In the terminal, she collected a suitcase half-stuffed with money. When she emerged from Arrivals, Dadya was waiting.

He too looked tired. Cherry-coloured pouches cushioned his dark eyes.

"Dadya." She hugged him; she smelled soap, and tobacco, and the scent caused by days spent worrying.

"Thank you," he kept saying, "thank you, thank you, thank you. Thank you, Anna, for what you are doing. God bless you and your Canadian. What is his name?"

"Hank."

"God bless you, and Hank, and all others like you."

She pulled away and looked up at him. Despite his roughened appearance, there was a calm in his eyes she couldn't quite fathom.

"Inshallah," he said, "this'll be over quickly."

In Pulkovo's small car park, Dadya led her to an old, battered Lada. She climbed in unsmiling. "Is the car of a friend," he said while starting the engine. The engine whirred, and coughed, and finally came to life with a hiccupping jitter. Streams of oily blue vapour shot from the exhaust pipe. Anna gazed out of her window, at drizzle and dark clouds and Unreal City clamour. As they drove, she observed her birthplace's dark, soulful glory, until the whole of the city began calling out to her. Oh yes—the canals all whispered, the gargoyles sang operas, the spires reached skyward in a gesture to heaven. It all looked stormy and regal, like a king on his deathbed.

I, Anna thought, *won't again leave you.*

Upon entering the Apraxin Dvor market, Dadya slowed, and the car crept through dim and rain-splattered laneways. When blocked by crowds, he craned his head out the window and began gruffly yelling. They came to the lane behind the repair shop, and Anna thought of the times she'd been here with Ruslan. It was quiet and cold and more than a little mysterious—a place where bats built their nests on old, rotting crossbeams. For a moment they sat, listening to muffled market sounds and their own skipping heartbeats.

They each opened a door and stepped into snowfall. Dadya swore in Avari: the ground was littered with candy wrappers and cigarette butts and tossed-away cans of gin mixed with tonic. Anna looked down and saw a leaflet promoting a ska band from Ossetia who were playing that night at the Lenin's Tomb rock club.

"Are you ready?" Dadya asked.

She followed him around to the storefront. He unlocked the wooden door that opened onto the cellar. They walked down uneven steps and sat in a room lined with white, empty wood shelves. Anna sighed and unzipped her suitcase. She reached inside and pulled out a sweater, which she handed to Dadya.

In one of the sleeves she had hidden most of Hank's money. Dadya began pulling out bundles of euros.

"I have more," Anna said, "if that's not enough—"

"No, it's good," Dadya said. "I talked them down a little each day. I'll call and get this over with. I'm pretty sure we can trust them."

"You have their number?"

"Yes."

"Dadya, who are they?"

"They are a group, Anya. One of many. They are not fooling around."

"From the market?"

"No. Of course not. They're from out near Kupchino."

"Are they . . ." She could barely say it. " . . . with Shamil Basayev?"

"I don't know. Who knows if he's even still alive? Sometimes I think he never even existed, that he was something Putin made up to put a face on the bad guy."

"You have met them?"

"They've come to the shop. Several times. They saw I had nothing. How they knew about you—I don't know. They have people everywhere, you know, in every city in every country."

Dadya was punching numbers into an old Romanian-made telephone. He waited, and began talking in the language that Ruslan had always reverted to when senseless with passion. This went on for five or ten seconds, and then he looked at her. "We wait," he said, and Anna realized she was shaking. "We wait," he said again, "until they contact us. Are you hungry?"

"No."

"Then have a rest."

Anna went to Ruslan's room and lay down on his bed. She stared up at the ceiling and felt blank all over, as though what they were doing were not really happening. After a bit she rose, and played card games with Dadya. This went on for hours. They played cribbage, and rummy, and a game from the Caucasus involving black cards and jokers. Meanwhile, Dadya told her things about Ruslan that she only knew partially.

"Anya—did Ruslan ever tell you how he came to St. Petersburg?"

"Not really."

"He came in the trunk of some crazy cousin's Lada. This was in 1999, the year the fighting spread to Dagestan. Apparently, Ruslan loved it. Loved every minute. Did you know all this?"

"Some of it."

"And did you know that once upon a time he was a pretty decent athlete?"

"What?"

"Oh sure. Polo was his game—Dagestani-style. We play with pistols and mallets and prayer mats tied to our stallions. It takes days and days, and we play it over whole mountain ranges. I never saw Ruslan play, but I heard stories."

"Dadya, you're kidding—I would never have thought. I didn't think he was the athletic type."

"Oh yes. He could have been a champion. He rode like Khadji Taran him*self*. But then"—here Dadya exhaled—"the foolishness of youth. It happens, it happens. He turned seventeen years of age, is the long and the short of it. I tell you, that was the *real* reason they sent him to the North. They thought: okay, okay, maybe in a big city, with more to occupy him, he won't run like a wild horse. I don't know if they ever really worried about him getting killed by a stray bomb."

That night they heard nothing more from Ruslan's captors. Anna stayed in Ruslan's room, where she was kept awake by jet lag and worry and the detectable scent of her abducted ex-lover. She tossed and turned, fretting under the watchful grimace of a snarling James Hetfield. Awake as awake *can* be, she listened to the noises made by a market after midnight: cats shrieking, odd calling voices, the passing of tires over cobblestoned laneways. As the night wore on, these sounds grew further and further apart, the market sinking slowly into a thick, gloomy silence. Anna finally nodded off around the time the market began to lighten. She awoke in mid-morning and drank dark, bitter coffee.

They stayed in the next day, by the phone waiting. Whenever it rang, she would leap on it, saying *Da? Da?* to a person who, more often than not, did not speak any Russian. Breathless, she would pass the receiver to Dadya, who would take it and listen and then shake his head slowly, as if to say, *No, no, Anya. I'm sorry. It's not them.*

As the waiting continued, she paced, and ate nothing, and retreated to her room for intense spells of crying. "Please," Dadya would beg her, "everything is all right. You will see. You will see. They won't touch him. I know this."

The hours crept by. A dozen times she thought she should telephone her mother, only to shudder at all the lies she'd have to come up with. (How many times had her *mamochka* said that her love for Ruslan would end in disaster? That he would drag her headlong into the murk of the Caucasus? That they were all savages, his people, and they would do things to hurt her? Under no circumstances, Anna thought, would she let her *mamochka* find out she'd been one hundred percent right.) For dinner, Dadya went out and came back with a goat stew. Anna couldn't eat. Darkness fell, and she once again listened to cats and market shoutings and, when everything was quiet, the distant slow gurgling of black canal waters.

She woke in mid-morning, to a day that was darkened by chunky grey rain clouds. The store was empty. She made herself tea. As she drank, she felt crushed under the weight of her worries. When Dadya returned, they resumed playing cards while awaiting a message. The phone rang shortly after noon. Anna answered; the voice said something in a language that sounded (at least to her ears) like Avari. She passed it to Dadya, who patiently listened, lifting his palm when she whispered, *Dadya? Dadya? Who is it?*

She could hear a babble of words coming from the phone's earpiece. Dadya hung up the phone without ever once talking.

"Okay," he said. "Everything is ready."

They walked out into flurries. They pushed through babushkas and vendors and robed shashlik blessers. Anna walked with her head down, every breath, blink, and thought devoted to Ruslan. She, believe it or not, imagined him shrugging off the whole thing, as though it had been no more inconvenient than a poorly done haircut. (And yet, underneath his blasé and uncaring attitude, there would be gratitude for his young Russian Anya . . . gratitude for the weird way that life had worked out . . . gratitude that would grow, and grow, until finally he would have to accept that he, oh yes *he*, was totally and inescapably in love *with* her. *Oh yes,* Anna thought, *that's what would happen.*)

They left the market and kept walking until Dadya stopped outside of a café. It had glass walls and a few tables and was directly across from Sennaya Ploschad. Anna stood outside; in her jacket's right pocket she could feel a brown paper bag stuffed full of money. She watched Dadya enter and walk to the front as though perusing the menu; he then came to the door and motioned her over. Her heels clacked against stone. They bought cherry cakes and coffee, and sat slowly eating. Long minutes passed. When a half-hour was over, Dadya bought two more coffees. They sat and they sipped, the coffee warming their hands and dampening their dry throats. More time passed. Anna wanted to leave, and said so to Dadya.

"No," he said, glancing over to a door at the side of the café.

Anna turned and saw two men. One was tall and thin and the colour of brown leather, the other squatter and olive and with his head shaved to stubble. They wore trimmed beards and cheap suits, and each had an air that seemed to her poisoned. Yet it wasn't their scowling presence that chilled the room and started it swaying. No—in front of them, being pushed forward by hands on his shoulders, was a man who was pale and rail-thin and far-away staring. Relief blossomed in Anna. This whole thing was a mistake. This man didn't swagger, or saunter, or look at all Viktor Tsoi–like. This man had broken teeth, and dead skin, and eyes slightly bulbous. This man (who, yes, it was true, bore a passing resemblance to her sweet Dagestani) was shaky, and weak, and mumbling to himself.

This man, she saw plainly, had a look in his eyes that was broken and haunted.

All three sat. Not a word was spoken. When Dadya nodded at Anna, she hesitated, thinking, *Why would we pay for this man whom we don't know?* Dadya then glared at her; startled, she reached into her pocket and snuck out the brown bag. She passed it under the table.

The Chechens left, leaving the Ruslan imposter.

"Nephew?" said Dadya.

The man opened his mouth, as though its use hurt him. "Da?" he said in a voice that, too many times, had like a drug coursed through Anna's whole body. He turned; Anna shuddered as she watched his eyes slowly focus. "Anya?" he said weakly. "Is it Anya?"

Oh, little one. All time turned to vapour, and all vapour to fine mist, and then this mist sifted away into a skin-pricking nothing.

Anna stayed on with Dadya and Ruslan. It was a decision she made without being invited—they needed her, and she wasn't about to stand on decorum. To accommodate her, Dadya borrowed a neighbour's old mattress and put it in a storeroom right next to Ruslan's. He also made space in the TV shop's bathroom, and he bought her a bath towel that came from the market, featuring small coloured drawings of St. Petersburg attractions. Then, to squash rumours amongst the old beetroot vendors, Dadya told everybody that Anna was a Russian friend of the family, and was staying to help Ruslan with his recovery.

She got to work, her movements infused with a purpose that felt foreign. The first thing she did was buy them a blender, so that every morning she could serve juice made from broccoli or carrots. At lunch, she fried fish—either sturgeon or cod or fresh salmon fillets. She'd read that omega-3s were good for the memory, and it seemed that, above all else, Ruslan had been rendered forgetful; whenever he emerged from his room, where he spent most of his day sleeping, he would look at her as though he hadn't yet met her. But then, slowly, after he'd swallowed the cod oil tincture she slipped into his juice glass, a look of recognition would flit across his gaunt features.

"Good morning," he'd then mutter, be it morning, noon, or evening. "Good morning, Anya, how have you been?"

For dinner, she made him all of his Russian favourites: pelmeni and borscht, cabbage rolls and boiled buckwheat, stroganoff and cheese bread and soup made with kidneys. And while Dadya appreciated this motherly cooking (he'd look up from his plate and say, "By Allah this tastes good!"), Ruslan had to struggle with the small portions she gave him. Often he'd inspect each stabbed forkful as though it were covered with ants or tiny red spiders. Other times he'd stop chewing, his mouth filled with food and his eyes looking straight through her.

"Do you like it?" she'd ask.

A second would pass by. Suddenly he'd seem to remember where he was, and say in a voice disembodied, "Yes, thank you, I like it."

How she slaved over Ruslan, in the hope that expressions of kindness would counteract what (she thought) those damn Chechens had done to him. And yes, yes, she often wondered what *exactly* had been done to him, only to chase away the question as she was afraid of the details. Still, one afternoon, when Ruslan was asleep and Anna and Dadya were having coffee together, she could stand it no longer.

"Dadya," she said, "do you . . . I mean . . ." Her voice grew quiet. "Do you know what they did to him?"

"*Bah,*" Dadya said. "They're savages, they're animals, you don't want to think about it."

"Please, Dadya."

"No, little beauty. Is better we don't know."

A long moment passed.

"Anna," he said, "you do know what today is?"

"Yes," she said, suddenly remembering; it had been so easy to forget in this sad, Muslim household.

"Wait," Dadya said, before rising and disappearing into one of the back rooms. He returned, smiling, his hands held behind him. Sitting, he handed Anna a gift wrapped in red and green paper.

"Oh, Dadya," she said. "I feel awful. I didn't get you anything. I thought, since you were—"

"Bah. Is nothing. Is your holiday, anyway. Open it."

She pulled open the bow and lifted the lid off a cardboard box about the size of an apple. Peering in, she saw an antique brooch lying on a bed of cotton batten. She pulled it out. It was metal and old and had a red stone in its centre.

"Merry Christmas," said Dadya.

"Thank you," she said, her eyes facing downward.

"It belonged to one of my aunts. From Dagestan."

"Thank you," she said again, and when she rose to hug him, tears dripped on his shoulder.

She baked bread, she kept Ruslan's clothes freshly laundered, she went out and bought flowers to decorate his room. In the evenings, she'd sit by him, watching the nighttime crime dramas that filled Russia's airwaves. Every other afternoon she would fill a tub with warm water and then wait outside the bathroom while Ruslan bathed himself. Then, when he emerged, she'd towel that hair that had once had such an effect on her, the whole time singing folk songs her babushka had sung to her during long-ago bath times. She sang him the one about wood nymphs who lived in a larder, and the one about the woodchopper who swung an axe filled with magic, and the one about the young woman who longed for her husband.

Ruslan, after a time, got to know them. "Anya," he asked her one afternoon, "sing the one about the lonely Russian woman."

"Which one?"

"The one about the woman. Who is waiting for her . . . for her husband. The one who thinks her husband is up to no good."

"'Along the Petersburg Road'?"

"Yes."

"You like this one?"

"Yes."

"All right," she said, and by the time she had finished faking her way through verses she could barely remember, he was staring straight ahead, into the centre of nothingness, as though the melody had whisked him to a place where things didn't matter.

Meanwhile (and mysteriously), the shop was filling with second-hand TVs. If Anna hadn't been so distracted, she might have wondered why this was—why Dadya was now spending his days as he always had spent them: hunched over and fiddling, the room filling with the tang of sweat and burnt solder. Some days this would please him. On others he'd grow frantic, and bellow in Russian or Avari: "These cheap sets from Bulgaria aren't even worth saving!" It was a sentiment he'd cap by sweeping an arm over the table, sending a hail of old parts onto the floor crashing.

And Ruslan, if nearby, would hold his ears and look frightened. One time when this happened, Anna suggested they go walking, at least until Dadya had regained his composure. Ruslan nodded, and they headed to one of the smaller, and iced-over, canals in the city. Like old persons they walked, arm in arm slowly, their faces awakened by cold air and the clamour around them. She struggled to ignore his elbow's extreme thinness, and the tragic way in which his steps were tentative and halting. Mostly he was silent. To fill the time, Anna rambled about things unimportant: the weather, ice hockey, what was on at Mariinsky.

"Ruslan," she asked, "you are listening?"

He stopped, and looked at her. "Yes, Anya. Yes. What were you saying?"

They took a few more steps. She could hear water trickling beneath cracks in the surface. The sounds made by traffic were muted and distant.

"Ruslan," she said, "tell me one thing. Tell me one small thing that happened. This will help you."

"No."

"Please, Ruslan. It is good to get things off your chest."

"NO!"

He stormed off, his back looking so, so narrow as he walked away from her. Anna stood watching, tears welling, the urge to steal something mounting inside her. She swallowed, and trembled, and to a street kiosk headed (where she paid for some water and nicked a small box of candy). This helped, though for a few minutes only. She knew, yes she *knew,* that if she wanted to discover what had happened to him, she would have to listen to the ravings that he made when he was sleeping.

So she did. She couldn't sleep anyway. She would lie in her bed with her arms wrapped around her. When she heard him start moaning, she'd rush to his room and find him eyes-wide and shivering. "Shhhhh," she would say, "I'm here, it's all right, I am right here beside you."

It was during these moments—Anna rocking her Ruslan like a scared, knee-scraped toddler—that she heard details that confused her, Ruslan muttering about insects and trees and the different odours of soil, till she began to wonder if he had been imprisoned outdoors. Another night she heard him railing about white pines and she wondered if he'd been kept in some kind of forest.

These were the good nights. On others, she heard words and phrases that caused her to shudder. She *learned*, little one, that he had begged them. He had begged them to stop, and they hadn't listened. As she softly sang to him—*Along the Petersburg Road, along the small lane, to the Tverskoi–Yamskoi quarter, with a little bell ringing*—she heard desperate pleadings, garbled and repeated as though he were back there. She heard: *please* and *I beg you* and *for God's sake have mercy*. She heard: *oh God not again* and *I'll tell you anything*. And, on a night in which Ruslan's nocturnal screaming had been far worse than normal, she heard: *please, please, just kill me, I'll pay you*.

And though she couldn't know exactly what had been done *to* him, her imagination took over, and they would both shiver together, as though the two of them had shared the very same torment. With time, he'd grow quiet, and fall asleep, occasionally with his eyes just a little bit open. Only then would she return to the stockroom beside his, and pull cold, scratchy sheets to her damp nose. She would try to breathe deeply and think of things that had nothing to do with Ruslan, or Chechnya, or modern-day Russia. It never worked—slowly she'd drift into her own blood-soaked nightmares. Soon, Ruslan wasn't the only one who bolted upright in his sleep, eyes blank and skin damp and hands clutching at bedsheets.

Greyish blue sacs sprouted beneath both of her eyes. Her hands succumbed to a slight all-day trembling, and her figure acquired a grim, nervous leanness. She struggled to keep cooking, but often found herself too exhausted to face the crowds in Apraxin. While she tried to keep fresh flowers in the repair shop, she now often forgot until the last bunch grew wilted and dreary. She was also frightened of being discovered. Once, when out buying potatoes, she spotted Natalia, a dozen rows away and looking at jackets. Anna froze. She ached to see a friend who had nothing to do with the Caucasus, and yet she couldn't imagine telling Natalia she was living with Ruslan in Dadya's repair shop. In the end, she ducked behind a stand selling cabbage and rutabagas.

There was another problem. Among the Apraxin Dvor vendors, rumours were spreading about the young nurse of Ruslan. It seemed that every time she passed by, some small thing would vanish: a bunch of carrots, a small bag of shallots, a segment of ginger as gnarled as a tree root. Though it was never a lot, it seemed there always was something.

One day, one of the babushkas stopped Dadya on the lane outside of his shop.

"What is it?" he asked, for he could tell she was angry.

She pointed toward the shop. "That girl," she croaked, "that *Russian*. We are starting to think that her fingers are sticky..."

"Who?" Dadya answered. "Anya? What are you talking about, old woman?"

"She steals. She's a *vor*. She can't go outside without taking something."

"Oh no, you're mistaken. She's been a godsend."

"I tell you, she thieves."

"And *I* tell you she's a good girl. By the grace of Allah, do not bother me again with your petty suspicions."

THE CULPRITS

Yet even as he said this, he thought of small things of his that had been disappearing from his shop: a screwdriver, a knob used for attenuating volume, a dish where he put small change and tokens (the small change and tokens dumped out where it had been). *Could it be that . . . no, no, these babushki are all crazy, out of their minds with grief caused by sons lost in battle . . .* And yet the accusation had planted a grain of suspicion in Dadya's mind. Instead of marching straight into the shop, he stopped on the steps leading down to the cellar and peered through the window set into the wood door. Anna was at his table, looking so haggard and thin it was as though she were turning into Ruslan. He waited, and was still watching when she reached out and touched a pair of old wire strippers. She took them in her hands, rolling them around and around in small, dainty fingers. The most meagre of grins crossed her near-pretty features. With a sudden sharp breath, she closed her eyes, crossed her heart, and put the wire strippers in her pocket.

Look at us, Dadya thought sadly. *Look at us all in this crazed, all-day jihad. Nephew tortured, Anya taking things that don't belong to her, me cutting deals with radical Sunnis. Look at us, sweet and yet judgmental Allah—every one of us corrupted by this evil called Chechnya.*

The next afternoon, Dadya again returned to his shop and found Anna at his work table, her face in her hands. She straightened as he came in, and smiled wanly at him. Her eyes were as red as apples at harvest. A long moment passed in which no words were uttered.

"I can't help him," she said.

"Nobody can."

"I tried. I am sorry."

"It is not your fault. Listen to me, Anya. I didn't want to tell you this. Ruslan was given something that scrambled his mind. He was given a terrible drug that turned his life to nothing. He is in God's hands now. We can only pray that some good comes from this. We can only do what we can to make sure that something useful comes from all of this . . . from all of this torment." He sat, and lied to her. "I am sending him home."

"Home?"

"To Dagestan. His parents' farm is well away from the Chechen border. There's no fighting there now. There hasn't been for some time. There are chickens and green fields and fresh watermelons. Did you know this about the Caucasus? That the watermelons grow wild? That they are as juicy and sweet as anything God has ever made? It is peaceful and, best of all, it's far from here."

"He can't travel by himself."

"I'll take him."

"How?"

"By bus."

She swallowed, and felt real pain. She had failed, again. She had failed at everything, at *everything*, she had ever in her life tried.

"When will you go?"

"Soon. He is in pain."

"Today?"

"No. But soon."

Her chair scraped against the cement floor, and then Anna was behind him, wrapping slender forearms around both of his shoulders.

Dadya stood when she released him. "Thank you," he said. "Thank you for everything. Ruslan would not have lived without you."

"No, Dadya, it's not—"

"*Anya.* Thank you."

There was a short burst of awkwardness, both of them painfully smiling. Dadya left. The shop door wheezed open and then dropped back into place with a loud wooden banging. Anna sat beneath pipes and hot air ducts and wondered what she should do. Her options were not pretty—really, she had no choice but to return to her mother's, the only problem being that her mother's was not her mother's, not since she'd rented their *communalka* to unregistered Ossetians. If she went, she'd be sharing a sofa in her aunt's small apartment, amidst cousins and parents and her uncle's old father (who, it was said, was prone to getting loose and wandering the city).

And yet . . .

She thought of Ruslan, of what had become of him. She rose and walked down the hall to where he was sleeping. Lightly, she knocked. She heard murmurs and bedsprings. She knocked again, and this time heard nothing. She opened his door and tiptoed inside. She forgot about breathing. In her head was one thought and one sad thought only: this place had once been a place of such intoxication. And now? It was the room of a sick man, who would never be better.

She lowered herself to the edge of his bed. The only light came trickling in from the hallway. He lay on his back, head slowly tossing. With each of his breaths came a scent warm and sour. His eyes danced beneath eyelids as thin as pink tissues. Anna wondered what he might be dreaming. She took his hand, and his eyes opened partly. Slowly they focused.

"Anya," he whispered.

"Yes."

"You're here."

She pushed hair off his forehead, and then tried weakly smiling. "You are going home."

He blinked at her curiously. "I am?"

"I understand there's fresh air there." She made an attempt at a small joke: "And all the watermelons a Chechen like you would ever care to eat."

Ruslan still looked at her, puzzled about this talk of returning to Dagestan. Instead of saying farewell, Anna bent over and placed her mouth on his lightly. There her lips rested, neither kissing nor parting nor in any way moving. The whole time she marvelled at how his mouth had once charged her. Now it felt like the flesh of a corpse that had momentarily risen.

Little one: thin fingers alighted on the tip of her right breast. She flinched. His hands—those weak, spindly instruments—began to roam over her body. Anna gulped, and breathed deeply. When he fumbled with her skirt clasp, she robotically helped him; pity, of course, was the ultimate culprit. Then they came to her—those words she'd waited so long for. Those words she'd once have given anything to hear, if only he'd said them when he was still the old Ruslan.

"Anya," he whispered. "Always, I've loved you . . ."

She felt her heart groan, like an old person dying. The weight of their history like blood passed between them. He pulled down his blanket and directed her hand to where he'd grown swollen. Anna touched, and felt sickened—there were divots, and gouges, and bumpy scar tissue. She grew nauseous, not just at the ruin of his body but at the frustration and pain she'd endured these last few weeks. In the room's dusty gloom, she prayed he'd mistake her disgust for desire.

"Do you want me to?" she whispered, and he moaned once again that he'd love her forever. She shifted her weight, and was not at all ready. Her sorrowful breasts were now being chewed on. Tears fell from her eyes upon his once-beautiful cheekbones. He seemed not to mind; as they rolled past his mouth, he caught them on his tongue. "Do you want me to?" she croaked, hoping upon hope that he'd wither before her. Instead, he groaned and nodded and said again that he loved her. *Do it,* she thought. *Think how he's suffered.* Her hips shifted forward and took the warped thing inside her. It felt like a corkscrew, against dry flesh revolving. She prayed to Jesus, and Onuphrius, and Allah, and whatever other god might be looking down on her. This helped; with just two or three rockings, Ruslan neck-arched and groaned and filled poor *mamochka.*

Then.

He exhaled and she smelled it—that scent that is the hallmark of a soul lost and darkened. It was mulchy and vile, like a matting of leaves left to rot in an eavestrough. She fell off him and lay trembling. Three inches of mattress stood like a brick wall between them. Ruslan murmured. Anna touched him, and her fingers felt frozen. This was not Ruslan. This was some dark replacement. She touched herself between her legs, sniffed the tips of her fingers, and discovered what it is like to shake hands with evil. It was the same putrid stench that had infected Ruslan's breath, only *it* was a dozen—no, no, a hundred—times stronger. It was the scent of something distorted, of something dark, of something monstrous and big-headed and sickly omniscient.

It was the scent, my half-*seestra,* of yours truly.

And so, there it was—my tentative stage entrance. I'd arrived just shy of New Year's, in this harrowing tale of the Tushino bombing— just a few random cells, jiggling and humming and with life mutating. *Mamochka* sobbed and packed her small suitcase. She stuffed the rest of Hank's euros inside her bra cups, where they abraded her skin like a fine grade of sandpaper. She then bolted through Apraxin with the face of the shell-shocked.

The city that night ran with ghosts, spooks, and goblins. With every step she could see them, perched grinning on rooftops and pointing with talons. She ran faster, and faster, her face tilted down to avoid stares and glances. She reached the Sennaya metro station. Under chandeliers and marble statues, she boarded a subway heading north to Devyatkino. Here, she took a ten-ruble minivan, and rode with cauliflower-eared men who'd been all day drinking; she could smell diesel and turnip and home-distilled vodka. She rode into a clanking and cold Russian suburb, and got out before a building that loomed high above her.

She looked up, feeling awful. White-skinned, coughing children played on the pavement around her. The building's vestibule was unlit; in shadows she entered the old cage elevator. It ground upward for a minute before stopping between floors. She was too exhausted to start crying; instead, she looked out along a grimy, unswept floor. When she saw ankles, she called, "Hey, I am trapped here."

Two young men crouched over and looked at her, smiling.

"*Dyevushka*," one said, "what are you doing there?"

"What does it look like?"

They laughed. "But why did you get on at all? That thing hasn't worked right since Gorbachev."

"I forgot. This is my aunt's building. I don't come here often."

"Ah well," they laughed. "Your aunt should have told you."

They each pulled hard on the door until it was pried mostly open. Reaching over, they took Anna's hands and lifted her upward. She brushed against filthy wrought iron and the lip of the fourth floor.

"Thank you."

THE CULPRITS

They nodded and walked off, still chuckling. After uselessly wiping the front of her clothing, Anna climbed up dark stairs toward her aunt's small apartment. She knocked on the door. She waited, and heard the clicking and shunting and scraping of deadbolts. It was Aunt Katya who opened; her hair was in curlers, and she was wearing her bathrobe. Her eyes widened, and her mouth hung wide open: before her, unannounced, was the niece who had gone off to marry in Canada, her clothing badly rumpled and a smudge of oil staining her right cheek.

"Paulina!" she called. "Paulina! Come quickly . . . it's *Anya!*"

Anna forced a smile. Within seconds she was standing before her young cousins Sasha and Tanya, Katya's husband, Yuri, and Yuri's elderly father, Ivan. And then it was her mother, Paulina Borisovna, stopping inches from her daughter, smelling of Georgian tobacco and soapy dishwater. A long moment followed. The two women embraced lightly, their bodies barely touching.

"My daughter," said Paulina, "you have come for a visit? Or did things not work out in Canada?"

Anya pulled away and felt her skin crawl with the history between them. A second later she was encircled by her family, Katya saying, "Anya, Anya, my God, you look skinny," and Yuri saying, "Welcome, welcome, stay as long as you want to," and both Sasha and Tanya piping up together, "Yes, yes, you can sleep in our room," while Ivan turned in half-panicked circles while saying, "Who's Anya? Who is she? Who is *this* girl?"

"I," Anna said with a weak smile, "am tired."

"Yes!" Katya cried. "Of course you are! Of course you are! After such a long trip you must be exhausted! Why didn't you call us? We could have picked you up at the airport! Little beauty, what were you thinking?" Her aunt took her elbow and led her to the bedroom shared by the cousins. "Here," her aunt said, "you can sleep *here*, for as long as you want."

"Thank you," Anna said.

"Not at all, not at all."

"Thank you."

"Is there anything you need?"

"No, I am fine, I just need to rest . . ."

. . . and with that, she was kissed on both cheeks and left alone in the room decorated with Avril Lavigne and Linkin Park posters, along with a framed poster advertising Paul McCartney's St. Petersburg concert. Anna crossed the room and pulled off clothes smelling of my foul, ghoulish essence. She left them all in a heap and crawled under the covers. She yawned and felt numb; this feeling spread, like a chill, over all of her body. Her throat constricted and turned sore. She rolled into a ball and held herself, whimpering.

When her eyes next opened, she was in pitch darkness. She rolled over and pulled the sheets over her head. Here she stayed, her dreams blood-soaked and lurid and rooted in forests. When she next awoke, it was the middle of the afternoon. She could hear a radio playing—some middle-of-the-road station, pulled in from Finland—and her aunt Katya humming. She yawned, and stretched, and felt terrible all over. She rose, and dug a robe out of her suitcase. In the kitchen, she found Katya peeling vegetables while listening to the soft hits of yesteryear. Her aunt looked up, and smiled at her house guest.

"Tatya," she said, "what are you listening to?"

"I think it's a song about a girl. Is it? Sometimes I think I'll learn English just to understand the words on this station."

Anya listened more closely. "Yes, Tatya. The girl's name is Brandy."

"Brandy? Like the drink?"

"Yes."

"And the singer—he is in love with her?"

"In this song he is."

Katya smiled broadly. "I bet you hate this music."

"No," Anna lied. "I like it. It's . . . calming."

"You are not at all telling the truth. But that's okay, you come and sit down and have some breakfast. It is late, but of course your body is bothered by jet lag. Would you like some tea? Some toast, maybe, to go with it?"

"Yes, all right, thank you."

Anna sat. Katya stood and put on the kettle and put two slices of bread in the toaster. The song changed, the room filling with the banter of a Finnish announcer. Katya put Anna's breakfast on the table in front of her. Anna took a sip of tea; it was hot and strong, and it passed with some difficulty over the lump in her throat. Katya sat back down and looked at her niece for a moment. She put a hand on the girl's forearm. It was the kindness of this gesture that caused Anna to put down her tea, and put her face in her hands, and let regret surge through her like a bubbling river. Katya reached over with her free hand and rubbed Anya's shoulder.

"It did not work out? In Canada?"

The answer came out muffled.

"Is okay, little beauty. In life there are always challenges. You can stay for as long as you want."

"There isn't enough room."

"We'll make room."

"My mother. She doesn't—"

"Oh no, Anna, you mustn't think that! She is delighted you are here! It's just that, well, with Paulina it is difficult for her to show this. She has always been this way, ever since she was a little girl. Trust me, I know her better than anyone."

"She wishes I wasn't here."

"It's not true. She loves you with all of her heart and soul. Anna, you must understand that with parents it is like this—with love there comes sometimes a quickness of anger. It is only because we want the best for our children."

When it came time for bed that night, everyone insisted that Anna continue to sleep in the room of Tanya and Sasha. And while Anna protested, her aunt insisted, "No, no, Anyachka, little beauty, you have had much travel and you must have some real rest." (The reality, of course, is that they assumed her Internet Canadian must have been a real monster, and for this reason they all felt acute pity for her.) Anna protested once again, this time looking to her mother. Paulina nodded and said, "Anya, yes, it's better that you're comfortable."

This meant that the twins would sleep on the fold-out sofa with Anna's mother. Aunt Katya and Yuri (who was her second husband, the first having perished somewhere near Kabul) would continue sleeping in the apartment's main bedroom, while Yuri's father, Ivan, stayed in a cot in the kitchen, where he liked to drift off to the refrigerator humming.

And so, Anna took to bed, spending most of her days sleeping. Whenever she awoke, she felt sluggish and weak and ragged with emotion. The one thing she didn't feel was nauseous, so it never once occurred to her she was pregnant. This went on for days, Anna blaming her fatigue on the sadness she'd acquired from Ruslan. She only emerged from the twins' room to pick at her meals or take short, exhausting walks along the neighbourhood's main boulevard. Often she awoke in the middle of the night, the silence of the apartment causing her thoughts to go to bad places. One time she arose and tromped dead-eyed into the kitchen. As quietly as possible she put on the kettle.

The old man's eyes opened.

"Natasha," he croaked, which was the name of his daughter. She had married a Russian naval officer and now lived ten times zones away, in an isolated region that stretched north of China.

"No, Ivan. I'm Anya."

"Natasha."

"No."

His eyes were like marbles, grown glassy with the things he had in his life seen. They focused on her. "They say . . . they say you were in Canada."

"Yes."

"Yes?"

"Shhhhhhhhhh, Ivan. Sleep."

"What was it like?"

"Shhhhhhhh. I'm sorry I woke you."

"No, please tell me."

She paused. "It was nice."

"Nice . . . how?"

Everything felt heavy—the air, her thoughts, Ivan's questions, the small wire glasses that sat on her nose bridge. "There is no Chechnya there," she said. "And no businessmen gangsters, out in the street and killing each other. The people work too hard, and are boring because of it. They live in nice homes, and watch hockey on television. The cities are clean, or at least the one I saw was. The people do not like opera or ballet, and they have no famous writers. They are polite to one another, without ever being friendly. They keep their problems to themselves, and don't know how to laugh properly."

"Really?"

"Yes, Ivan."

"It doesn't sound so good to me. But you liked it?"

"I don't know. Things were . . . complicated there."

Ivan looked away from her, as though some other thought had suddenly come to him. He closed his eyes for a moment. When he opened them next, he said, "Natasha, please, my little Bing cherry. Don't forget your school books."

The family grew tired of Anna's all-day-and-night sleeping. The twins, who had been so solicitous at first, started barging into the room to look for school books or clothes, or to have twice-daily arguments about the things brothers and sisters fight over. Katya and Yuri began to spend more time in the refuge of their bedroom, emerging only to work, or eat meals, or go to the one, tiny bathroom. Anna's mother began to complain loudly to anyone who would listen—"Ahhhhh, Katya [or Yuri, or Ivan, or for that matter Olga, the neighbour with whom she often had coffee], I am kicked all night long by a pair of thirteen-year-olds, both of whom are going crazy with hormones and after-school beer drinking . . ."

While Anna heard this, and wished she could do something about it, she felt the sort of exhaustion that harries the mind and makes the muscles feel tender. She continued to sleep, and have nightmares, and occasionally eat in the small, moonlit kitchen. One morning her mother rushed into the twins' room, wearing her work blouse and newly applied lipstick.

"Get up!" she hissed. "Get up!"

"What is it, Mother?"

"You can't keep doing this!"

"Mother, please, I am tired."

"Always, always, you are tired. You have to get up and get a job or go back to school or something. I'm tired of watching you wallow. I'm sorry, but we all are. Okay, okay, so things didn't work out with your Canadian—I am sorry, I really am, but it doesn't mean you can feel sorry for yourself forever. I'm sorry, little bird, but this has to end and it has to end now."

For no reason she could think of, Anna opened her mouth and said in a whisper, "Ruslan's dead." Her mother looked stunned, and Anna was glad that she said it.

"How?"

"A car crash," she said. "That car of his—it was always a death trap."

Paulina approached. "How do you know this?"

"I called his uncle."

"Why did you call?"

"I still had things there I wanted to pick up."

Paulina sat on the bed and looked at her daughter. "Life," she said, "has not been easy for you, these past couple of months." She then reached out and brushed a lock of Anna's hair away from her forehead. As she did this, Anna again had her memory: her father, late at night, dressed in a blue athlete's track suit, his left wrist adorned with a platinum Rolex, his muscles still big from years of weightlifting, doing the exact same thing to her. It was their little ritual, performed every evening—stroking her hair, kissing her forehead, saying, "Tomorrow, little beauty, will come to you quickly," Anna never realizing that one night he would leave for work and disappear into thin air.

Two hours later, Anna forced herself to get up, take a shower, get dressed, and put on her makeup. She then took the train into the city and went to the employment office near Ploschad Voostaniya. She entered a room filled with beautiful young women in heels and tight dresses, all waiting for interviews with one of the counsellors. Anna took a number and sat beside a willowy girl who looked like the tennis star Maria Sharapova (albeit with stiletto heels and a shirt tight as cling wrap). Anna tried to read a magazine and found that she couldn't; she kept glancing at the woman beside her, all the while thinking, *Now she's the type who gets work in Russia.* Anna waited, and waited, and then left. On the street, she found a kiosk where the owner was distracted by that day's newspaper.

The weather turned warmer. She spent the next week roaming St. Petersburg's neighbourhoods and parks, trying to reconnect with the city she had once found so lovely. She couldn't: behind every archway and shadow she saw the souls of dead Chechens. Often she'd stop, and turn around suddenly, certain that someone had called to her. Resting on a bench, she would watch young men and women walk by her talking, and she would think: *How can you carry on? How, when there are dark forces at work in this Unreal metropolis?* She contacted none of her old friends or classmates, though she knew sooner or later she'd run into one of them. Occasionally she found herself thinking of Hank Wallins; he was such a sad man, and she'd made him sadder. At night, she'd go home and eat a meal cooked by Katya. The twins took back their room, and Anna slept next to her mother. It was like before she had left, though this time they were surrounded by family instead of drunk *communalka* neighbours. While this should have made her feel better, it didn't; she started stealing every day, her body on the verge of complete disappearance.

And then, on a night in which the lights in the apartment had been off for an hour, and Anna was lying awake next to her mother, Yuri suddenly flicked on all the lights and yelled, "Get up, get up, Ivan's gone missing!"

She pulled on jeans and a sweater. Sasha and Tanya emerged, having done the same. Soon, all of them were dressed in their coats and running down flights of stairs, Yuri calling out, "Ivan! Ivan!" in case his old father was still in the building. They stopped for a moment in the building's graffiti-scrawled lobby before heading outside across a wide, snowy car lot. For a moment they paused at the edge of the thin, white pine forest, and then headed into woods criss-crossed with small trails.

"Spread out," Yuri yelled. "Spread out, this shouldn't take long."

Anna walked along with her young cousin Tanya, who was sulkily chewing gum while looking down at her footfalls. "This always happens," she complained. "They always find him after a few minutes. They don't even *need* me. Tomorrow I'll be tired for school!"

The forest was littered with bottles and crack pipes and left-behind condoms. The air was still and polar; with each breath her lungs cooled. "Ivan!" Anna called. "Ivan! Ivan!" When she heard no answer, she continued walking forward, her niece right behind her and resentfully silent. Anna kept her head down; though the woods were lit by the light of a full moon, she was worried she might trip in the shadows. And if she wasn't exactly paying attention to where she was going, it hardly mattered, for the forest was small and Tanya knew every inch of it—she often cut through it to reach a friend in the next block. So Anna kept walking and calling and feeling sorry for Yuri—he was a good man, and he treated all of them nicely, and he didn't deserve to be burdened with Ivan. Suddenly she noticed she could no longer hear Tanya's boots crunching behind her. She turned, and saw nothing but bare trees and shadow and the floor of the forest.

"Tanya?" she called. When no one responded, she yelled, "Ivan!" in a voice showing the first signs of worry. She stopped, and listened, and heard only the shifting of wind in trees sparse and swaying. "TANYA!" she hollered, this time feeling stupid.

There were pines and cold earth and noises all around her. She looked in every direction, and when her heart began to pound, she said out loud, "Stop it, *dyevushka*." She breathed, and breathed deeply. It was only a matter of catching her breath, and keeping her head, and finding which way would lead her out. Yet each path was winding, and every few feet would branch into two or more paths that, too, were curving and in every way going. And the shadows—they were sage-coloured and breathing and they folded around her. She kept walking, her heart beating madly, hoping she would stumble upon Yuri, or Katya, or her bedraggled mother.

She spotted a diffused light, far off in a clearing. She went toward it, the light taking on a hue that was the slightest bit yellow. It too was difficult to reach: all of the paths seemed to run around it or simply head off in a different direction. She finally found one that led her close enough to see that the light was shining from a tent made of canvas. City folk, she figured, who'd lost the use of their dacha. She looked once again for a way that led to it. There was none. She inhaled once or twice, and decided to leave the safety of the footpaths. She trampled over mushrooms and around saplings and over fallen, gnarled branches; twigs scratched at her face and threatened her vision. As she approached, she could hear a buzzing noise coming from inside the tent walls. This confused her; it was now curiosity, more than desperation, that kept her thrashing forward.

She stopped outside of the tent.

"Hello?" she called.

The buzzing grew louder, and she noticed a strange scent, like meat being charred over the heat of a fire.

"Hello?" she half yelled, thinking that whoever was in there was cooking up something that smelled vaguely off-putting. "Hello!?"

Again there was only the buzzing, and the scent of food burning. For a moment Anna thought about leaving; she looked in all directions, and felt trapped by the forest. She tried to knock on the tent flap, and found this was useless. With a quick, shallow breath she threw back the rough flap.

She gasped, yes she did, her eyes blazing with horror.

She saw a man wearing a bandolier, aviator sunglasses, and the sleeveless khaki shirt of a soldier for hire. In his hand was some sort of skin-searing flesh wand, and he was using it to burn a faceless cadaver. He looked up, smiled, and said, "*Dyevushka!* What took you? I have been here waiting *for* you!"

Anna awoke and bolted upright, trembling all over. Tears fell from her cheeks and dampened the bedspread. She looked at her mother, whose stress lines seemed to soften when she was sleeping. For no reason she could think of, Anna touched the older woman's hair and said, "I'm sorry, *mamochka*, for being so crazy."

The next morning, after everyone but Katya had left the apartment, she showered and dressed in her best clothes. Katya caught her as she emerged from the washroom.

"Anya!" she said. "Do you have a job interview today?"

"Yes," she lied.

"But what for? What kind of job?"

"It's nothing, Tatya. Just an office job till school starts up in the fall."

"But that's wonderful!"

"No, no, I won't get it, don't get excited."

"Still, Anya, after only looking for one week, it's good to have an interview already. Only you may want to put on a little makeup, you look like maybe you didn't sleep well last night."

Anna, who felt weak from both her dreams and my growing inside her, shivered as she walked through the cold winter weather. Forty-five minutes and two train rides later, she arrived at the Church of the Saviour on Spilled Blood, where Alexander II had been killed as a thanks for serf-freeing. She showed her student card and got in for nothing. Inside, there was only a handful of penitents, babushkas, and muttering Old Believers. The air was heavy and dank, and her footfalls made echoes. After a bit of wandering she found a Saint Onuphrius icon, set into a recess near the right of the pulpit.

She fell to her knees and said precisely the following:

"Please, Onuphrius, I have never before felt so lost, or so tired, or so disgusted with myself. If somebody of your holy stature could give me some guidance, or perhaps even the slightest clue of what it is I should be doing, I would be most thankful and appreciative and I would follow your advice to the letter."

Now. Little one. You can choose not to believe what then happened. Or, you can attribute it to a moment of depressive psychosis, or a *dyevushka*'s fertile imagination, or the religious experiences that occur to those who are troubled. *Or,* you can accept that miracles do happen—that dead people talk, that love conquers sorrow, that a man like Hank Wallins could over subway tracks hover. You can simply accept that Onuphrius, the patron saint of wandering the desert—of packing up and buggering off every time things grew stressful—could look down at poor Anna and say to her clearly: "Take it from me, my supplicating rabbit. The politicians are corrupt here, criminals run everything, and when water pipes break in the winter, nobody bothers to fix them. Old people die like dogs in the street, clutching to their last sprig of window-box parsley, and for a young woman like yourself to get ahead she has to either marry a drunkard with bad teeth and connections, or dress like a call girl and show her midriff in winter. And don't even get me started on Putin, that karate-practising fascist. So do yourself a favour, and get the hell out of this country."

She thanked him and rose slowly, surprised by the relief his answer had brought her. She then went to Nevsky. As always, it was swarming with people, thousands and thousands, as if the whole city had fled cramped, dark apartments. It was warmer that day and light snowflakes were falling. Around she looked calmly, realizing she would miss not only its buildings but those who'd survived here, for if a city's story is created, it is created by its people.

And so, she stood watching, amused and besotted. Oh yes—she could see them in doorways, and on benches, and on the cool *prospekt* striding. She saw shoppers and office workers, going about normal business. She saw tomcats and stray dogs and kind, smiling midgets. She saw Paris Hilton–like "students" winking at male tourists. She saw bustier-wearing angels and fresh-out-of-jail misfits; Ural Mash heavies and gun-toting athletes; tattooed *businezmeni* and FSB agents. She saw tomcats and mongrels and members of pro-Putin youth groups; zipper-scarred fall guys and oligarch patsies; sickos and saints and do-gooding weirdos. She saw yarmulke wearers and livid Islamists; jackbooted skinheads with teeth-baring pit bulls; vixens and bosses and doomed U-boat commanders; crime lords and virgins and virally infected sex workers. She saw handout-seeking saviours and drug-addicted young mothers; press barons and models and jailed Yukos chairmen;

nervous Koreans and in-fear Nigerians; lovers and haters and porn movie directors. She saw drunkards and teetotallers and solvent inhalers; giants and endomorphs and kids wearing nose rings; sex-crazy preachers and radiated Belarusians; sopranos and violinists and lesbian pop duos; chess masters and physicists and long-limbed tennis wonders; mystics and magicians and those who flagellated themselves with birch sapling branches; metalheads and b-boys and flannel shirt–wearing rockers; kitten sellers and kiosk vendors and drug peddlers whispering, *Hey you, hey you, would you buy some green hashish?;* engineers and film stars and ruby-eyed fixers; jesters and servants and plutonium dealers; gem thieves and Gnostics and judo-practising fascists; jackals and thinkers and stoned, dead-eyed soldiers . . . oh yes yes yes, she saw club-footed wife beaters and black market corpse dealers and swirling-gas politicians and motion-sick travellers and on-the-make cosmeticians and beer-drinking children and—believe it or not—those who still yearned for Stalin and the vast college campus that had once been Mother Russia.

And Anna, our Anya, our near-pretty and cross-eyed and *vor*-blooded and (oh yes *and*) unknowingly pregnant *mamochka* . . . well.

She felt a love in her heart for every one *of* them.

A week later, she stuffed the last of her money inside of a bra which, despite her weight loss, was growing mysteriously tighter. She then boarded the same coffee-scented airplane and wrinkled her nose through the same Moscow transfer and the same pelmeni dinner. She slept through the same Moscow crime flicks and awoke to the same light of a moon that was orange and twinkling. She then poked at the same hardened rolls served with coffee and quince jam and, with her stomach in turmoil, she landed in the city of good plumbing, clean air, and citizens so polite they smiled at just about anything.

Hank was on his porch, in his parka and toque, replacing a board in the railing. When he heard steps, he looked up, his expression turning to a mix of disbelief, and startled joy, and the fear caused by getting the unlikeliest of wishes.

"You've lost weight."

"Yes, Hank."

He gestured at his house. "I'm selling," he told her. "I don't have a pot to piss in. That's the gist of it, right there. Cards on the table."

She looked at him curiously. "You not having pit in which to piss?"

"A pot. Not a pit. A *pot*. And I don't."

"Perhaps is expression? Meaning you do not have much money?"

"Yeah. It is."

There was a pause.

"How," he asked, "is your brother?"

"Hank. I do not have brother."

"Yes. I know."

"You do?"

"Yes."

"And yet you still to me giving money?"

"Looks that way."

"Hank," Anna said. "You are truly, truly strange man." Her throat seized with emotion, and her face burned with the heat caused by Hank's kindness—it was a heat she'd never known, and which felt to her wondrous. When she smiled, she smiled warmly, as if her soul were a lantern. "I will help you," she told him. "Please let me."

Hank said nothing.

"Things . . . things they falling to shit in Russia."
"I'm sorry," he said, and went back to his hammering.

Over the next week, she earned her keep by finishing the job that she'd started. She painted, she hemmed curtains, she got on her hands and knees to fasten loosened floorboards. She fixed cracks in the ceiling, and plugged holes in the basement, so that the house wouldn't flood when all the snow melted. She turned up the heat, and made the small house a sauna, and took off her clothes even when Hank was near her. Over dinners, they talked, as though for the first time; though neither knew why, the walls between them were gradually toppling. Then, on a Friday night in which her skin felt warm and pulsing, and she craved nothing more than a feeling of safety, she rose from her bed and snuck down the hallway. Slowly, she opened Hank's door. As she tiptoed toward him, she could tell he wasn't sleeping.

Lifting the blankets, she slipped in beside him.

"I am sorry," she said. "But I must know you not hating me."

Hank wriggled his body close to her. His hands touched her face, and his skin pressed hers in a way that was lovely. Then, to make the act of love pleasing, they both started size-changing—Anna grew larger, and Hank he grew smaller, until their bodies fit together like spoons in a drawer. She kissed him, feeling at first like a guilt-ridden sister. This guilt lasted a second before changing into something that was solemn and grateful. Her mouth then grew hungry, having not eaten for ages. Her fingers stroked a back that was light pink and freckled. Their bodies writhed to the tones of a white noise generator. Hank closed his eyes and, for the first time in eight years, kissed a woman while not thinking of Martine.

THE CULPRITS

That's when it happened. There came the presence of God and his best friend the Devil. There was the touching of flesh, and the cupping of shoulders, and the bucking of hips toward unknown territory. Oh yes—the culprit was need, and it raged in both *of* them. And while it was nothing compared to the mad ruttings Anna had once known with Ruslan, she also knew that Ruslan existed no longer, his mind all but lost in some sad, lonely ether. She also had to admit that, on this evening, in this cold, far-off city, in this little room smelling of wonder and gratitude and flannel pyjamas . . . well.

It was more than enough, and that was saying something.

NINE

So that's it, then—boy meets girl, boy loses girl, boy gets girl back. Story over. Time for Moldovan champagne, Caspian fish eggs, and delirious lives lived happily forever. Were it only that easy. Were life only that accommodating. (Were life only as simple as a walk in a forest!) Remember: this is not my story, or your story, or the story of two innocents who got caught up in something. Oh no, this is the story of Tushino, and the bombs that went off there.

Little one.

There is still terror to come, in the homeland of Anna.

In the meantime, strangers were traipsing through the small house on Craven—all of them couples with a baby in a blue Peg Perego. The type, *seestra,* who claimed to love both the area's multicultural flair and the autumnal colours coating the walls of the living room. Thirty-six couples saw it the first day. Of these, a good dozen lingered, the father checking in the basement for cracks in the foundation, the mother in Hank's office, picturing new blinds and a change table from Nestings.

The agent handed out cups of mulled cider while sibilantly making claims that were more or less truthful. Hank, to make himself scarce, was out buying new jeans. That left *mamochka*—who, as the open house wore on, walked down the street to the nearest Shoppers Drug Mart, where she bought a pregnancy test, a bottle of Tylenol, and, just in case, a paperback copy of *What to Expect When You're Expecting*. She returned as the last of the couples were leaving. In the home's sudden quiet, she went to the bathroom and sat on the toilet. Her hands were shaking as she wrestled with plastic. She then held the test underneath her and directed a stream of pee on it.

When Hank returned, toting a bag from Mark's Work Wearhouse, he was stopped dead by the expression on her face: part solemn, part delighted, part afraid of what he might have to say on the matter. She got off the sofa and went over to him. They both stood for a moment, looking at each other.

"Hank," she said. "We going to have baby."

Hank then gained his own odd expression: part joy, part fear, and part suspicion that maybe, *maybe*, this was just another con that they practised in Russia. She sensed his trepidation. "Please, Hank. Say to me something. Say to me you are happy."

A long time transpired. Inside, I flip-flopped, and felt mirthful about what was going to happen. (My omniscience, at times, does come in handy.) *Hhhay-pee*, Hank thought. *I love the way that she says that*. At first his smile was weak, like something unpractised and a little bit perilous. But then it grew, slowly brightening the room like a ray of white sunlight. Anna beamed too; it was the first time she'd ever seen him so joyful. Inside her I performed an in vitro cartwheel—it is the job of a son to make his father figure feel merry.

"Hank? You are pleased?"

His eyes glistened with the thought of a life with direction. "Yes," he croaked. "I am."

"You are, mmmmm, how you saying . . . *bloody* pleased?"

"Yes," he said, grinning. "I'm bloody pleased. And I wanna get married."

Two weeks later, after a breakfast of eggs and orange blossoms at the downtown Sheraton, the two traversed the open-air plaza that fronted the City Hall complex. Twenty minutes later, they stood before a Justice of the Peace. Hank wore a suit he'd purchased at a Harry Rosen sell-off. *Mamochka,* of course, looked just shy of beautiful, in a cream-coloured dress that showed off her slight thickening.

And their witness? Their testifier before God? He arrived late, huffing and puffing, hair tamped down to one side, saying, *Forgive me, Hank, forgive me. I got a little bit held up. Now come on, brother, let's get you married.*

The ceremony started. The Justice of the Peace was a young woman with nice hair, who had them both swear they weren't already married. When that was over, she got to the good part.

"I do," said Hank.

"I do," said our Anna.

They kissed. The Justice of the Peace grinned. Manuel yelled, "Hurray!" and threw both his arms upward.

Hank and Anna looked at each other, glimpsing a future in which they'd never be parted.

So.

They were young (or in Hank's case, youngish), married, with a baby on the way. Anna grew quickly, thanks to yours truly. By three months she was bloated, and by four was beginning to irrepressibly thicken. For this Hank felt just a little bit guilty. *He,* he confessed, had weighed eleven pounds and change on the day of his own birth. "Thank God," replied Anna, "they have strong drugs to give me."

The house sold easily, for much more than Hank had paid for it. "Anya," he told her on the night they took offers, "you've more than repaid the money I gave you." And Anna, despite the pleasure this brought her, could only burp into her hand and look grossly dyspeptic. Despite her new happiness, things weren't easy for her. She suffered from gout and spasms and bad nighttime cramping; from mood swings and thinning hair and digital tingling; from a pregnancy cough that left her throat ravaged, a craving for sardines mashed with cold turnips, *and,* on nights in which she awoke feeling startled, a feeling that some new tragedy was about to befall her. She got bigger and bigger. Only an ultrasound convinced her I was not sharing quarters.

"Just wait," her ob-gyn told her while smiling. "You'll soon start to feel better."

Which she did; her ailments receded around the time the bulge in her middle began to draw glances from strangers. Her only symptoms *now* were the kicks I dispensed whenever she stopped moving. "Babies," said *What to Expect When You're Expecting,* "are often calmed by the rocking that comes when the mother is in motion." This was an understatement. Whenever Anna failed to provide me with motion, I thrashed and flailed and behaved like a gymnast. In other words: I kept her awake. She didn't mind, or at least she didn't mind greatly. To pass all those hours, she paced the living room while knitting—misshapen boots, droopy-collared buntings, sweaters that sagged where the arms met the body. Hank, meanwhile, did the things done by fathers—he shopped for strollers and cribs, he bought checkered Lamaze toys, he told

Anna she was beautiful when, on one oddball morning, she awoke stricken with acne.

The day arrived when they were to move back to the building Hank had once lived in. It was the third week of May, and a bank of humid air squatted on the city like an overweight bully. Far off, in the east, the sun cast a weak orange glow—the towers downtown looked gauzy and saffron, and the sides of the houses looked caught in a half-light. They were on the porch drinking coffee. Vapour coiled from their mugs and hung in the air like the webs of two spiders. Everything was quiet. The neighbourhood kids were still dreaming, and the greasy spoons along Queen Street were not yet serving breakfast. Hank and Anna sipped without talking, and listened as the street came alive slowly. They heard mothers yelling, radios being turned on, and the low coughing rattle of cars old and dented.

The movers arrived around nine. They were all from Newfoundland. Two were tall, with round, hulking shoulders. The third, meanwhile, made up for his lack of size by being all the more intense—he cursed and he growled, and his forearms were kelpy with tattoos acquired in prison. Whenever he lifted anything that weighed more than a toaster, the veins in his forearms plumped up and turned rope-like.

Over the next couple of hours, they loaded Hank and Anna's possessions into the truck that the movers had backed into the front yard. Hank and *mamochka* helped, though mostly with smaller items—Hank's ankle still had a tendency to become painful, particularly when stressed by hard work or fast walking, and Anna's girth made lifting and bending a problem.

After the truck was loaded, Hank called a taxi. Within a half-hour they had all rendezvoused in front of the old building on Wellesley. Here the traffic was thicker, and the day's heat had risen. Hank's shirt was sticking to his skin, and a sheen had come up on Anna's pale forehead. The movers, meanwhile, were beginning to give off a scent faintly goatlike. Still—within minutes they were hauling up chairs, lamps, a fake wood kitchen table, a sofa as lumpy as overcooked oatmeal, a desk filled with papers that Anna had once pored over, and the mattress that Hank and *mamochka* thought I'd been conceived on. The only thing hindering their progress was the building's freight elevator, which was running even slower that morning than usual. This prompted the lead mover to pound his fists against the doors and yell, "Fer chrissakes would you hurry the fuck up!"

When they were done, the furniture had all been dropped more or less where Anna wanted, and the boxes had been stacked into piles high and teetering. Hank paid them and they left, leaving Hank and Anna alone in their new home.

They sat on the sofa, their thoughts emitting a faint insect buzzing: life, they considered, had a way of coming full circle, thereby offering clues of its mystical nature. And while this thought wasn't particularly earth-shattering, it was enough for a while, after all that had happened.

"Okay, rabbit," Anna said, attempting to heave herself forward. She failed to gain altitude until Hank firmly pushed against the curve of her backbone. This worked. She stretched and yawned, her shirt revealing a white, ballooned belly. "Okay, *malchik*. I am having long and cool shower. I am hot as, mmmmmmmm, how you saying? Hot pavement? In the hot state of Georgia? By the way, sweet one, I would much like it for you to come with me . . ."

"In a minute," Hank said, amazed by how proud, and how frightened, he felt at that moment. To punctuate this thought, he slapped the cushion beside him; a cloud of dust drifted into the air slowly. He coughed, and heard something. It was Anna, his Anya, like a child, really, singing under a rain of cool water. He looked around the apartment, his eyes damp and blinking. He couldn't help but question how all the moments of his life had turned into *this* one, with not a thing to his name but a young Russian who loved him.

(And me, oh yes *me,* inside of her writhing.)

Hank rose. He moved around boxes, careful not to stub his toe, or topple a lamp, or kick over plants that were brown-leafed and drooping. He opened the bathroom door and stepped inside slowly. The room was filled with a cool mist. To *mamochka*'s soft singing he took off his clothing. This wasn't easy: the bathroom was small, and his ankle had a habit of playing tricks on him. He sat on the toilet while removing his trousers. He rose to unbutton his shirt and step into the shower. This startled Anna, who had been busy singing Viktor Tsoi love songs. She jumped, and then laughed at the way nerves controlled so much of her behaviour.

She smiled, and looked at him. Her hands reached up and held pink, sloping shoulders. She looked through a right eye that faced more or less forward and a left eye that pointed about fifteen degrees inward. "Okay, boy," she uttered. "Big plans. They are what I having for this place. Maybe some paint, maybe some wallpaper. But whole house? *Pluh,* was too much. Back home, as you know, everybody they live in apartments so tiny you can barely breathe . . ."

She rose up on tiptoes and placed her lips softly against his; a river of water coursed between their two bodies. He started washing her with a cloth that was orange and soapy. He attended to her back, her neck, and her protuberant stomach. He then moved to her breasts, which were blue-veined and firm and as bulbous as softballs. Here he lingered; her nipples grew as wide as asparagus. Soon, Hank's warm, soapy washing turned into something that had nothing to do with cleanliness. Anna swayed, and closed her

THE CULPRITS

eyes, and to her Hank murmured, "Okay, rabbit, okay, *malchik*, let us leaving this shower and, mmmmmm, how it is you say? Christen our new palace?"

She turned off the water and stepped out from the shower. A trailing of drips led toward the lone bedroom. Hank followed, his ears gently *ping*ing. He found her damp and nude and on his old mattress sitting.

"Come," she said, patting beside her. He sat. Anna smiled weakly, as if to comment on this joy that had cropped up between them. Fingertips trailed across skin hot and softened. Hank relaxed further, and his cochlear *ping*s turned to a warm, grateful *mmmmmmmmm*ing. Goosebumps rose. The hairs on arms and legs stiffened. An ache invaded parts of the body where an ache can feel lovely. Soon, pulses meshed and became a single, new energy. Because of Anna's condition, there was only one way to express their moving-day ardour. Hank held her at the place where a woman's body sweeps in from the hip bones, and they found a rhythm that was close to their hearts' unified beating. Meanwhile, I closed my salamander eyes and enjoyed this sweet rocking.

Ah yes. *Lovely*. Nothing pleases a child more than the affection that exists between those who care for him. When this tenderness is present, you don't care what they have done or what they're capable of doing. Trust me, the motion is like no other—it's a rocking and a stroking and an in vitro shiatsu, all into one rolled. It made me sleepy with joy. It made me foggy with promise. It made me forget my horrific envisioning. I yawned and writhed giddily as it all started building—this rhythmic back-and-forth jostling, this soothing and unmade-bed shaking, this brief and oh-so-pleasing sensation. Suddenly it stopped. All was stillness and warmth and minor-chord striking. Giggles replaced groans and the crack of forked lightning.

I heard Hank's voice, a croaking near whisper, try out three new words.

And Anna, who was by surprise taken, felt like laughing and crying and so, in the end, chose to do neither—she only lowered her head and whispered something that was not in any way a deception.

"Hank. I love you too."

A scent penetrated my cavern—a blending of tobacco, and perfume, and the musk caused by human carnality. Moments passed, and passed deliciously. *Mamochka* lay grinning. She rubbed the underside of her forearms, where the mattress knobs left button-shaped impressions.

"Look," she said, laughing. "Look at what you have done to me!"

"What?"

"*This.*"

"Jesus . . ." Hank said, and when his expression signalled that he really was worried—that he really believed he'd in some small way hurt her—she chortled and rubbed his head and said, "Do not worry, rabbit. I soon will recover."

They both rose, their nudity now the nudity of children. They looked through boxes labelled *Bedroom,* searching for linen. They then made their bed, Anna Verkoskova humming. A second after that, they were lying on sheets made of cotton, their chests rising and falling in a slow, blissful concert. Anna turned and rested the side of her face on a pink, fleshy shoulder. Her arm crossed Hank's chest, and her fingertips traced the French girl's striped sweater.

"My father," she said in a voice growing sleepy. "He too had many tattoos. They were green and all over his body. Is one of many things I remember about him." At this mention of family, Hank grew quiet; the silence of his boyhood came howling in his ears. "And I have told you, when I was little, he would talk about them—what they mean and what they, mmmmmm, *signify*? Yes? He would say: This one, *dyevushka*, it mean honour. And this one, it mean truth. And this one—oh, how I remember, it was big and ugly and all over his chest—he would say that this bird it mean freedom, which is something you had better be careful about. Free will, he would say, is like curse wrapped in chocolate. Liberty, he would say, is like evil coated in honey. Truth, he would say, is something that frightens." There was a pause. Hank still looked doleful. "He was strange man, my father. I did not know him for long."

"What'd he mean?"

"I *think* he mean that once you have choice, you have sin. That once you start living, you have to start lying. He used to say we *all* are guilty. Every one of us. Probably was some Russian thing."

"I suppose."

"You *have* to be Russian to say such things, yes? It make no sense to your ears, yes?"

"It does, sort of."

"It does?"

"Yeah. A little."

"Maybe you are turning Russian. And maybe I am turning Canadian, because I think these words they are, hmmmm, how do you say . . . bull crap?"

Hank gazed at the ceiling. "What happened to him?"

"Oh, well. Is old story. Is something that happens. He stayed out a lot, and one day he stayed out for good. I cried and I cried and I cried and still it did no good, which is lesson we all learn sooner or later. Some say he was *vor*, picked up by those who no longer needed his services. I don't know. He once was a sportsman, a, mmmmm, weightlifter, from Tambov. He was big man, like you are, Hank."

"What's a *vor*?"

"Is like thief. Only, is thief not like you have here. Is thief who is, mmmmm, *like,* proud to be that way. Who doesn't want to be any other way. It's like part of class system we have in Russia. It's like here, you have rich, middle, poor. At home, we have superrich, very poor, and those who say fuck it to everything, and these are *vors.* They seem to be all over and everywhere when democracy it came to St. Petersburg. They seem to come out of wood working, yes? I say this correctly? They work for the mobsters. They needed by gangsters. But then, kaboom, overnight, the mobsters become the new *businezmeni* and they no longer need *vors* to do their chores. But I don't know if is true my father was *vor.* I think they were ugly rumours, thought of by, mmmmmmm, crones. Yes, by crones, from our neighbourhood. My mother, she never speak of it. Of course, he *did* have many tattoos. They say this is sure sign . . ."

They continued talking, mostly about the things that young people discuss when they're expecting a family—where the baby will sleep, the colours of curtains, the pros and cons of disposable diapers.

"I hoping the baby is calm tonight," Anna said after a long, blissful silence.

"I hope so too," Hank sleepily answered. His thoughts were beginning to swirl. His breathing deepened, and his blood pressure lowered. Oh yes—he twitched, and sputtered, and through his nose lightly whistled, before beginning to snore like a congested bull terrier. *Mamochka* didn't care; she too was balancing on the knife-edge of dreaming. She struggled against it—she couldn't believe that love had so determinedly pursued her, only to track her down in this parquet-floored apartment. Maybe, she thought, that's what life is—the constant evolving of what can possibly happen.

After a time, she surrendered. Her limbs lost their rigidity. Her eyes drooped shut and rotated upward. All the functions of her body slowed—pulse, breathing, the rate at which her skin absorbed oxygen. Unlike Hank, who tossed and ground his teeth, Anna turned to a stone that was warmth-giving and supple. Her face glowed white with the ghost of near beauty.

And inside her? Inside our with-me-pregnant *mamochka*? Little one. I settled in, motionless and knowing, wishing only to please her. But then my omniscience ignited: I trembled, I winced, I felt a discomfort I wouldn't wish upon anybody. Without the motions of her body—movements that caused me to float gyroscopically within her—there was nothing to distract me. Without all that wonderful side-to-side sloshing, there was nothing to stop my prognostications from coming. (There was nothing to stop bombs falling on Tushino!) I tried, *seestra*, I promise: I turned my head, I thought about puppies and mushrooms and the skin-tight skating outfits of Irina Slutskaya. I prayed that my eyelids would turn into dark velvet curtains. For all the good it did me, I might as well have been whistling show tunes—I began to see things that had not as yet happened. Oh yes, they came to me, bloodied and awful, smoking and too real, until finally I was left with little or no option.

Even though it caused *mamochka* discomfort, I stirred with what little I had to stir with. Gently, I tried to create my own waves—my own in vitro frothings—so as to calm the omniscience I'd inherited from my DNA-altered *papochka*. When this failed, I felt the beginnings of panic. I took my huge head and pounded it against my own womb wall. I pulled my hands from my ears and slugged my own amnion. I took my Scottie dog–like tail and from side to side swept it, like a baby Godzilla wreaking carnage upon Tokyo—oh yes oh yes, I was light-standard toppling, and on low buildings stamping, and flinging Toyotas through air blackened by fires. I didn't care, for fear is the worst of all culprits. I chopped and I smashed and inside her I hollered. Only this time I went too far. I admit it. I'm too fiercely energetic, a trait that came from my skirt-chasing father.

Anna wakened and held herself, gasping. "Hank," she whispered. When she got no response, she elbowed his rib cage. He awoke to find her groaning and crying.

"Bloody hell," he blurted. "Is it the baby?"

She didn't answer; she was too busy sputtering and holding her stomach. Between her legs there was a sinister pool, bordering on black and soaking through bedsheets. He leapt up and dressed before scooping up Anna. He rushed from the apartment, leaving the front door wide open, the top sheet still hanging from his wife's writhing body. He reached the elevators and pressed the button with his elbow. It was eight o'clock in the evening, and I was aware of one thing and one damn thing only: the very fluid that succoured me, that brought me oxygen and nutrients and carbon dioxide, *that kept my marble-sized heart consistently beating,* was from my hideaway flowing. Hank knew this too; his French-girl tattoo was receiving a warm, bloody soaking.

The elevators grunted and wheezed and produced the discordant clank of rusted chains turning. From inside the shaft, Hank could hear pulleys and a motor's loud grinding. He waited and waited, growing more and more frantic. Having no idea that the elevator was just a floor and a half away from them, he came to the errant conclusion that it had chosen that moment—*goddamnit, goddamnit!*—to once again stop working. He so loudly cursed that *mamochka* took a moment to stop moaning and look at her husband. Her head then lolled back against Hank's tattooed forearm.

He trundled toward the stairwell, the ding of the elevator lost to *mamochka*'s loud bellows. They were on the sixteenth floor, and though Hank was a large man, he was also a fat man, and the fact that he smoked heavily didn't help him much either. Blood pounded in his temples, and a stabbing pain came to where he felt that his heart was. And his ears! His damn ears! In the stairwell's clammy silence, they erupted with clicks and with buzzes, with bags of glass breaking and small babies crying and, as always, that maddening underlay of *ping ping ping ping*ing. He made it down four floors, and then another, correctly understanding that his wife could be dying.

He started to feel dizzy, and his pin-pricking arms turned numb altogether. Ten seconds later, his peripheral vision started to blur and turn wavy. With the last strength he could muster, he lumbered out of the stairwell and onto the tenth floor. He stopped and leaned against a wall, panting. He was about to call out for help when the elevator doors opened and a pair of men in wigs, silver dresses, and sheer white lace stockings came out laughing, their destination a Judy Garland-athon about to start in suite 1011.

Their names were Jeff and Ronald, though on evenings like this they went by Lola and Bridget. They heard Anna's groans, which by this point were noticeably weakening. They turned, their mascara-caked eyes opened widely, and swung into action. First, Lola held open the doors of the now-waiting elevator. Bridget came running and swooped-up *mamochka* in arms muscled by daily Y workouts. They piled into the elevator, Hank gasping for air and covering both his ears. After one or two floors he started stroking Anna's damp hair and telling her that everything was going to be all right.

Which it was, actually. What they didn't realize was this: I'd splayed both my frog's legs, a move that blocked my passage so effectively it would've taken a team of oxen to yank me into this world. All outward signs, however, were to the contrary—Anna had grown silent, and Bridget's gown was messed with a burgundy discharge. When they burst from the building, Lola sprinted curb-ward and hailed a cab in the possession of a driver named Mohammed. He pulled over, and grimaced: not only was the woman who had hailed him a *man*, but there was a second one coming, this one carrying what looked like a cadaver. Before he could protest, they all piled in, followed by a wheezing, orange-haired fellow who had been struggling to keep up. Mohammed pulled away, hardly needing to be told where they would be going.

Anna lay across the laps of three men, two of whom were chewing on red, painted fingernails. She had grown cold and still.

"Oh well," she murmured.

"Shhhhhhhhhh," said Hank.

"Maybe we trying again, okay, rabbit?"

"Shhhhhhhhhhhhhhhh. Everything's okay."

"I suppose. The Russian soul is forged by suffering. Or so they always say."

"No, Anya, *Jesus*, shhhhhhhh."

"That, and our talent for dreaming, yes?"

She laughed darkly, and started to drip tears on top of Hank's lap. Seconds passed slowly. There was something in the way that Hank stroked her hair away from her crown—in the way he used his fat fingers so tenderly—that touched Lola and Bridget. Within a few moments their mascara started to moisten, making both of them look a little Halloween-ish.

Mohammed turned onto the circular driveway leading to Wellesley General Emergency. Hank bundled up Anna. Lola and Bridget ran ahead, only to be stopped by a security guard who assumed that the two men, by virtue of their appearance, were suffering from drug trips that had turned into nightmares. His attention was diverted, however, when he spotted Hank and *mamochka*, the latter now unconscious and entirely pallid. Everyone came running: doctors and nurses, interns and orderlies, even a religious fanatic who—for no other reason than it was a late Friday evening—had been hiding behind a plastic-leaf ficus, shaking branches and quoting the Bible in a voice thin and hollow. Within moments Anna was on a gurney, an oxygen mask over her mouth and both eyelids spasming. They rushed her away. Hank was led to a corner by a sandy-haired doctor, where they stood next to the glow of a machine serving coffee.

"It's her first child?"

"Yes."

"And is there a history of miscarriages in her family?"

"I dunno. She's from Russia."

"I'm sorry?"

"She's Russian. She's from Russia. I'm not . . . Jesus, I *dunno*."

The doctor scribbled, his brow furrowed. "How has the pregnancy been?"

"Lousy. The baby kicks like a horse."

"That's common enough."

"No, I mean he *kicks*. He kicks her *hard*."

"How about dizziness?"

"Yes."

"Gout?"

"Yes."

"Anemia?"

"I don't think so."

"Vomiting?"

"No, not really. That's the one thing she didn't really have."

"Hypertension?"

"Yes, a little. Listen, doctor, will she—"

"Diabetes, migraines, cramping?"

"No, yes, yes."

"Any bleeding?"

"Any *bleeding*? Christ, did ya *see* her?!"

The doctor inhaled slowly. "No, I mean before tonight."

"A little. Here and there. Jesus, doctor, is she gonna be all right?"

"Has she taken any drugs today?"

"No."

"Nothing? Aspirin, cough medicine?"

"No."

"Street drugs?"

"Christ, no."

"Is there anything that might have caused this? Any falls? Did she work excessively hard?"

(*There.* You can see it as well as I do—the tilt of Hank's head, the falling of his shoulders, the automatic belief that he was the culprit.)

"We moved," he said in a voice almost whispering.

"You moved?"

"Yes."

"You mean . . . your place of residence? Today?"

Hank nodded. "There was . . . lifting."

Hank followed the young doctor down a fluorescent-lit hallway. They manoeuvred past corner after corner before arriving in a room filled with anxious people all waiting.

"You can wait here," said the doctor.

Hank nodded, and squeezed into a chair between a wall and an old woman. The room was full and smelled of over-bleached cotton. At some point the old woman left, and it didn't at all register that the seat beside Hank was empty. Sometime after that, the doctor reappeared. Hank studied the man's eyes, looking for the barest hint of promise.

The doctor said something in a voice sounding tired.

"Pardon me?"

"Everything's fine."

"Really?"

"Yes, Mr. Wallins. Fine."

Hank breathed deeply. "Really?" is all he kept saying. *"Really, really, really . . ."*

"We're fairly sure that a portion of the placenta came away from the wall of the uterus. Our primary objective was to stem the bleeding. We've given Anna a unit of whole blood and something to help her sleep. But the baby's heartbeat is good and strong—we had no trouble picking it up with a stethoscope. What we'd like to do is confirm our suspicions, and determine the extent of the tearing. I've got her scheduled for an ultrasound in the morning, when the department opens."

"So she's going to be all right?"

"She might have to take it pretty easy until she's due. But yes, essentially, she's fine. If her previa is really bad, she'll have to stay in the hospital to avoid movement. But that's only in extreme cases. What's more likely is that, when she's ready to have the baby, she might have to opt for a Caesarean. But yes, she's fine."

"Totally fine?"

"Mr. Wallins," the doctor said with a half grin, "would you like to see her?"

There was a single soft light, and a machine somewhere clinking. On the far side was a bed, and in that bed Anna lay sleeping. He walked up and leaned over. Her chest rose and fell softly, her breath coming in slow, measured whispers. He kissed her cool forehead and rested a hand on her belly.

This touch I felt—I felt its warmth, its need, its tentative pressure. It was, I knew, the hand of a man who would love me for each moment of my short life. I knew this for certain. My little heart pounded, and blood through my veins gurgled hotly. To show poor Hank that I wanted nothing more than what every boy wants—the love of a father—I punched the top of the cavern with a fist raised in triumph. It was my own way of saying, *I'm here! Your little Canadian-born Russian is alive and kicking! I am wishing to taste the sweetness of life! Every iota of me craves maple syrup and pelmeni, back bacon and vodka, Beaver Tails and shashlik and snowflakes and chess and body-banging ice hockey . . . oh yes, oh yes, my ersatz papochka, it's me, it's me, wishing to whole-heartedly sample all of life's magic!*

His hand popped off Anna's belly as if singed by a fire. He smiled, but for one second only—tears sprang into his eyes, for the first time he could remember. They were tears of love and pain, of gratitude and hope, and they kept right on coming, a veritable deluge, Hank bending over and resting his face against his wife's mounded stomach. And oh, how it felt good, his tears tapping my home like a rain warm and salted. He couldn't stop. He just couldn't. His chest heaved; his face turned red and puffy. This went on and on, until the pain that lived inside him had been just a little expended.

He started. Anna's eyes were wide open. Because she had always suspected that the soul of her Canadian was marred by some misery, she blinked, and smiled, and looked at him sadly. "So," she said weakly, "we still to have bright, bouncing baby, yes, Hank?"

He nodded.

"I am glad. This being-pregnant business—*pluh*, is for birds. It would be shameful to have nothing to show for it."

Hank squeezed her hand. "You have to take it easy."

"Taking it easy I can do. After the year we've had, is something I can do with pleasure."

"We'll be all right."

"Yes, rabbit. We will be all right. I would like to call him Mikhail, after my father. As for middle name, I would call him after you. Mikhail Henry Wallins. In Russia, they would call him Misha Henryevich. Yes, I like. It has, mmmmmm, nice ring. *Now*. Come and lie beside your poor wife and hold her hand. My head is foggy, and I feeling like I have been kicked by a horse."

Hank crawled into the small bed beside her. They linked fingers, and felt lucky. Much later, after they'd slept, her breakfast arrived; Anna pushed it away while sighing loudly. "Rabbit," she said. "Please. Could you go and get me something eatable. A cruller, maybe, with strong tea?"

Hank nodded. He left the room and went down to the main floor. Outside the front entrance he had two cigarettes quickly. He returned with a pair of crullers and paper cups filled with hot, dark brown liquid. In Anna's raised bed they sat, chewing and talking of things in the future.

Anna said: "You know where I want to go, rabbit? Where I have dream of going since I was little?"

"No, Anya. Where?"

"*Norway*. Where they have those, mmmmmmm, how you saying in English? Those little, like, streams or rivers?"

"I dunno."

"Yes you do, rabbit. *Think*. Is like name of, mmmmm, popular car."

Hank grinned. "Fjords?"

"*Yes*. That is it! Fee-ords. Is very nice there, I think."

An orderly came and took away the untouched tray. A nurse also came, and escorted Hank and Anna to the ultrasound department.

The technician had frizzy hair, and freckles that were Hank-like. "Now," she said, "just lie down and relax."

Anna moved slowly, not wishing to dislodge me. Hank took the chair reserved for boyfriends and husbands.

"So," the technician said, "you had a little bleeding last night?"

Anna chuckled gravely, in that manner of Russians. "*Da*. You could say this."

"Well then. We'll just have a look and see what's what."

She lifted *mamochka*'s gown and started rubbing warmed jelly over the patient's stretched stomach. The technician smiled, and flicked switches and buttons. There was a patchwork of snow against a deep sea-green background. "Now," she said, "at this stage you might be able to tell what the sex is—so don't look if you don't want to know."

"Is okay," Anna said. "I already know is boy. I have feeling in my bones and I have had it for much time."

"Even better," said the technician. She rubbed a wand over Anna's skin in slow, measured circles. "You've already had an ultrasound, am I right?"

"A while ago. We could see nothing. The doctor said maybe the baby it was hiding."

"Well, that happens."

"The baby, I think, was still very small."

"Well, no chance of that *this* time."

The technician's voice trailed off, her attention diverted by the image that was forming on the screen. Hank and Anna looked on as well, blinking.

"Okay," said the woman, "we're in luck, we're going to get a pretty good . . ." Her hand stopped moving, and this froze the image. Oh yes—suddenly I was there, before the whole world embarrassed, a photograph in snow and green light and flickering diodes. Hank covered both ears without thinking. The technician head-swivelled and said, "I'm sure that it's . . ."

(*What?* I want to yell. *A mistake? An error? God's idea of eternal justice? Well?!?*)

Only *mamochka*, bless her heart, kept looking at me. She was my mother and nothing would stop her. The only sounds in the room were machine-made and beeping.

The good news was that Anna's in-her-bones feeling was correct. I was a boy like no other; my genitals were in place and noticeably dangling. The bad news, however, was that they could see all of me. They could see how I was formed. They could see the size of my head bone.

They could see, little one, how I *would* be.

Seestra.

Life, basically, is a kaleidoscope, continuously turning, the crystals in the lens all the moments that we have. Only with life the crystals aren't uniformly lovely. Oh no—some are glorious, most are neither here nor there, and some are so hideous they are best soon forgotten.

I was a snowy green picture on a TV-sized monitor. I was an accumulation of flecks, revealing the life inside Anna. I was an apparition, a spectre, a causer of one hell of a ruckus. Anna finally winced, and her eyes filled with moisture. Hank still smothered his ears while gazing straight at me. The technician was frozen, her wand tip on strike against an ointment-smeared belly. All three struggled to process the entity before them. In return, I wiggled and I waggled, my only real way of *Hello, out there!* saying.

Still. I could imagine some of the adjectives they were all trying to banish. Bulbous, for example. Protuberant, surely. Elephantine, probably, in the head bone department. Or, the worst of the lot—*fused*. I ask you—was there ever a word that sounded so judgmental? So accusingly pious? You almost had to laugh at how unfair all of this was. If I was this way, it was because nature (and N20) had teamed up to cause me.

The muscles in Anna's neck were distended. Hank and the technician heard an intake of breathing.

"Anya..." Hank started, his voice trailing to nothing.

(And what were you about to say, my red-haired semi-papa? That everything was okay? That everything was going to be *all right*?!?)

"Anna," the technician said, "there are many..." (Many *what*? Cure-alls? Remedies? Tinctures? Balms for what *I* was?) Her voice faltered. She put a hand on Anna's shoulder, which had started shaking.

When Hank tried to calm her, she swatted his hands and told him to leave her. This swatting turned to howling, and this howling turned to words that were high-pitched and piercing. "He is in pain!" she cried. "My baby is in pain! Somebody do something to help him..."

The technician bolted from the room. A doctor and nurse both hurried in. Anna arched her back, slapped the mattress, and yelled for someone to help her suffering baby. (She needn't have; it was only my ego that had taken a bruising.) Pills were placed in a cup white and little. Anna whimpered, and swallowed them with a glass of cool water. Slowly she calmed, her eyes halfway closing. When she was completely asleep, it was decided she would stay in the hospital for the rest of my gestation. From this moment on, *mamochka* was bed-bound, bathroom privileges only. This meant no hallway wanderings, no getting up to pray before Saint Onuphrius, no visiting the gift shop when she felt herself fading. Honestly—it would be as hellish for her as it was for yours truly.

A spare bed was found, and *mamochka* was moved to a room semi-private; one other patient was asleep behind a curtain. The light in the room was appropriately gloomy. Anna was unconscious, a fetal monitor stretched tightly around her. Hank approached the bed. He took one of her slight hands and stroked it. Here he stood for a moment, his skin shining palely.

"Anya," he said in a voice low and croaking. "I'm sorry, I am. Bloody hell, please forgive me."

As they waited for my arrival, Hank did all he could do to help the time pass for Anna. Together they watched television, propped side by side, a pale little hand inside a big one covered with freckles. He brought her books—her Pelevin, her Sorokin, her fast-paced and diverting Dashkova—and he went all the way to the Arbat, where he bought copies of *Izvestia, Kommersant,* and the Russian edition of *Vogue* magazine. He also bought her pelmeni and borscht, sticky cakes and blini, sausage and kebabs and salads tasting of dillweed. To wash these down, he smuggled in half-bottles of white wine, which he served in paper cups pulled from a dispenser. Oh yes—he spent all day with her, having taken an emergency leave from Quality Assurance.

"I love you," he now said often.

"I love you too," she said with a grin that looked tired. "Now, please, join me on this bed. I am hungry for some of your delicious shashlik . . ."

(Little one—what *passes* for humour between newlywed lovers.)

She had medicated ups and unmedicated downs. One moment she'd look fine, sitting up and watching *Survivor,* and the next she'd take her eyeglasses off and start unashamedly weeping. When this happened, Hank would hug her and say, "Shhhhhhh, Anya, shhhhhh. We'll get through this together."

Time mutated under the pressure of waiting. Here, in room 327 of Wellesley General, it was no longer measured in minutes and hours. Here, it came in the number of naps per day taken, or in meals barely poked at. It was measured in halting trips to the bathroom, Anya moving like an old woman who was worried about falling.

Each day, a nurse listened to my heartbeat (which was as strong as a drum, and a sign that wonders do happen). She also listened for uterine contractions; hearing nothing, she would smile, and say "Good" to *mamochka*. Every third or fourth day, a technician came for another ultrasound; whenever they spied me attempting to roll, or swish my bent legs, or bring a hand to my forehead ... well. There were sighs of relief, and words of encouragement offered. I, knowing this, timed my activities duly. It was a fine line I walked. It was finesse that I needed during *mamochka*'s bed-resting. If I moved too much—if I thrashed or started flailing—I put us both in grave danger. And *yet*. If I moved not at all, the visions started coming, lit up blood-red and soaring, like the flares used by drivers when on a lonely road stranded.

And then?

It was hello Tushino, it was hello outdoor rock concert, it was hello sunshine and hot weather and the bedlam that followed.

Anna was in her hospital room, resting. I had kicked a little that day, though no more than I'd had to. She was foggy-headed, and her lower body was swaddled in towels replaced hourly. Chinese whispers came from beyond her roommate's pulled curtain.

Hank was beside her. His eyelids were heavy, and he looked tired all over.

"Hey, *malchik*."

He took one of her hands.

"So," she said weakly. "We are to do what, now?"

Hank said what he thought was expected—what he imagined a strong character would say in the movies. "Everything's going to be all right."

"Oh no, rabbit. Is not true."

"Anya. Please."

"Oh yes, *malchik*. This is a real and not-going-away thing. The doctors, already they saying our baby's days will be numbered as soon as he take his first breath. They told to me this, rabbit. Can you believe? Can you believe saying something so cold?"

"Anya, the doctors, they—"

"They are what, rabbit? They are always wrong? They are in business to frighten people? They are *bastards*? Yes, of course, of course. Only not this time. You know this, rabbit. So once again I ask you. How we surviving this thing? We are not strong people, Hank. We were not blessed in this way. We were born fragile, you and I. We are people who grow ill with worry, and who spend our days fretting. So, again, how we preventing this from killing us?"

"We just do."

Hank took a deep breath and decided to spend not only his days but his nights right there with her.

Which he did. He went down to the gift shop near the hospital's entrance. He bought toothpaste, a toothbrush, and a kit used for shaving. When she wakened that night, he was right there beside her, on his chair dozing. She looked over at him. His face was tilted backward and his mouth partly open. Anna then smiled, for the first time in ages.

Later, he wakened. They played cribbage, and dominoes, and a Russian version of Parcheesi. They ate food taken out from Slavic cantinas. He brought in more wine, Hank saying *Cheers*! and Anna *Noz drofstnyy*! They watched more TV together, and he bought her a teddy which she hugged like a lifebuoy. He bathed her with sponges, and washed her hair in a basin. When she napped in the daytime, he stayed right beside her, reading a newspaper. At night, nurses found him struggling to sleep while sitting slumped over; they brought in a chair that folded into a twin-cushioned mattress. When Anna's roommate grumbled—why was *her* husband not allowed the same privileges?—the nurses silenced her with glares and grave, saddened gestures.

And then, late one night, Anna awoke to a clawing of worry. Slowly she sat up, pulling sheets off her. She felt a slow, growing weightlessness, as though there were nothing inside her. She swivelled, and slipped her feet into slippers. Beside her, in his bed, Hank wriggled and rolled over. She stood—frozen, breathless, her body still lightening—until he resumed his faint, pug-like snoring. She poked her head from the curtains. Her roommate was sleeping, chest rising and falling. In the dim light of the room Anna could see the woman's purse on the nightstand, not quite all the way zippered. *Mamochka* crept forward, on tiptoes advancing. She moved stealthily and silently, her hand slipping inside.

And oh, oh, the uplifting touch of a brown leather wallet! The energizing stroke of cool metal house keys! The restoring caress of Kleenex-brand tissue! The soul-lifting arias sung by things to be stolen! She settled on a tube of cherry red lipstick, which she took back to her nest like an oriole, hoarding. Sitting on her bed, she opened the tube and considered the colour—it was the deep red of apples, of stop signs, of fire trucks and billboards and a clown's bulbous nostrils. She then thought of another thing that was red—*blood flowing from her*—and as she did, her guilt rose inside her, quickly growing into a dislodging torrent. Sniffling, she rose, and put back the lipstick. Back in bed, she felt a sharp pain in her back, and she knew, yes she did, for her sins this was payment.

The pain stopped. A few minutes later it came back, feeling like a muscle beginning to spasm. Anna breathed, and thought, *It is happening*. She lay there, in silence, during her early contractions. An hour went by, and then another. When she began to feel like her muscles were tearing, she moaned and reached for Hank, who came awake blinking.

"Oh Jesus," he said in a way almost mournful.

Anna took quick, huffing breaths. Between them she muttered, "We will have a beautiful baby..."

Hank darted from the room. He stopped at the nurses' station, where he stuttered and pointed with a pink sausage finger. The nurse looked up and understood in an instant.

She strode into the room's twilight and pulled open the curtain. Anna had broken by then into a fine perspiration; her upper lip was damp with translucent droplets. The nurse took her pulse and placed the back of her hand on the patient's moist forehead. With the help of her watch, she measured the intervals between Anna's loud gaspings.

And then there were interns, lots and lots of them, running into the room like a herd of chased bison. This awakened Anna's roommate, who immediately asked what was happening. Nobody answered, and nobody needed to: the young Russian girl had gone into labour. They shifted Anna onto a gurney; she was moaning and weeping and clutching her stomach. They wheeled her to delivery, Hank hurrying along behind them. A doctor arrived, along with a trio of nurses.

Mamochka, in a fever, heard several voices.

A female one: *It's happening quickly.*

Another, inappropriately calm, saying: *There is some bleeding.*

A third voice, the doctor's, saying: *Breathe, Anna, breathe, everything's going to be all right.*

Meanwhile, in all the excitement, I struggled to stay calm and as still as I could manage. It didn't help. Anna cried out, her lips spanned by spittle. Her back arched again and her nose started running. Someone barked orders, and they all worked twice as quickly: syringes were filled, an IV inserted, and a fetal heart monitor was clipped to yours truly. An anesthesiologist came galloping from open-heart surgery. Another doctor arrived, this one older and grey-haired and sporting a knowing expression.

Anna's blood pressure had dropped, and the sheet under her abdomen had sprouted a large crimson puddle. This was bad news. The hour was nigh, and like a bad wolf upon me. Believe me—if I could have put it off, I would have, for with my omniscience I knew—I *knew*—that the beginning of my life would mark the start of its ending (and while this is true of everybody, it was particularly true in my case). But there was no point complaining. It was time to swallow my medicine and face the grim music—time to muster my courage and do what I had to. Besides, I had little say in the matter. Nature is the beast who decides, when you come right down to it, and already she was bearing down like a bastard. The walls of my cavern were rumbling. The floor was quivering and shaking and in figure eights twisting. Life, oh yes life, was caving in *on* me.

But.

Just when I was about to be spat into this world gasping cruelly, there was a break in all of this cataclysmic shaking. My rib cage spasmed. Sensing reprieve, I gasped for oxygenated liquid and futilely grabbed for my blue and green lifeline. Oh yes, I had changed my mind: I would do anything, *anything,* if it meant a few hours more in my warm place. (*That,* little one, is the hold life has on us. You think: just a little bit more, just a little bit more, and maybe its meaning will reveal itself to me.) But then, suddenly, the respite was over. There was a downward heave-hoing, and a rapid uncoiling of enraged, spasming muscles—my frog legs widened, my arms spread-eagled, my skin turned blue (or at least bluer than normal). None of this helped, not when time was the culprit and it had given out on me. It felt like I was being pulled down a chute, along with thick, swampy water. And let me tell you—it felt just like hell, this being-born business. With no other recourse, I began loudly squalling. I balled malformed hands and started screaming bloody murder. "I won't go!" I hollered to myself. "I refuse! I reject your deception-filled world! I will fight you full on, my little arms spread and both frog legs kicking!!!"

Quite a production, this. I was as coated with guilt as I was with thick mucus. Despite loving her with all my soul, I was giving *mamochka* a run for her money. She shuddered, and once again called for Hank to come save her. (But what could he do, beyond stroking her face and saying, *Breathe, Anya, deeply?*) Seeing her torment, the doctors slipped so many painkillers into Anna's epidural that, after a minute or two, she lost the ability to breathe by and for herself. No problem! They wheeled in two respirators, the big one for her and the smaller for you-know-who. Soon she was lolling and leg-spread and not in any way coherent.

Those fiends. Those ghouls. Those not-fighting-fair bastards. With *mamochka's* pulse now a slow thump-thump-thumping, they shrugged and produced just one more needle. You should have *seen* it: as long as a riding crop and every bit as subtle. And though needles like this don't really exist, I am the teller of this tale and you'll just have to accept it. Little one: *two fully grown hands were needed to use it*. They held it up spurting, and I started panicking. *Mamochka*, I hollered, don't just lie there! Or Hank! Henry Wallins! My father in spirit if not in seminal fluids! Don't just *stand* there, peering through fingers a little bit parted . . . do something, for Christ's sake! Use your heft! Throw some of those fists that are pink-fleshed and ham-sized! I love you like a father, goddamnit, so go ahead and save me and my puckered-skin bottom!

It did no good. The tip of the syringe touched the apex of belly. From within, I watched it all: flesh pricked by needle, blood on skin bubbling, a serum from their world into mine seeping. *Good,* someone said. For a while, all was peaceful. I tricked myself into thinking that the worst of it was over. But then—*Jesus*. Like a horse it came kicking. It took hold of my head and yanked madly at it. The rush was cyclonic, and far more than I could handle. And so, I gave in. To tell the truth, I was tired. I gave a last token holler—*Fuck you all!*—and, with an inhale, pointed my flippers and toes and hara-kiried myself toward a small slit of daylight. As I let go of all that was sacred (*life,* little one, this thing we call *living*!) my thoughts were not on *mamochka* or Hank or Tushino, or the way my brief existence would make everything all right.

Oh no no no.

My thoughts were on my real father, and how soon I would join him.

TEN

So. The main event. No looking away as things start to get ugly. No averting the eyes from all that is coming. No saying to yourself: *This is just a story made up by a child wanting attention.*

If only, little *seestra*.

If only.

Ruslan opened his eyes in darkness. It was the middle of the night. He sat. A thin slash of lamplight came from his small window, hitting Metallica's James Hetfield right at midsection.

Ruslan listened carefully, for his dream of the forest had not dissipated fully—he could still hear crickets and tree rustlings and from-the-tent screaming, along with all the other sounds that had come to his cold, earth-floored burrow. He held up his arms and saw burns, freshly smoking. His head and back ached with a Biblical fury.

He blinked.

He looked around.

The girl? he thought. *Where is she? The one with the crossed eyes?*

He rose and went to the storeroom beside his. He pushed the door open. Amidst a heap of old stereos, he saw a bed empty save for sheets and a pillow. *Not here,* he concluded, and he moved to Dadya's room, where the hallway opened into the repair shop. From outside, he listened; he heard snoring and rustlings and occasional mumbling.

Also he heard his own maddened giggling.

Dadya, he thought, *this city, it's funny, it was supposed to keep me safe . . . remember that, Dadya? Remember that's why they sent me from Dagestan? So I couldn't get in trouble with all the guns and the Arabs who were running around down there?*

Something startled him and his giggles turned to a sudden, rough panic. He took a deep breath and realized it was nothing: no OMON fighters, no *militsia* or FSB killers, just some market-street stirrings—leaves, perhaps, or a blowing milk carton. He calmed, put his boots on, and walked out through the wood door. Upon reaching the lane, he looked in both directions. The market was empty, and lit only by the occasional lamppost. He moved through pockets of shadow. The clack of his boots echoed off tin wood-stall facings. In the gloom he saw phantoms and wharf rats and smudgy-faced urchins. He reached the edge of Apraxin. The avenue, at this hour, looked black-topped and empty; he heard the occasional whine of passing car tires. One driver honked, thinking Ruslan a drunkard.

Still—he crossed the near-empty street without watching for traffic. Light fell on the Fontanka in a refracted shimmer. He began walking beside a low stone canal wall. He followed it along, past Nevsky and the Russian Museum, and when he reached the Summer Garden he turned and walked all the way back to where he had started. This took more than an hour. He stood on the bank wall and, for a moment, gazed at his ghostly reflection. Then he fell forward calmly, his face smacking first against chilly dark waters. His body followed. He sank a few feet, feeling nothing but coldness, and as he descended through gas-scented waters he amused himself by watching serpents and mermaids and the waterlogged corpses of mob hit-men victims. *I'm coming*, he thought, *I'm coming*, yet when his thin body was a foot from the bottom, the air in his lungs propelled his form upward. His body then rolled as he rose to the surface. Soon he was floating and up at stars looking. He stayed this way for a while, on small cold waves bobbing. He started to drift, blue-lipped and shaking, until he came to a rest against a concrete abutment. With each sloshing wave his face was washed with dark, dirty water.

In the eastern sky there were ribbons, light orange and shimmering.

He clambered onto land, and cut back through the market. Nobody stopped him. Even though he was dripping and shivering and talking to himself, nobody so much as looked at him, and he considered this a sign that his future, and what he planned to do with it, held promise. Still, he couldn't believe it. He threw insolent stares and got no reaction. He stole apples from fruit stalls and wasn't at all noticed. Then it came to him: he, Ruslan Bhaiev, was an apparition—as Unreal as the City he had escaped to. The only sign of his presence were wet, puddly footmarks. Oh yes—he was a ghost, a spook, an Apraxin Dvor spectre. (Irony of ironies—didn't they use the word *phantom* to describe Chechen fighters?) To test his new theory, he walked the Sadovaya: though it was filling with early morning cars and pedestrians and kiosk attendants, he was unnoticed. In fact, the crowds in front of him kept mysteriously parting. He reached Sennaya station; in a subway car packed full with people, no one seemed to notice that Ruslan was dripping black water, and filling the car with the scent of canal brine.

As they headed to the suburbs, far more commuters got off than got on. Soon he was sitting all alone, water pooling on his seat as he stared ahead blankly. He reached Veteranovsky Prospect and took a minibus farther, de-boarding in front of a crowded expressway.

This, he thought, *will be my last test* . . .

. . . and he took a step onto the highway, this time causing mayhem. Horns blared, drivers started shouting, cars screeched to a stop in clouds of burnt rubber. Ruslan looked ahead like a zombie, taking step after slow step, until his foot hit the curb of a median island. He tripped and fell forward, landing face down in crabgrass. Up he got, smiling—one more half to go and *he,* he would do it. His right foot met tarmac, as well as more screeches and honking and sudden car swervings. A Lada stopped just inches from him, the driver yelling, *What the hell are you doing, you goddamn* chorny zhopie*!?* Ruslan took no notice. He took a second and a third deliberate step forward. His foot touched the curb on the far side of the freeway. A hundred old buildings were lined up before him. He walked up and down until he found the correct one.

He went through the dark entrance. He adjusted to gloom, clammy air, and wall markings in Arabic. He trudged up concrete steps and walked down the hall filled with robed children playing. Here his presence was noted—the kids stopped to stare curiously as Ruslan walked past them. He knocked on the door of the al Qaeda hideout.

It was Khassan who answered. His eyes roamed Ruslan's damp body.

"I am here," Ruslan mumbled. "One of your soldiers."

Al Qaeda's newest recruit was given a duster, a can of coarse cleansing powder, a djellaba that felt soft on his shoulders, and—last but not least—a copy of the Quran with the passages concerning virgins highlighted with markers. Thusly equipped, he passed his days awaiting rapture. He cleaned, and tidied, and made bulging lamb sandwiches for visiting Wahhabis. When the local *militsia* came for their bimonthly payoffs, Ruslan hid in his room, silently rocking and muttering and wishing them harm with a fury.

And always, from the room right beside his, came laptop computer tappings and fax machine gurgles and the customized ringing of a half-dozen cellphones—everything from a tinny call to prayer to the *Doctor Zhivago* theme music. The television in the living room blared Al Jazeera. Five times a day, Ruslan learned to kneel facing Mecca (and he thought, yes he did, of the number of times Dadya and Vakha had bugged him to do this). One afternoon the phone rang; when Khassan answered, Ruslan could hear the faint voice of Dadya, speaking in what sounded like a mix of Russian and Avari.

"No," said Khassan.

He could hear Dadya's speech grow more frantic; he wished he could make out what his uncle was saying. Khassan's face, meanwhile, bore no emotion. "No," he said sternly. "Ruslan is in seclusion. Do not come here. If you do, we will deal with you."

Ruslan heard yelling coming through the receiver.

"Do *not*," Khassan stated before hanging the phone up.

Ahmed and Ayman, the two who had been there before, had gone away. Meanwhile, the apartment hosted Wahhabis and Salafists and radical Sunnis, each one wearing a beard and a long, flowing white robe. Four came more than the others. The first, of course, was Khassan, Vakha's son, the only member who actually hailed from the Caucasus; as far as Ruslan could tell, he was also the only good speaker of Russian. There was the plump Jordanian Karim, who giggled like a girl and, all day and all evening, smoked grassy green chunks of the Taliban's finest. Mohammed, meanwhile, was Karim's funhouse mirror reflection—he was solemn, tall, and as thin as a plant stake. *He,* it was said, was from the Sudan, and had lost family members there to Clinton's medicine factory bombing. Ruslan only knew that he spent most of his time in the far sofa corner, leafing through the Quran, terrorist cell correspondence, and well-thumbed copies of Cyrillic-script *Hustler.* (He put the latter away whenever Khassan was nearby.) Finally, there was dark, brutish Omar. *He,* it was said, came from the Saudi peninsula, and for a while had been in contact with the one and only al-Khattab. Quickly, Ruslan learned to give him a wide berth, for there was something about him that was ugly and menacing. A hundred ant-sized scars speckled his scalp like a frosting. He had shadows beneath his eyes, and a face as muttony and round as a sheep's rearmost quarters. He also gave Ruslan lingering glances every time he accepted a glass of mint tea, an American cigarette, or a serving of falafel balls with Kraft Thousand Island dressing.

Ruslan was praised, and praised often.

Khassan: "You are a martyr, a saint, a true jihadist. You're a gift sent from Allah to help with our mission. Now, please, see to the bathroom—it's as filthy as I've ever seen it."

Or this, from Karim, in elementary Russian, looking like a pudgy and green-smoke-breathing puppet: "Paradise awaits you, my Dagestani brother."

Or Mohammed, giving him back pats and thumbs-up as he spoke not one word of Russian.

Or, Omar, entering the room, stroking at the stubble on his face, his breath smelling of Chivas and non-pork salami, an always-lit cigarette between thick, greasy fingers, the whites of his eyes netted with veins red and spidery, saying, "You do good, you do good," while leering at Ruslan.

(Oh my father, oh my N20-ruined *papochka*. Run. Run away. Run away now, and run away quickly.)

Days turned to weeks. Ruslan at times forgot why he was in the apartment—he became lost to routine, and in this there was comfort. One day, as he lay on the apartment's old sofa, eyes closed and listening to the squeals of small children, Khassan entered half smiling. He carried a brown package. Ruslan jumped, concerned he'd been caught doing nothing.

"No, no, Ruslan, my brother. Sit, sit, please, don't worry."

Ruslan sat. Khassan sat beside him. The paper package sat on Khassan's gowned legs.

"Look at me," Khassan said while rolling up the sleeves of his djellaba. "Please look, my brother."

Khassan's arm was covered with mashed potato burn marks. Ruslan turned away, visions of the forest popping before him.

"No," Khassan repeated while waggling his arm at him. "*Look*, it's important. It's important you know this . . . my whole body, covered, everything but the face."

"When?" Ruslan peeped.

"In 1999. After Putin bombed the Moscow apartments and blamed it on Chechens. While *you* were still lucky enough to be living in Dagestan. All of Apraxin was a ghost town in those terrible days. They grabbed me in a café and held me for eight weeks. I can't believe Vakha never told you. Finally, I was dumped in a laneway. Vakha found me whimpering like a dog. It took me a year to recover. It was a miracle I survived. Of course, they weren't yet using N20."

Ruslan could picture it clearly. He shivered, and wished that Khassan weren't there with him.

"Ruslan," Khassan said calmly. "I speak Russian, Arabic, Farsi, three Caucasian dialects, and a smattering of English. I am good with languages. I always have been. This is my curse. Do you understand? Are you following me? They need me, here. We are making the transition, you see, from a logistical to a direct-strike cell, and it is difficult. The money we got from your *dyevushka*—it will fund our first action." Though the apartment was empty, he lowered his voice and moved closer. "The others are all idiots. They are all simpletons and hypocrites. No better than puppets. Without me, *plah*, they'd be hopeless. Otherwise, I would martyr myself. It would be my honour, my greatest joy. *I* would do what you are going to do. I wish I could, Ruslan. Let Allah be praised for his wisdom, but I wish that I could . . ."

The words hung there, clanging. Seconds passed. *He is right*, Ruslan thought. *It will be a way out of this eternal torture.* For the briefest of moments, and without even realizing, Ruslan grinned slightly, his visions having turned to lilies and waterfalls and glossy-lipped virgins.

Khassan tossed the package to Ruslan. "Here," he said, "put this on."

Ruslan blinked.

"Go ahead. You will wear it. It is your disguise."

Ruslan carried the package to his room. He sat on the bed and pulled the string wrapped around it. The paper came away with the sound of light rustling. He upheld each item. There was an embroidered peasant blouse, a fine cotton head scarf, and a long grey skirt that felt in spots almost worn through. He held these garments to his body, inspecting every angle, neither happy nor unhappy nor even neutral. He walked back to the living room and showed the outfit to Khassan.

Khassan smiled, and explained: "You'll need women's clothing to hide the belt you'll be wearing."

Everything seemed to change at that moment. Now, when Karim wanted some bread with tahini, or Khassan decided the apartment needed cleaning, they no longer looked insistently at Ruslan. New faces started coming and going—they were young men like him, bony-armed and hollow-cheeked, their eyes swimming with the madness caused by omniscience. *They* started to do the cleaning, the cooking, the general Wahhabi-pleasing. Ruslan, now that he dressed like a widow, rested unbothered; he took long baths, drank black tea, ate watermelon toffee. A television set was put in his room; he spent most of his time there, smoking cigarettes and watching Russian ice hockey. One night, as he lay in hot bathtub water, Omar entered the room and stood over him glowering.

In a moment Khassan was there, smacking Omar in the head while yelling in Arabic.

Ruslan was given pomegranates, chocolate, and non-alcoholic beverages. He played chess with Khassan, as well as he was able. One afternoon, shortly after the first warm day of spring had arrived in north Russia and Khassan had let Ruslan take one of his castles, Khassan paused and looked at him. "Ruslan," he said. "You are restoring the honour taken from you, from your parents, from your brothers and sisters, and most of all from your homeland, which will soon officially join the anti-Crusade in the Caucasus. This is what you are doing. You are following the proud tradition of the blood vendetta. You must never wilt, nor vary from your chosen path. This is what you are doing, soldier."

Ruslan's heart beat a little bit quicker.

"Here," Khassan said, handing him a tube of Bulgarian lipstick.

Ruslan took it—it was the dark brown-red of blood, and he found this so fitting. He put it to his lips and began roughly pushing.

"No," Khassan said, "more like *this*." He leaned over forward and helped guide Ruslan's fingers. "There," he said, and they both went to the bathroom to look in the mirror. *It's me*, Ruslan thought, for the makeup restored some of the colour that had been lost in the forest.

"Is there more?"

"Yes."

"In other colours?"

"Yes."

"Will I wear them?"

"Yes."

There was a pause. It seemed to go on forever.

"Why?" Ruslan asked.

"It's far more disturbing if they think you're a woman."

Ruslan went out with Khassan beside him. At first they drew stares from the robed hallway children, who all felt that they knew this young head-scarved woman. Ruslan looked ahead, feeling the heft of deception.

They walked into a hazed evening sunlight. Khassan stopped for a minute, letting Ruslan adapt to his black widow persona. They slowly walked to a market that was three large blocks over. It was muddy and makeshift, with stalls tacked together and covered by blue nylon tarpaulins. Ruslan's legs felt jittery. Matted-hair dogs ran in tight, panting circles. There were children, and babushkas, and old drunken men passing bottles in circles.

Khassan gave Ruslan some rubles. "Buy something," he said.

"They won't even notice. You are only visible to them as a group, as an entire people. They only see you when you're a threat. They will not look at you as an individual."

Ruslan approached a stall. There was a fat Russian woman with a mole on her forehead; she gave Ruslan the hard look reserved for all *chorny zhopie*. But then she looked away. Khassan smiled. Ruslan chose soap, a loaf of bread, and a bottle of oil. He passed over money in a hand slightly shaking. She gave him the change, and turned her back to him.

"Good," Khassan said. "Now let's do some exploring."

They did, for the better part of an hour. They strolled past kiosks and freeways and battered Soviet buildings. They moved through cracked-tarmac playgrounds, the swing sets all broken and ignored by thin, violent children. They wandered past babushkas selling family mementoes, and beside roadways crowded with rusting old Ladas. At one point, next to yet another impromptu market, this one selling pipes and hardware and old plumbing equipment, Khassan turned to Ruslan and said, "Look . . . look . . . no one is noticing anything out of the ordinary . . . you can move about freely, like a sad Chechen widow."

As Ruslan walked, he watched other women. Yet he didn't watch them the way he did before. Oh no—this time he did it with the object of mimicry. He studied that sway of the hips, that swing of the arms, that mix of deference and contempt that breathes in all Russian women.

"Let's get back," Khassan said, and he held a hand out in traffic. It took minutes and minutes for a cab to pull over—they were both clearly Caucasians, and Khassan was wearing a telltale djellaba. A car stopped finally.

"You do it," Khassan whispered, and when Ruslan hesitated he gave him a shove with his elbow. Stuttering, Ruslan negotiated a price back to their building. And though the driver may have wondered about this woman's strange vocal tenor, and may have blinked once or twice at her oversized larynx, he nonetheless let them into his backfiring Volga.

Ruslan left the building more and more often now, so as to roam St. Petersburg in his long skirt and kerchief. This felt strange— like being a tourist in the city that had killed him. He was looking through eyes that were somebody else's. He was a Caucasian phantom, taken to wandering. He visited monuments and churches and onion-domed mausoleums, a young Muslim widow amidst hundreds of tourists. He went to the Hermitage for the first time; here he saw an immortality in the paintings that left him breathless and elated. Oh yes—he saw himself as an artist of sorts, like Chagall or Kandinsky, the only difference the palette. One afternoon he took a train out to Peterhof, where he wandered the gardens like a young, awestruck peasant. He couldn't believe it! The trees! The palaces! The *fountains!* In the cascade of water, he heard other-world voices. In the light, misting spray, he heard the singing of virgins. He smiled, and he smiled, and then something happened: his grin fell from his face, making a splash in the water.

Seestra—his nose turned sniffly, and his dark eyes grew wide with an N20 vision. (It sometimes was like this—heaven switching to hell in the depths of his wrecked mind.) As he peered into the spray of the fountain, kind other-world voices melted to nothing. In their absence came the cawing of hawks, and the whistle wind makes when blowing through near-empty places. Oh yes— Ruslan saw Chechnya, he saw Grozny, he saw old women drinking tea in the Minutka Square market. And though he had never been to this neighbouring republic, he was there now in spirit, and he could see that nothing, not a thing, had been left untouched by the twin rounds of fighting. Minutka Square—the heart of a city once dubbed "the Paris of the Caucasus"—had been reduced to rubble, and craters, and packs of skinny dogs who roamed the empty streets whimpering. And the *buildings*. Those that remained (which were only a handful) were strafed, and hollowed, and so battered by carpet bombs they looked ready to topple. The blackened husk of an oil truck—the fire had smouldered for two days, the locals using the smoke to cure sausages for winter—glinted in the first bleak light of the morning. There were corpses still trapped under rubble, and the children who played here didn't know what it was like to breathe air that wasn't reeking and awful.

But humans, they cope. It is, as I've said, what they're known for. (It's why self-deception exists, and all of its adjuncts.) The actual fighting had died down, the residents of Grozny now suffering an occupation of Russian soldiers (who came in the night and took away anyone who they claimed might be colluding with Shamil Basayev or the Arab al-Khattab). One block down and another two over, a man and two women had just opened a hair salon. The university had reopened, though without heat or electricity or any sort of plumbing. Buses had once again started running, though the roadways posed every sort of obstacle. Though the circus hall was ruined, people could still be found there, juggling under low lights with saddened clown faces.

In this catastrophe of death, mud, and rubble—in this wholesale degradation of what once was Minutka—tea-drinking old women tacked together a market each morning (for it is always, *always,* women who keep things running during times of disaster). Every day except Fridays, they set out turnips, beets, browning celery, bundles of radishes, heads of frozen iceberg lettuce, smoked fish that had been pulled from muddy Chechen rivers, buckets of beer made from ginger and sugar, and—of course—the watermelons that sprang like dandelions from the black earth of the country. Beneath the cloths covering their tables, they put out their *real* stock: cardboard boxes filled with grenades, and Kalashnikovs, and just slightly oxidized guns used for taking down airplanes. Little one—in the sick joke that was Chechnya, the unpaid Russian soldiers sold weapons to the very people they were supposed to be killing.

As the sun rose bold and flaring, the old women began removing layers of sweaters. The shadows falling over Minutka Square shortened, and then altogether vanished. The plaza was now skylit and hot and wispy with smoke from smouldering fires. A mother washed her daughter in a red basin nearby. Another pushed a stroller over debris and wrecked concrete. As late morning approached, the women stopped chattering to one another. The stillness was punctuated only by the barking of dogs, and the call of a muezzin, and the motors of the Jeeps driven by *contraktniki*. A wind blew from the west, rustling head scarves and irritating dry throats, and there was the occasional glop of feet stepping in mud. Otherwise, there was silence. Business was not brisk. Of the 400,000 souls who once lived here, only a tenth remained—these were the *podvalshchiki*, or "basement people," so named because they lived in the only structures still standing, their root cellar doors decorated with signs reading *Please! People live here!* so that the Russians wouldn't throw grenades in them while their children were sleeping. Yet the real irony? The thing that made one laugh darkly? The majority of these basement dwellers were ethnically *Russian*, the native Chechens all having had dachas to flee to, or country relatives to visit, or footpaths to follow into hills green and tree-covered. Oh yes. After eight or so years, the Chechen conflict had dissolved into Russians killing Russians, with everybody too numb and dead-dog tired to notice.

It was into this vision of chaos, of devastation, *of complete and still-going-on desecration,* that Ruslan watched a young girl appear out of nowhere. Her skin was olive, and her eyes gleamed with an anger that flared inside of her. She was wearing a head scarf, a loose blouse, and a skirt long and mud-fringed. She waited. The sun beat on her shoulders. As time wore on, others joined her—mostly old women traders, returning to villages with wares they'd try to sell again the next day. A small bus arrived. Tottering, yes; backfiring, yes; bouncing and heaving over sun-glinting debris . . . yes. Its door craned open. The girl climbed on with the others. After having a quick smoke, the driver closed the door and then revved the engine, black plumes of exhaust knifing the dense air. They went slowly. The bus was bouncing so badly over rubble and black, muddy ridges that the girl held on to her seat not to bump her head on the metal roof. Once the driver reached the main artery, he went a little faster—the destruction was at its worst in the heart of the city. The bus passed the black and reduced-to-rubble Chekhov Library, the Swiss-cheesed football stadium, the teetering and flame-licked brandy factory. Schools, mosques, factories, churches, theatres, apartment buildings, shops—all had been strafed, or mortared, or (as was the case with President Dudayev's palace) reduced to nothing. As they chugged past an old plastic boot factory, the girl noticed that it now bore a hole so large a tank could have driven through it.

And then they passed the mansions built by *air people*—so named because their wealth seemed to appear out of thin air once the Chechen war started—oh yes, the bus passed *air*-Mercedes parked in driveways, and shiny new *air*-BMWs, and leather-upholstered *air*–Lexus SUVs. Grozny then petered to nothing—to a filthy bad memory in a jiggling mirror. The loveliness of the countryside seemed an impossibility after the foul and nightly assaulted city. The fruit trees were in bloom and the hills were dotted with outbursts of colour. Bees hovered, birds swooped, and everything was fragrant with the essence of lilac. In the distance, mountain peaks reached toward a blue thin and depthless.

And Ruslan saw it all. With his N20 omniscience, he watched the young girl travel to Khasavyurt, and then Astrakhan, and then the wetlands of the Volga, and then to the city of Tambov (known for producing Tchaikovsky, Rachmaninov, and track suit–wearing hit men) . . . Oh yes, as Ruslan took the subway back to the Wahhabi headquarters, his face gone white and his dark eyes flickering with live apparitions, he watched as her bus headed north, along the exact route he had once taken, toward a city known for its past and its beauty and its all-over Unrealness, oh yes yes yes, Ruslan ran up the building's dark stairwell, past Salafist children and pro-9/11 graffiti. Inside, he stepped into the al Qaeda apartment.

He stopped. Of course, she was there, quietly sitting.

"Ahhhh," Khassan said, "it's Ruslan! Ruslan, come here, you must meet our latest guest. Her name is Suleimanovna Ali Hadjaeyeva, but she calls herself Suli. She has been kind enough to join us from Grozny. In fact, she just got here. We are proud and extremely fortunate to have her. You and she will be working together."

Suli was wearing a kerchief and the blouse of a peasant; she looked at him through eyes as round as egg cups. Her skin, Ruslan noticed, was the dark, supple purple of a harvested eggplant. And her features—he'd never seen a face so narrow, or an expression so riddled with fear and suspicion.

A thought popped up and by surprise took him.

THE CULPRITS

This girl. This Chechen.
She is almost pretty.

Suli slept in the office, on a cot by the window. Khassan unplugged the fax and brought the satellite telephone (which they used to keep in contact with the frontiers of Pakistan) into the living room. Meanwhile, the boys who'd been coming just vanished; Ruslan began to question whether they'd ever really been there. No matter. Suli did what the boys had done before her, and what Ruslan had done before *them*—she cleaned, she ran errands, she added a solemnity to an already grave climate. The apartment filled with smells of Chechen home cooking. She made mutton dumplings, and thick porous bread, and kebabs from the meaty part of an oxtail. Meanwhile, other men came—mullahs and imams and long-bearded zealots. After a surfeit of head bows, they'd all have long meetings while sitting cross-legged. These councils were conducted in Arabic, with a smattering of Farsi thrown in for good measure. When they left, their stomachs would be filled with rice, and flatbreads, and lamb chops served with a sauce made from garlic. (And always, *always*, there was unspeaking Suli, working grim-faced in the apartment's small kitchen.)

With nothing to do, Ruslan helped her. She'd hand him vegetables to peel, or lettuce to wash, her instructions relayed with nods of her scarved head. She never spoke, or looked directly at him, or was in any way friendly. Still, he liked helping. There was something about her—some recognizable suffering. One morning, when the apartment was empty and a fog had enfolded the whole of the building, Ruslan tried talking to her.

"You are from Grozny," he said in Russian.

She stopped working. Her arms were covered in nicks, and small burns, and welts that were reddish. Without the briefest of glances, she went back to her cooking.

"You are from Grozny," he said, this time in Avari. When she didn't so much as pause, he decided that she really did speak nothing but Chechen, the language of phantoms and wolves and skies filled with bright half moons. He studied the side of her face—the way her jaw muscles worked beneath the curve of her cheekbones.

Was it a husband? he wanted to ask her. *A brother? Your beloved papochka? Whoever it is, I know. I know what happened to him.*

Two days later, the sun came up white and bleary. It was early June in St. Petersburg, a time when the Summer Palace embankment became thick with pale Russians tanning. Suli served lunch to Ruslan, Khassan, and Mohammed. The two bearded men ate quickly, and left their plates on the dining room table. Ruslan was helping to clean up when he and Suli came face to face outside of the kitchen; they each motioned to the same side before feinting to the other and then awkwardly smiling.

In a whispery Russian she asked, "Did you like it?"

"Yes," he said, startled. "It was delicious."

She nodded and passed him, going into the kitchen. The very next day, Khassan gave her some rubles. The two conversed briefly in Chechen, and the girl fetched the jute sack that she used to carry groceries. Ruslan was in the living room. She paused at the door and looked over at him through eyes slightly narrowed.

"You coming?" she asked with a hint of impatience.

He found it hard just to keep up—she moved as though chased by whatever demons lived in her. She trundled along the thoroughfare that bisected the neighbourhood; they passed block after block, roaming farther and farther. His skin grew damp and his breathing grew ragged. Finally, they came around a building that was coated in graffiti (oddly, most of it was in English, as though the Chechens who lived here hoped for international exposure—fuck Putin, fuck Basayev, fuck George Bush and Tony Blair and what those sociopath bastards will do to get oil). They moved over a lot that was weedy and strewn with glass bottles. They crossed rusted train tracks and came to a market in a wedge of tamped brown earth. There was a modicum of shade thrown by a few spindly pine trees.

"I like it here," Suli said while picking out peppers and ground coffee (as well as cheese and mint used for salads). "Many Chechens come here." Ruslan stayed right beside her. They were like two women, thumping melons and sniffing meat and looking for herbs fresh and bushy. The last thing she bought was a tin of small orange biscuits. She walked home much slower than she'd come, and as she did she chewed one after another.

Out of the blue she said, "There's now a shortage of women."

There was a brief pause. Ruslan was puzzled—he thought that maybe her words meant something else altogether, snared by his ears and in error translated.

"Pardon?"

"They're running out."

"Out?"

"Of young Chechen women. The *contraktniki* are taking us before we even have a chance to be married, never mind become widows. First they took all the young men to filtration camps built in forests, and now they're taking away women. Why do you think you're dressed that way?" She looked at him, her gaze running disgustedly over his clothing. "Why do you think they're passing you off as a woman? If the Russians knew we were running out of women, they'd start taking away children and old people and then there'd be none of us left. We'd be all of us gone."

They walked a few more paces. There was something about her theory that didn't quite make sense. Or maybe it did—he couldn't, at that moment, understand what she was saying.

After a minute of silence she said, "I was taken at Urus Marten."

They each took a few steps. U.M., as they called it, was a known rebel stronghold.

Finally, Ruslan said, "They took me near Apraxin Dvor."

"What? *Here*? In the city?"

"Yes."

"Hmmmm. The Russians are widening their horizons."

Ruslan said nothing—he knew that with women there are other methods of debasement. He wanted to open his mouth and ask, *How did you survive? How did you do it? My uncle had televisions to sell to get the money for my ransom. But what about you? What did you think about while waiting?* Yet he didn't. Her eyes had grown steely. Unnerved, he looked forward. He could see it all. He knew what she was thinking. She wanted to kill with the venom of glances. She wanted to destroy, using the lethality of wishes. Even with his mind as it was, Ruslan understood something.

She hadn't survived.

Nobody does, really.

Most afternoons now, they went out together to visit Caucasian markets. "Look," she would say with a scowl. "Only children and old people. Everyone else is hiding. Even all these months after *Nord-Ost*. This is what has become of my people, of my feared warrior nation. *Hiding*."

Or they'd be at the kitchen table, dicing vegetables for soups or minty salads, and she would suddenly stop.

"How much?" she spat one morning, her peeler pointing at him.

Ruslan said nothing.

"Your family. How much are they getting?"

He thought of old Dadya and his shop in Apraxin filling with TVs.

"I don't know," he said.

"You don't know!? What do you *mean* you don't know?"

Ruslan shrugged.

"But you know who is getting it?"

"My uncle. He sold all he owned to buy me back from the Russians."

"Your uncle?"

"Yes."

Suli snorted, and went back to working. "My aunt is getting ten thousand euros. The bitch. She always hated me. She says I stole a brooch from her. What do I want with her fucking brooch? It was as ugly as a donkey's ass. *Bah*. At least, who knows, maybe this will restore honour to our side of the family. *Only* . . ." She paused and leaned closer. "You know what they say, don't you? That these Wahhabi fuckers, after they grease some wheels and pay their expenses and dip their sticky fingers into it, there'll be maybe a thousand left, if even that. Sometimes, I hear, there is nothing."

Ruslan's head spun, and he suddenly felt frightened. "No," he said. "My uncle has already received some payment."

"Really?"

"Yes."

"Hmmm." She paused. "They must think he'll be some use to them later. Because other families they get nothing. At least, this is what I've heard. I have known other girls who have done this. *I* knew Zarema Mazhikhoyeva, the Tverskaya bomber. And afterward, I heard whisperings, about promises and money and how the two had added up to nothing. I bet you my aunt ends up getting zero. I tell you, *malchik*, I'd laugh if that happened. I'd laugh all the way to paradise."

Another time, the two of them lazing on the apartment's old sofa, they fended off boredom with a game they'd invented.

"Mountains."

"Quince jam," countered Ruslan.

"Dancing the *zikr*."

"The taste of malted rye flour."

"Goat's milk."

"The sound of wild dogs braying."

"Firing guns during weddings."

"Ha! That's a good one . . ."

"Go."

"Caucasian autumns."

"Wrestling matches."

"Sweetening tea with jam instead of sugar."

"Mountain polo."

"We were always better than you."

"Not on your life."

"I used to play, you know."

"Really?"

"Yes."

"Were you good?"

"I don't remember. I mean, I do and I don't. Everything is a jumble."

Pause.

"Watermelons," said Suli.

"Mmmmm. Yes. Watermelons. Why do you suppose they grow so well down south?"

"I don't know. I don't care. I only know that I'd like one that hasn't been battered all day in a bouncing truck."

"Fresh curds."

"Really?"

"Yes. And dandelion tea."

"Yes. Dandelion tea."

"I know!"

"What?"

"Big families."

"Yes. Rooms full of aunts and uncles and a half-dozen children. These Russians—how they can live with only one or maybe two children. I don't understand it. I don't know how they can do it."

"No, me neither."

"It must be so lonely."

"Yes."

There was a pause.

"There's not much else, is there?"

"No," said Ruslan.

"There's rubble."

"And checkpoints."

"And mortar rounds off in the distance."

"And the buildings of Grozny, looking like vegetable graters."

Suli looked as though she might start crying.

"You know," she said, "who is behind this, don't you?"

"Behind what?"

"Chechnya, the bombings, *this*."

"I don't know."

"Everybody."

"I don't understand."

"Everybody is at fault."

"I don't—"

"When it comes to something as fucked up as Chechnya, everybody is a culprit. Putin is a culprit. Bush is a culprit, for supporting the 'anti-terrorist' forces in Chechnya. Shamil Basayev is a culprit. Khattab is a culprit, with his videos of hostages losing their fingers. General Dudayev is a culprit, Aslan Maskhadov is a culprit, and Boris Yeltsin—now *he,* he was a culprit, and drunk as an uncle on top of it. Chevron and BP are culprits, if only for funding the protection of the pipeline. The OMON are culprits and the *contraktniki* are culprits and the FSB are culprits. The Russian police are culprits, as are the soldiers. The Russian *people* are culprits, though no more than the Chechens—yes, yes, I'll admit it, after beating the Russians in 1996, what did we do? At the first glimpse of freedom we turned to kidnapping and smuggling and narcotics trafficking. Stalin was a culprit, for shipping us all to Kazakhstan in the forties, and making us all so pissed off in the first place. General Yermolov was a culprit, for saying, 'The only good Chechen's a dead one.'" She paused to catch her breath. "The Cossacks were culprits, for using the Russian word 'terrible' as the name for our capital. Three hundred years of fighting and resistance and stupid blood vendettas are the culprits. Everybody and everything is a culprit. When something like this goes on for so long, things like right and wrong, justified or not justified . . . *pluh.* They go out the window. They don't exist any longer. There is only business and vengeance. And after a while even business goes out the window, until none of it, not one moment, makes sense to anybody any longer. Everything, that is, but the desire to get even."

She stopped, her hands shaking with anger. Ruslan didn't know what to say; with his mind as it was, he hadn't understood most of it. The apartment door opened. Mohammed sauntered in with a loud, laughing Karim. Suli rose and lowered her head and rushed into the kitchen. Ruslan went with her. A minute later he smelled the rosemary scent of green Taliban hashish. Working over the sink, Suli lowered her head and began furiously peeling.

She brooded for days, before again speaking.

The weather outside grew hotter and hotter. As June wore on, Ruslan and Suli learned they had another thing in common: they would both wake in the middle of the night, sweat-soaked and shaken by hellacious nightmares. One evening they awoke at the same time; he heard her yelps and she heard his moaning. They both emerged in the hallway. Nodding, they went to the kitchen and sat in half darkness. Suli made tea, and they moved their chairs next to the window. Sipping, they watched the sun rise over a landscape of buildings. This helped. There was something about the morning's first sunshine that made everything simpler, and easier to fathom.

And though Suli never laughed—she treated the slightest of grins as though it caused pain in her jawbones—there *was* that time in which the two of them were side by side in the kitchen, Ruslan in his skirt chopping up spinach. Suli, meanwhile, was stirring a pot bubbling with chard leaves and mutton. Both of them had grown damp in the apartment's humidity. They were talking about Khassan and his three stupid henchmen.

"*Omar,*" said Suli.

"What did he do?"

"Many things. And nothing."

"Tell me."

"It's the way he looks at me. Like he wants to throw me to the carpet and then do things to me."

Ruslan's N20 fog cleared for one second, just long enough for the old Ruslan—the Ruslan who was witty and jaunty and a charmer of women—to open his mouth and say, "I'd like to punch him in the mouth, that fat, lascivious mongrel."

Suli was tasting the soup at the moment he said it, and she laughed so hard broth from her nose spouted. Ruslan chortled too, and pretty soon they were both holding their bellies and riotously laughing. But then, one moment later, the thought of that fat, leering Omar aroused in Suli an ugly emotion. Her face bloomed hotly, and she began softly weeping for the first time in front of him. Ruslan watched silently. She moved to the stove, and still Ruslan stood there, listening to her tears land in soup flavoured with tarragon.

"I begged them," she choked. Though she no longer seemed to be crying, her tears kept coming, as though a sorrowful rain were falling inside her.

"I did too," Ruslan told her.

(And later, after they'd served lunch to the Wahhabis, roly-poly Karim came up to Ruslan. "Hey *dyevushka*," he said in his bad Russian, "the borscht it had, mmmmm, anchovy? It taste, like, salty or something?")

Khassan was coming less and less often; apparently he was busy with what Karim described as "last-minute, mmmmmm, details." Ruslan began reading the Quran, especially the parts highlighted in light blue. June gave way to July, and the air it grew denser. The sun blazed in the sky like a vengeful pariah. Ruslan felt his mind slipping deeper and deeper into the future. Often, he gazed out the window and saw paradise form in heat rising off pavement. Oh yes—he saw jungle vines curl over Soviet apartments. He saw babushkas transform into garlanded sirens. He saw pines turn to trees bursting with sweet fruit.

On the evening of July the fourth, Suli came to him. It was just before midnight, and Ruslan was lying awake, listening to insects and jaguars and aroused howler monkeys. He heard her timidly knocking. Tomorrow was the day, and both of them knew it.

"What is it?" he whispered. She stood in the shadows, dressed in a skirt and a T-shirt. She said nothing, and for a moment Ruslan wondered if he was imagining the whole thing. "Suli?" he said.

She crept forward sniffling, and crawled into his bed of matted-down vine leaves. She turned her back to him. No warmth came from her body. For the longest time they both lay there, trying to understand this strange, awkward moment. Finally, Suli reached behind her and took hold of his right hand. She put it onto her belly. Ruslan was surprised, for it felt slightly bloated.

"You see?" she said softly. "You see why I have to do this?"

Seconds went by. Her voice, when it came, was a rasping.

"I can feel it. Inside me. Moving. Breathing. One of *theirs*. I have dreams, Ruslan. It's a ghoul, I know it, a little living Putin. Whenever I sleep, it practises its judo kicks on me. It sees things, it knows. Ruslan—it knows what I'm thinking, it knows what I'm *feeling*. Thank God I'll die before this thing is born. This world . . . this world already has more than enough sorrow."

Ruslan said nothing. What she said had overwhelmed him, and he had closed his mind to it. He was now on a raft, floating along a green, lustrous river. Fish jumped, and swans drifted, and the native girl next to him had glistening soft bronze skin. He moved closer to his virgin, who looked a little like Suli. She accepted his closeness. They both slept so deeply that nothing would rouse them—not the passage of hours, not the first hint of sunlight, not the round-the-clock ringing of satellite telephones.

It was Khassan who found them, curled together like puppies, one of them stone-faced and the other one smiling.

The whole world was quiet save for the soft, idling hush of a Mercedes sedan. The driver was Omar. When he heard footfalls on pavement, he looked at them, scowling. Khassan opened the rear door and Suli climbed inside. Ruslan followed, the green of the jungle replaced by fine leather. Khassan sat in front. Omar put the car into gear, and was about to pull away when Khassan said something in Arabic. Omar braked. Khassan turned.

"Ruslan," he said in Avari, "you and I will trade seats. I don't want you distracted by your sweetheart."

And so they changed places, and rode through a day slowly dawning. No one spoke. In the absence of conversation, Ruslan listened to the thrumming of tires against an undulating roadway. Khassan and Omar smoked so many cigarettes that the air turned blue and scratched at Ruslan's throat like a three-week-old kitten. Every few minutes he opened his window and let the air of the morning ruffle his head scarf.

The car left the city, Khassan choosing a rural route to avoid the *militsia*-packed freeway. The sun rose above, over fields grey and grassy, and a bank of pink light fell upon the Mercedes. They passed timber-house towns and spurts of pine forest. As Ruslan looked out of his window, he saw old Orthodox churches, built from nothing but wood beams fitted tightly together. They passed streams of clear water and fields of alfalfa, and they even saw the odd tacked-together pyramid, which in the countryside was said to cure everything from disease to bankruptcy. As the morning progressed, the sun became hot and white-blazing. Inside the car, Omar turned the air conditioning up so high that Ruslan's skin sprouted goosebumps, and he resisted the temptation to curl his arms around himself. Somewhere in the flatlands between Malaya Vishera and the town of Bologoye, they pulled over; all four wandered into dense, white-barked forest, each picking a place where he or she could privately make water.

Otherwise, they didn't stop. At one point Khassan asked, "Is anyone hungry?" This startled Ruslan: it was the first time anyone had spoken in more than an hour. Suli said nothing, feeding a silence broken rarely by quick, jabbing comments. For example—outside the city of Tver, a place where prisons housed the homeless who'd been arrested in Russia's two major cities, Omar gestured and said in bad Russian, "I have there friend, a good one. Maybe he dead now."

They kept to country roads, their progress impeded at times by horses and wagons. Villages turned into towns. They passed through Kiln, and Gorodnya, and along the maple-lined banks of the wide Volga River. At one point they got stuck behind goats walking slowly. Omar honked, and cursed, and leaned his nicked head out to yell at the herder. When the road finally cleared, he hard-gunned the engine, spewing up earth that was black and mushroomy—this caused the herder to wave his fist and at them curse loudly. And yet, aside from that one confrontational moment, the trip acquired a tranquility that defied its true nature. Ruslan's mind stilled. Tiny details seemed to take on a spiritual significance: the play of wind in pine branches, the slow, lazy movements of a cow's mouth while chewing, the latches on the doors of small wooden churches. They all, it now seemed, pointed at some higher order. (He glanced over his shoulder at the girl he'd spent his last night with, only to find that her brow was furrowed and the muscles around her mouth angrily tightened.)

Finally, the skies of Moscow appeared in the distance, Khassan mumbling something that had to do with a nest and its vipers.

Soon there was smog and more cars and the market in Mitino, where pirated copies of Lotus or Excel sold for three euros. Omar merged onto a multi-lane ring road, and then followed signs to the aerodrome at Tushino. Ruslan took deep breaths. He closed his eyes and imagined what Allah might look like: bearded and smiling, with a touch soft and caring.

What he saw was a world so little like *this* one.

Omar pulled onto the road that led into the aerodrome. As they approached the huge stadium, Ruslan saw that a market topped by tarpaulins had cropped up beside it. From the car, he could see hordes of young people, all long-limbed and heavy metal–loving and having no idea—no idea *at all*—what was about to befall them. They were innocently buying cold drinks, and T-shirts, and pills that would cause them to see mighty things and grind their poor teeth together. One by one, they were joining the forty thousand or so who were in the stadium already. (As Ruslan watched, a single sad thought kept coming to him: *I once was one of you. I once liked heavy metal. I once would've liked to have come here.*)

The Mercedes passed the drome's public entrance and headed for a lane marked *For official vehicles only*. They stopped at a checkpoint. Here, Omar nodded at a narrow-faced Russian who wore high lace-up boots and olive green fatigues. The soldier checked the licence plates, looked over at Khassan, and then waved the car through with a dismissive gesture. Omar pulled onto a lane that skirted behind Tushino, toward a place filled with lorries and vans and trucks used for towing airplanes. To their left was the drome, and on their right were the airstrips, looking hot and deserted in the day's blazing sunshine. Through the smoked glass of the Mercedes they could hear bass notes thumping from inside the stadium. Omar kept driving. The bass notes faded. They approached a small hangar at the end of the airfield. Another

THE CULPRITS

paid-off Russian waved the car inside; a second later they were sitting in a damp, gloomy blackness.

Someone flicked lights on, illuminating the hangar in hues pale and orange. Ruslan saw they were parked amongst forklifts and trucks and other vehicles used for loading. Khassan got out, and the rest of them followed. While they waited by the car, he walked toward a dark pocket at the rear of the hangar. From this distance Ruslan heard shards of a conversation in Russian. Omar lit a cigarette and blew smoke into air that smelled strongly of diesel. From outside the garage, Ruslan could hear the *beep beep*ing of large trucks reversing.

Two minutes passed. And though Ruslan's head was a maelstrom of knowledge, certain memories broke through in these last minutes of his life. Playing in fields dotted with flowers. Racing on stallions that snorted with fury. Jiggling and bouncing in the trunk of a Lada (before squinting in the sun of a big Unreal City).

A Volga filled up with every colour of primrose.

The feel of his back against rugs made from tigers.

Kissing—really *kissing*—a near-pretty girl whose left eye turned inward.

Khassan returned carrying vests built from thick, dark grey nylon.

"Open your shirts," he commanded Ruslan and Suli.

Suli hesitated, and glanced over at Ruslan.

"Go on—open them," Khassan stated.

Ruslan began fumbling with buttons; seeing this, Suli reluctantly followed, her tiny breasts clothed in a bra beige and wispy (and yes, oh yes, they all couldn't help noticing the slight bulge of her stomach). Ruslan's mind went blank, or at least as blank as it could go. Khassan was fastening his vest, which contained nails and ball bearings and one-half a kilogram of explosives. Khassan tightened the straps, making sure they wouldn't come loose. He then tried to slip a finger between Ruslan's skin and the nylon; when he found this was difficult, he grinned and stared into Ruslan's blank, dark eyes. A moment passed. Khassan leaned forward and into Ruslan's ear whispered, "If you give yourself up, or lose your nerve, we pay your precious Dadya a visit. Do you understand, *dyevushka*? Do I make myself clear?"

Ruslan nodded. Khassan grinned and turned his attention to Suli, who was breathing in short gasps. He worked at the straps, clasps, and buckles, careful to avoid the protruding wires of her TNT-filled vest. When he was finished, he leaned over and whispered a threat into her ear—no doubt it was directed at the aunt who was receiving Suli's payment. There was a long moment of silence. Then came the girl's razor-thin chuckle. Everyone froze, as though they'd heard someone screaming. Suli straightened, and her eyes regained the steeliness that was her most pronounced feature.

"Go ahead, motherfucker. See if I care."

Khassan lifted his hand as if about to strike her. Suli didn't shrink, or step backward, or so much as blink at him. Instead she smiled, and took the two wires that hung from the bottom of her bomb pack, her little twig fingers never looking so potent.

"Go ahead," she said again. "Go ahead, you Wahhabi cocksucker."

"How dare—"

"How dare *you*, ruining our country, making our fight into a business. Giving that bastard Putin his election platform. I know who you work for, and it's *not* Osama bin Laden. I hope you rot in hell. I couldn't care less if I kill Russians or Wahhabis—they are both the same enemy, and every Chechen knows it."

THE CULPRITS

There was a long, pregnant silence. Ruslan thought she might even do it. Khassan stared at her, his eyes burning hotly. He finally spoke in a voice slightly lowered. "Into the car," he said, and then Suli, oh yes Suli, took enough time to show this was all *her* decision.

Omar restarted the car, and soon they were driving back over the tarmac. Throughout, Suli sat muttering insults in Russian, and not once, not *once*, did Khassan or Omar do anything to silence her. Finally, she stopped and closed her eyes. To Ruslan it looked as though she was praying.

Stop, Ruslan wanted to say, *you are making me nervous,* and when the lunacy of this notion occurred to him, his mind went elsewhere. They passed biplanes and small jets and Russian transporters. As Suli kept praying, Ruslan's head emptied, and then refilled itself with nothing more profound than the voice of Metallica's lead singer, the knees-bent and grimacing James Hetfield.

Omar directed the car to the aerodrome's main entrance. They stopped. Khassan turned and passed something to Ruslan. He took it and saw they were identification papers from Chechnya. He opened them and discovered that, on this day, he was a 21-year-old woman named Zulikhan Likhadzhiyeva.

"Put them in one of your pockets," said Khassan.

Ruslan did so and stepped into eye-blinding sunshine. Suli circled the car so as to be right beside him. Slowly, they began walking toward the drome and the impromptu tarp market. As they did, a line from Ruslan's favourite song by Metallica kept circling inside his mind, as if to take him away from all that was happening—*say your prayers, little one, say your prayers*—and, as he walked forward, that snarling, dark lyric replayed over and over, it not mattering one whit that Ruslan's English was so rudimentary he could not understand *it* or the next line, oh no no no, he didn't know what it meant when James Hetfield growled *say your name, oh small one, oh baby one, oh . . .*

little one.

And then he and Suli were in the ad hoc market, the young Russian vendors calling, "Hey, how about T-shirts or hackey sacks or some blistering green hashish?" and as the two black widows kept moving, deadened eyes facing forward, they drew glances and odd giggles, for who could figure out what two country bumpkins were doing at the Krylya All-Day Music Festival, where the Russian heavy metal band called (believe it or not) Crematorium was just taking the stage to cheering and whistling. When those outside heard the first thrashing guitar chords, they all started running toward the front entrance, for Crematorium was a band of true stature, and their last compact disc was a work of thunder and power and heavy metal brilliance.

Suli was shaking and dripping tears from her dark eyes, and none of it, not one moment, meant anything to Ruslan. Oh no— he could focus only on the true masters Metallica, a band so much better than the group now onstage that he chuckled dismissively as James Hetfield's words thundered inside him, *say your prayers, little one, don't forget, my son,* and it was at *that* moment that the first Russian security guard noticed that Suli was crying, and pointed at her while yelling loudly in Russian. This caused Suli to shriek curse words at Putin, and the Wahhabi movement, and the *contraktniki* baby who was fouling her insides. She finished with an ear-piercing *Allahu Akbar!* and then she rushed straight ahead at the tin-roofed ticket kiosks. A pair of guards tackled her. As she lay on hot tarmac, she again yelled *Allahu Akbar!* and then touched together wires protruding from her peasant blouse, and none of it—not the ensuing explosion, not the ripped-apart Suli, not the deaths of the two guards who'd around the knees grabbed her—registered with Ruslan, for his head was now screaming with guitars and drums and, above all else, James Hetfield's snarling lyrics, *tuck you in, warm within, keep you free from sin, till the sandman he comes.*

Only a portion of Suli's charge had gone off. She was still alive and stomach-oozing onto hot, jet-black tarmac, where her insides were starting to cook like eggs fried in butter. Meanwhile, most of those struggling to get inside the drome thought that the explosion was something Crematorium was doing live and onstage, and—*yes oh yes!*—if the band was bringing out pyrotechnics for their very *first* song, just imagine what their set closer would be like, so the crowd pushed and heaved harder to get in the stadium, and it was only when some girls at the rear of the crush heard Suli moaning that they turned to see a pair of dead guards and a peasant with her insides out-flowing. They began loudly screaming, and all hell then broke loose. A male voice yelled, "Oh my god, there's another!" and Ruslan looked up and saw a dozen hands pointing and still, *still,* his favourite song dominated his mindscape, *sleep with one eye open, gripping your pillow tight,* and for a moment—for the briefest of microseconds—it occurred to him that none of these people had ever done anything to him, that the youth of Moscow overwhelmingly hated Putin, *that none of these E-tab-swallowing concertgoers was in any way a culprit,* but then the thundering in his head grew louder and his thoughts grew more disordered and James Hetfield's voice screamed louder inside him—*sleep with one eye open! gripping your pillow tight!*—and really, it didn't matter, it really didn't, Ruslan having left his life back in a filtration camp forest, his mind N20 ravaged and his backbone pressed against cold, wormy soil. Oh yes, he'd left his life behind in a freezing OMON pit, and as the Tushino guards all pulled guns and pointed them at him, he closed his eyes and tightened his fists as the best song of all time screamed through his blown mind, *exit light, enter night, take my hand,* and so he did, he took James Hetfield's imaginary hand and together they pitched headlong into the heart of the people just as Ruslan touched two wires hanging from his vest and then oh yes then he blew himself to bits with the words *off to never never land!* in his head screaming.

The carnage! The wreckage! The horror caused by bombs filled with nails and ball bearings! Hundreds of metres away, people were hit by shreds of muscle and tissue. Blinded by shrapnel, others fell to their knees, screaming, *My eyes my eyes* bozhe moi *I cannot see!* Others were deafened; these were the ones who walked aimlessly in circles, tapping the sides of their ears as though they were watches that had stopped ticking. Others ran screaming, and others fell praying, and others cupped their faces in fits of uncontrolled weeping. And still they wouldn't stop coming, these Tushino-born horrors. Columns of smoke were rising up darkly. In them were tiny bits of clothing, and hair snatches, and kopeck-sized portions of skin singed and tattered. The force from the blast had blown holes in the tarmac, and from these came fountains of foul sewer water, loosened from pipes that had been in-two broken. Suddenly there was shit, and shit everywhere, running muddy and dark and pooling with spilt blood. Above it all—above the blind and the bleeding and the deaf walking in circles—smoke from the explosions formed a thick, darkened matting, such that the sun from the sky seemed to retreat to a safe place. Oh yes yes yes, dusk had come in the middle of a day white with sunshine. Those with their vision intact craned their heads upward, wondering if this eclipse was a sign that God had finally thrown up his hands and said, *That's it, I give up.* And still there was screaming, and howling, and the first of many shouts for retaliation. There came ambulance sirens and the *beat-beat-beat* of news helicopters; as reports of the event spewed from government-controlled media, the ring roads of Moscow became jammed with parents frantically rushing to Tushino.

Seventeen died, and they died on Hank's nickel. And yes, this figure is little more than a whispered insignificance when compared to what happened in *Nord-Ost,* or what *would* happen at a school in a small Ossetian town called Beslan. Still—seventeen deaths meant seventeen ruined families, and seventeen sets of devastated parents, and seventeen sets of traumatized siblings, a healthy percentage of whom would succumb to depression and the bottle and a pathological hatred of Chechens. And if there were seventeen deaths, it is easy to forget there were hundreds of injured—hundreds who lost their vision, or who would forever be deafened, or who had lost parts of their viscera to the nails that were flying, such that the daily practices of feeding and evacuation would, for the rest of their lives, be a long, painful challenge. And if hundreds were *injured,* it meant that hundreds more, perhaps even thousands, would be traumatized by what they saw *and,* more specifically, by what they heard. For when the witnesses at Tushino started giving interviews to police and to media, they over and over gave the same tearful story, a story whose very repetitiveness was what became eerie: When the second bomb went off, the limbs of its victims were hurled violently skyward, only to noisily land on the roofs of the kiosks.

And that sound, my little half-*seestra,* was nothing less than a *ping ping ping ping*ing.

ELEVEN

And, because terror begets terror, and horror begets horror, at the exact moment that Ruslan blew himself up to "Enter Sandman," thousands of kilometres away, in a room filled with green tile and beeping machines and bright overhead light, Anna Verkoskova née Mikhailovna was, like the concertgoers at Tushino, screaming. You see, little one—I, your humble and world-weary narrator, months premature and cursed with a smart car–sized forehead, was coming into a world I knew to be gorgeous and cruel and filled with deception. Oh yes, little one, I was saying my prayers, I was counting my blessings, I was plummeting headfirst into cupped and pink-palmed hands.

The lunacy! The madness! The ensuing pandemonium! I tell you—things were more restful at the Tushino concert. Nurses gasped, machines beeped loudly, and doctors started throwing orders about as though this might accomplish something, and still, *still*, Anna reached for me, as though I were the most beautiful baby ever to grace a Gerber bottle label.

In the past, I suppose, I would have been stillborn. But this was July the fifth, the year 2003. Doctors rushed to the room like bears to spilled honey. They produced syringes and all sorts of medical devices. I wished that they hadn't. Just *look* at me, I wanted to yell at them. Just look at what this story has left *of* me. Were it up to yours truly, I would have been wrapped in a warm towel and placed into the arms reaching out for me. Once there, I'd nuzzle and burrow, letting that dim spark of life seep from me sweetly.

You can imagine what happened instead. The same pair of hands that had caught me whisked me to a lamp used for warming up babies. Meanwhile, *mamochka* was hysterically wailing: *My baby! My baby! Oh God, let me see my baby!* An oxygen mask was slipped over my features. My chest was pressed by the thumbs of a doctor. When this didn't come close to working—I was a robin's egg blue, and heading toward purple—a tube was slid down my throat and into my small lungs. Through this they pumped oxygen and a squirt of epinephrine. This worked. Life's spark was mine, however jarring. Worse, I now wanted more *of* it. It was like a bad habit—no matter how hurtful, I craved life's sore presence.

And so, I fought like a Russian in a World War II battle (by which I mean unarmed and reckless and aware of my own doom impending). I let out a holler that was desperate and whinnying. When they slid a tube in my nostril, I swatted it roughly, causing the doctors and nurses to know that they'd saved me. They placed me in a box with Plexiglas windows; I looked like a hairless suckling lamb in a farm incubator. No matter. From my cube I could see them giving a shot to *mamochka*. "My baby!" she shrieked. "My baby! Please give me my baby!" Slowly, her pleas to hold me turned to incoherent mumblings. Her arms stopped waving, and the tears on her face dried like cracks in a desert. She tumbled toward sleep with one eye half-open.

The room was invaded by a ghostly, sad quiet. Everyone watched as Hank Wallins approached me. He looked down, his sad green eyes brimming. He had never before felt such a sense of belonging.

My son, he thought, wishing only to touch me.

He turned. The doctors and nurses were all looking at him, their expressions betraying the tragedy of this moment. "Please," he murmured to them, "could I be alone with my son?"

Awkward seconds ticked by. One of the nurses, a Jamaican woman who had been there the longest and had made peace with the taste and texture of sorrow, stepped forward and said, "You go right ahead, Mistah Wallins. Don't pick him up, you might take out a tube and deprive him of his supper, but you go right ahead. You go ahead and touch that darling baby all you want to."

So he did. He lightly stroked my mottled skin, just above the diaper. He learned about the way that my hair felt, all soft and rabbit-cottony. His ears stopped *ping*ing, for he was at peace now that his worst fears had been realized. I started gurgling and kicking and fluttering my eyelids. And then, for just a second, Hank swore I was smiling. This helped. It just *did.* He smiled as well, and I wanted to let him know I could see all he was doing. So I did. I sounded off inside his ears, Hank hearing the coo of a baby delighted with living. Despite his not being my real papa, we were genuinely, and in the manner of lucky sons and even luckier fathers, connected.

It's all worth it, I told him, *if just for this moment.*

It's all worth it, I told him, *if just for this feeling of being here with you.*

Hank smiled again, sadly. The flesh padding his jawline was shaking like jelly.

"I," he mumbled, "will love you forever."

They put me in a room with Hank and *mamochka,* my cube connected to machines that made ominous beepings. And though no one told Hank and Anna that this was done rarely, and only under the direst of circumstances, they knew. This was the saddest thing about all of this: they both understood what was happening to us.

Nurses came on the hour, disturbing the room's quiet with quick heart rate checkings. Hank spent his time pacing, or holding *mamochka*, or smoking cigarettes outside of the hospital. Anna, meanwhile, refused any more sedatives, or tranquilizers, or postpartum soporifics. She knew her time with me was God-given (and about to be God-taken) and she wished to make the most of it. All day long she whispered into my ear, singing little songs that made a music of Russian. She covered my face with warm, dill-flavoured kisses. She held my non-prehensile hands as though they would one day learn to throw and grip a pencil and handle the controls of an Xbox.

She held them as though they would one day grow large and be able to hug her.

This was the blessing of my life, and the reason I wouldn't have traded places with anyone. I was having a lifetime of love packed into a few days. I was discovering that when you are a child only a mother can love, that love is far more intense than is usual. I was discovering, little one, that love can be so fierce it has the power to strengthen flesh, and bind wounds, and keep a prune-sized heart beating just a little bit longer. And so, I hung on. I'm nothing if not a fighter, and I clung to my life like a fierce Chechen phantom. Half-Slavic and half-Caucasian, I took on all comers.

And still her love heightened with each passing second. *Aren't you a beautiful boy?* she would coo, meaning every word of it, before kissing my nose as though it were candy. *Aren't you the most beautiful little boy in the world?* she would whisper to me, and it was only when her arms grew tired and her legs grew achy that she would reluctantly place me back under my heat lamp, mindful of the tubes in and out of me running. Then she'd sit beside me, her heart so filled with love it felt angelically weighted, until she could no longer stand it. Out I'd come once again. She'd rock me, and kiss me over and over, and say, "Mama she loves you, oh how she loves you."

Seestra.

Every child should know this. Every baby should feel this. I tell you—there'd be less hate, and corruption, and wars started by vanity.

Days passed. Hank and Anna began to look haggard—there's a price, little one, that comes with so much bliss-knowing. I too started to go under. My heartbeat grew more erratic, my kidneys deteriorated, my lungs deflated like a tent in a blowdown. In the face of these problems, the doctors attacked as though *I* were the enemy: I was kept alive with drugs and machines and medical ponderings. I was kept breathing through wishes and prayers and scientific Hail Marys. (They regarded me as a challenge, and I can't say I blamed them.) Still, I grew smaller, and weaker, till I was doing nothing for myself other than periodic leg kicking. And so, they gave in. They pulled all the tubes from me, lifted me up from my Plexiglas condo, and placed me for good in the arms of *mamochka*. I burrowed into her breast like a flu-sickened puppy.

I didn't immediately expire, which is saying something.

I spent two happy days, Anya and Hank taking turns holding and nuzzling me. In those two days I was treated to a severity of love you never will know. But don't worry—we are talking of Hank and Anna, and you *will* have your fair share. It's just that you won't ever need the type of love I was for two wondrous days given. For this, you should be eternally grateful: you will have your health, little *seestra,* and all that comes with it.

THE CULPRITS

On the rare occasions in which *mamochka* had to get up—to use the washroom or stretch her legs in the hallway—she'd give me to Hank. He'd keep her bed warm while talking to me, his voice turned to gravel from so much tobacco. He'd speak of bike rides, and ball games, and long father-and-son strolls we'd one day take together. And always, *always,* he'd look into my salamander eyes as though they were something inspiring. I, in turn, would cast my gaze upward, and in so doing I'd erase the loneliness that had always run through him. (It was the least I could do, given the troubles I'd caused him.) Hank's eyes would mist over, and he would try hard not to blubber. I liked this. *You are all right,* I'd telepathically inform him—and, because I am who I am, I know he believed me.

Mamochka returned, and saw Hank snuffling. She touched his round shoulder, which brought on real emotion.

She said, "That is it, rabbit. Let all of it out."

So.

It was the middle of the night. *Mamochka* was sleeping with yours truly in her arms. Hank was on the fold-out chair snoring, having one of the best sleeps he'd had since I'd come into this world. The nurse on duty—the same Jamaican woman who told Hank it was okay to touch me—came in for a look-see. She right away noticed. My monitor showed nothing but weak, plaintive cracklings. My chest barely moved, and my skin was the light blue of a bird's egg. And she knew, yes she did, there were things that she should do. There were alarms she should sound, and bells she should ring, and young snot-nosed specialists who should immediately be summoned. Instead, she did nothing. She thought of the parents and this cruel, hard prolonging. She let her eyes fill, and her soul channel sadness.

With plump hands she reached over and woke up *mamochka*.

"*Da*," Anna said, not knowing where she was.

"Honey?"

"Yes?" Anna answered, rubbing sleep from her crossed eyes.

The nurse pushed hair off the patient's small forehead. With glistening eyes, she smiled fully—she was a Christian woman, and she believed that hidden within the seams of tragedy existed crumbs of truth and love and God's infinite virtue. She pulled in a breath and said, "It time, honey."

Anna looked at me, and gave me a squeeze that would send me off feeling much loved. I said a wordless goodbye to her, *mamochka*'s sweet face now an all-over grimace. I bid farewell to Hank, who woke just then with a strangely calm feeling. I gave final thanks to the Creator, for such things are important. I then slipped away, sacrificing myself so that Hank and Anna might start over. I gave myself to God, so that they might be innocent and given a fresh new slate gleaming.

I let myself go, so they'd no longer be culprits.

Such moments, such moments . . .

Anna was sobbing, and wishing she could have gone instead of me. For a second, Hank was confused. He rubbed sleep from his eyes and looked over, groggy; an instant later he knew what had happened. His ears started to ring, but with the piping of angels. It was beautiful, it was, he couldn't help but feel lightened. He glanced at the nurse, and found that she too looked contented. Oh yes. Both she and Anna could hear it—the noise in Hank's ears was now filling the warm room.

"You 'ear that?" the nurse asked.

"Yes," said Hank Wallins.

"Isn't it beautiful?"

Hank nodded, and climbed into bed beside my weeping *mamochka*. He rubbed the brown moss that grew over my soft spot. This helped. It made the transition easier. Though there are few rules of life, this is one of them: few things feel better to a boy than the touch of a father. Few things make a small boy feel safer than a father's deep timbre. (Oh, Hank, oh, my tall and ersatz *papochka*—you are pinch-hitting wonderfully.) And so, it was easy. I hovered, I floated away, I left my body behind as though it were a pair of worn trousers. The room filled with a light that everyone noticed. It was all right, this feeling, and it made me feel silly for struggling so hard over the last hundred hours. I was a butterfly, wafting. Below, Anna was crying so hard the bed was noticeably shaking. Hank, meanwhile, was experiencing something that was closer to wonder. That left the nurse—she was rubbing Anna's shoulder while saying, "That's it, you say goodbye now, honey, you go ahead and cry all that you want to."

The funeral was two days later. The guests were few—Manuel and his family, and the ghost of a French girl who went by just one name. You can probably picture it, so I'll give just the highlights.

Bright blue summer skies, with not a chance of rain coming.

An Orthodox priest, reading psalms in the languages of both Hank and *mamochka*.

Hank, a big man dissolving, his tears like rain on a warm forest falling.

Anna, totally quiet, for she had been crying for two days, and had become so dehydrated that even one more tear was impossible. This was too bad; in the absence of tears, she discovered a deeper pain will develop, one that punctures the soul with a sharp, twisting dagger. In her hands was a small and wooden Saint Onuphrius icon (he being the saint of far-away going). When I was lowered to my grave, Anna tossed him in with me.

A polished wood casket, about the size of a bread loaf.

Manuel's small children, looking nervous and awkward.

Manuel and his wife, both head-down and praying.

Martine's ghost, smiling, for she knew of the things that were awaiting in heaven.

A throwing of soil.

Hank's ears, deathly silent.

Wind rustling tree branches.

O Jesus, we are gathered . . .

Hank and Anna took to a bed still surrounded by boxes. At night they lit candles, and during the day they fed on Hank's medications. Oh yes—they gobbled fistfuls of Zoloft, and Elavil, and enough lorazepam to still the heart of a hippo. This went on for a month. Quality Assurance accepted that Hank was out for the long haul, his job now performed entirely by Manuel (who still had hours to kill, standing alone outside determinedly smoking). One day Anna awoke, as best as she was able, and understood that this painlessness was a betrayal of my memory. She flushed Hank's pills and felt a searing hurt for it.

The phone occasionally rang, the news having spread to the far side of the ocean: Anna's mother in St. Petersburg, along with the odd aunt and uncle. Each time, Hank or Anna checked caller ID and let the phone go on ringing. Flowers arrived from Hank's employer; they stayed in their wrapping, turning brittle and flaking. Motions were made to plant a tree in my honour; when they were better, Hank and Anna promised, they'd select a location.

They ate, although rarely: cheese and crackers, takeout chicken, noodles ordered in from a nearby Chinese restaurant. In the middle of the night they'd meet on the sofa, which they positioned so it had a view out the window. This somehow helped, though neither one knew why—there is something soothing about the lights of a city when everything you know is inside of you, dying.

Then.

The day was a Tuesday, in the middle of September. A cool wind had ushered away the summer's humidity. Dawn broke crisply, on a day of harsh reckoning. Hank started moaning. In his ears was the sound of metal screeching on metal. Without any of his pills, his anguish was a summit that he had to go through. This went on for two hours—Hank writhing and squirming on the apartment's sofa, cursing his Anna for tossing his Xanax. When he could stand it no longer, he rose and dressed and went to the Wellesley subway station. He marched downstairs and stood at the edge of the platform; beneath his toes there was air, and a four- or five-foot drop. He heard the train coming. In a few seconds' time he'd let himself fall forward, and this time hovering would not happen to him. The train entered the station and came barrelling toward him. Hank was just about to do it when a voice arose in his ears and spoke loudly to him. (And I tell you—I had to yell to be heard over the screeching of train wheels on metal.)

Are you crazy? I hollered.

You have a woman who loves you.

Two days later, with Hank outside shopping, rock bottom came to poor Anna as well. She ran to the living room, semi-nude and bent over. In a carton marked *Kitchen,* she found a knife used for shashlik. She placed the blade against her wrist and felt her pulse in her fingers. A droplet of blood fell; once hitting, it smeared on linoleum tiling. She was about to start slicing when she paused, and had a momentary think about what death just might feel like—all that emptiness, all that space reaching forever.

All that slow fading to nothing.

This frightened her. She knew what this was like, just as she knew there is nothing more unsettling than this thing called infinity. Her hand started trembling and her mouth levered open. The knife then dropped to the scuffed parquet flooring. She followed, collapsing. Pain burned like jet fuel through all of her body. She convulsed, and vomited, and gasped for short breaths over a heart speeding madly.

This went on for an hour, and then the worst was all over.

Hank was cooking with groceries he'd purchased. Or at least, he was trying—he was a klutz in the kitchen, all thumbs and big feet and worried expressions. By the time he had finished, the potatoes were lumpy, the carrots were mushy, and the roast was reduced to a blob of dark cinders.

He stumbled from the kitchen, looking hot and worked over.

"Sorry," he said.

She could smell smoke in his hair and burnt meat on his clothing. She smiled; she couldn't help it. She'd never known anyone who could at times be so useless. "Is okay," she said. "Please, come here, rabbit."

She hugged him; sometimes the smallest gestures of kindness can act like an earthquake. He returned her embrace, and their mouths came together. One second passed; their lips pressed tighter together. Skin surfaces warmed, and hands started caressing. Anna unbuttoned her blouse in a way that felt sacred. They moved to the floor in a slow-motion tumble; here they both discovered that there is nothing like misery to unlock one's capacity for pleasure. The room filled with yelps and groans and curse words in Russian. Boxes toppled and plants overturned and two sets of arms flailed with abandon. Anna never imagined she could feel this impassioned about her sluggish Canadian. And *Hank*—he'd never felt so unlocked from the prison that was himself. His ears sang with Barry White records and then he felt a lightness come to him. He was air, he was essence, yes yes yes the two of them started to above the floor hover. Just when it seemed that they would both tumble back down and drop back into their skins, they succumbed once again to a force born in heaven, the two of them floating for what seemed like forever.

The neighbour next door began pounding the wall and in a croaky voice yelling. It was then, and then only, that they fell back to the parquet. They lay holding each other, until the moisture on their skin began to evaporate and they both started to shiver in the room's autumn coolness. They rose, and walked hand in hand to the bedroom. Once there, they lay on clouds, two skin-stinging survivors of a parent's worst nightmare.

After that, they still rarely, if ever, left the apartment. There was, however, a big difference—long periods of suffering were now interspersed with eruptions of soul-wafting carnality. Relying on memory, Hank showed her all the things he'd done with his Martine—the Spread Eagle, the Flying Wallenda, the acrobatic (and somewhat bruising) French Inquisition. Anna, meanwhile, couldn't believe it—next to these, her episodes with Ruslan were benign teenage fumblings. Next to these, her meetings with Ruslan were like platonic handshakes. Furthermore, it was during one of these bouts that *you*, little one, were created. And though Anna doesn't quite yet know it, she has her suspicions, and is about one week away from a pharmacy visit. (*This* time, when she pees on a wick and it turns a summer-sky blueness, she'll be correct in assuming that Hank, oh yes Hank, is the orange-haired father.)

Yes, my semi-*seestra,* you are already in her, no doubt wishing your half-brother would once and for all clam up. And if you are wondering why I have forced this macabre tale upon you, with its rhythms of Russian and nursery school stories, I will tell you:

It was because I wanted you to know something. With my death, Hank and Anna were absolved for this thing called Tushino. I made it okay for them to have you. In other words, *seestra,* you'll have no concerns or great worries. This I did for you. You'll be born healthy, and happy, and with a normal-sized head on your pretty-girl shoulders. You will know the love reserved for children who are living in paradise—it will be eternal and brilliant and, best of all, something that you'll take for granted. Oh yes, you'll grow up thinking that the world is a nice place, despite a mountain of evidence that it's no walk in a forest. You won't know the default fear that makes life a burden. When challenges crop up, you won't run away panicking—you won't follow the example of Saint Onuphrius!—for you'll have a little voice inside you saying things will be okay.

As for your parents: I wish I could say that Hank's prescient ear *ping*ings will end with the joy you will cause him (they won't, though they will get a lot milder) or that *mamochka* will stop her pilfering, having found in her life another kind father figure (she won't, not completely, though it's true she'll feel the urge far, far less often). The truth is this: bad habits have a way of blazing forever, even without wood or oxygen to fuel them.

So, goodbye. Adios. Ciao. *Do sbidaniya.* My time is now and now it is my time. I will duck into shadows and stop blabbing at you. Papa is waiting—my real one, that is, and not the lightly freckled version who's still mourning my passing. I'm quite excited, really. Ruslan tells me my new home is warm all the year round and never too humid. He says that war is unknown, and

THE CULPRITS

the fields are dotted with wild grasses and flowers. He says that people can laugh without having to cry first. He says that children stay young, even when they get older. He says that smiles hide nothing (except good intentions). He says that the cities are places of imagination. He says that guilt is reserved for those who enjoy it. He says that deception occurs, though only as white lies. He says that locks don't exist, nor the concept of envy. He says the water tastes like water, and not Chernobyl fallout. He says the air smells of tarragon, and sometimes snapdragons. He says the soil grows crops like there is no tomorrow. He says there's a lightness to living that borders on floating.

He *says:* there are watermelons, everywhere, and that they're juicy and sweet and through black soil sprouting.

ACKNOWLEDGEMENTS

No yoos, no *Culprits:* Susie, Sally, Ella, Anne, Jackie, Tatiana Smirnova, Kasia Szymczyk, every Russo-Canadian who ever told me what was what and why, Bill Evans, Anton Newcombe, Jeff Tweedy, Black Rebel Motorcycle Club, Wes Anderson, Alejandro Gonzalez Inarritu, www.larrycarlson.com, Jerry Garcia, Randy Weston, Don Cherry (*not* the hockey guy), Salman Rushdie, David Mitchell, Richard Flanagan, Jeffrey Eugenides, DI.fm Ambient, Gary Shteyngart, the Don Valley mountain bike path, Gunther Funk, blue agave, Sri Krishnamacharya, Batifole, the capybara rodent, Antibalas, Cinematic Orchestra, *Waterland,* illuminated highway signs, Alan Ball, Kate Winslet, Mark Rothko, Susie, Sally, Ella, and, of course, those little jars that anchovies come in.

ABOUT THE AUTHOR

ROBERT HOUGH has been published to rave reviews in fifteen territories around the world. His first novel, *The Final Confessions of Mabel Stark*, was nominated for the Commonwealth Writers Prize for Best First Book and the Trillium Award, and is in development for a motion picture by Kate Winslet and her husband, Sam Mendes. His second novel, *The Stowaway*, was longlisted for the IMPAC International Dublin Literary Prize and is a Globe 100 Best Book. Critics have compared his work to that of Conrad (*Library Journal*), Zola, Camus, and Calvino (*The Globe and Mail*), Thomas Berger (*Kirkus*), Robertson Davies (*USA Today*), Angela Carter and Peter Carey (*The Times*), and Margaret Laurence and Carol Shields (*The Vancouver Sun*). He lives in Toronto with his wife and two daughters.

A NOTE ON THE TYPE

The body of *The Culprits* has been set in a digitized form of Caslon, a typeface based on the original 1734 designs of William Caslon. Caslon is generally regarded as the first British typefounder of consequence, and it is believed that these original fonts were used in the first edition of Adam Smith's *The Wealth of Nations*, a pioneering work in the field of systems thinking. Caslon is widely considered to be among the world's most "user-friendly" text faces, and hence is ideally suited to The Human Factor.